A
LIGHTHOUSE
FOR THE
LONELY HEART

SCOTT WILLIAM CARTER

FLYING RAVEN

PRESS

FOR R.B.

AMONG GIANTS,
YOU WERE ALWAYS
ONE OF THE TALLEST.

Chapter 1

The ocean churned, wild and unforgiving, buffeting the boat from all sides. It wasn't much of a boat, a pathetic fourteen-foot aluminum rust bucket with a pitiful ten-horsepower outboard motor that threatened to fly apart as it rattled violently in its casing, but Gage didn't care. He kept the throttle cranked to the max, his fingers on the handle already so numb he barely felt them. The roaring wind in his ears, the cold rain in his eyes—he might as well have been blind and deaf for all the good his senses did him.

Yet still he strained, squinting into the murk of night, searching for the yacht he knew had to be out there.

His bruised and beaten face, his left eye almost completely swollen closed, made it even harder to see anything. For now, he saw only the next ocean swell, white-capped and ferocious, sweep toward him out of the swirls of blues and blacks. The boat crested the wave, catching air, and slammed down hard in a spray of salty mist. Gage knew he risked capsizing, pushing the little boat with such abandon, but what other choice did he have?

If he hurried, he might still save them.

The storm had come on suddenly, following one of the most beautiful September days they'd had in years. Sunny and still, high sixties, with an extended forecast of many more days like it to come—and then, out of nowhere, *this*. A raging monster that surged out of the west with all the suddenness of a heart attack.

Nothing. He saw nothing. He blinked away the stinging salt water, hoping, praying for some sign. Was he even heading west? Dizzy, disoriented, his head still ringing from all the punches he'd taken to the face, he was no longer sure. He could have been heading up or down, his sense of direction was so out of whack. He glanced over his shoulder, trying to reaffirm his course, and was reassured when he saw the telltale glow high up on Heceta Head.

The lighthouse.

It was still there. Of course it was still there. It was hardly more than a yellow smear, but when the rest of the world was black and full of hidden dangers, a yellow smear could provide all the hope a person needed. The source of so much strife, the focal point of so much of his effort the past few weeks—and yet there it was, still persisting, still true to its singular mission regardless of all the chaos. Show us the way. Save us from the rocks. Bring us home. He hoped it would do the same for him. Once he found the yacht. Once he saved them.

"Garrison."

His first name, a whisper in all that howling wind, should not have been something he could hear. Yet he had. He'd heard it as clearly as he'd heard it spoken so many hundreds, thousands of times before. He would have known that voice if it had been seven years or seven hundred.

He turned, with all the slowness and apprehension of a man who feared that any sudden movement would prove this all to be a dream, and saw her perched at the front of the boat. A dark, pleasing shape. Long black hair whipped around her face. Her eyes flashed momentarily white as the boat lurched over the next ocean swell. Like her voice, he should not have been able to identify her from these sparse details, but he could. This was no dream. How could it be a dream? The way she gripped the metal bow with both hands, the way she arched her back and leaned into the storm—it was all too real, all too particular, all too *her* for this to be a dream.

"Janet?"

"It's me, sweetie."

"What are you doing here?"

She said nothing. He felt a terrible quench of loneliness, the worst he'd felt in all the years since she'd died. His wife. His true love. The woman who'd meant everything to him, and the woman he'd failed not once, but many times, and in the end, too. In the end, he'd failed her in the worst possible way. Someone had come to kill him and ended up killing her instead. He could move three thousand miles away to try to forget his failure, and in an instant, with nothing more than his name, all that time and distance was gone and it was as if his failure was yesterday.

"Don't give up hope," she said.

He blinked and she was gone. He blinked a few more times, hoping to bring her back, but he saw nothing but the raging storm ahead.

"Janet?" he said.

The word had barely fallen from his lips when a fiery explosion—an outline of a yacht briefly visible within the most intense oranges and yellows he'd ever seen—lit up the western sky.

Chapter 2

One week earlier, as the sun slipped behind an indigo ocean as smooth and shiny as a taut ribbon, Gage crammed the last of the plastic totes into the white Corolla and shut the trunk. A bit too forcefully. A slam, really.

Even reflected in the rear window, the ocean and the sky, glimpsed through the fir trees and over the tops of the houses down the hill, were full of the kind of vibrant colors usually only seen in the many artist galleries that populated the Oregon coast: a mix of warm crimsons, pulsating yellows, and a wide spectrum of blues that ranged from the most somber shade to the lightest and cheeriest.

It had been a particularly stunning sunset, the latest in a long stretch of stunning sunsets, but Gage was in no mood to enjoy it.

"I just don't know why you have to take the cat," he said.

Zoe's answer, if she'd even heard him, was the distinctive clink of a seatbelt. He took a step around the car and saw her leaning over the cat carrier, a massive orange crate she'd bought on Amazon when he'd refused to give her the older, smaller, and, honestly, infinitely inferior cat carrier they'd had ever since he'd inherited the cat and all its paraphernalia from his deceased house cleaner—and Zoe's grandmother—three years earlier. Through the gaps in the carrier, he saw the cat peering out at him with its large yellow eyes, seemingly happy to the point of smugness. The color of the carrier matched the color of the tabby's thick orange fur, which, knowing Zoe, was probably deliberate.

A breeze ruffled the arbor vitae that separated his house from his closest neighbors. Down below, on Highway 101, a truck downshifted as it prepared to haul its load up the many hills of Barnacle Bluffs. Gage took another couple steps toward Zoe just as she turned, and, because the gravel driveway was loose and uneven—another sore point because he'd refused to pave it even though he had the money—his right foot came down in a divot. This created an awkward twist that predictably sent a painful shiver into his worthless right knee.

Seeing his grimace, Zoe shook her head and crossed her arms, looking so much older than her nineteen years. Of course, she'd always been older than her years, even when he first met her and she was still in her Goth stage: black, baggy clothes, black hair, and so many earrings, nose rings, and other jewelry affixed to her face that she set off metal detectors at the court-house when they went to her adoption hearing. Now all that remained of that rebellious time was a single diamond stud so tiny some people had mistakenly pointed out to her that she had a bit of glitter stuck to the side of her nose.

As for the rest of her? Gone was the near-religious com-mitment to the color black. Her hair, a luxurious auburn high-lighted by just a few threads of blond—a look that some women spent a small fortune to achieve in a salon and yet was entirely natural, flowed in gentle, billowing curls to her shoulders. The hip-hugging jeans, the V-neck gray cardigan over the powder-blue T-shirt, and the leather mesh sandals—all of it could have come straight from a J.Crew catalog. Even her toenails had been painted the same blue as her shirt.

Yet it would have been a mistake to think that the young woman before him was a carbon copy of some preppy who frequented Martha's Vineyard, or that she'd suppressed her fierce intelligence behind a conformist facade. A while back, he'd made the mistake of asking if she was making a deliberate choice to blend in with people better, which prompted her to unleash a blistering two-hour tirade about the real definition of feminism in the modern era.

"Acting up again?" she said, nodding toward his knee.

He shrugged.

"You know—" she began.

"Don't," he said.

"I was only going to say—"

"I know exactly what you were going to say. You were going to remind me, as you and others have done many times before, about the wonders of modern medicine. Let's just pretend we had the conversation this time, shall we? I want to stay focused on why you're stealing my cat."

Zoe rolled her eyes. "The reason everybody keeps bringing up knee surgery is because you're so damn stubborn about it. You were never supposed to have just that one surgery, but you refuse to go back. Cobalt-chromium and titanium plating, wear-resistant plastic molded just for your knee—"

"Boy, you've done a lot of research."

"It'll change your life!"

"It's an unnecessary expense."

"God, you're impossible. That's not why you don't get it done, and you know it. You don't get it fixed because you *want* to suffer."

"Now you sound like Tatyana—right before she left me, too."

This gave her pause. He knew it would. Zoe, with everything she'd been through, had one of the hardest shells to crack. She didn't break easy. She didn't break at all, really. But for her to even get misty-eyed, that was a rare event. He definitely saw a bit of glistening there, maybe even a tear if pushed to the brink. It wasn't really fighting fair, bringing up Tatyana, but he didn't feel like fighting fair.

Truthfully, Tatyana hadn't left him—they'd left each other, or he'd left her and she'd let him do it, but in the end it was all a muddle, as the ends of relationships often were. His lovely girlfriend of nearly six months, a doctor who'd emigrated from Ukraine when she was a young woman in search of a better life, had finally decided that all the troubles in her homeland demanded some personal sacrifice, whatever that meant, so she'd announced one morning over pancakes and scrambled eggs that she was going back. A month, a year, she didn't know for how long. Did this mean they were through? She said she preferred to think of it as taking a break. He said he preferred something a little more definitive.

There'd been shouting. Scrambled eggs thrown against the wall. That whole business about his knee had been brought up out of the blue, along with lots of other long-simmering minor feuds all folded into the bigger one. Deep down, though he hadn't said it aloud, he'd actually preferred to wait for her, call it a break, a reset, a long-distance relationship, whatever. He'd wanted to hold on to whatever she would give him, but he didn't think that was fair to her. She was going home to finally deal with the guilt because of her choices, the people she'd left behind, the people she'd hurt. He didn't want to give her any more reason to feel guilty.

If anyone was well acquainted with all the dangers of piling on the guilt, it was Gage.

But damn it, he had to draw the line somewhere.

"Let's get back to the cat," he said.

Zoe groaned. "You're just deflecting."

"And you're stealing my pet."

"It's not stealing if you own it! Grandma actually got Carrot for me, after I came to live with her. That's his name, you know. Carrot. Not 'the cat,' as you so lovingly refer to him. If you can't even use his name, why in the world do you think he belongs with you?"

"I use his name. I use it all the time."

"Uh huh."

"Carrot. See, not so hard. Carrot, would you like Zoe to steal you away from me? If you don't answer, I'll assume you're blissfully happy in this life. See, no answer. I knew it. He's silently outraged at this injustice you're foisting upon him. Upon Carrot. Because that's his name."

"Congratulations, you passed the first test in pet ownership. Now, when's the last time you fed him?"

"Well …"

"Changed his litter box? Took him to the vet?"

"He goes to the vet?"

"When's the last time you even petted him, for God's sake?"

"Last week, when I sat down near him, he started purring. Does that count? At least, I think that sound was him. It might have been the furnace acting up again."

He smiled. She didn't. He tried a wink. She ignored it. It was becoming abundantly clear that he'd taken his concern for the cat—for Carrot—as far as he possibly could. He knew what this little song and dance was about. She did too. What was that line? Something about partings and sweet sorrow? He thought about saying as such, to see if he could get her into another bantering contest to determine who could remember the most lines from Shakespeare, a common game of theirs, but he knew she'd see right through that ploy just like she was seeing through this one.

"Term doesn't even start for another week," he said.

"I need time to settle in," she said.

"What about Todd? How's he handling this, you moving away?"

"First of all, his name is Zachary. And second of all, when did you suddenly become concerned about what he thinks?"

"I know he cares about you a lot. I just don't like to think of him heartbroken."

"Uh huh. You told me if I ever married a cop, you wouldn't attend the wedding."

"I never said that."

"Yeah, well, he's got his job here, and we're trying the long-distance thing for a while and seeing how it goes."

"This was his idea or yours?"

"What difference does it make?"

"Ah! It was yours."

"Will you stop? This isn't about Carrot, Zachary, or any of that stuff. You're just cranky because I'm leaving."

"Portland's a big city. I worry about you there."

"Dad, you lived in New York for years. Portland is tiny compared to it. You know I'll be fine. Mostly I'll be sticking to the campus, anyway. My apartment is a block from PSU. Between that, the college library, and maybe Powell's bookstore now and then, I really don't need much else. I'm going to bury myself in books and learning. It's going to be wonderful! I know you never really wanted me to go to the community college, you wanted me to go straight to a four-year school, and now here I'm going and you're not happy about it. You should be excited for me."

He barely heard anything after the word *dad*. She'd called him *dad*. First word out of her mouth. He doubted she was even conscious of it. In fact, he was quite certain she wasn't, considering how rarely she called him that, but it didn't blunt his joy any. She seldom spoke about her real parents, drug addicts who'd spent most of her childhood in and out of prison, both now deceased, and if she'd thought of anyone as a mother, it had been Mattie, her grandmother. Did she think of Gage as a father? Really think of him that way, after three years and all their ups and downs? How strange that a three-letter word like that could affect him so much. He'd never wanted kids—at least, that was what he'd told himself because Janet hadn't wanted them either—but right now there was nothing more important than being a father to the young woman in front of him.

"I *am* excited for you," he said quietly.

"You've got a funny way of showing it."

"I just don't know what I'm going to do without my cat."

"Ah, well. You can come visit him."

"I can?"

"Absolutely."

"Tomorrow?"

"Let's try for two weeks."

"Hmm."

"And I'll bring him down to visit you too."

"He'd like that."

They stood there for a while, nodding. The breeze picked up, stirring her hair across her face and neck. The tops of the arbor vitae shimmied against the deepening sky. At some point in the last few minutes, most of the fiery oranges and yellows, even most of the blue, had disappeared, leaving indigo fading into black. The color matched his mood, but he steeled himself against it. The big A-frame house was all lit up, every light on as she'd scurried from room to room packing the last of her things. It seemed incongruously bright for how empty it was. How empty it would be.

"Well," he said, shrugging.

"Yeah," she said.

"Don't get too smart for me, all that book learnin' you're gonna do. I still want to be able to talk to you."

"Uh huh. This coming from a guy who once read Encyclopedia Britannica cover to cover just for fun."

"I was out of crossword puzzles that month. Besides—"

Before he could finish, she burst into tears. She could have shot him with his Beretta and it would have shocked him less. While he was still fumbling around, trying to figure out how to respond, she seized him in a fierce hug. It wasn't exactly a loving embrace. It felt as if she was trying to squeeze all the air out of his lungs. Despite how small she was, she was certainly strong enough to do it. It took a moment to respond in kind, partly because she'd wrapped her arms in his own, and partly because they hugged so infrequently he always felt like he had to relearn how to do it with her each time they did. But he eventually got his arms around her, and he didn't want to let go, not ever.

At some point he did. She got in her car, wiping her eyes, feigning a smile. She mumbled something about loving him. He mumbled it back. That was what they did. When it came to the important stuff, they mumbled. She shut the door and started the Toyota. He thought that was it, she was gone, and he felt as if a sinkhole had opened up beneath him, but then her expression turned puzzled.

She pulled out her iPhone and answered it. There was a brief conversation he couldn't hear, then she clicked off and rolled down the window.

"It was Alex," she said.

"Oh?"

"You really need to get a cell phone."

He let this pass without comment. It would just bring another long-simmering feud to the front burner.

"Anyway," Zoe said, "he wants you to come down to the bookstore."

"Now?"

"Now."

"Why?"

"I don't know, something about a woman who wants to hire you."

"Did he tell her that I'm—"

"Look, I'm not your secretary, okay? Just go down there. Maybe without me around all the time you'll finally have to get a phone."

She rolled up her window and drove off. He watched her taillights disappear around the bend, listened until he couldn't hear the crunch of the tires on the gravel, and then stood there a while longer, wishing he could have ended their conversation on a better note. Then again, maybe that was appropriate. An argument, a hug, and capped off with just a bit of flippant attitude.

It was all Zoe.

Chapter 3

Except for Books and Oddities, the rest of the little, ramshackle Horseshoe Mall at the edge of town was dark by the time Gage got there. The antique shop, the baseball card store, the auction house at the back—all the owners had long since gone home by seven o'clock on a Sunday in mid-September. This was true for most of the shops in Barnacle Bluffs. People would often stay late during the height of the summer, hoping to make one more buck when the sun was shining and Highway 101 was choked with tourists, but after Labor Day it was tough to find a storekeeper who even managed to stay true to his posted hours.

The light from the store's front window spilled onto the boardwalk, a yellow rectangle on weathered wood. The neon orange *open* sign pulsed in the deepening darkness. Gage parked his Volkswagen van, his sputtering, grumbling, old beast, his mustard-yellow monster that he planned to drive as long as people were still allowed to drive, in front of the shop next to Alex's green Toyota Sienna and killed the engine. On the other side of Alex's van was a black Lincoln Navigator, a big SUV monstrosity with tinted windows and a California plate.

He saw the woman right away. She saw him, too, or at least she looked in his direction from her place at Alex's front counter, probably drawn by the van's emphysema-like wheezing that persisted long after he'd killed the engine.

And he knew, at a single glance, that he'd seen this woman before. He didn't know from where, but he definitely recognized her.

She didn't make it easy. The banks of fluorescent lights may have been bright, even for a bookstore, but they hardly warranted the hazel-tinted sunglasses that took up half her face. She wore a black, oversized beret tilted low on her forehead, the mounds of curly, dark hair framing her face as surely as a hood. It was a nice face, what he could see of it, a little round but in a good way, exuding a sort of vibrant wholesomeness that penetrated even her concealing ensemble. She was short, even standing next to Alex, probably not much over five feet tall. A black wool trench coat, the collar turned up high, was big and bulky enough, especially with how short she was, to mostly hide her figure, but he did get a tantalizing sense of a bosomy, curvaceous form underneath.

How did he know her? He sat there in the cooling van mulling it over until Alex looked over his shoulder at him, raising those big expressive eyebrows as if to ask just what he was doing. Then Gage donned his fedora—two could play the hat game— and went inside, hobbling up the steps with his cane. He wished he could have left the cane in the van. He always did when meeting a pretty woman. But the aches were just too piercing.

The familiar scent of old books, an intoxicating odor if there ever was one, greeted him as soon as he stepped inside.

"Took your time about it," Alex said.

Bald, perpetually rumpled, and armed with the kind of thick, envy-inducing mustache that only a rare few men could ever hope to grow, Gage's old friend perched in his usual place on his stool behind his counter, mountains of dog-eared paperbacks, glossy kid books, and hardcovers with chipped and nicked jackets piled high around him. The day's trade, most likely. Gage barely acknowledged him with a glance, he was so distracted by the woman's smile.

She'd lit up as soon as he walked through the chiming door, flashing him a row of pearly whites that would probably make men and women alike weak in the knees. And actually did, because it was her smile that finally allowed him to place her. He hadn't met her after all, though he did know her. Millions of people did.

"Nice hat," Gage said. It was the first thing that came to mind.

"Yours too," she said.

"Nora West?"

"You know me. I'm flattered."

"I like your music."

"Thank you."

She smiled again. The compliment sounded inane coming out of his mouth, so pedestrian, the type of thing he was sure she heard dozens of times a day. He wished he could have said something more insightful, maybe something about how her music was a wonderful mix of jazzy R&B, modern pop, and solid folk music that gave it a timeless appeal. Her songs, not all of them, but most, were the rare kind that you could not only sing to in the shower, they actually stayed with you in a lasting way. If most of the popular songs on the radio were as fulfilling as fast food hamburgers, hers were home cooking all the way, the good kind.

That was what he should have said. Yet her thank you was impressively genuine, or at least seemed so. It might have still been practiced, but she was good at it. In the way she spoke just those two words, she made him feel like he was her only fan.

And he was, if he admitted it to himself, a fan, as much as Gage was a fan of anything.

"Here buying books?" he asked. Another inane comment. He was really on a roll.

She laughed and took off her glasses, placing them on the counter in front of her, looking at him with big brown luminous eyes that were just as rich and genuine as her smile. They were soulful, those eyes, and they were a perfect fit for her music. "No," she said, "though Alex does have a very nice shop. But I'm here to see you."

"Ms. West surmised," Alex said, with a wry grin, "as most people who want to get in touch with you eventually do, that the best way to reach out to you is by contacting *me.*"

"It's that stupid series of articles Buzz Burgin wrote," Gage said. "He made you seem like my Dr. Watson."

"That's part of it. The other part is your absolute commitment to a nineteenth-century hermit lifestyle."

"Hey, I have Wi-Fi."

"Uh huh. Are you going to keep it now that Zoe's moving out?"

"We'll see."

"Exactly." Alex looked at Nora. "I'm sorry. It's an old beef I have with him. I don't mean to make you feel bad for coming here. It's fine, really."

"No, no, no," Nora said, "it's all right. You're old friends, obviously. That's nice. I always like seeing that, you know, the way old friends get along. Even when they bicker, they don't, you know? Anyway, it's good. It's fine."

She'd tried to say this in a lighthearted way, but Gage detected a poignancy there, a barely detectable undercurrent of sadness, or longing, a hint of something missing or broken, and it was the first time, but not the last, that he realized something remarkable about Ms. West: she was lonely. Profoundly so.

"Well," Gage said, "I do want to punch Alex in the face now and then. So far, I've managed to restrain myself—only because his beautiful wife would kill me if I made his face any less pleasant to look at than it already is."

"Hey, I'm a handsome fellow," Alex said. "Back when I was a young man, still in the FBI, I had to fight women off with a stick."

"Oh God," Gage said, "not more of the 'when I was a young FBI lad' stories ... Nora, don't listen to a word out of his mouth. Most of it is about as true as what's in the novels in his store."

"How about the part where I kicked you out of the academy?"

"I dropped out."

"You dropped out because I was going to kick you out."

"No, I just didn't like the weather in Virginia."

Alex shook his head and turned to Nora. "You better tell him quick why you're here. Otherwise this Abbott and Costello routine will go on for hours."

Nora chuckled. "Abbott and Costello. Alex, that reference really dates you. Just how old *are* you, exactly?"

"Ah," Gage said, "I think I'm really going to like Ms. West."

"Nora," she said. "Please, just Nora."

"Fine. Garrison for me. Alex. Or Old Man Alex, as we call him around these parts. That works, too."

"Hey!" Alex said.

"Anyway," Gage said, "I'm still waiting for the big reveal here. I assume you didn't come all the way out here to the ends of the Earth to meet me just because rumors of my dashing good looks and my one-in-a-million personality have finally spread far and wide?"

"One in a million," Alex muttered, "that part's certainly

true."

"Would it break your heart," Nora said to Gage, "if I told you that wasn't the reason?"

"A little," Gage said, "but I'll get over it. Can I ask you something? Is that a rental out there, or did you drive all the way from Los Angeles?"

"I drove. It's mine."

"Ah."

"From San Francisco, actually. I have a place in LA, but I actually live most of the time in my condo in the Bay Area."

"That's still a long haul. Ten hours?"

"I went up the coast, so it took more like twelve. But I didn't want to risk the airports, not for this. The paparazzi, you know. I didn't want the attention."

"Okay, now you've *really* piqued my interest."

"I hope so," Nora said. "I really want to hire you. I know it's kind of crazy, me just jumping in a car and driving up here, but I had no choice. I'll pay any price, really. Money's not an issue. So whatever it costs—"

"Hold on now," Gage said. "Before we talk rates, I need at least a sense of what you want me to do."

"Wow," Alex said. "I'm surprised."

"What?" Gage said.

"You almost sound ready to say yes already. It's not like you. I warned Ms.—Nora, I warned Nora that she was probably going to be disappointed, considering how often you tell people no."

"Maybe I need the work."

"Uh huh."

Gage, not liking his tone, let it pass. He nodded at Nora, encouraging her to proceed. She took a deep breath.

"Do you know about the suicide at Heceta Head

Lighthouse?" she asked. "Last Wednesday?"

"Yeah. Just what I read in the *Bugle*. A volunteer there, an old guy, let himself in late at night when no one was around. He threw himself from the top—took a header right onto the ... I'm sorry, did I say something wrong?"

Nora's face had visibly paled. She swallowed as if she had tasted something unpleasant, started to say something, then shook her head and gestured for him to continue.

"It'll become clear in a minute," Alex said.

"Okay," Gage said. "I read they found a suicide note on him. Something about him having Alzheimer's and not wanting to wither away. I don't think the Florence police released his name, did they?"

"No," Alex said. "Not officially. But Nora here already had an idea who it was, and I made a few calls to some of my friends in the FBI before you got here. Does the name Ed Boone ring a bell?"

"It sounds familiar," Gage said.

"I'll give you a hint. You know that hole-in-the-wall diner you like to eat at now and then?"

"McAllister's?"

"That's the one. You remember what it was called originally?"

"Yeah, I think it was Ed's Diner ... Wait. Ed Boone. That's where I'd heard it before. He was the original owner, wasn't he?"

"Good job. Not many people even know that. He sold it over twenty years ago."

"I didn't think he was alive."

"I guess almost nobody did. Yet he's been living right here in town the whole time—not far from you, it would seem. You know that apartment complex on Driftwood Drive, the one on the other side of that undeveloped forest area behind your house?"

"He lived there?"

"Apparently."

"And he volunteered at Heceta Head Lighthouse? That's an hour away." He looked at Nora. "Okay, what exactly is going on here? What does this have to do with you?"

She no longer seemed like she might lose her dinner, but she was still having trouble speaking. She tried a couple times, shook her head, and then retrieved a wrinkled business envelope from the inside pocket of her trench coat. She handed it to him.

"It's—It's probably easier if you just read this first," she said.

It had already been opened. Both the address and the return address were handwritten in blue ink, the letters small but uneven, as if from a shaky hand. The sender was Edward M. Boone, and just as Alex had said, the address was the apartment complex not far from Gage's house. Nora West's address was her condo in San Francisco. The T in her last name was slightly smeared, the paper around the letter warped, as if it had gotten wet but then dried. From the rain, perhaps. Or tears.

The letter inside was a single sheet of white paper, folded twice. The text was typewritten—not from a computer, but an actual typewriter, the darkness of each letter faded and uneven, as if the ribbon was on its last legs. It was on the front and the back. Most of the lowercase t's were chopped off at the top, so they looked more like i's. A few of the words were scratched out with a blue pen, and Gage could see that most of them were just garbled versions of the words that followed. The letter was still filled with plenty of typos and other errors:

Dear Nora,

I am writing you now becaus I dont

havemuch time before thingsreally go south and I cant remember even the important stuff. But Ive never been a very lucky man so I dont want to wait.

I want to get the hard part out of the way straight off.

Im your father.

There I said it. Im sure you get all kinds of kooky letters from fans so your liable not to believe it. Thats OK. But keep an open mind now. I want you to know the truth. Its important I think. Your mother didnt want me in her life and I honord her choice. She didnt want me to never tell you and I honord that for a long time to. Even after I heard she died I didnt write you.

Butyou deserv to know the truth. Your mother and I had an affair. It just happend. She worked at the casino as a waitress. I was married with two boys, had the diner, a lot of stress. Deedee was a lot of fun, easy to talk to. Then she got pregnant. She didnt tell me for a long time. She finally said I had to choose her or Kathy. I chose Kathy. My boys really needed their father and I still loved Kathy. I loved your mom too in a different way so it wasnt easy.

So Deedee told me that was fine but I couldnt never see you. If I tried shed tell Kathy and the boys. I saw you aroudn town sometimes and you were so cute but I kept my distance like she wanted. Sad thing is things went south with Kathy and she moved to California with the boys. Most of it was my drinking but some of it was just us growing apart. I thought about trying to reconnect wiht Deedee but she was with that other guy by then and I saw you with him in the Jaybee's parking lot and saw the way you looked at him and knew he was the daddy you desrved. Then he got a job in Nevada I guess from what I heard and you all moved away.

I been alone ever since. Lots of years alone. Boys grew up and didnt want nothing to do with me and I cant blame them much since I wasnt very good to them after I took to the drinking. Sad right? I chose Kathy because I wanted to be there for the boys and I wasnt anyway. I worked the diner for a while but really lost heart. Sold it at a good price. Sold everthing really. The house had a lot of painful memories. I moved into this little apartment and just lived off what I had. Amazing how long you can do that if you dont spend much.

I did eventually get so bored I started volunteering at Heceta Lightouse. It was something to do in a place where nobody knew me. Not that anybody really knows me in Barnacle Bluffs either. They did once. I was Ed at Ed's Diner.

Its okay though. I just wanted you to know who your real father is. I know your mother didnt put down my name on the birth certificate so Im not sure there is a way to prove it except through a DNA test so you can do that if you want. Im sorry, Nora. I watched you become a star and many times I thought of writing you but I just didnt know how. I wish I could have been better. Not just for you but for everybody.

Please forgive me. Itd be nice to have at least one person who doesnt hate me when Im gone.

Sincerly,
Ed (your father)

P.S. I have a little money saved. I know you dont need it so Id like to donate it to the library here in town. I wrote up a will saying so and Im leaving it on the bookshlef.I named you Executor. Its in an envelope filed under Boone between the books. The library was real good to me. I dont want my boys to get it since they dont even care whether I live or die. I also heard from some people that they became real bad sorts. Anything else I have can be given to Goodwill. Its not worth nothing. But your the Executor so you decide whats best.

Gage looked up when he was finished. "Wow," he said.

"That's quite a letter. You lived here?"

Nora nodded. "Until I was thirteen."

"You'd think that would be known around these parts. It's not like we have all that many famous people from Barnacle Bluffs."

"Well, I didn't go to school a whole lot back then, and Mom didn't care. Plus I was still Nora Storm-Tree."

"Nora what?"

She laughed. It was more of a sharp snort than a laugh, but considering how out of sorts she'd appeared moments ago, he was glad to see any expression of levity from her. "My mother was part of the Kayok tribe. You know, the ones behind Golden Eagle Casino? I was born on the reservation. Storm-Tree was my actual last name until I changed it when I turned eighteen."

Gage glanced at the letter. "Do you have reason to think this is true?"

"I don't know. It *could* be. Why would he make it up? That's why I'm here. I want to hire you to find out. You're going to keep all this to yourself, right? Based on your reputation, I kind of figured you would keep it confidential. I really don't want all this stuff out right now. I guess I should have asked this before. This whole thing is so impulsive. Kind of stupid of me, talking so much about everything before—"

"Don't sweat it, Nora. Your secret is safe with me. What did your mother tell you about your father?"

"Not much. She said he was a fisherman out of Newport. She said they were only together a little while before he died in a bad storm at sea. I asked her his name many times, but she said his family didn't approve of them and she didn't want me to go snooping into their business. I always kind of figured it was a lie, but I didn't know how to go about finding out the truth. She was pretty stubborn about it."

"How'd your mom die?"

"House fire," Nora said. "But she always drank and smoke. She'd fall asleep with a cigarette in her hand. I told her how dangerous it was—at least when I was still living with her. That was a long time ago. I ran away from home when I was sixteen and never looked back. Mom was … a difficult woman. And that was before Larry split. After that, she was difficult *and* a drunk."

"Larry?"

"Oh, that's the guy Ed mentioned in his letter, the guy that was kind of like my father. But it was just for a few years. We moved to Las Vegas with him because he got a job with a construction company down there. I think he did drywall. Can't remember. Anyway, we weren't even there a year and he took off to New Orleans with some stripper. He *was* nice to me. I remember I started calling him Dad and it kind of wigged him out, though. For a long time I blamed myself for him leaving. Figured I scared him off. At least until he tried to make contact again once I hit it big and asked for money. Then I saw him for the shallow asshole he was."

"I'm sorry."

She shrugged. "Water under the bridge. The nice thing about being rich? I can afford a lot of therapy."

"What did your mom think? You know, when you became such a big star?"

"Honestly? I don't think she even knew who I was."

"Really?"

"Yeah. I mean, it's not like I told her when I legally changed my last name to West, and by the time my first single went big, I think she was pretty much out of it. If she did, I'm surprised she didn't try to do what Larry did and hit me up for some cash, since she was living in this crappy trailer park in Henderson. I thought about going to her funeral, but I was too afraid the paparazzi would find me. I don't know why I wanted to go. It's not like she meant anything to me."

Gage thought the truth was probably more complicated, as the truth about family often was, but he saw no reason to point that out. He looked at the letter again, considering.

"So," he said, "you want my help."

"Desperately," she said.

"To find out if he's really your father?"

"Yes. And everything else about him. About his life. I want to know who he was, really. I wish ... I wish he hadn't done this. I wish we could have had some time together. It just doesn't make any sense. Why kill himself? He could have waited. We could have—could have had some time."

Her voice cracked. She blinked heavily, her eyes misty. Alex produced a box of tissues and placed them on the glass counter in front of her. She took one, mumbled a thank you, but didn't use it, balling it up in her fist instead. The tears didn't come.

Outside, a big RV rumbled up the highway. The neon *open* sign pulsed a brighter orange, mirrored in the deepening black of the window.

"I'm sorry," she said. "I cried a lot on the way up here, but I thought I was past it."

"You're entitled," Gage said. "Look, I'm happy to help you. But I do wonder, why not just do it yourself?"

She sniffled. "I can't. Think about who I am. I mean, I'm not trying to sound egotistical or anything, it's just—"

"The press," Gage said, nodding.

"The paparazzi," she said. "All those vultures. I start asking around as me, and ... well, it'll turn this city into a madhouse. I don't want that for me. I don't want that for Barnacle Bluffs either."

"If it's true what he said about the will," Gage said, "your name's going to get out there soon enough."

"Yeah, but they don't have to know I'm *here*. If I'm not here, it can look like some crackpot fan made it all up. But if I'm here …"

"I get it," Gage said. "If you're here, the press will automatically treat it like it's true. I don't know how long that will work, but at least it might buy you a little bit of time."

"That's all I'm hoping for," Nora said.

Alex, who'd been silent for most of the conversation, drummed his fingers on the counter. "I wonder about that will," he said. "It doesn't sound like he had witnesses or had it notarized. I redid mine last year, and I know from what my lawyer told me that Oregon is a terrible state for wills without solid proof. He said without good witnesses, an estate will go to probate in Oregon for sure, and it's almost guaranteed to be a messy and expensive. I think his boys would get his money no matter what he wrote."

Gage said, "He called it a 'new will.' Which, of course, implies that there's an old one."

"Which means it will be even messier," Alex said.

"I'll worry about that later," Nora said. "If it's true, if he is who says he is, I'll just write a check to the library for whatever he had. I mean, it can't be much, right?"

"Probably not," Gage said, though something about the note made him wonder. Why would Ed make a point of expressing that he *didn't* want his sons to get the money if there wasn't much money to have? "Like you said, we can worry about that later. Right now we want to find out if any of this is true."

"So you're really going to do it?" Nora said. "You're really going to help me?"

Hopeful, eyes bright, she leaned forward and squeezed his arm. It wasn't much of a touch, most likely an automatic gesture, but there was still something electrifying about it. Even through his jacket's leather sleeve, he felt the sparks. There was definitely an attraction. Or was it just the thrill of being touched by the famous Nora West? He didn't know. In any case, she must have felt something, too, even if it was the mild embarrassment that accompanied unconsciously overstepping social norms, because she dropped her hand.

"Yes," he said, "I'm going to help you."

Alex chuckled. "Get it in writing."

"And your fee?" Nora asked. "The amount isn't really a concern, but do you want me to pay you something up front? What do they call that? A retainer?"

"We'll worry about that later," Gage said.

"What he means," Alex said, "is that you shouldn't worry about it at all. Paying my friend here for his help is even tougher than getting him to agree to help you in the first place."

"Oh, I won't accept that," Nora said. "I *will* pay you. I won't accept anybody's charity."

She said the last part with a fierceness that surprised all three of them, because all three of them fell silent. The brief flare of defiance actually made her seem even more attractive to him, the way those big brown eyes lit up with a hidden fire. It was a stark contrast to that vibrant wholesomeness that emanated from her no matter how much she tried to play the part of the celebrity, a glimpse of determined independence behind that aura of goodness that surrounded her. She came off like a people pleaser, someone who just wanted you to like her, but the show of anger revealed a more complicated woman.

"Sorry," she said, "that came out a little harsh."

"No worries," Gage said. "I will send you an invoice at the appropriate time. Fair?"

"Fair," she said.

"Good. Now, how can I get in touch with you? I assume

you're heading home in the morning."

"No, I want to hang around here for a while. I don't have a concert for two weeks, and the other stuff I can just reschedule. I wanted time to write some songs, anyway."

"Really? It's going to be hard to keep a low profile. Even checking in to a hotel—"

"She can stay at the Turret House," Alex said. "But we're mostly booked up right now, meaning there will be lots of other guests around …"

"Yeah," Gage said, "not a good option. Don't get me wrong, Nora. The B&B that he and his better half run is the best place to stay in town, no question, but not great for maintaining your privacy. I'd recommend the Inn at Sapphire Head, one of the best hotels in town, but I don't think you'd be better off there. Everyone has to come through the lobby. But if you don't mind staying in something not quite so fancy …"

"I don't need fancy," she said.

"Well, then there's this place down the hill from me called the Starfish Motel. Right on the beach, so you get a nice view. All the rooms have their own doors to the outside. Most of them have little kitchenettes, so you wouldn't have to eat out much. I'll book the room in my name so they'll never even see you, and I could even pick up groceries for you."

"Wow," she said, "sounds perfect."

"And if you like Greek cooking," Alex said, "I can almost guarantee you that my wife will be providing you with a few Meals on Wheels deliveries. She's a *huge* fan. She wouldn't be able to live with herself if she thought you were surviving off microwave dinners or something. I just hope you like baklava."

"I *love* baklava. That's so nice. Why are you both being so nice?"

Gage looked at Alex. His friend was just as dumbfounded by

the question as he was.

"What other way would we be?" Gage asked.

"I don't know," Nora said. "I'm just so used to people who aren't nice to me. I seem to attract them like flies. They usually want something from me. But I don't get that sense from you two."

"I hope not," Gage said. "All I usually want from people is for them to go away."

She laughed.

"It's true," Alex said. "The fact that Garrison is being nice to you is even more unexpected than the fact that he's agreed to help you. It means he likes you. Treat him well and he'll be loyal forever."

"You make me sound like a dog," Gage said.

Alex shrugged. "Well, if the bone fits …"

"I'll try not to take it for granted," Nora said. "And Alex, your wife? You said she's a fan. I hope you're not offended by my asking, but, well, she won't …"

"Tell anyone?" Alex said. "God no. Your secret is safe with her, too. Once you meet her you won't worry about it either, trust me."

"That's putting it mildly," Gage said. "Eve is the kind of person who is impossible not to like. I don't think there's an ounce of meanness in her."

"I once heard her curse in traffic," Alex said.

"Really?" Gage said.

"It may have only been 'darn,' but it definitely sounded like a curse. It was only once, though. Twenty years ago."

"I don't believe it."

"Yeah, well, I don't either. I probably dreamed it."

Nora laughed. "You two. Don't you ever quit? Seriously, I really appreciate all this. Maybe it's all nothing, anyway, just another crazy letter from a fan. But I *have* to know. And it will get out that I'm here, trust me. Plus, if Ed really turns out to be my father, well, it will really get nuts around here. I want to apologize right now."

"No need," Gage said. "You have just as much a right to be in this city as anyone else."

"Seriously, though—" Nora said.

"Seriously," Gage said, "don't worry about it. If they find you at the Starfish, we'll find you another place. We'll put you in a tent in the forest if we have to. If you want to be here, you can be here. Trust me when I say, *the press is not my friend.* The only people I like less are the police. Any opportunity to disappoint either group is seen, by yours truly, as a pure good."

Alex said, "I can attest to the veracity of all of that."

"Okay," Nora said. "But if it comes to it, I do have a backup option that might be a bit better than a tent in the forest."

"Oh?"

"My yacht."

"You have a yacht?"

"Yes. *La Vie Sans Regrets.* That's what I named it. A life without regrets, just to remind me to focus on living now. It's one of my few indulgences, and it's not that big, nothing like what Spielberg or Clapton have. Only a hundred feet. I can even sail it myself if I had to, though I do have a two-person crew. It's down in the Bay Area, of course, but all I have to do is give them the word and they'll sail it up here. If we have to, we can just stay a few miles out in the ocean and nobody will bother me."

Alex shook his head. "I'm stuck on the 'only a hundred feet' part."

"Really, it sounds more impressive than it is," Nora said.

"Oh, I imagine it's still plenty impressive," Alex said.

"Well." She shrugged.

"Let's hope you don't have to go to that kind of trouble," Gage said. "You've got two weeks, right? Maybe we can find out what you need to know in that amount of time. First things first. You need a room for the night."

Chapter 4

To Nora's credit, she didn't even wrinkle her nose when she saw Gage's van. Most people, he found, looked at his beloved Volkswagen as an alien creature, something that certainly didn't belong on the road and may not have even belonged on planet Earth. He told her just to follow him to the Starfish, then wait in her Navigator until he came back out with the keys.

The night breeze still felt warm, and Gage drove with his window rolled down, marveling that the headlights in his side-view mirror actually belonged to the great Nora West. It didn't feel like it was really happening. Maybe he'd dreamed the whole thing, and he was in the throes of some kind of trauma-induced hallucination due to his grief over giving up his cat. Sure, that might be it. How else to explain the surreal coincidence of the musician who'd meant so much to him, probably more than any musician in his whole life, showing up out of the blue in Barnacle Bluffs, desperate for his help?

He didn't tell her, nor was he sure he ever could, but her third album, *One True Love,* had really helped him through those dark years after Janet died. That first month especially—when the image of Janet submerged in the tub, eyes unseeing, skin already turning blue, would not subside, would not fade even the slightest no matter how drunk he got himself—the title song of the album had acted as a sort of lifeline preventing him from losing his sanity altogether. It was strange that he had not recognized Nora immediately, when her pretty face was on the back of all of her albums, but then, he hadn't spent a lot of time looking at the back of her albums. Mostly he'd been sitting in the dark, carried away by her soulful voice.

He also hadn't listened to her at all in years, at least not by conscious choice. Sometimes he'd catch one of her songs when picking up milk at Jaybee's, or on the jukebox at McAllister's Diner on one of his infrequent visits, and he'd feel the combination of gratitude and nostalgia one got toward an old friend from the past who'd been there for you when it mattered most but eventually, life being what it is, had to chart a different path. Or you did. In the end, it was all the same.

Yet she was here now. What did it mean? Coincidence? Of course. He didn't believe in fate. Still, it was interesting. He was no big believer in psychoanalysis either, especially the self-administered kind, but he would have to be a complete idiot not to see why he'd so quickly jumped at the chance to help her, especially by his own curmudgeonly standards.

A debt was due. He needed to pay her back for what her music had done for him, and here was his chance.

Five minutes later, he parked in one of the few unnumbered spots near the office of the Starfish Motel, a plain, two-story building on the west side of Highway 101 and down the hill from his house. It wasn't much to look at, to put it mildly, especially from the backside, with its flaking gray paint and rusting metal staircase, but he knew that the sweeping ocean view it afforded all of its occupants more than made up for its drab exterior. Plus, the rooms themselves, although plain, were pretty nice for the money.

He motioned for her to park in the empty spot next to him, then gestured for her to wait in the Navigator. The hodgepodge of houses and other small motels that lined the street seemed quiet, many windows dark, parking lots less than half full, which was no surprise for a Sunday in September. A good night to slip in unnoticed.

The clerk, a kid who smelled like cigarettes and was more interested in the episode of *Pawn Stars* playing on the TV mounted in the corner of the lobby than in Gage, said they had five rooms available that could be booked for the week. Gage chose one on the first floor on the corner, easier to get in and out without having to walk by a lot of people, and was back outside with the keys before the show had gone to commercial.

She powered down her tinted window, once again wearing her sunglasses. He laughed.

"What?" she asked.

"Do you always wear sunglasses at night?"

"Oh." She took them off. "Sorry. It's just, you know, habit."

"So people won't recognize you?"

"I guess."

"Does it really help that much?"

"Probably not. It's not just that, though. It's like ... you don't have to make eye contact, right? If people know you're looking at them, they think that's an invitation. It's weird, but it does make a difference."

He didn't know what to say to that, so he handed her the keys and told her where the room was. They carried her bags to her room, fortunate not to encounter anyone coming or going. She didn't have one guitar, but three, and he carried all of them. He was proud to do so.

The room smelled faintly musty, but otherwise was quite

nice: a queen bed with an appropriate starfish comforter, paintings of seashells, pastel-blue walls. The kitchenette was more like
a kitchen corner, in that the oven, sink, microwave, half-sized
refrigerator, and white laminate cabinets were all crammed into
a space hardly bigger than a phone booth, but at least all the
pieces were there. She could live there unobtrusively for quite a
long time, which was the important thing.

After tossing her bags on the bed, she opened the screen
door. The waves crashing on the beach, the salty breeze rustling
past the curtains—the sounds and smells of the ocean quickly
invaded the space.

"It's so dark out there I can't even see it," she said.

"It's not more than fifty feet away."

"Good. I like it."

"So the place will work?"

"It's great."

She turned and smiled. He smiled back.

"You okay for the night," he said, "or do you want me to go
to the store?"

"I'm okay tonight," she said.

"I'll bring some food by in the morning."

"All right. And what's your plan? Who are you going to talk
to first?"

"I need to think about it. I'll let you know in the morning."

"You'll keep me in the loop, though?"

"Absolutely."

"Wait, you don't have my number. We need to exchange—"

"I don't have a number."

She smiled faintly. "What?"

"I don't have a phone."

"You don't have a phone?"

"Nope."

"Why not?"

He sighed. "Not this again."

"Excuse me?"

"Nothing. I'll update you in person, okay? We'll figure it out as we go along. Let's just start with tomorrow morning."

She still looked a bit confused, but she nodded. He should have left right then. A wish goodnight, a perfunctory nod, that was all the moment dictated. But he wanted to say something more, something about her music. Maybe nothing quite so personal as what her music had really meant to him, but *something*. She must have taken the uncomfortable silence the wrong way, because she stared at the floor and chewed on her bottom lip, obviously troubled.

"I need to say something," she said.

Already, he knew something was off. She sounded nervous.

"Okay," he said.

"We're not, you know, having sex."

"What?"

"I just feel I need to get that out there right away."

Gage was so taken aback that words failed him. He found her attractive, certainly, but the last thing he'd been thinking about was making some sort of pass at her. She looked up at him. Again, she must have read his silence the wrong way, because she took a stutter step toward him, her expression now troubled. When she spoke, her words spilled out in a jumbled rush.

"I know that was blunt," she said. "I'm sorry. I hope I didn't your feelings. It's not ... I mean, you're obviously attractive. I'm sure you have no trouble with women. I'm just saying— you know, if things were different, if I was ... I'm just not in a place, you know? I made a pact with myself. I got so messed up with men I decided—three years, that's what I told myself. Three years without … Okay, I'm babbling. I've said too much already. It'd be helpful if you said something now. Really."

"Okay," he said.

"Okay?"

He shrugged.

"That's it," she said. "Okay?"

"I guess."

"Okay to what?"

"Okay to … your request."

"Huh."

"What do you want me to say?"

She didn't answer for a moment. He heard footsteps on the landing above them, laughter. In the room next door, someone turned on a television and he heard a male voice, steady, droning, like a news anchor. Above it all, the ocean waves continued their rhythmic dance on the beach.

"I don't know," she said. "I guess I expected … I don't know."

"You expected me to put up more of a fight?"

"No. I mean … I, um, I'm just confused."

"I'll say."

She looked at him sharply. "Excuse me?"

"You're confused. I appreciate you putting up the red flag, but honestly, Nora, I wasn't even thinking along those lines."

"Oh," she said.

"Obviously you're an attractive woman. I doubt you have any trouble with men, especially if you're so accustomed to them throwing themselves at you an hour after meeting them that you make them sign some sort of terms of service agreement just to have a conversation with you."

Her face reddened. "That's not—that's not what I was saying!"

"Well, good. Because I'm not one of your groupies, Nora."

"I didn't—I didn't say—"

"And I'm not some celebrity sycophant out to get his jollies by trying to bag the great Nora West like some sort of trophy. The last thing on my mind was how I could get you into bed. I mean, we just met, for God's sake."

"I know! You just—I mean, if you lived my life … If you—if you had to deal with—"

"Oh, I'm sure. If I lived your life, and had men throwing themselves at me all the time, and probably women, too, I might just become self-absorbed enough to think that all people are that way. But not everybody's that way, Nora. I'm not that way. Some people actually believe in, you know, romance. Or letting things go as they will, whether something develops or not."

"I believe in romance."

"Good. I do too. But I wasn't thinking about that either. All I was really thinking about was how to help you. Is that okay? Does my motivation have to be more complex than that?"

She was all wound up with another fiery retort, but his question stopped her. She blinked several times, her pupils so dilated he saw only a sliver of her brown irises. The pink in her cheeks had deepened into a shade of crimson, spreading to her ears, her forehead, and her neck. She took a deep, shuddering breath, then looked at the floor.

"I think you should go now," she said.

He nodded, though she wasn't looking at him. Had he been too harsh? Of course he'd been too harsh. Navigating the troubled waters of interpersonal conflict had never been his forte. When someone poked him with a stick, he hit back with a club. It was his way. Garrison Gage, master conversationalist.

"I'll be by in the morning with groceries," he said.

She didn't say anything, but when he started for the door, she followed him. The atmosphere between them had been poisoned, but he wasn't sure what to do about it. Partly it was her fault, partly his, but there was no point in assigning blame—it was what it was, and here they were. He opened the door. An elderly couple was shuffling past at just that moment, so he waited, smiling politely at them until they'd passed, making sure to use his body to block Nora from view.

When he turned to say goodbye to Nora, hoping to part on at least somewhat more friendly terms, she was still glaring at him with enough intensity to turn sand into glass.

"I'm not self-absorbed," she said.

"Okay," he said.

"Really, I'm not."

"Okay."

"Will you stop saying *okay*? I don't think you believe me. It's fine, you don't believe me. But I'm not self-absorbed. I'm *not*. I just wanted to correct you on that."

"I stand corrected," he said.

He hadn't meant to say it with a smug tone, but he could hear himself, and he certainly sounded smug. His rudeness was apparently unstoppable. Once out, there was little hope putting the jerk inside him back in the bottle. He knew this from experience. Unfettered, unchained, unbridled, here was the side of him that he'd worked to soften in recent years—mostly failing, but still he'd tried. Garrison 2.0, Zoe had jokingly called his feeble attempts at a softer approach. In a strange way, it always felt liberating allowing his pure, raw self out into the light, but he still felt bad it was happening with Nora.

She started to say something else, sputtered a little, then shook her head and started to close the door. He felt a sudden pang of remorse—not so much at what he'd said, or how he'd handled things, but simply that their first night was going to end in such a rotten way. He wanted to salvage it somehow.

"Nora?"

She stopped and looked at him through the crack in the door, eyes weary.

"I really like your music," he said.

It felt phony coming out of his mouth, even if it hadn't felt phony saying it. So much for an eloquent explanation of all her work had done for him. He might as well have sent her a greeting card. She tilted her head down, part nod, part act of surrender.

He was about to try again when she closed the door.

Chapter 5

For his first five years in Barnacle Bluffs, Gage had lived alone. The house on the hill, purchased outright for cash by parting with the brownstone in New York and all of its blood-soaked memories, had offered him the kind of solitary refuge he'd so desperately wanted. Alex had already been in town, of course, and that might have factored into his plans on some minor level—the recognition, even then, that a completely hermit-like existence probably wasn't healthy—but it was the house itself that had really committed him to the move. With the hill below, the undeveloped forest of firs and oaks behind, and the wall of arbor vitae that separated the house from its nearest neighbor, it had resembled a private retreat as much as any two-thousand-square-foot A-frame on only half an acre could.

There may be people a stone's throw away from him on three sides, and a sprawling apartment complex a short jaunt through what only seemed like a massive forest behind him, but the feeling of isolation, of being cut off from the world and all of its problems, was real enough—even if it was only an illusion. A view of the ocean, the night whisper of the trees, and years to stew in his guilt unencumbered by the annoyances of other people: it was all he'd needed. The illusion had worked, at least for a time.

Yet there was another way to look at the seclusion of his house, and the way it had been used to separate him from the world. It wasn't until he rounded the corner on his gravel drive, coming back from dropping off Nora at the Starfish Motel that Sunday night, that he finally realized what should have been obvious to him when he bought the place. The wall of firs to the east, black and textureless in the night, was so solid it could have been concrete. The dozens of column-like arbor vitae, in nicely spaced parallel lines, resembled giant metal bars. This house, his private little compound, wasn't a retreat.

It was a prison.

This was the feeling he carried into the house with him, of being an inmate of a jail of his own making. He didn't bother turning on any lights, settling into his armchair, brooding. The digital oven clock, a beacon of green in the dark, read 9:32. He watched it until it turned to 9:33. He felt an impending depression weighing him down, like the way the air thickens with a coming storm, and shrugged it off with a morose resignation. What would come would come. He listened to the sounds of the house, the dissatisfied hum of the refrigerator, the sigh of the wind against the windows, the wincing creaks and groans of support beams high above him, and wondered if the house missed Zoe too. Maybe it only missed the cat. After all, the cat had spent a lot more time in it.

"Carrot," he said to the dark.

Without quite realizing it, he found himself standing in the doorway to her room. He flicked on the light. She'd tidied it up quite a bit, much tidier than she'd kept it when actually living in it: the bed was made, the floor was clean, the tops of the dressers were organized, agates, shell shells, and other knickknacks she'd picked up on her beach walks neatly arranged. She'd left her Radiohead posters, her packed bookshelves, and most of the framed black-and-white photos. They were hers, photography something she'd been dabbling with since he'd known her, taking them with her Nikon DSLR and printing them on a compact photo printer he'd bought her for Christmas a couple years back.

Some of the photos pictured popular places on the Oregon coast—a sunset view of Haystack Rock in Canon Beach, the Devil's Churn outside of Florence on an overcast day—but most actually pictured small, unremarkable things. Or perhaps remarkable, if seen for what they really were: a piece of driftwood that looked like a hunched old man, a lonely seagull pecking at a piece of gum in the casino parking lot, a rusty, abandoned lawn chair half buried in sand. She'd taken a few pictures of people, too. He smiled when he realized that the one of she and Gage standing in the yard behind the Turret House, taken by Alex, was gone.

He also saw that she'd taken her camera and her printer. Why this made him sad, he could not say.

Struck by the sudden urge to call her, he started for the front door. In five minutes, he could be on the phone at the gas station down the hill. Or was it too late? He stopped, his hand on the doorknob, and realized how foolish he was being. No, he would not succumb to his loneliness with such self-pitying melodrama. What was happening to him?

Instead, he bustled from room to room, as much as a man with a bum knee could bustle, turning on all the lights and directing his sudden burst of energy into a flurry of cleaning. It soon became clear that the house didn't need cleaning, as Zoe had apparently done it recently. This deepened his sadness: one, because she'd cleaned the house and he hadn't noticed, and two, because he'd told her many times over the years that she didn't need to clean at all; he'd be happy to pay for a housekeeper again. She'd always taken offense to this suggestion, as if he was throwing shade at her cleaning prowess. He'd often wondered if the real reason was because her grandmother had been the last housekeeper, and the thought of replacing her with a stranger was just too much for Zoe to bear.

Somehow, with great effort, Gage still managed to collect half a bag worth of garbage, mostly piles of mail she'd left for him to go through, but it was enough for him to feel like he'd accomplished something.

He tied off the string and carried the bag outside. It was going on midnight, and the crescent moon was half obscured in strips of clouds like a belly dancer spinning amidst rippling scarves. The night felt warm, the heat of the day still lingering, but the darkness was deep enough that the firs, the arbor vitae, and the many varied colors of the ivy, juniper, and the rest of the underbrush had all seeped away, leaving a mottled black. All the light emanating from his house, yellow squares on the gravel, made the darkness that much deeper.

His garbage can was in a small, fenced-in enclosure on the south side of his house, the one area that the porch light didn't reach. With the arbor vitae looming behind it, and the firs towering to his left, even all the brightly illuminated windows of his house couldn't alleviate the impenetrable darkness. It was blackness all around, so black he couldn't even see the lid of the can and had to feel for it. The odor of rancid meat—he guessed Zoe had taken it upon herself to clean the fridge, too—left no doubt he was in the right place. He tossed the bag inside, slamming the lid down in the hopes of trapping the smell. No go. He still got a good whiff of rotten foulness, and he cringed away from it, backing out of the clearing with a hand over his nose.

That was when he saw someone standing in the trees.

It was the silhouette of a man, or at least what seemed like a man, standing between the trunks of two firs, just far enough back in the shadows that his form was almost, but only *almost,* indistinguishable from the rest of the darkness. It was only the man's torso, the hedge of junipers on that corner blocking his lower form from view, and the branches of a young sapling next to him also blocked part of his face, but Gage was still sure it was a man.

"Hello?" Gage said.

The man didn't move, so still that Gage began to doubt whether he was a real person at all. They both remained absolutely still, a standoff of sorts, and Gage was determined to wait him out. He didn't even want to look away. If the man fled, he wanted to see it, as proof he was real. His Beretta ... it was back in the house, and he felt defenseless and exposed. He didn't even have his cane, not that a pursuit through the trees was even a possibility. Was the stranger armed? He could have been aiming a handgun at Gage right now, using the waist-high juniper to block the view.

Gage's heart began to pound, a steady drumming in his ears. Still, the stranger didn't move. An eerie stillness enveloped them. Gage started to doubt himself, wondering if hallucinations, strange imaginings, and, yes, maybe even invisible friends would soon become part of his everyday life. Why wouldn't his invisible friend be an ominous shadow in the dark? It fit him, didn't it?

Then, just as the gentlest of breezes whispered along the tops of the firs, just when Gage was about to give up this silly game and go searching for a better one, like how fast he could find the bottom of a bottle of bourbon, the stranger moved.

He simply turned and stepped deeper into the shadows, not running, certainly not fleeing, but not walking away with obliviousness or indifference either. He left like a man who wanted Gage to *know* he was leaving.

And yet the stranger's departure only lasted a second before he vanished completely into the shadows.

THE NEXT MORNING, after a night spending more time reassuring himself his Beretta was within reach on his nightstand than actually sleeping, he ventured into the forest behind his house for some sign of the stranger. The fog that wreathed the trees, thick and wet on his face, did not make his job any easier. There were no obvious footprints or broken branches. Somehow he almost expected something blatant and sinister, like the words *I'm watching you* carved into tree. He searched until his fingers and toes were numb from the cold, growing increasingly frustrated, and thinking about those years after Janet's death where she sometimes appeared to him.

She'd seemed so real, as real as a person could be.

Knowing little good would come from continuing to dwell on it, he pushed the whole thing from his mind and left for the grocery store. The empty aisles at Jaybee's, and the lonely highway, should have been some clue to him how early it was, but it wasn't until Nora opened her motel door, rubbing her eyes and squinting up at him, that he realized he'd never checked the time.

She wore a baggy white T-shirt and gray sweatpants with holes in the knees, the kind of thing that millions of women wore to bed but that he somehow found surprising on the great Nora West. He didn't know what he expected—a black silk gown with a ruby-studded collar? It wasn't the sort of ensemble that was designed to show off her figure, that was sure, but there was still something tantalizing about how her body filled out the clothes in certain places, tight here, loose there, a curve of a hip, a slope of a breast, as if he was glimpsing her naked body through shifting vapors of smoke. Gage always found it more provocative when a woman wasn't *trying* to beautiful.

"Are you always such an early riser?" she asked.

"Almost never," he said. He shifted the two bags of groceries in his arms. "Do you always answer your door without asking who it is?"

"I looked through the peephole," she said.

"Not for very long. You should be more careful."

"Okay … Is there a specific reason I need to be more careful?"

"No. Can I put these on your kitchen counter?"

"Oh, yeah, sorry. Come on in."

She took one of bags from him and led the way. He would have protested, but the truth was that without his cane, his situation was too precarious to pass up the offer. As it was, he was glad she was in front of him, because she didn't have to watch him limp into the room. He was also afforded a very nice view of the sway of her bottom inside sweatpants that didn't seem at all baggy from the backside.

He realized he was staring, and caught himself. Hadn't he learned anything from the previous night? The last thing he wanted was start the next day on another awkward misunderstanding. Don't go there, Gage.

Pale gray light rimmed the closed curtains, the surf crashing on the beach loud enough that she must have had the screen door cracked open. He hoped she hadn't slept with it open. She put the bag on the tiny kitchen counter and started to unload it, but then must have read his concern on his face, because she stopped and looked at him.

"Okay, what is it?"

Gage put his bag on the counter next to hers. "Nothing."

"It's obviously not nothing. What happened?"

"Nothing happened. I just …" He thought about telling her about the man he'd seen in trees, but if he was going crazy, he'd prefer to keep that fact to himself a bit longer. "Look, this whole thing is just strange, that's all. The letter. His suicide. I've just learned to be careful when all the pieces don't seem to add up. Can you just, you know, take extra precautions?"

She studied his face for a long time, the sleepiness in her eyes already completely gone. In the end, though she didn't appear satisfied with his explanation, she nodded and emptied the bags. He helped her. She offered to pay and he told her he'd put it on her bill, knowing full well he'd never put it on the bill because there would never be a bill. She asked him if he wanted some coffee, and he said yes. While she was making it, he opened the curtains.

The fog still lay thick over the western horizon, only a small strip of beach and flat gray ocean visible before everything blurred into white. The grass on the narrow strip between her concrete patio and the white picket fence glistened with moisture. A lone seagull stood on the fence, staring at him petulantly, like an impatient diner glaring at a waiter, but otherwise Gage saw no one. When he turned around, he saw Nora wincing and shielding her eyes.

"Ouch," she said.

"You want me to close them?"

"No, no, it's good. You weren't lying. It's really close. It's just, I'm not much of a morning person, you know?"

"Sorry again."

"No, it's fine, really. I'm here for a reason. I can't expect you to adjust to my schedule."

With the room now full of light, he saw what he had not

seen before: her acoustic guitar perched on the couch, and an open spiral notebook on the bamboo coffee table near it. In the lined pages of the notebook, he saw a mixture of handwritten words and musical notes written in blue ink, lots of scratched-out passages. He realized he was staring, looked up and met her gaze, then felt guilty, as if she'd caught him snooping in her underwear drawer.

"Yeah," she said, "I wrote a little last night."

"New song?"

She shrugged, turning her attention to getting down some mugs. He didn't press, though he was dying to know what she wrote. Her cell phone, plugged into a socket at the edge of the counter, vibrated. She glanced at it and wrinkled her nose.

"It's been going crazy this morning," she said. "Everybody's pretty upset that I took off."

"Everybody?"

She shrugged. "My personal assistant, Jewel, mostly. But she called my manger, Harry, and he got everybody else worked up into a tizzy. Some of the guys in the band even called. You know, it's mostly my fault. I just left a message for her yesterday telling her I was taking off for a few days and I'd be in touch. Then, because I'm a pretty horrible liar, I didn't answer her calls or texts."

"Do they know where you are now?"

"No. Not yet. I did text them telling them I'm fine, so they'd lay off, but I just don't want to deal with that right now. And honestly, if I tell them I'm in Oregon, I know it's going to leak to the press. But I don't know how long I can hold them off before they send out a search party for me." She laughed, though it came out a bit hollow. "I'm only joking a little."

"Well," Gage said, "I guess the upside is it's nice to have people who care about you so much."

She didn't say anything, though he sensed it was uncomfortable terrain for her. She poured their coffee and put his cup on the counter, along with the creamer he'd bought. Even with a healthy dollop of half-and-half, the coffee tasted strong and bitter. He put in more creamer, which made the taste at least tolerable. She drank hers black. They stood like that, sipping their coffee in silence, the gray faux-marble counter between them like a fence between two pens. He felt like he was in a different world from her.

"So," she said, "what's your plan?"

"Well, I'm not sure yet. It depends on how fast things have been moving with your f—with Ed Boone's personal affairs. Has his next of kin been notified? I'd like to see his apartment. It'd be a good place to start, and there's got to be a lot of clues in there, maybe even some things about you. There's the will, of course. We want to get that into the right hands. His neighbors. The library. Heceta Head. Anyplace he's spent some time. I usually just start asking questions and see where it leads."

"Hmm. Doesn't seem all that complicated."

"What, did you expect Sherlock Holmes?"

"No. No, I just ... I don't know."

"Most of the time it's not complicated at all. Usually this kind of work is just brute effort when it comes down to it. Being relentless, following one lead to another. There's a lot of dead ends, a lot of conversations that lead nowhere, a lot of hours spent following people or on stakeouts that don't amount to anything. Most PIs are bad not because they lack brilliant deductive reasoning but because most PIs are lazy."

"Well," she said, "it's a good thing *you're* not lazy."

"Oh, no, I'm lazy too. Just not when I'm working."

"Somehow I have a hard time believing that."

"Do you want to know how many hours I've spent just sitting in my armchair doing crossword puzzles? Civilizations have risen and fallen, I assure you, while I was filling my days putting tiny letters in tiny boxes."

"Hmm."

"Anyway," he said, "I'll know more when I start asking questions. In the meantime, sit tight. Write some songs. I'll swing by at least once a day, if not more."

"Okay," she said. "One request?"

"Sure."

She smiled. "Can you not make it so early next time?"

Chapter 6

Feeling better about how he parted from Nora this time—
there was still an awkwardness there, a residual tension
from their spat last night, but no rancor—Gage headed into
town in the van. His first instinct was to check out Ed Boone's
apartment, but it was still too early for that. Besides, he needed
some breakfast, and he knew the perfect place to do it.

The fog pressing down on the ocean was already lifting, the
ocean extending farther to the horizon, more blue than gray. He
had the highway mostly to himself, the road slick and black, the
headlamps of the occasional passing car a soft and gauzy yellow.
The cast iron clock mounted on the sidewalk outside the U.S.
Bank, at the edge of the most touristy part of town, read a quarter past seven, and all the little shops were still dark. Kites, surf-
boards, T-shirts, saltwater taffy, knickknacks of every size and
shape—the windows were filled with all the kitschy stuff that
was common in a beach town but would have been out of place
just about anywhere else in Oregon. Gage, usually indifferent to
this sort of thing, felt strangely morose at the sight of all those
empty sidewalks.

A couple blocks after the clock, he turned east and parked

on the street. Unlike the highway, cars were parked on both sides, as well as in the little parking lot right behind McAllister's Family Diner. This was its official name, of course, the latest in a long series of names over the past few decades, but almost everybody just called it "the diner." Or Ed's Diner, if they were real old-timers and remembered its original name. Unfortunately, there weren't many of those folks around anymore, since most of them had been old-timers even back then, and the thing about old-timers was that their time eventually did run out.

Gage hoped to find at least a few of them.

He donned his fedora and walked with his cane to the front door. The humidity from yesterday still lingered, and his jacket would have been unnecessary if not for the moisture in the air. Water beaded on the leather. It was quiet enough on the highway that he heard the ocean over the tops of the stores on the other side of the road. The diner was in a low, squat building, a laundromat on one side, a tax preparer on the other, moss growing in the crumbling sidewalk along the front. Through the big front windows, he saw two old guys at separate booths and his heart cheered a little. Maybe luck was on his side.

Most of the booths and tables were taken, so Gage took a seat at the counter, leaning his cane underneath. That was the thing about the cane. He always had to find a place to put it. The hubbub of conversation was loud enough that he could only barely make out Otis Redding's "(Sittin' On) The Dock of the Bay" playing from the jukebox. The diner might have seemed surprisingly busy for a Monday in September, especially for a town that lived and died by the tourist trade, but it was no surprise to anyone who actually lived in Barnacle Bluffs. The peeling black-and-white checkered tile floor, the yellow stuffing spilling out from all the rips in the vinyl booths, the grease stains that dotted the plain white walls—these may have been off-putting details to some of the ritzier tourists from the valley, but they were signs of familiarity and comfort to the locals who actually kept the place in business.

A few people glanced at him, but mostly he was ignored. It was why Gage liked the place. Though gossip certainly traveled fast when there was something worth talking about, like any small town, for the most part the locals didn't bother you unless you wanted to be bothered. Be friendly, you usually got friendly back. Keep to yourself, and they'd do the same, no hard feelings. Gage, of course, almost always opted for the second.

Today, however, he needed to dig deep for his best social self. He drummed his fingers on the counter in time to Redding, and when Judy, the waitress, asked him if he wanted coffee, he actually smiled at her.

It seemed to catch her off guard, as if she'd just witnessed a rare phenomenon she'd never expected to see. She smiled back, furtively, and when she went to pour his coffee, she splashed a little on the counter. She apologized and dabbed at it with a washcloth from her apron. He hadn't talked to her much over the years, but he'd never seen her spill coffee. He hadn't known it was possible.

"Good morning, Judy," he said.

"Good morning, good morning," she said.

"Got quite a crowd today."

"We do."

She stood there with her coffee pot in one hand, the soiled rag in the other, looking at Gage as if not sure what to do next. It was as if she'd forgotten that she was a waitress. He knew she knew who he was, about his past. She'd said some kind words to him during a few of his cases before, so they weren't exactly strangers. A stout woman with stout red hair, not exactly a natural color, but certainly one that matched her bright red lipstick.

On someone else, seen someplace else, her appearance might have seemed anachronistic, straight out of the seventies, but since the diner was also straight out of the seventies, it fit. It fit so well, in fact, that he couldn't imagine her outside of it. Maybe she didn't exist outside of it, like a character in a *Twilight Zone* episode. He thought of mentioning this, as a sort of joke, but couldn't think how to say it without it coming out more like an insult, so he went with the basics instead.

"I'll have the ham and eggs number two," he said.

"Oh, right," she said.

When she started to turn away, he said, "Judy?"

"Yes?"

"Have you worked here a long time?"

"Um, I suppose. Why do you ask?"

"How long?"

"Oh gosh, sweetie," she said, "I don't know. Let me see. I moved to Barnacle Bluffs after my divorce, and it was the following winter … Yes, a little over twenty years."

"So you didn't know the original owner?"

"Ed Boone? No. I mean, not directly. I think Bart Jellstone had owned it a good five years by that point, and of course the Wellseys after that. I've seen a lot of owners come and go. But I did hear stories about the old days when Ed owned it. Why? What's this about, Garrison?"

Gage knew he should have anticipated this question, since it was obvious he was going to have to answer it and he couldn't very well tell people the truth, but he hadn't put any thought into a cover story. It may not have been public knowledge that Ed Boone had been the name of the volunteer at Heceta Head who'd committed suicide, but it would be soon enough, so he couldn't very well pretend this was about something else. It had to be something that involved his death that made sense.

"I'm writing a book," he said.

"A what?"

"A book. You know, with words and everything."

"You're writing a book?"

"Yes."

"What about? Your cases?"

"No. Not exactly."

Gage wished he'd thought of something better, but it was too late now, so he had to go with it. Bill Withers launched into "Lean on Me," and the conversation had lulled just enough that he could actually make out some of the words. It also meant a few of his neighbors might hear his answer, so he wanted it to be a decent one. Fortunately, Judy gave him a bit more time.

"Hold on, sweetie," she said, "let me get your order in first, and put down this coffee pot. I want to hear everything about this, though! Be back in a jiffy."

She sounded sincere, and probably was. The advantage someone like Judy had was that she probably didn't have to fake sincerity when it came to small talk. She actually wanted to hear what people had to say, and it made him feel bad lying to her. He watched her clip his order to the cord that ran along the window to the kitchen, his mind skipping past a dozen different book possibilities. By the time she returned to him, he thought he had something at least somewhat plausible.

"It's called *Barnacle Bluffs Blues: The Secret Stories of a Small Coastal Town*," he explained.

"Oh!" Judy said.

"History, humor, anecdote. You know, a little bit of everything. I've learned a lot about this place from all the work I've done, and I thought it might be fun to put it into a book."

"Certainly. I mean, I can think of lots of stories for your book. I hear all kinds of things working here."

"I'm sure you do. That's what I'm hoping."

"Like the Johnson twins," Judy said, leaning in. "You hear about them? This was, oh, maybe seven, eight years ago. The little one, she—"

"Actually," Gage said, "I want to stick with Ed Boone first, if you don't mind."

"Oh. Why—why do you want to know about him? I'm not sure I—"

"Did you hear he died?"

"Died? Oh, gosh, no. How? When?"

"I can't say more right now, but you'll read about it in the paper soon enough. I heard it from … one of my sources in town. I think they're trying to notify the family."

"Oh my."

"Otherwise I'd tell you the details. But I'm very interested in his life for my book. Seems like he could have been quite a person in his day, knew everybody, that sort of thing. And yet, when he died, nobody seemed to know he was even living here."

Judy raised her eyebrows. "He was living in Barnacle Bluffs?"

"That's what I mean. He just faded into obscurity."

"I have to be honest. Until you told me just now that he died, I thought he'd probably already passed on. But it's not like I thought about it, really. It's just one of things I kind of assumed. Will you excuse me for a sec?"

"Sure," Gage said.

She grabbed the coffee pot and filled the cups of everyone at the counter. She took an order from a man in a UPS uniform. The hubbub in the room rose again, drowning out the jukebox. When Judy returned, she touched her bob of hair, looking thoughtful.

"I really don't know much about Ed, I'm afraid," she said. "I've been racking my brains, but I … well, I heard he was real good to the staff. At least, according to Ronnie."

"Ronnie?"

"She was a waitress here when I started. I think she was Ed's first hire, so she'd been around quite a while."

"Where is she now?"

"I don't know. Might not be, you know, with us anymore. She filed for social security a few months after I started, and retired a few months after that. I guess she had some pension money, too, from when her husband was in the military. She was a sweet gal, Ronnie. Always something nice to say about everybody. Oh, you know, I just remembered—her son's still living around here, I think. He's an accountant or lawyer or something. Name's ... oh, geez, just slipped my mind. It will come back to me in a minute. But he used to come here when he was in high school all the time and have milkshakes at the counter. He might know a thing or two about Ed."

"Do you remember Ronnie's last name, at least?"

"Meyer. Ronnie Meyer. Or Veronica, I guess, was her real name. And if you— Howie! That was her son's name. I knew it would come to me. Howard. Sweet kid. Very shy, but sweet. Always 'thank you, ma'am,' and 'please, sir,' talked so soft you could barely hear him. Which was the opposite of Ronnie, let me tell you, always gabbing up a—"

"Did she tell you anything about Ed's family life?"

"What? Oh, no, he really didn't come up much. Or if he did, I don't remember. I just remember her saying what a good boss he was when somebody asked about how the diner started in the first place."

"So she didn't say anything about him possibly being ... unfaithful?"

"Unfaithful! Heavens, no. I mean, if he was, Ronnie would never say such a thing. She was far too sweet to talk about things like that. She'd get cross if someone even said the word damn. Just a sweet, sweet soul. Why, did you hear Ed was unfaithful?"

Gage shrugged. "Just rumors. I want to be careful I don't make those rumors worse, you understand?"

"Oh sure, sure. I'm trying to think of someone else you could talk to, but she's the only one I knew who worked with him. The cook, the busboy—everybody else was almost as new as me. I could tell you *a lot* about some of the other owners, though. Like the Wellseys. Oh boy. What a crazy bunch of—"

"I *do* want to hear about the Wellseys, but I want to stick with this chapter on Ed Boone first. Makes it easier if I, you know, see one topic all the way through. Are you sure there's no one else you can think of who knew him?"

She winced, as if his rebuffing her comment about the Wellseys had shocked her, but she quickly turned thoughtful again. He liked that she recovered fast. It was a good quality for a waitress, getting over small slights in a hurry. It was a good quality for anyone, in fact. She brought a finger to her lips, her eyes turning distant, gazing over him at the crowded room. Gage saw that the ends of her fingers were chapped and bleached, full of tiny fissures and cracks from all her years of hard working.

"Hmm," she said, "I'll really have to think on that one. Maybe the mailman? Carl. He retired, too, but only a couple years ago. He told me he'd been working this route thirty-two years, so he must have known Ed at least a little. But other than that ... *Oh!*"

"What's that?"

She pointed in the direction of the window. "You could always talk to those two."

He turned and saw that she was pointing at the two old-timers sitting in booths back to back, the ones he'd seen when entering the diner.

"Frank and Wilford," she said. "They've been coming here *forever*. Like, to hear them tell it, they were already sitting here when the diner was built up around them. I bet they have a thing or two to tell you about Ed. Frank's the one on the left, the one in the hat with the buttons on it. But be careful."

"Why's that?"

She smirked. "You'll see. I don't want to ruin the fun."

Gage thanked her for her help and told her that if she thought of anything else about Ed to let him know. She seemed disappointed that he didn't want immediate access to her treasure trove of Barnacle Bluffs history, and he again felt a little bad lying to her, but nothing good would come of it if Nora's presence in town was made known. He took a sip of his coffee and made his way as inconspicuously as he could to the two old guys sitting in adjoining booths, their backs to each other, looking about as approachable as wounded dogs.

"Hello, gentlemen," Gage said.

Neither of them acknowledged his presence. He thought it might be the loudness of the music, so he tried again. Still nothing. Frank took a sip of his coffee and gazed out the window. Wilford, most of his meal gone, pushed what was left of his hash browns around with his fork but didn't take a bite.

Something was going on between them. Gage could feel it. The hostility was thick, the anger simmering just beneath their deep scowls, and it wasn't just toward him. They were quite the pair. At a glance, Gage had thought them so similar in appearance they could have been twins, but up close they were more different than alike. They were both wrinkled, jowly men with weathered faces, but Frank was stocky and slouched, both his sun-faded blue hat and his fishing vest adorned with buttons. Gage saw a Reagan button and a Dukakis button. He saw Mickey Mouse and Superman. He saw buttons for the Oregon

State Fair, St. Patrick's Day, and the American Heart Association. His face had a lumpy, uneven quality, as if it had melted for a while in the hot sun and dried in cool weather. Uneven tufts of white hair sprouted from various places on his chin and cheeks, particularly thick on the mole on his sagging neck.

Wilford, on the other hand, sat ramrod straight in his seat, with the kind of still dignity of a Buddhist monk. His face, though also deeply wrinkled, was more precise and symmetrical in its lines and angles, like a sculpture by Rodin. His silver hair, what was left of it, was neatly parted and slicked with enough hairspray to hold it down in hurricane-force winds. He wore a similar army-green fisherman's vest, but so bright and clean it could have been bought off the rack that morning.

"Are you talking to me?" Wilford asked suddenly. "Or are you directing your words toward somebody else in this vicinity?"

Frank snorted.

"Well," Gage said, "I guess I was hoping to talk to both of you."

Wilford replied with a quick shake of his head. Frank rolled his eyes and took another sip of his coffee.

"What?" Gage said.

"I don't know who *else* you're talking about," Wilford said, "but if you're addressing me, I'm afraid I have to decline your invitation. I'm just finishing up momentarily, then I have an appointment to keep."

Frank snorted again. Wilford's nose and cheeks reddened slightly, and when he spoke, his voice was even more clipped.

"Though it may be hard to believe," he said, "*some* people actually have lives. I have a routine teeth cleaning with the dentist, if you really must know. So whatever insurance you're selling, good man, I'm not in the market at this time. Perhaps there are more gullible participants for your wares somewhere nearby."

Though he glanced at Gage when he spoke, as if talking to him, it was obvious that most of his remarks were meant for Frank. His button-adorned companion sighed again, then looked up at Gage, squinting with his right eye. His left was a milky white color, the iris tanner than the solid chocolate brown of the other one.

"You're that detective fella," Frank said.

"That's right," Gage said.

"Figured. Some folks around these parts may not be very observant, but I do try to pay attention."

Wilford gave a quick, curt shake of his head. Frank didn't look at him, but even with his back turned he seemed to know that Wilford had reacted because his scowl deepened.

"You know," Frank said, still looking at Gage, "just because a man's busy don't mean he's really, you know, *busy*. He can be doing a lot of somethings that all add up to a lot of nothings."

"There's wisdom there," Gage said. "You have just a minute? I want to see what you know about Ed Boone."

This piqued their interest, but Wilford, other than sitting a bit straighter in his booth, tried not to show it. Frank raised his unruly white eyebrows.

"The guy who started this joint?" he said.

"So you know him?"

"Sure I know him. Like I said, I pay attention."

Wilford shook his head again, this time vigorously enough that Frank probably felt the vibration through the booth. He shook his head in return. Judy, smiling a bit too smugly for Gage's taste, brought his meal to him and asked where he was going to sit.

"Not *here*," Wilford said.

Gage looked at Frank, who, after a moment's hesitation, finally shrugged. Judy deposited the plate and Gage slid into the other side of the booth with his cane, now with a clear view of Frank's bedraggled face and the back of Wilford's rigid neck, the redness deepening by the second. Steam rose from the hash browns, the smell of cooked potatoes buttery and rich. Judy brought his coffee. Gage ate for a moment in silence, trying to let their curiosity grow. The ham was a bit dry, and the scrambled eggs were on the runny side, but since the whole thing cost not much more than a latte at Starbucks, he couldn't complain.

"Well?" Frank said. "What happened with Ed? There been some kind of wrongdoing or something? I figure there must be, you involved."

"Nope," Gage said, "I'm just writing a book."

This got both of their attention. Frank, reaching for his coffee, paused. Wilford, though he didn't turn, sat straighter in his seat.

"A book?" Frank said. "What kind of book?"

Gage told them what he'd told Judy. By the end, Wilford was half turned toward him. When Frank started to talk about the early pioneers who settled in Barnacle Bluffs, Gage interjected by saying he specifically wanted to know about Ed Boone right now, because he was new at this whole book-writing thing and taking it one chapter at a time so as not to get confused. And it wasn't going to be a definitive history, more just historical anecdotes.

"Sounds like bathroom reading," Frank said.

"What's wrong with bathroom reading?" Gage said. "People need something to read in the bathroom, don't they?"

Wilford, with a great show of haughtiness, said, "Well, if someone was asking me—"

"No one's asking you," Frank said.

"If someone was asking *me*," Wilford continued, louder, "I would say I think it's an *excellent* idea."

"Well, you would."

"Excuse me? What's that supposed to mean?"

Frank, looking at Gage and not Wilford, shrugged.

"Go ahead, then," Wilford said. "Whatever insult you've saved up this time, spit it out."

"Oh, I thought you weren't talking to me?"

"Don't be ridiculous. I'm not the one who severed our friendship."

Frank laughed. "Severed. God, only you talk like that. It's like you think you're on *Downton Abbey*. And I didn't *sever* anything."

"We had an arrangement—"

"There you go again. Arrangement. What are you, Jane Austen?"

"We had an *arrangement,*" Wilford pushed on, his face now nearly as red as the ketchup bottle, "one we both agreed on, and you—you changed things without discussing it with me first."

Frank held up his index finger. "One time," he said, still directing his comments at Gage even though Gage was merely a bystander to whatever petty feud this was. "One time, I had breakfast with someone else, and it's like it's the end of the world."

"It's the principle of the thing," Wilford said.

"Oh, it's not about that, and you know it. It's about who I had breakfast with."

"I have no idea *what* you are talking about."

Frank shook his head. "What do they say about denial and a river in Egypt? For God's sake, she doesn't even live here anymore."

"I done with this," Wilford said, spinning back around in his seat. "I'm absolutely done. There's no sense in treading this ground again. Good day, sir. It was the principle of the thing. It's all about the principle. Good day."

"Yeah," Frank said, "the principle of her liking me and not you. That's what you can't get over."

"I can't even stand to look at you."

"Fine. Why don't you eat somewhere else, then? You've always had that option."

"I will *not* change *my* routine," Wilford said. "I'm not the one who changed things. *You* should eat somewhere else."

"Fat chance," Frank said. "I like this joint too much to leave because of your stupidness."

"Stupidness!"

"If the shoe fits."

"Stupidness is not— It's not even a word. It's stupidity, if you have to be so crude as to use such a word."

"I guess I'm just too dumb to talk to you. Maybe you shouldn't even bother. I liked it better when you were giving me the silent treatment."

Wilford said nothing, but in his rigid stillness he emanated all the impending doom of a ticking time bomb. Frank, who'd appeared smug and irritated when this dust-up started, now stared despondently into his coffee. Here, finally, they'd come to the source of their strained relationship, and Gage wasn't at all surprised it was about a woman. He would have liked to sidestep the whole thing entirely, but he didn't see how he was going to get any information out of them when they were more concerned about their feud than about helping him.

"How long has it been?" he asked.

They both looked at him.

"Since this, uh, woman — What's her name?"

"Vicky," Frank said.

"How long has she been gone?"

"A little over two years," Frank said.

"Twenty-seven months, to be precise," Wilford said.

Frank rolled his eyes and seemed prepared to say something, but Gage held up his hand.

"And all this time you two have been sitting at separate tables?" he asked.

Neither of them answered, which Gage took to be a yes. They both appeared to be hunkering down, preparing for mortar fire, and Gage knew little good would come from tackling their hurt feelings head-on. He had another idea in mind.

"Which means," he said, "that you've been wasting this diner's money for twenty-seven months."

Frank looked up sharply. Wilford spun around in his seat. Now it was time for Gage to press his advantage.

"Does this place look like a soup kitchen?" he asked.

"Excuse me?" Wilford said.

"It *is* a for-profit business, right?" When they both started to sputter an answer, Gage forged ahead. "I eat here too, guys. You know how often I come here and don't find a table? It gets busy. Sometimes I'll eat at the counter, but other times I just go somewhere else. I'm sure I'm not alone. If you're taking two tables when you could take one, you're hurting this business. Is that what you want to do? Hurt their bottom line?"

Embarrassed, chagrined, they mumbled "no."

"It's hard enough for a restaurant to make it into this town with everything going right," Gage said. "They certainly don't need to be wasting a booth because two guys old enough to know better are acting like jealous high schoolers. I don't know who this Vicky was, but she's gone now. You can get over this thing or not, I don't care, but if you're going to eat in this restaurant, you better get back to eating in one booth or you should *both* find other places to take your sorry asses. Because I don't want to see this place go under because you're acting childish."

While they were still recovering from his withering assault, Gage got out of his seat. He pointed at Wilford, then at his booth. Head bowed like a scolded toddler, Wilford slid out of his seat and sat across from Frank. Neither of them would meet each other's eyes. Gage went back to eating his breakfast, not saying a word. He was aware of people in the room watching them, but paid them no mind. The jukebox was between songs, which made the silence in the room all the more noticeable, every clink and clatter of dishes jarring.

Gage went on working on his breakfast, studiously ignoring the attention, until finally Sonny and Cher were singing on the jukebox, the conversation began to rise again, and the room was back to what it was before Gage's outburst. By then, Frank and Wilford were fidgeting in their seats, which was exactly what Gage wanted.

"Now," Gage said, "as I was saying before, anything you can tell me about Ed Boone would be much appreciated."

"Well—" Wilford began.

"If I recall—" Frank said at the same time.

"Oh," Wilford said. "I'm sorry. You go ahead."

"No, no," Frank said, "you go first. I'm sorry for interrupting"

"It's no problem. You weren't interrupting. You really are the one who should—"

"*Guys,*" Gage said, "your newfound politeness is really quite endearing, but one of you has to speak first. Frank, tell me what you know and Wilford will chime in."

Frank shrugged. "All right. I really didn't know him that well. I don't think Willy did either." He glanced at Wilford, who nodded, before continuing. "He kind of kept to himself. A loner, you know. We started coming here, what, about a year after he opened?"

Wilford nodded. "After the Pancake House burned down."

"Right. Damn, they had good coffee. You remember that coffee, Willy?"

"It was indeed superb."

"Anyway, Ed would sometimes stop at the booth and say hello, chat a little, but it was mostly about the weather or complaining about the tourists, you know, the usual. So I don't know. Maybe loner isn't the right word. He did talk to everybody, but it never seemed to be about anything. Everybody seemed to like him, that's for sure. Everybody knew Ed. Why are you so interested in him, anyway?"

"He died last week," Gage said.

"Oh. Natural causes?"

"I can't say more right now, but it will come out soon enough."

"Wait a minute," Wilford said. "Wait a minute now. Last week. He wasn't that fellow who committed suicide by jumping off Heceta Head, was he?"

Gage took a sip of coffee.

"Aha," Wilford said. "How did you find this out? The paper didn't mention his name."

"Let's just say his recent death piqued my interest in him, okay? Here's a guy everybody in town knew at one point. He was Ed of Ed's Diner. Then, after he sold the place, he faded into the background, to the point where people are surprised to find out he was even still alive. What happened to him to make him do that?"

"Well," Frank said, "that's kind of the thing with him. Everybody may have known him when he had the diner, but he was still part of the background. He was just part of the background that everybody saw, you know? It's like if you pass the same tree every day on your way to work. You see it but you don't really see it."

"Excellent simile," Wilford said.

"Thank you," Frank said.

"You know anything about his wife and kids?" Gage asked.

"Oh, sure. She was hard to forget. She didn't come in all that often, but when she did … boy, she was a shrew. What was her name, Willy?"

"Hmm. I remember it started with a K."

"Kathy! Right. She was a piece of work. Now if there was ever a woman who could drive a man to suicide, it was her. Wouldn't be surprised at all to find out that was the reason."

"Apparently," Gage said, "she actually divorced him and moved to California before he sold the diner. So she'd been gone a long time."

"Oh! He never said a thing about it. Not surprising, I guess, the way he was."

"What about his sons?"

"The boys?" Frank said. "They were even worse than her. Spoiled little brats. I mean, she only came in when she needed cash for something, and she usually just dipped into the till and took it. The boys were usually just running wild, climbing all over everything, yelling, fighting with each other—real snot-nosed little brats, you know. Tells you how bad they were, I remember them so well. You remember their names, Willy?"

"Not a clue."

"Yeah, she avoided this place like the plague. I do remember them coming in sometimes on their own when they were a bit older. Same deal. Just to get money from the till. They were just a year apart, I think. Big boys. Built like bulls. I think Ed was a little scared of them by then, and they were only in middle school."

"All right," Gage said. "This question is going to seem a little out of the blue, but do you know if he had an affair?"

"What?" Frank said. "Ed? No. If he did, he hid it pretty darn well." He glanced at Wilford, who had grown noticeably quiet. "What is it, Willy?"

"I was just … Do you remember Ronnie?"

"Of course. Best waitress we ever had. Sweet gal. Wait a minute, you're not saying … she and Ed …"

"No, no," Wilford said. "I mean, I don't know. When my mother was still alive, she lived down the street from Ronnie's place. I saw Ed drop her off a few times, back when her car was always having trouble. Do you remember her complaining about that?"

Frank scratched the stubble on his chin. "Ronnie and Ed. Come to think of it, they did seem to have a way about them, little smiles they had just for each other. But … nah. They were both just sweet people. No way they could have been carrying on something and keeping it hidden from everybody."

"If they were," Wilford said, "they were certainly very good at it."

"Didn't she have a kid? I remember her mom stopping by with a little boy a couple times. She didn't seem unhappy. But then, it would be hard to know with someone like Ronnie. The world might be falling apart around her and she'd probably go on smiling."

"Anything else you remember about him?" Gage asked. "Did he have any hobbies or interests?"

"Don't know," Frank said. He glanced at Wilford, who shook his head. "Like I said, he kept a pretty tight lid on himself, and we didn't really know him that well."

"What about the casino?"

"How's that?"

"Did he say anything about gambling? Playing cards, that

sort of thing?"

Wilford straightened in his seat. "Oh! I do remember something. It was back when the Golden Eagle Casino was first going to open. I overheard him talking about it with another customer. He was really quite animated about it. That's why I remember it so well. I remember thinking it was strange to hear Ed so animated about anything."

"He was happy about it?" Gage asked.

"No! Quite the opposite. He was dead set against it opening. He said casinos were like catnip to gambling addicts. He said they soaked up money in a community and ruined lives. He said it was the worst mistake the city of Barnacle Bluffs had ever made, letting the Kayok tribe open the Golden Eagle, and we'd all be dealing with the aftermath for a long time to come."

"Interesting," Gage said.

Gage pressed a bit more, but other than Frank remembering Ed making a few positive comments about the Portland Trailblazers during one of their runs to the finals, they couldn't remember anything else distinct about him. They seemed to feel a little bad about it, too, that he'd been such a distinct presence in their lives for such a long period, and yet they knew so little about him.

After Gage finished his breakfast, he paid his tab and thanked them for their help. Outside, he glanced over his shoulder to see what the two of them would do once Gage left. He told himself he didn't care, that whatever the two old guys did wasn't his concern.

And yet, when he saw that Frank and Wilford were still sitting at the same booth, talking happily, Gage couldn't help but smile.

Chapter 7

If nothing else, Gage drove away from the diner feeling like he had a few more people to talk to about Ed Boone. There were his sons, of course. He'd need to talk to them. Ronnie, the waitress, if she was alive, and maybe her husband or son. There was also something there concerning his strong negative reaction to Golden Eagle Casino coming to town. A recovering gambling addict, maybe? In his experience, gambling addicts were often like ex-smokers: militant and outspoken in warning people about the dangers of their particular vices.

Yet that made it hard to believe Ed would play the slots at the casino just to relax, as he'd mentioned in his letter, but why lie in the letter? Something didn't quite add up, though Gage couldn't say what yet.

He also felt a growing connection to Ed Boone. He'd assumed Ed had been a real man of the town, a social butterfly, but he sounded more like Gage: private, keeping his personal life personal unless it couldn't be helped. He might have been a little more outwardly polite, a better and more willing listener to the trivialities of people's lives, but in temperament and personality,

Gage sensed a kindred spirit.

Or maybe he was just projecting onto Ed what he wanted to be there. He'd been guilty of that before.

For now, Gage decided the next step was to visit the man's last residence. The digital clock under the outlet mall sign read 8:47, the red letters glowing in the wisps of fog that wreathed the sign. Plenty late enough to knock on people's doors. Traffic was heavier, but he didn't have far to drive, turning onto the road just past the one that led to his house, a wider road that wound up into the firs and around the hill.

The apartment complex, appropriately called Hidden Hills Village, was a dozen buildings tucked into the trees like a private commune, each building with ten units, five on the first floor, five on the second. Most of the buildings had been recently painted a tint of bright yellow that should have been reserved for bananas and rain slickers, and the other half of the buildings may have once been a jolly shade of red but were now a faded and diluted pink. The colors may have been someone's attempt to make the place seem cheery and welcoming, but they seemed like a feeble effort to camouflage the drabness of the place. Moss and pine needles coated the sagging roofs. The sidewalks were crumbling and the parking lot was full of potholes. The grassy common area could only be called grassy by a narrow margin; most of it was weeds and mole holes.

The complex may have been less than a hundred yards of forest away from his house, a fact that was highly evident by the number of cats from the complex that wandered through his property, but Gage had never visited it. There'd never been a reason. When he went on his walks, he always went to the beach. But it was about what he expected. He'd seen a half-dozen other apartment complexes like it around town, and they were all about the same—full of twenty-year-old cars and trucks, rusted out and missing hubcaps; children's plastic outdoor toys crammed onto tiny balconies; haggard men and women in too-tight T-shirts smoking on their postage-stamp patios or in their open doorways.

It was about what Gage expected because it didn't take him long, after moving to the city years ago, to learn about the highly bifurcated nature of Barnacle Bluffs, which had no industry except tourism. People didn't like to talk about social classes in Oregon, or really anywhere in America, in Gage's experience, but that didn't mean there weren't any. With rare exceptions, the people of Barnacle Bluffs could be divided into two groups: the rich, either full-time retirees or part-timers from the valley with second homes on the beach, and the service class. They were the people who worked in the knickknack shops, the restaurants, and the grocery stores, which made up the bulk of the available jobs.

The best off among this group may have ascended to working at the casino, or perhaps, if they were lucky, the city or the county, with its more generous pay and prized benefit package. The worst lived primarily off welfare checks and food stamps, and there were plenty of those people, too. There wasn't much of a middle class—teachers, police officers, nurses who worked at the hospital—and those people always seemed to struggle to find their place in Barnacle Bluffs. If they could afford it, few of this smaller group wanted to raise their families in an apartment, even in one of the rare upscale ones, and a decent house in their price range was always tough to find.

Gage had Ed Boone's address from the letter he'd sent to Nora, number 608. As luck would have it, it was located in the building farthest from the front, which meant there were fewer curious neighbors who might spot him if had to break into the apartment.

Yet when he parked his van, he saw that breaking into the apartment was going to be a difficult prospect. The first problem was that number 608 was on the second floor, with no access to windows or screen doors. The second problem was Unit 6, where the apartment was located, was the building currently being painted, and a crew of two guys was working on the wall directly adjacent to Ed's door.

That left returning late at night, or seeing if someone with a key would let him in now. The shades of the windows were drawn, and no light seemed to come from within. Had anyone been there since Ed died? If they hadn't, it wouldn't be long, and Gage really wanted to see the man's place before too many people started picking over his belongings. That made waiting until night less appealing.

He'd passed the office on the way in, a first floor apartment marked with an orange neon *open* sign in a window, so he drove the van back there and parked. The sign had been on when he came in, but now it was off. Just his luck. Not far from the door, a man in tan overalls was emptying a lawnmower bag into a green barrel, a big, lumberjack-like guy with an unruly black beard. The patch of lawn in front of the office was one of the few areas that had healthy, growing grass.

When Gage got out of the van, the man eyed Gage suspiciously.

Gage waved politely. The man glared. Obviously the friendly type.

"The managers in?" Gage asked.

The man shrugged. His face was like churned-up mud, lumpy in some places, hard-edged in others, his tan a deep but uneven brown. It was still cool enough that Gage saw the man's breath fogging in front of him. The air smelled of freshly cut grass and gasoline.

Since the conversation wasn't getting him anywhere, Gage walked to the door, leaving his cane behind because it was such a short distance. Plus, he felt self-conscious about it with King Kong watching. He tried the door. Locked. He looked at the yard man, who'd since turned his attention to putting the bag on the mower.

"Any idea when they'll be back?" Gage asked.

This time, the guy didn't even bother with a shrug. The blinds on the window next to the door were closed, but there was light inside. He also thought he heard faint voices. Not regular voices, though—hollow, like from a television. He knocked on the door. No answer. He knocked again, harder. Still no one. The television implied that they were either inside, and ignoring him, or they were somewhere in the complex and didn't bother turning off the set because they knew they'd be back soon.

Gage returned to his van. The yard man pushed the lawnmower off the grass onto the sidewalk, passing Gage without even a glance. Gage watched the manager's office for any sign of activity. It hadn't felt cool inside the van before, but now, sitting in stillness, it did. He tapped his fingers on the steering wheel to warm them. So much of his early years as a private investigator in the New York area had been spent waiting. Some people even said that was what separated the good PIs from the bad ones— the ability to wait. Gage had never liked waiting, the endless monotony of it, but he was certainly good at it. He could outwait the best of them.

He was sitting there practicing his waiting skills when there was a partial eclipse of the sun. That was what it felt like, a sudden darkening of the interior of the van, but when he turned toward the driver's-side window, he saw that the thing doing the darkening was, in fact, the yard man.

His huge, bearded face loomed so close to the glass that

Gage flinched. Other than a few rhythmic blinks, the yard man barely moved, studying Gage with the kind of passive curiosity that a boy forced to visit a museum might have when peering at a rare insect under glass—like everyone told him how rare and interesting this insect was, and he was trying to judge for himself but so far was unimpressed.

Gage, his heart slowing, rolled down his window. He didn't sense any violent intent from the big guy, but still his hand moved to the Beretta holstered inside his jacket.

"Can I help you?" he asked.

The man just went on staring, his utter stillness even more unnerving than if he had raised a clenched fist. He smelled of wet earth and garlic.

"Is this a staring contest?" Gage asked. "I stopped doing those in fourth grade, so I'm pretty out of practice."

"Ron," the man said.

"Excuse me?"

"Name."

He spoke in a whisper, but his voice was so deep that it would have rumbled like a locomotive if he'd talked any louder.

"That's your name? Well, nice to—"

"No. Your name. What is it?"

"Oh."

"Don't lie."

"Um … I wouldn't even think of it. The name's Garrison. Garrison Gage."

Ron tipped his head. It might have been a nod, but it was so slight that Gage immediately began to doubt whether the man had moved at all.

"Is there something you—" Gage began.

"I knew it," Ron said.

"Sorry?"

"You're that detective."

"Um."

"I heard about you."

"Okay. I'm still not sure …"

Gage trailed off because Ron abruptly turned and walked away. No goodbye, no acknowledgement of any sort, not even another one of those barely perceptible nods. And here he thought he'd made a new best friend. He watched Ron walk—it was more of a lumber, really—down the sidewalk toward the management office.

He assumed the big fella was going to report Gage to the managers, tell them just who, exactly, was biding his time outside their office, and his belief seemed confirmed when Ron took a key from the center pocket of his overalls and unlocked the door. Instead of entering, Ron turned, looked at Gage for a long beat, and walked away. This time, he headed away from Gage's van, rounding the corner and disappearing.

Despite Ron's slightly less than optimal communication skills, it only took a moment for Gage to realize what the big guy had in mind. He'd unlocked the door because he wanted Gage to go into the office.

Why? Gage sensed some kind of trap, but couldn't for the life of him think of any reason why Ron would want to do such a thing. Did he already know why Gage was there? How would that even be possible?

Still, whatever Ron's motive, Gage was not about to pass up the opportunity to look inside the office. He checked his Beretta, ensuring it was properly loaded, and returned the piece to its holster with the outer strap unbuckled. Approaching the door, he didn't see anybody watching. The sun, piercing the clouds, warmed up the air in a hurry; what was left of the dew on the grass was nearly gone. A crow cawed at him from up in the branches of the oak, but otherwise he was alone. He knocked. Again, nobody answered. When he thought he'd waited long enough, he tried the knob. Unlocked.

Steeling himself, he opened the door.

If there was a trap waiting for him, it wasn't an obvious one. Standing in the doorway, he found himself looking upon a messy but rather ordinary office. Mounds of paper littered the top of the L-shaped wood laminate desk. A dozen blue spiral notebooks, each marked with a year in black marker, filled the matching bookshelves. A sad goldfish swam in lazy circles in the bowl on the metal filing cabinet. In the corner, a behemoth of a television, even by current standards, was showing an episode of *Modern Family.* There was a *no smoking* sign on the corner of the desk, but the place smelled strongly of cigarettes.

There were two doors along the far wall, one that was open and led to a tiny bathroom, and another that was closed almost all the way but not completely. He saw light under the crack.

Stepping close to the door, he heard sounds from within—grunting and heavy breathing, along with distinctive flesh-smacking noises, that, when combined, could usually only mean one thing. Gage didn't want to open the door, he really didn't, but it might be an opportunity to get a bit of leverage.

Sure enough, when he gently pushed open the door, the nature of the spectacle that greeted him was about as he expected, though even less pleasant to look at than he'd prepared himself to see, and he'd prepared himself to see something fairly unpleasant. It wasn't just that the two people currently copulating on the floor were of the extra-large variety—a pair of walruses came to mind—or that the overhead fluorescent lights were particularly harsh. It was that the view he'd been afforded, of a hairy bottom and lots of quivering folds of flesh, was about the worst way to see two people in that position imaginable.

The storeroom, filled with industrial shelving, all of it packed with boxes, bins, and totes, was a fairly good size, but the massive girth of the two occupants made the aisle between the shelves feel extremely narrow. Neither of them were completely naked. The man's baggy jeans and white briefs were pooled around his ankles. He still wore white socks and even whiter tennis shoes. The woman's dress, lavender with pink stripes, was hiked up over her mountain-sized breasts. One of her open-toed sandals had been kicked off. Both the man and the woman were flushed pink, and the room stank of their sweat.

Gage wondered if this was what good old Ron had wanted him to see, a perverted joke, and then he saw the needles.

Two syringes, both empty, sat on a pair of pastel-pink panties tucked partially under one of the shelves. Based on the frantic fornicating of the room's occupants, he guessed that the contents of the syringes had been methamphetamine in liquid form, or another stimulant, and not something with a more subduing effect.

Why good old Ron was willing to reveal his managers' illegal activities was still unknown, but Gage could guess that these people violated some personal code the big man had. As a big believer in keeping true to a personal code himself, Gage was starting to like Ron quite a bit.

Since the man and the woman still hadn't taken notice of him, and Gage had no desire to go on witnessing their rabbit-making ways, he decided to bring this show to a quick end.

"Heavens to Betsy," he said.

That did it. If he'd set off a flash grenade, it couldn't have had a more profound effect on the aspiring porn stars. They sprang off each other surprisingly fast for two people of such profound size, scrambling for their clothes.

"Fuck!" the man cried.

His face had all the round whiteness of a snowman with none of the cute appeal, what little blond hair he still possessed so fine and pale that it was almost indistinguishable from his scalp if not for how it glistened with sweat. He glared at Gage with beady, recessed eyes. The woman, who had a thin mustache about the same color as the man's hair, burst into tears. She didn't have a neck so much as a series of chins—at least four of them—that spread all the way around her neck in a way that made Gage think of those African tribal women with the metal hoops around their necks.

"Sorry," Gage said. "The door happened to be unlocked."

The woman, hurriedly covering herself as best she could with her dress, wailed at the man, "I thought you locked it, John!"

"I did, I did!" he sputtered, hiking up his pants.

"Well, obviously you *didn't*!"

Gage, averting his eyes as much as possible, said, "I'll be waiting in the office. That'll give you two some time to … well, time."

He shut the door. Though part of him had enjoyed the shock of surprising them, the tiny part of him that just couldn't help poking a nest of snakes with a stick even when he knew no good would come of it, he did not enjoy watching them fumble around in their nakedness. In fact, he would have very much preferred purging that image completely from his mind, though he didn't know if that was possible. It was there to stay, he feared, the price he'd paid for his insolent ways.

A commercial for a fabric softener was playing on the television. He took refuge on a padded folding chair opposite the desk, listening to the ongoing commotion inside the storeroom: the rustle of clothes, whispered cursing, the bump and rattle of bodies banging into the shelving and the walls. This went on for some time, then there was a long period of near-silence, in which he could just barely make out a strained conversation between the man and the woman.

Finally, the storeroom door flew open and the man emerged first, slicking back what little hair he had with a sweaty hand. He smiled furtively at Gage, rushing to his desk as if he expected it would protect him from incoming mortar fire. He may have been dressed, but the fly of his pants was unzipped and the collar of his green golf shift was flipped up on one side. He wore tiny, wire-rimmed glasses, but they did little to make his face seem less round.

"Well, well," he said, nearly missing the chair as he dropped into it. "Yes, um, I assume—that is, are you hear to apply for one of the vacant units, Mister ..."

"Gage. Garrison Gage."

"Right, Mr. Gage." Unlike his yard man, he showed no sign that the name meant anything to him. He rifled through the mounds of paper on his desk, producing a glossy full-color brochure, one that had been well used, a coffee stain on one corner. "Um, we have several to choose from, Mr. Gage. Let me—let me show you some floor plans ..."

"I'm here on another matter," Gage said.

"Oh?"

The man swallowed with an audible *glump.* By this time, his partner in crime had shuffled out of the storeroom. She appeared to be trying to slink her way past the desk without being seen, a comical effort considering not only her size but the vivid lavender color of her dress, and she stopped when Gage made his comment. He turned and looked at her. She'd made some attempt to put her platinum-blonde hair back in its bun, but loose strands stuck out in every direction. Judging by the depth of her brown highlights, she was due for another coloring any day now.

"I'd like to talk to you both, really," Gage said. "Assuming you're both the managers of this complex, correct?"

"Um," the woman said. That was it.

"Well, certainly, certainly," the man said. "We are indeed. But what is this—"

"And your names?" Gage asked.

"Our names?"

"No, the names of your superhero alter egos. Of course your names."

"Oh," the man said, "yes, I'm John Krohn. This is—this is my *wife*, Mel. Mel Krohn." He put extra emphasis on the word *wife*, as if he wanted to be sure that Gage knew that the woman he'd been having sex with was his proper spouse. "We're the managers. But you already knew that. Heh, heh. How can we help you, sir?"

"I'm here about Ed Boone," Gage said.

John Krohn's face was actually quite hard to read, due to its roundness and heavy amounts of flesh, all of which functioned to mask the movement of any facial muscles, but Gage thought he detected a flash of fear in the man's eyes.

"Who?" he asked.

"Come on now, John. Let's not play games."

"I'm sorry?"

"Ed Boone lived in 608. He died last week. I'm sure you heard about it."

"Last week ... Oh, right! The guy who jumped off Heceta Head. Right, right. Just took me a moment there to ... to connect the dots. A lot of people live here, you know. Heh, heh." He fidgeted in his seat, the swivel chair squeaking from the strain of holding his weight. "So are you—are you representing his son?"

The fear had returned, a blackening of the pupils already mostly black to begin with. Gage wasn't quite sure what to make of this new information, or John Krohn's reaction. A lawyer for the brother? He could have played along, pretended to be legal counsel just to see where this would lead, but with the leverage Gage already had, he didn't think that would be the most expedient way to get what he wanted.

"His son was here?"

John noticeably relaxed, his shoulders slumping. "So you're not a lawyer?"

"Heavens no."

"Oh, good."

"It's worse, though. I'm a private investigator."

"A what?" The eyes flashed wider again, at least as wide as they would go. "You're a private—a private—"

"Private investigator. Yep, I do private investigating. Detecting, sleuthing, you know, that sort of thing." Gage glanced at Mel, who still stood in the same place. "It's like being a lawyer in one way, I guess. Most people hate you."

Gage smiled, but poor Mel looked like she wanted to throw up, so he returned his attention to John.

"Well," John said, "I'm not sure—I'm not sure what you—"

"Let's cut to the chase, shall we? We're all busy people—I mean, you two were *definitely* getting busy—and as much as I enjoy small talk, I think we'd all be better off if I moved things along. I'm guessing you're both nervous because you're afraid I noticed the needles in the storeroom, the needles that might lead someone to assume you regularly partake in a drug-related activity that's most definitely illegal. But I want to assure you that I *didn't* notice those needles."

John stared, the incomprehension a beautiful thing to behold. It was so beautiful that Gage was tempted to let the moment stretch for a while longer, but he still had that awful image of John and Mel in the storeroom stuck in his mind, and the only hope of ridding himself of it was getting them out of his life as soon as possible.

"I'm sorry," John said.

"I'm sure you are."

"No, I mean, I don't quite—"

"Let me finish. See, I didn't notice those needles, but I did see them. Do you know what I'm saying? Not to get all Zen on you, but we all know there's a difference between seeing and noticing, right? So while I didn't notice them, I did see them, and it's still possible that if I were to focus on what I saw, I might remember something I didn't notice at first. Like those needles."

Mel whimpered. She didn't seem to realize she'd made the sound until Gage looked at her, and she stopped.

"So here's the deal, you two," Gage said. "If you keep me happy, it's highly unlikely that my mind would drift back to that image I now have imprinted firmly in my mind of you two doing your … business in the storeroom. If I did, I might notice those needles, and if I noticed those needles, I might feel obligated to inform the owner of this complex that there might be illegal drug activity taking place in this office. I might even feel compelled, as a sort of extension of the law myself, to inform the police."

Gage had their full, rapt attention. He'd had their attention before, of course, but now he had their attention in the way a grizzly had the attention of a pair of hikers who'd had the misfortune of crossing its path.

"What do you want?" John asked, his voice soft and pinched.

"Answers, first," Gage said. "You said Ed's son was here. When was this?"

"Yesterday," John said.

"What was his name?"

"I don't know."

"John," Gage said.

"Elliott!" Mel said. "His name was Elliott Boone! Or Younger, actually. He said his dad's last name was Boone but his last name was Younger."

"Very good. And why did you think I might be a lawyer? Did he want into the apartment, but you wouldn't let him?"

"We can't," John said weakly. "If someone dies, or is missing, the company policy—the policy is that we need proof that the tenant wanted the person to have access. If they were listed as an emergency contact on their contact sheet, that would do it. Being a relative isn't enough. A search warrant, an order from a judge … There's other ways. I told him he needed to talk to the police, see what they could do. Our hands were tied."

"I imagine Elliott Younger was not very pleased," Gage said.

"No, he wasn't. He threatened to sue us. That's why I thought maybe you were a lawyer."

Gage remembered the man he'd seen in the trees last night. Could it have been this Elliott Boone? He wondered how long this guy had been in town, and what he knew about his father's death.

"Did he say where he was staying?"

John shook his head. Gage glanced at Mel, who did the same.

"Did he mention his brother being in town?"

"No," John said.

"Okay. How about why he wanted into the apartment?"

"He just said he was Ed's son and he needed to get inside right away. I assumed he was probably looking for a will."

"Probably so. Anything else about him you can tell me?"

"No. Just, like, he was dressed in a suit, real polished sort of guy. He wasn't all that big, but … I don't know, there was something about him. The way he looked at me. It wasn't fun, him being mad at me."

"Okay, let's move on to Ed himself. What can you tell me about him?"

"Nothing."

"Oh, come on now. You can certainly do better than that."

"Really! All I can say is he must have paid his rent on time. If you pay your rent on time around here, you don't really get noticed."

Gage rubbed his temples with a great theatrical flourish. "John, I'm starting to remember something. This thing I saw earlier, in the storeroom, it's coming back to me."

"I'm telling the truth!" John protested.

"He is, he is!" Mel chimed in, her voice high and shrill. "We didn't know him. We wouldn't even recognize him if you showed us his picture. We've only been here for three years, and he was here a lot longer than that. He paid with the drop box, not in person. He never complained about anything. When the son showed up telling us he was dead, we had to look him up just to see if he really lived here. The name didn't ring a bell."

"How long has he lived here?"

"A long time," John said.

"How long, exactly?"

"I don't know. You want me to look it up? Let me get the file; it will just take a second. I got it out when his son showed up." He dug through the papers on his desk. In his haste, a couple manila folders and a blue binder clattered to the floor. He found a folder, discarded it, found another and opened it. "Yes, I've got it all right here. Looks like … Wow, he moved in only a year after it opened. There was just one other tenant in the apartment before him. Twenty-two years. Twenty-two years and two months, to be exact."

"Can I see the file?"

When he hesitated, Gage gestured to his temple again and

John quickly handed it over. There were three documents inside, all yellowed with age. The first was a one-page "tenant information" document detailing all the basic information: Ed Boone's name, phone number, unit number, and the like. It listed his lease as "month to month with first, last, deposit." The notes area was blank. So was the place for emergency contact information. The second document was a handwritten application, front and back, which listed Ed's place of employment as Ed's Diner, which fit the time period. Twenty-two years ago, he still owned the place. The last document was a multi-page rental agreement, which spelled out all the terms in tiny print. Ed's signature was at the end of it.

Gage thought about asking John to make a copy of everything, but he didn't see any useful information that he didn't already know or couldn't get easily. He handed the folder back to John.

"That's it?" he said. "That's all you have?"

"I'm sorry," John said.

"All right, next step. I want to see his place."

John swallowed.

"I promise not to take anything," Gage said.

"Um, well, it's highly irregular."

"Hmm. Do you really want to start a discussion about what's highly irregular?"

John swallowed again, chewed at his lip for a second, then picked up the phone on his desk. He hit one number on the keypad. It rang a long time until someone answered, during which John smiled at Gage nervously and Mel bit at her fingernails. The exchange was brief, and mostly involved John yelling at Ron to turn off the leaf blower so they could talk, but he finally managed to communicate that he wanted Ron to meet Gage at unit 608 in five minutes and let him in. There was something in John's tone that Gage didn't like, a way he spoke to Ron that sounded a bit too much like a plantation owner barking orders to a slave.

"Ron will let you in," John said, putting the receiver back in the cradle.

"Good. This Ron, he's your yard guy?"

"Yes. Among other things. General maintenance supervisor is his title. He's all right. Just got to keep him in line, you know. It's hard to get good help."

"Seems like a nice guy. Talkative fellow."

John laughed, a sharp snort, but then his eyes changed. They hardened, like the surface of a pond freezing right before Gage's eyes. He put two and two together, just as Gage hoped he would—the unlocked door, the sound of the mower right outside.

"You met him," John said.

"I did. He was helpful."

"I see."

John drummed his fingers on the desk. Nobody said anything for a moment, though Gage felt their expectation weighing on him. They were waiting for him to leave.

"How much do you pay Ron?" Gage asked.

"Excuse me?"

"It's a simple enough question."

"What does that have to do with anything?"

"Humor me."

"I don't know. I think it's twenty bucks an hour."

"If I ask Ron, that's what he'll say?"

"Well, maybe it's fifteen."

"Maybe?"

Mel joined in with her high-pitched squeak: "It's thirteen seventy-five an hour. I know, because I just processed his paycheck."

"Wow," Gage said, "that's not much for a man of Ron's abilities. How about we give him a raise?"

They both stared at him as if he'd just spoken in tongues.

"Excuse me?" John said.

"Excuse you for what?"

"Huh?"

"You really need to stop saying that. Excuse you for what? What did you do that you want me to excuse you for?"

John, whose face was reddening by the second, must have realized that the collar of his golf shirt was folded up on one side, because he reached back and folded it down then tugged at it. "I'm sorry, I'm afraid I—"

"Don't say 'I'm sorry' either. I don't like empty apologies. The next thing you should say is, 'How much?'"

"How much?"

"Good. You said it as if it was a question about the question, not the question itself, but it was good enough. Let's go with twenty dollars an hour."

"What! I can't do that. We have—we have a business—"

"I changed my mind. Twenty is too low. Someone would steal him away from you. Let's do twenty-five."

"Twenty-five!"

"Still too low? You think we should do thirty?"

"But twenty-five is more than I make!"

"Let's make it twenty-six, then. Seems fair."

John stewed in silence. He wasn't a complicated man. Watching his gears turn was like watching a child's engineering kit, one with all the moving parts made obvious. Mel made a sound that was half sigh and half whimper.

"Okay," he said.

"Say again?" Gage asked.

"I said okay. I'll give him the raise."

"Good, good. I think that's a wise choice. Ron seems like just the sort of person I want to keep in touch with, by the way. He seems to know things. So I figure I'll stop by from time to time and see how things are going. I'll expect he'll be here for a long time. Wouldn't you agree?"

John mumbled something.

"What's that?" Gage said.

"Yes," John said, "he'll be here for a long time."

"Fantastic." Gage got to his feet, then turned back for one last remark because he couldn't help himself. He tapped his forehead. "Because, you know, I'd hate to think what I'd remember if I couldn't get in touch with Ron. Think of him as a way of distracting me from those unpleasant memories."

If John or Mel had even one ounce of real courage, they might have given Gage a nice, cold stare, but instead they barely lifted their gazes from the floor. When he left, Gage almost felt bad for them.

Almost.

Chapter 8

Ron was waiting for him when Gage parked the van in front of Unit 6. He leaned against one side of the doorframe of Ed Boone's apartment, so broad-chested his other shoulder nearly brushed the other side. The potted geraniums on either side of the door looked like dandelions in child-size paper cups next to Ron's work boots. He was such a massive physical specimen that Gage felt self-conscious about taking his cane, but trying to take the stairs without it was a risk he wasn't willing to take just for his pride.

When he managed to trudge up to the top, Ron nodded to him.

"I read about what happened to your knee," he said. "That's the shits, man."

This comment surprised Gage on two levels. First, and most embarrassingly, Gage wouldn't have expected Ron to be much of a reader. The second surprise, of course, was that Ron had not only read about the encounter with the mafia hit man who'd maimed Gage and killed his wife, but remembered it, felt bad about it, and decided he should express some sympathy. This embarrassed Gage because he knew he'd typecast the big guy, both in his literacy level and his ability to express empathy.

"Thanks," Gage said, because he didn't know what else to say.

"Why don't you get it fixed?"

"What's that?"

"The knee. I got mine fixed after I got back from Iraq. Ortho doc was great."

"Oh. I don't know."

"You should."

"Yeah."

"It'll make you feel loads better. I know how it is. You feel like maybe you're a pussy for not just toughing it out. But it's not worth it, man. Just get the sucker fixed."

Gage nodded, not knowing what to say. He had no intention of getting his knee fixed, but somehow, hearing it from Ron instead of all the other people in his life, he found it hard to muster any indignation. He just felt a little sorry for himself, and that wasn't a feeling he wanted to dwell on for long.

"Can I see the apartment?" he asked.

Ron backed inside and gestured for Gage to enter. He stepped into a tiny foyer, a square of pebbled yellow vinyl that was probably original to the apartment, but in surprisingly good shape. The wildflower design was scuffed and faded in a few spots, but it looked more like two years old than twenty. Beyond the vinyl was, just as John predicted, white-and-blue checkered carpet, and it was in even better shape than the vinyl. It did show some wear here and there, especially down the middle, but it also still bore tracks from a recent vacuuming. There was a pair of men's brown felt slippers on a black iron shoe rack by the door, as well as rubber boots, a pair of brown loafers, and a set of well-worn tennis shoes with sand stuck to the treads.

Gage made a quick first pass. The hall led to two doors, a

bathroom and a bedroom. There were picture hooks on the hall-way walls but no pictures. He peeked in both rooms and found their condition much like the hall: old, but well maintained, with only the minimum amount of furnishings. There was a well-worn toothbrush in a glass on the counter in the bathroom, a metal-frame bed and a dresser in the bedroom. The dresser was a golden color that was meant to look like pine but was probably just pressboard.

Three hardcover books with glossy protective covers sat on the matching bedside end table, all three bearing library labels on their spine. The first book was a biography of Howard Hughes, the second a history of the Civil War, and the last a historical novel set during the Great Depression that had won a Pulitzer. Gage knew it had won the Pulitzer because he had read it himself. The books were the only sign of personality in an otherwise sterile room. No photos on his end table. No paintings, posters, or prints on the walls—walls that were utterly white and bare except for a handful of picture hooks that somehow made the walls seem even more naked and barren.

"Ed sure liked to read," Ron said.

Gage looked at him. The big guy leaned his bearded face into the bedroom without entering it, like a giant peering into a dollhouse.

"You knew him personally?" Gage asked.

"A little. He was always going back and forth from the library. He used to buy a lot of books years ago, he said, but now he just uses the library. I like to buy mine. You know, for writing notes in them. Especially the heavier stuff, philosophy, that sort of thing."

An image of Ron scribbling notes in Plato's *Republic* popped into Gage's mind, nearly derailing him. "Where are the pictures?"

"What do you mean?"

"On the walls. Here, the hall. There are picture hooks, but no pictures."

"Oh." Ron shrugged. "I think those were here, you know, before."

"From the previous owners?"

"Yeah. They left them behind, I guess."

"Twenty years ago?"

"I guess so."

"And he never hung his own pictures?"

"I guess not."

Gage looked at the picture hooks again. For some reason, the sight of all those empty hooks made him feel a deep wellspring of sadness. It wasn't that the walls were bare. Usually that just showed either obliviousness or indifference to what a few pictures could do to change the mood of a room. But what kind of man moved into an apartment and not only didn't hang any pictures, but didn't even bother to take down the picture hooks the previous occupants had left behind? Maybe there were people who could remain oblivious to empty picture hooks for a week or a month, but twenty years?

That was an active choice, ignoring those picture hooks for that long, and what did that choice say about Ed Boone? To Gage, it said that Ed Boone refused to see this apartment as his home. No way he'd planned to live here twenty years. It was temporary, until other opportunities presented themselves, whatever those were.

Gage thought about himself. He had pictures on his walls, didn't he? Zoe certainly did, but what about him? Strangely, he couldn't recall, though he was sure he did. He distinctly remembered buying some prints of sunsets on the Oregon coast, though he couldn't remember actually hanging them. Yes, that was right, one in the living room and one in the hall. And, of course, he had those framed pictures of Janet by his bed.

But he didn't have a lot. More than Ed Boone, but that wasn't saying much.

He perused the kitchen and the living room, Ron dutifully following. If not for the sheer size of him, and the smell of garlic and cut grass that pervaded any room he occupied, the man was surprisingly unobtrusive. If it was possible for a mountain to be invisible, then Ron fit the bill. Gage wondered if any mountains smelled like garlic.

The living room also sported blank white walls with empty picture hooks, but, just as Ed Boone had indicated in his letter, there were lots of books. The books were contained in three six-foot adjoining bookshelves, the cheap kind you could buy at Walmart. The shelves were packed to the brim with a wide assortment of hardcovers and paperbacks of every size and color, neatly alphabetized by author.

The couch and loveseat were a muted gray that might have been the original tint or might have been muted because it had faded; in either case, there was so little wear Gage doubted either had been used much. The brown leather recliner next to the couch, however, looked well used indeed, with wear marks on both the seat and the arms. There was a cheap maple end table with a lamp on it, positioned to provide maximum lighting for the chair. Another library book, a recent Stephen King, lay on the end table.

The kitchen, a tiny nook beyond a simple oak table with four chairs, was just as a bare. The blue Formica countertop, a color and style Gage doubted existed anywhere else in the world other than this apartment, shone as if it had been recently installed. He checked the cabinets and the drawers, half expecting them to be empty, since the house had the feeling of Hollywood make-believe, but there were pots and pans and forks and knives and everything else a person would need. There were spices in the cupboard, milk, cheese, and other things in the fridge, even if it all felt a bit too sterile and organized.

"He spend a lot of time here?" Gage asked.

Ron shrugged.

"I thought you knew him?" Gage asked.

"Not that well."

"But you didn't get the sense that he actually lived somewhere else, did you?"

"No."

Gage stepped over to the bookcase. He saw a whole section of books on Heceta Head Lighthouse, all filed under H, but everything else was alphabetized by author. Between two hardcovers by Block and Bukowski, Gage thought he spotted a sliver of something white, like an envelope. He debated whether to pull it out in front of Ron. It might be better to look at it on his own, but he didn't know when he'd have a chance to do that, and he had a hunch there might be an advantage to extending some trust to Ron. It was just a gut feeling, but he had the sense Ron was holding back, something he knew, and if he felt like Gage was willing to trust him, well, then maybe Ron would trust him back.

"Can you keep a secret?" Gage asked him.

Ron stood there staring for a long time, as if nothing had been asked of him but to do just that.

"I asked—" Gage began.

"I heard you. Is it something about Ed?"

"Yes."

"Soon as I saw you, back in the van, I knew that's why you were here."

"What makes you say that?"

Ron shrugged. "I knew it was Ed who they said jumped from the lighthouse. I knew because that's where he went and he didn't come home. Then the police showed up and asked questions, but he's got no family so they told John and Mel to hold tight for now. Don't know why else you'd be here. What's the secret?"

It was quite a monologue for somebody like Ron. He visibly sagged, as if all those words strung together had depleted him. Gage reached between the books and pulled out a slender white envelope. The words "My Will, Ed Boone," were handwritten on the outside. The envelope was sealed.

He showed it to Ron.

"Oh," Ron said.

"I think it's a good idea that you just saw me do this," Gage said. "In case there's ever a challenge in court, now there are two of us who found this here."

"How'd you know it was there?"

"I can't say just yet."

"But that's part of the secret?"

"Yeah."

"And you're not going to tell anyone about it?"

"Not just yet. If I open it now, people might think it's been tampered with. I'm going to put it back and make sure the police are the ones who open it. I just wanted to confirm it was here."

Gage studied the envelope for a moment, then slid it back into place.

"Question," Ron said.

"Sure," Gage said.

"You think somebody's not gonna like what's inside there? Like his kids?"

"I think it's a distinct possibility."

Ron's expression turned sullen. Gage searched the rest of the apartment, hoping to find some hints of Ed's life, especially his life before coming to the apartment. He did find a wall calendar in the bathroom, one with several hand-written appointments throughout—not many, but a few. There were appointments with a Dr. Keene, one each month going back a year, plus other, more frequent visits with doctors the last few months. One, a Dr. Hambly, had *OHSU* written after it, which had to be Oregon Health Sciences University in Portland. A specialist for his Alzheimer's, no doubt. Dr. Keene was probably the local doctor.

There were also weekly notations, every Thursday, for HHL, which must have stood for Heceta Head Lighthouse. Other than that, the calendar was pretty barren. There were two appointments, six months apart, for BBAH, but Gage couldn't think what that was. Barnacle Bluffs was obvious, but nothing jumped to mind for the AH.

"What's BBAH?" he asked Ron.

Ron shrugged. The handwriting was clearer earlier in the year, shakier later. The ballpoint pen he'd probably used was in the top drawer, along with manual razors, shaving cream, and all the other basics for personal hygiene. In the medicine cabinet, a wide range of pills was on display. Beyond the usual, Aleve, Imodium, Sudafed, and the like, there was Donepezil and Rivastigmine, which Gage guessed was for the Alzheimer's. No Xanax, Lexapro, or other drugs to treat depression or anxiety, which didn't surprise Gage. This was a guy after his own heart, somebody who might take some pills for physical pain but would rather die than admit he couldn't keep his mental house in order.

Satisfied he'd searched as much as he could for now, Gage headed for the door. He'd confirmed the will was here, and he also had the names of some doctors, people who might shed more light on Ed's life. Nothing about Nora—CDs, biographies, and the like—which did seem odd.

"I know what BBAH is," Ron said.

Gage stopped. With the front door on one side, and Ron, who was essentially a wall, on the other, Gage felt like he was stuffed in a broom closet. There was an edge in Ron's voice that made Gage hyperconscious of the tight space, how much of a disadvantage he was at if Ron wasn't the good guy he thought he was.

"You do?"

Ron nodded.

"Well?"

"It's Barnacle Bluffs Animal Hospital."

"The animal hospital? But why? Did he volunteer there too?"

"No."

"Okay. Because if someone goes to a vet, that usually implies—"

"Yeah, he had a dog."

The big guy didn't appear to be joking. Gage hadn't seen any signs of a dog.

"He had a dog?"

"Didn't I just say that?"

"Right. What kind of dog?"

"A little one."

"You don't know the breed?"

"It's black. Some white. Funny snout."

"And you have it at your place?"

"You don't see it hiding around here, do ya?"

"All right. Why didn't you tell me this before?"

Ron hesitated. "I wasn't sure about you. He really loved that dog. For the short time he had her, he already loved her almost as much as his books."

"How long did he have it?"

"Not very long. A few months. He told me he got her from the Humane Society. I remember John and Mel making a stink about it back in May, but he told them to check his contract."

"And they allow dogs here?"

"Not anymore. But they did when he came here. I think his contract allows pets with a deposit. He told me he had a dog when he first got here, but when she passed he didn't get another until Lady."

"Why do you have it?"

"Sometimes he'd ask me to watch her. Like if he knew he was going to be gone a long time. Like when he stayed overnight in Portland for one of his appointments. Not a lot, just sometimes. He didn't want Lady to be lonely."

"The dog's name is Lady?"

"Yeah. Lady Luck, but he just calls her Lady."

"So I want to be clear about this, Ron. When did Ed give you Lady?"

The big guy stared at Gage, but didn't say anything.

"Ron?"

"He didn't."

"Excuse me?"

"He didn't give her to me this time. That's why I didn't say anything at first. I came and got her."

"When?"

"Right away."

"Like how soon, right away?"

"Like, right when I heard he'd jumped." Ron paused. "I have a police scanner. I like to listen to it at night. Helps me sleep."

"I see. Odd, but okay."

"I knew it was him as soon as I heard the police talking about a possible suicide at the lighthouse. I knew how much Ed loved that dog. I knew about his mean sons. I didn't want no mean-ass kids to end up with the dog. Figured she'd just end up at the pound. So I came over here very late, and since Ed wasn't here I knew for sure it was him that jumped. I took Lady home."

"You must have taken everything for her, too. I didn't see a bowl, dog food—"

"Yeah, I took all of it. Ed kept all her food and stuff all neat and tidy in the cupboard, anyway. I just took her bed and her toys. I didn't want there to be no sign of her. Figured I could always give her to the kids if they turned out all right. But I saw the son that came yesterday. Real prick."

"But Ed didn't ask you to look after her this time?"

"No. When he was just going to the lighthouse for the afternoon, he usually didn't. He'd just leave Lady in the apartment."

Gage took his hand off the knob, absorbing this information. It troubled him. If Ed was the kind of guy who'd make sure his dog was looked after while he was at OHSU, certainly he was the kind of guy who would make sure his dog would have a new home if he planned on committing suicide. Yet he hadn't. Of course, someone who planned on killing himself wasn't in his right mind, but he hadn't mentioned Lady in his letter to Nora, either. Why?

And he'd only had Lady a few months. Why would someone intent on suicide get a dog?

It made Gage curious about the will. He'd thought leaving it unopened would make it likelier that the will would hold up in court, especially with Ron as his witness, but now he really wanted to know if Lady Luck was mentioned.

"I need a favor," Gage said.

"Huh," Ron said.

"I need you to leave me alone in the apartment for a few minutes."

"Huh."

"I can't quite tell the difference between your various *huhs.* Is that a yes?"

"Why?"

"Let's just say I need to use the facilities and I'm a shy person."

"Right."

"Or we could say that I want to make sure you don't see something so you can't say you saw something if somebody asks you what you saw."

Ron nodded. "Plausible deniability."

"Yes. I could have just said that, I guess."

"I do read," Ron said.

"Of course you do."

"Will this help Ed?"

"It may."

Ron nodded and left. He didn't even look at Gage as he closed the door. Not a man for big goodbyes, apparently. Gage retrieved the will from the bookcase. He searched the drawers in the kitchen until he found some blank envelopes, ones that matched the envelope the will was inside. He found a blue ballpoint pen in the same drawer.

Then he opened the sealed envelope. He pulled out a typewritten single sheet of paper, holding it by the very corner, careful not to get his fingerprints on it. Using his sleeves and not his hands, he pushed out the folded edges so he could read it.

The will was one page, typewritten, signed and dated six months earlier. There was no mention of Lady, or any other pet. It was just as Ed had said in his letter: he'd named Nora West the executor.

Just like Ed's letter, most of the lowercase t's were chopped off at the top, so it was obviously from the same typewriter. Gage made a mental note to find out where Ed had typed the will. A friend's? A copy shop? The library? Six months earlier ... Well, that would explain why the dog wasn't mentioned. If Ron was correct, Ed didn't have the dog then. There were also fewer spelling errors and other typos, which also made sense. Ed must have had more of his faculties intact then.

Still, it didn't answer the most nagging question: why hadn't Ed mentioned the dog to Nora?

Chapter 9

Once Gage had carefully put the will in the new envelope, he sealed it, wrote "My Will, Ed Boone" in as close to the original handwriting as possible, and put it back where he'd found it on the shelf. He stuffed the old envelope in his pocket and made one more pass of the apartment. He came up empty, but when he was in the bathroom again he looked at Ed Boone's hairbrush, a wooden brush with black plastic bristles, and an idea occurred to him. He took the brush, slipped it into the inside pocket of his jacket, and headed for the door.

Outside, he found Ron sitting in the passenger seat of his van.

All right, strange. What, the guy wanted a lift to the mall? The van had never felt small to Gage, but the way Ron filled the front window made Gage think of one of those tiny clown cars.

The sun was not visible, but the sky had gone from gun-metal gray to dishrag dirty white. No traces of the early morning fog remained, but the air still felt thick, pushing against his face like wet cotton. The Douglas firs that separated the apartment complex from the forest were a vibrant, shimmering green. He took the steps slowly with his cane, trying to decide how he was going to break it to Ron that, despite the mustard-yellow color of his Volkswagen, he wasn't a taxi service.

It wasn't until he actually opened the driver's-side door that he saw the dog on Ron's lap.

"Oh no," Gage said.

The tiny black-and-white dog perked up its pointed ears. Gage's canine expertise ranked only slightly higher than his feline expertise—which was to say, not much expertise at all—but he did know this particular breed because he'd once had a client with three of them. A Boston Terrier. Though the three Boston Terriers of his client, which he'd been told repeatedly by their rich, artsy owner were certified purebreds, were enormous compared to the runt in his van.

It could hardly be called a dog, really, more of a giant rat, and not even all that giant if placed in a lineup with some of the rats he'd seen in New York. Compact and muscular, with a snout so flat it looked like it had just smashed into a brick wall, the dog blinked up at him with big, glassy eyes, eyes much too big for its little face. Most of its dense fur was black, except for its snout and its belly, which were white.

"This is Lady," Ron said.

"I gathered."

"I want you to take her."

"I was afraid you'd say that."

"I like the dog. It just doesn't get along with my cat."

"I could take the cat instead."

"No."

"I like cats. I'm more of a cat person."

"No."

Gage stood there with the door open, afraid that getting into the van might seal some unspoken compact to accept the dog. A breeze stirred the tops of the fir trees. Somewhere around the corner, a baby started crying. Gage felt a connection. The idea of taking the dog—any dog, not just this little runt of a dog—made him want to cry too. His mind stumbled through a dozen excuses not to take the dog, most of them untrue, and even the ones that were true were pretty lame (the dog's colors wouldn't match his decor, for instance), but before he could settle on one, Ron got out of the van. He left Lady in the passenger seat. All Gage could do was watch helplessly.

"You have to take her," Ron said.

"It's not a good idea."

"You have to. There's nobody else."

"You don't have friends or family who might—"

"No."

"How about the Humane Society? Or the pound?"

Ron's eyes narrowed, his face darkening. "Ed loved this dog."

"But—"

"Ed *loved* this dog," Ron repeated. There was no threat in his voice, but there was an undertone of anger that matched his scowl. "Her things are in a box in the back. Dog food, bowl, a sleeping bed. A couple of toys. She didn't have much."

"Kind of like Ed," Gage said.

Ron nodded. Gage still hadn't gotten in the van. He was still holding out hope that Ron would change his mind, or that there would be a divine intervention.

"You get done in there what you wanted to get done?" Ron asked.

"Yeah, but if you think of anything else I should know about him—"

"I didn't know him that well."

"I know, but if you do—"

"I won't."

"Okay."

"I told you everything."

"Sure."

"There wasn't much else. He lived a quiet life."

"All right. I appreciate your help."

Ron tapped the window on the passenger side with the flat of his hand, and Lady looked at him, ears perking up again. Ron matched her, tilting his head at just the same angle, then turned abruptly and walked away. He loped, shoulders hunched, arms swinging, reminding Gage of the grainy videos of Bigfoot.

He looked at Lady. Lady looked back at him. When he couldn't prolong the moment any longer, Gage got in the van. The two of them regarded each other in the confined space, sizing each other up, the resignation Gage saw in Lady's eyes surely matching his own.

"Don't worry," he said, "you won't be stuck with me for long."

"No," ALEX SAID.

Gage had barely gotten the question out of his mouth when Alex was already firing his reply back with all the force of a slugger pounding a baseball that had floated dead center over the plate.

Too late now, Gage realized he probably should have waited at least until the front door to Books and Oddities had closed before asking if Alex would be interested in taking home a very cute Boston Terrier that just happened to be in Gage's van at that very moment. In his eagerness—or perhaps his despair—he hadn't been able to help himself, babbling a hello and a "how are you" and the question all in one fervent rush. He could have been offering a brand-new Corvette and the answer probably would have been the same. It was hard to accept anything from someone who sounded so desperate.

The bells over the door still rang in the air, the breeze stirring the bookmarks hanging on the rack on the edge of the glass counter. Alex, hunched on his stool and pricing a stack of paperbacks, hadn't even turned to look at him. A snowy-haired old lady out in the stacks *did* look at him, clutching her green plastic basket already half filled with books a little closer.

"But I even brought you donuts," Gage said, holding up the white bag.

Alex turned, his eyes, behind his glasses, registering both surprise and suspicion. "Chocolate with sprinkles?"

"So fresh you can smell the goodness."

"Mmm. I appreciate that very much. But I still won't take the dog."

"But you haven't heard anything about her yet."

"Alas, it doesn't matter. I can't take a dog regardless of its character, breed, or history."

"You told me you loved dogs. You said you always had them around growing up."

Alex slid off the stool and sauntered over to the bag, digging out one of the donuts. He held it up, inspecting it like a jeweler examining a diamond before taking a healthy bite of it. "Both are true," he said, after swallowing. "However, as much as it pains me, and as much as it pained my daughters when they were living with us, dog ownership is not in the cards for our particular family. Eve, you see, is deathly afraid of them."

"Oh, she wouldn't be afraid of Lady. She's tiny."

"I once saw my wife flee in hysterical terror from a miniature poodle about the size of my slipper."

"Seriously? You're not just making this up?"

"Afraid not." He leaned past Gage, peering out the window at the van. "Huh. She's cute, though. How'd you end up with her?"

While Alex finished his donut, Gage explained not only how he'd ended up with this particular Boston Terrier, but also, in a whisper, how this dog wasn't mentioned in either Ed's letter or his will.

"One question," Alex said. "Did you ever actually say no to Ron?"

"Of course I did."

"You actually said the word?"

"Well, maybe not the actual word."

"Uh huh."

"But I definitely made it clear that I wasn't interested."

"Mmm."

"Okay," Gage said, "you're getting that tone again. The smarmy tone of the psychiatrist who's about to reveal to me all of my hidden secrets."

"All I'm saying is maybe on some level you wanted the dog."

"What?"

"Zoe is gone. The nest is empty."

"You're being ridiculous."

"Am I?"

"Yes. And you've got sprinkles all over your mustache. That makes you look even sillier."

Alex, his smile so self-satisfied and smug that Gage was tempted to crack him upside the head with his cane, dug into his second donut. Gage stewed in his indignation, but was having a hard time keeping up the front. Was Alex right? As he pondered this, the snowy-haired old lady brought her books to the counter—a mixture of romances and mysteries, from the looks of it, much the same that was on the counter. Alex wiped his face with the napkin in the bag, told her what her credit for the traded books was, and rang the difference up in the cash register. She handed Alex her credit card, then turned and smiled at Gage.

"I heard you talking about the dog," she said.

"Oh?"

"I like Boston Terriers. I had one years ago."

"Oh yeah?"

"I might be interested in taking her."

"No," Gage said, surprising himself.

"Excuse me?"

"I don't even know you."

"Oh."

"No offense. I'm sure you're a nice person."

"I am. I am a nice person." She seemed beside herself. "I'm nice to dogs. I'm nice to everyone."

"I'm sure you are. But I just can't give this dog to anyone."

"Oh. Well, you could come over to my house if it would make you—"

"No."

"No?"

"No," Gage said flatly. "It's just that I'm ... No. We should just leave it at that."

The woman appeared too stunned to speak, staring at Gage in stricken silence. She even smelled like freshly baked cookies, which made Gage feel all the worse. Alex placed her books in a flowery bag with the words *Readers Are the Best Kind of People* in a heartwarming design on the side, and handed them to her. She fled the store without a glance at either of them.

"Now, see, you didn't have to do that," Alex said.

"Do what?"

"You know. Be you."

"I was just being honest."

"Uh huh. And you still don't think you want the dog?"

"I just didn't want the dog to go to *her.*"

"Yes. Those rosy cheeks. All that white hair. She did seem

quite ... unsavory."

"Mock me all you want, but I will make sure this dog gets a good home."

"Like a lonely widower who lives by himself?"

"Exa— Hey, now."

"So what's your next move on filling in the life story of one Ed Boone? We can speak frankly now. There's no one else in the store but us."

Gage, tabling the dog discussion despite his frustration, caught Alex up on the rest of what he'd learned, both from his visit to Ed's apartment and from talking to people at the diner. Alex got him a coffee in a Harry Potter mug—strong, with just a touch of Irish creamer, just the way he liked it. It placated Gage somewhat. He may have been stuck with a dog, but at least he had a friend who knew how he liked his coffee.

"I've also got a favor to ask," Gage said. He took the hairbrush out of his pocket and placed it on the counter.

"Thanks," Alex said, "but I don't have a whole lot of hair left to make use of it."

"It belonged to Ed Boone."

"Ah."

"You've probably guessed the favor."

"You want me to use my elaborate network of former colleagues in the FBI to somehow get a DNA test of a sample of Mr. Boone's hair."

"Exactly."

"I'll need a sample of Nora's hair, too."

"So you'll do it?"

Alex sighed. "Only because I like Ms. West quite a bit. Let me get something to put it in."

While Alex retrieved a clear plastic bag from under the counter, Gage thought about telling him about the man he'd seen in the trees the previous night, but decided to pass. Alex worried about him too much as it was, and Gage was still too uncertain about the whole thing. Both of them sat there sipping their coffee. Outside, the gravel parking lot was mostly empty, half the open signs still off, par for the course for ten a.m. on a Monday after Labor Day. A motorcycle roared past the Horseshoe Mall on Highway 101, not more than fifty yards away. Otherwise, the store was so quiet Gage could hear the ticking of the overhead fluorescent lights.

"The library, his doctor, the Heceta Head staff," Alex said. "You've got some choices. This waitress he used to sometimes drive home, you said she had a son?"

"Yeah, Howie. Still lives in town, from what I heard."

"Sounds like Ed and his mom were at least friends, maybe more. The kid might know something."

"Worth a shot, I guess."

"You don't sound all that excited."

"It's the dog not being mentioned in the letter," Gage said. "It's really nagging me. I understand if he wrote the will before he got the dog, but what about the letter? He'd said nothing else he had was worth anything."

Alex shrugged. "Maybe your mountain man was wrong about how much Ed cared about it. Or maybe Ed was just too out of his mind to think clearly about who was going to end up with his dog. You've been assuming that his suicide was premeditated, but maybe it was a spur-of-the-moment decision. It would explain why he just left the dog in the apartment. When he left, he was planning on coming back."

"Maybe. They did find a suicide note on him. I haven't read it yet—I imagine it's with the Florence police—but it was at least premeditated enough that he wrote a note before jumping."

"It'd be good to see that note."

Gage nodded. "Might explain his state of mind a little bit better. I'm not quite ready to drive to Florence yet, though. But there's someone in town who might be able to get me a scan of it. I need to talk to him, anyway."

"Who's that?"

"I'll tell you if you agree to take the dog."

"Nice try."

"All right, then you'll just have to wait in suspense like everyone else."

"It's going to be like that, then?"

"Yes," Gage said, "it is."

Chapter 10

Ten minutes later, Gage parked his van outside a gray one-story building on the far side of Big Dipper Lake that looked more like an inflated manufactured home than the Barnacle Bluffs police station. The place hardly seemed big enough to contain all the people who'd parked the dozen cars out front, some cruisers, most not, but in his visits inside—far too many the past few years for his liking—the station was much larger than it seemed.

The grounds were nicely kept, with bark dust so fresh it hadn't yet lost its reddish hue, a large rectangular swath of grass as well tended as the finest golf courses, and rhododendron bushes trimmed to a uniform perfection, as if the police were well aware of the unimpressive appearance of their station and were trying to make up for it with top-notch landscaping. The spruces and oaks behind the building blocked all but a hint of the blue expanse of lake.

Gage got out with his cane. His knee was holding up all right, and he hated to take it with him when surrounded by so much machismo, but he'd learned his lesson from one unfortunate incident a few year earlier—stumbling through the front door like a drunk idiot—and he wasn't willing to chance it.

On the passenger seat, Lady stood on all fours and looked at him expectantly. She'd been so quiet this whole time, not a bark, not a peep, nothing at all, that he'd begun to wonder if she was mute.

"You sit tight," Gage said. "Hopefully this won't take long."

Lady produced her first sound since he'd met her: a brief but unmistakable whine.

"What?" Gage said.

The dog looked past him. Following her gaze, Gage saw only the big rectangle of grass in front of the building.

"Ah," he said. "Got to do your business, huh?"

She cocked her head to the side in that distinctive way of hers. Gage was in no mood for escorting a dog on her bathroom break, but he also was in no mood to clean up an accident in his van. He fished around in the box Ron had given him and found a leash; the brown leather still retained its original rich hue, seemingly confirming that Ed hadn't owned the dog for long. He snapped the hook on Lady's collar, who took the opportunity to lick his hand. Nice. Now he remembered why he never liked dogs much.

"Now, listen," Gage said to her. "This is going to be a short-term arrangement. But we'll get along much better if you act a little less … doglike."

Lady, peering at him with those big eyes, gave him nothing but the silent treatment. He led her to the grass, feeling like a complete idiot with this tiny ball of fur pulling him eagerly along. He wasn't a big guy, though he wasn't little either—about six feet tall, medium build—but he towered over Lady like a giant. She didn't have much of a tail, a tiny stub that curled in the shape of a question mark, but she more than made up for its size with plenty of wagging gusto. She took her time sniffing around, pulling him this way and that, until finally he castigated her to get busy or he was putting her back in the van.

And wouldn't you know it, that was the moment when an unmarked black Crown Victoria pulled into the parking lot and two of his least favorite people in the world got out.

"New job, Gage?" Trenton said, laughing. "You so hard up for cash you're walking dogs now?"

Except for their identical gray trench coats, which they wore as dutifully as a uniform, Trenton and his partner Brisbane had almost nothing in common. Maybe their weight was actually the same, though Trenton, looming over his more rotund companion, stretched his two-hundred-plus pounds over a lanky six-foot-six frame, where Brisbane, almost a foot shorter, packed his bulk into much less surface area. Trenton, a bright redhead, wore his clothes with a sharp attention to detail, the shirt starched to a brilliant whiteness, the blue tie puckered to perfection, every crease just right. Brisbane, he of the scattered gray hair, liver-spotted cheeks, and deep bags under the eyes, always looked like he dressed in the dark while nursing a bottle of scotch.

"I'm watching it for a friend," Gage explained.

"You have friends?" Trenton said.

"Is there something I can help you with, detective?"

"Nope, just enjoying the show."

"Maybe you could watch it somewhere else." This, Gage realized, wasn't the wittiest comeback in the world, but then he wasn't feeling particularly witty. Lady, as if mocking him, was taking her own sweet time. "We'll be done in a minute."

"You can't leave that there," Brisbane growled. A man of few words, he always sounded like he was battling indigestion.

"Excuse me?"

"Your dog's ... offering. You can't leave it on the grass."

"Right. And what do you propose I do?"

Scott William Carter

"Pick it up."

"Pick it up?"

"That's what I just said."

"With my hands?"

Brisbane sighed. He marched over to Gage, reached deep into his pocket, and pulled out a blue plastic roll. He tore off a bag and handed it to Gage.

"Oh, those things," Gage said. "You just keep those in your pocket in case you run into people with dogs?"

"I have a lab."

"A meth lab?"

"A Labrador, you idiot!"

"Oh right, right."

"How can you be so smart and yet be such a jackass?"

"I don't know. How can you be so charming and yet fail to get all the ladies? Except for Trenton, of course, and he only barely qualifies."

Brisbane, shaking his head and muttering to himself, walked past Gage to the police station. Trenton started to offer a retort, but Brisbane held up his hand without turning, and Trenton, glaring at Gage, loped after his partner. They disappeared inside. Gage felt a twinge of guilt, wondering if maybe he'd been too hard on Brisbane—the man had given him a free doggy bag, after all—but the ledger of slights and insults was still so heavily tilted on their side that he wouldn't beat himself up too much over it. Besides, they were cops. It wasn't like they were real people.

Lady finished her business, looking up at him as if she was proud of it, wagging that non-tail of hers. Gage cleaned up the mess and dumped it in the can at the edge of the parking lot. He was heading to the van to put Lady back inside when a late eighties F-150 pulled into the lot, ostensibly white, but so cov-

128

ered in dirt and grime that the paint was more like bleach spots on a gray cloth. He knew the truck even before he saw the man behind the wheel. Percy Quinn.

The police chief parked next to Gage's van. He sat there with the truck idling for a long time, staring at Gage as if debating whether it would be better to turn around and leave. He was dressed casually, in a red flannel shirt and a Mariners cap. His face, always gaunt and sober, even though his eyes exuded a grandfatherly kindness, appeared even more drawn out than usual.

With a shrug, he got out of the truck, a manila envelope under his arm. He was dressed in wrinkled jeans and cowboy boots. Gage ushered Lady into the van and shut the door, turning to face Quinn.

"It seems I don't even have to go inside," Gage said. "I just stand here with a dog and everybody walks by eventually."

"What trouble have you got yourself into this time?" Quinn asked.

"Now why would you say a thing like that?"

"You steal that dog?"

"Yes. Are you going to arrest me?"

"Where'd you get it?"

"A friend gave it to me."

"You have friends?"

"Why does everyone keep saying that? Am I not a good person? If you prick me, do I not bleed?"

"You know," Quinn said, "in this town I can probably have you arrested for quoting Shakespeare. What do you want?"

"What makes you think I want something? Maybe I just take great satisfaction from having my new canine pal take a dump on your front lawn. And what's with the getup? You getting ready for the rodeo?"

"Not that it's any of your business, but Ginger is sick today. I'm home taking care of her. Just needed to drop something off. Now, are you going to tell me what you want so I can tell you no, and save us both some time, or do we have to have a long, drawn-out conversation before I eventually give you the same answer?"

Gage knew that Ginger, Quinn's wife, occasionally suffered debilitating migraines. It was hard to tell, but Gage thought he saw quite a bit more gray in Quinn's bushy black eyebrows. The lines in his face were deeper, the grooves more pronounced. He'd aged. Gage may not like Quinn all that much, but he did have a grudging respect for him, and that respect made him reluctant to take his teasing too far.

"You have any information about the suicide at Heceta Head?" he asked.

"Huh. Now that's not something I'd expect you'd be involved in."

"You didn't answer my question."

"Your answer is in the question. It was a suicide. No reason for the police to be deeply involved. Besides, it was in Florence. What's your angle, Gage? Who are you working for?"

"Can't say right now."

"Ah. Of course."

"I'd tell you if I could."

"Sure, sure. You expect me to just willy-nilly hand over whatever information I have, but if I ask questions, mum's the word."

"Did you just say willy-nilly?"

Quinn frowned and started for the door. "Goodbye, Gage."

"Hold on. I can't tell you who it is yet, but I can tell you this much. I have a client who might be related to Ed Boone."

Quinn had only taken a few steps before he stopped and

turned around. "And what makes him think that?"

"It's a she, actually, and she received a letter from Ed Boone dated the day before he died. He wanted her to know who her real father was, and she has reason to think he might be telling the truth."

"Okay, that's somewhat interesting. Still not sure how the police fit into this, though."

"A couple ways. First, one of Ed's biological sons is in town, and he's lining up a lawyer to get access to Ed's apartment. I happen to know that Ed doesn't want his kids to get squat."

"And how, pray tell, do you know this?"

"Because there's a will in Ed's apartment saying so."

"Mmm. And you know this will exists how, exactly?"

"That's not important. What's important is that we need that will to be preserved before Ed's son accidentally misplaces it. I have a hunch you'll find it on his bookshelf, filed under Boone."

"Gage, you know I can't do anything about that. Not without a court order."

"What if there was foul play involved?"

Quinn's dark eyebrows arched. "In Ed's death?"

"Exactly."

"You're saying it wasn't a suicide?"

Gage didn't know where he was going with this until he'd said the words aloud, but now that he had, the idea bloomed in his mind. He didn't quite believe it yet, but something didn't add up about Ed Boone's death. "I don't have anything solid yet. I'm just saying there might have been foul play. Maybe it *was* a suicide, but he was coerced. Who knows. Things just might be more complicated than they seem."

"Complicated doesn't mean illegal," Quinn said. "You've got to get me some proof before I can get a search warrant."

"What if I told you I had reason to believe there was a dead body in there?"

"Is there?"

"Could be."

"Gage—"

"I'm just saying, the only way to know for sure is to search the premises."

"You're really stretching on this one, pal. What's got you so desperate? He was just a lonely old man who decided to end things in his own way before the choice was taken from him."

"Ah hah. So you *do* know something about him. Did you read his suicide note?"

Quinn pursed his lips. "I may have."

"Did they send you a copy?"

"Where are you going with this, Gage?"

"I'd like to see it."

"Not unless you're family."

"I told you—" Gage began.

"Yeah, you've told me a lot of things, some pretty creative, even for you. But Chief Leonard only sent me a scan because Ed Boone lived up here, and he wanted our help tracking down next of kin."

"What did the note say?"

"I'm not going to tell you that."

"But Leonard must have thought there was something in the note that could help. Otherwise why send it to you?"

Quinn shook his head. "Are we done here?"

"Come on, chief. I'll be honest with you. Maybe you're right. Maybe he was just a lonely old man. Maybe this is nothing but a suicide. But I still want to help my client get some closure."

"What am I, a psychiatrist?"

"Can you just tell me what the note *said*?"

Quinn shook his head, adjusted his cap, looked away, and

sighed, making quite a show of mild anguish, until finally he looked back at Gage with something akin to exhausted resignation. "I don't know why I ever help you. It's not like you've ever been anything but a thorn in my side."

"It's my sunny disposition. What did it say?"

"Pretty much what I just said. He wrote that he was jumping before the disease made him forget who he was. And he wrote that he hoped everybody who knew him and everybody who might have known him if he'd been a better man could find it in their hearts to forgive him for all the wrong he'd done."

"That was it?"

"That was it. A couple sentences on the lighthouse stationery from the gift shop. Real messy handwriting, lots of spelling errors. Signed his name, and except for the signature being pretty big, it matches what we have on file for his driver's license."

"And that was how he wrote it? Those were the exact words?"

"I don't have a photographic memory," Quinn snapped. "That was the gist of it. Are we done?"

"But don't you see? He said, 'everybody who *might* have known him.' He was thinking about my client even then. That's why you told me, isn't it?"

"All I know is I've got to get back to my wife," Quinn said, "and instead I'm standing here in the parking lot wasting my time with you. I don't have more I can tell you, and it's not just because you're not related to Boone. There isn't anything. The guy killed himself. It's sad, but that's the way it is. If you want to make sure that will is preserved, you're going to have to find another way. Are we done?"

"Just one last question," Gage said.

Quinn sighed. "Yes?"

"How does Ginger feel about dogs?"

"Nice try."

"She's real sweet. Be a nice companion for her when you're working all those late hours."

"Goodbye, Gage."

"I hear owning a dog helps with migraines."

Quinn, who already had his back turned, laughed. Gage watched him go. It wasn't just that the chief had more gray in his hair. He also looked thinner, more stooped, not quite as much bounce in his step. He was definitely getting older. They all were. One day they'd all end up like Boone, alone in shabby little apartments, a couple revolutions of the planet all it took for everything they'd done and everyone they'd known to be a distant memory to anyone but themselves.

It was a bleak thought, but when Gage turned to the van and saw Lady perking her ears at him, he suddenly understood why a lonely old man might get a dog even when he knew he didn't have much time left.

"Hey," Quinn called to him. He had his hand on the front door to the station and was looking over his shoulder at Gage. "I just remembered. Somebody told me you're writing a book. Is that true?"

"Boy, news travels fast in this town."

"That surprises you?"

"Not really. Who needs the Internet when everybody around here seems to have ESP?"

"What's your book about?"

"It's a joke book for cops," Gage said. "I'm keeping it very short, and all the jokes are written at a first-grade level."

Quinn shook his head and disappeared into the building.

Chapter 11

Knowing he couldn't very well drive around with Lady all day, Gage took the dog back to his house.

He didn't expect to stay for more than a few minutes, just long enough to get the dog settled someplace where she couldn't do much damage—the spare bedroom, maybe—and his mind was so preoccupied that when he rounded the gravel drive up to his house, he didn't see the man in the dark suit blocking his way until the last second.

He managed to slam on the brakes just in time, skidding to a halt. The man, a big guy, a real hulk with wide shoulders and a blocky face, didn't even move. It wasn't until a cloud of gravel dust drifted over him that he reacted at all, and it was only to blink a few times.

They stared at each other through the glass, Gage feeling his irritation rise even as his heart slowed. He didn't like visitors. He especially didn't like unexpected visitors. A white Ford Mustang, a newer model, was parked exactly where Gage usually parked, not on the side, where there was ample space, but right in front of the garage. The man's hair was cut so short, a military-style buzzcut, and the color was so fair, nearly the same shade as his pink scalp, that at first Gage thought he was bald. His skull appeared slightly uneven, dented, as if someone had pressed their thumb into a piece of clay.

Gage got out of the van. He hadn't wanted Lady to get out yet, but she jumped out before he could stop her. Even worse, she bounded over to the stranger, sniffing at his shiny black Rockports. Despite telling himself that he didn't care about the stupid dog, Gage still felt a sharp stab of possessiveness. Jealousy, even. He felt even more irritated at his own emotions.

The man, frowning, kicked at her—not hard, just a slight movement to shoe her away, but Gage still didn't like it.

"Don't do that," he said.

The man looked at him, eyes pale blue, a thousand-yard stare that made Gage want to turn and see if there was something behind him. The man had seemed tall and broad even from within the van, but now, standing across from him, Gage felt particularly dwarfed. He must have been nearly seven feet tall. Big, apelike hands. Gage hoped the tailor who'd made the suit had been paid double, because it certainly would have taken double the material of a normal-sized man. Even Ron, his new friend, would have been small next to this guy.

"This your dog?" the man asked. His voice was high-pitched and whiney, childlike, not at all what Gage expected.

"No," Gage said, "I stole her from an old lady at the bookstore."

"You did?"

Gage chuckled, but the man didn't. He just went on staring blankly. Gage hit the reset button in his mind. It was obvious he was going to have to operate at a much lower level with this guy.

"Is there something I can help you with?" he asked.

The man blinked.

"Who are you?" Gage said.

The man swallowed hard and gazed over his shoulder at the house. It was at that moment that a slender man in a similar dark suit rounded the corner from the back of the house, saw them, and moved to join them. The wet ivy he'd walked through had darkened the hem of his pants and made his Rockports—the same shoes as the big guy—gleam with moisture.

"What the hell are you doing?" Gage said.

The man, approaching them, smiled. He was small, with sharp, finely honed features, and when he smiled, he looked askance, as if he was amused by some private joke. He bore a striking resemblance to the larger man, not just in their clothes, which were identical, but with the same pale pink skin and fair hair. Beyond their size, there were other differences: his hair was slightly longer and spiked. His eyes were dark and dull, sitting solidly in their sockets like walnut shells. A faint diagonal birthmark over his right eyebrow made it seem as if he was perpetually arching one brow. Both of them were in their late thirties or early forties, Gage guessed.

"Just taking a look at your beautiful property," the smaller man said. His voice, although a bit deeper than his companion's, came off as the more feminine of the two, imbued with a soft, almost intimate whisper.

"Some would call that trespassing."

The man shrugged. "I'm sorry if I offended. I'm just drawn to beautiful things, and your place has a certain … quaint beauty about it, unkempt as it is. The view over the hedge of the ocean is spectacular. I assume you're Garrison Gage?"

"Who's asking?"

"Sorry, I'm Elliott Younger. And you're Garrison?"

Gage looked at the bigger man, who stood there, silent and staring blankly, like one of those blow-up snowmen people put outside their houses that eventually revealed how empty they were when not propped up by lots of air. It was obvious, just from the few moments spent among them, that the smaller man was the one doing the propping. "And what about you, big guy? Do you have a name, or are you totally incapable of speech?"

The bigger man looked at Elliott helplessly, and Elliott, smiling his askance smile, directed his remark at Gage.

"This is Dennis," Elliott said. "We all just call him Denny, of course. Please forgive his taciturn ways. He can't help it, alas."

"I'm a little slow," Denny said.

"Well," Gage said, "at least you're honest about it. A lot of people are slow but like to pretend otherwise."

"I'm a little slow," Denny repeated.

"Yeah, you said that."

"I'm a little—"

"*Enough,*" Elliott said.

The word was not shouted—in fact, it was said only with a hint more volume than Elliott's suave whisper—but it was spoken with such sharp contempt that it still startled Gage. It also had its intended effect, because Denny looked down at his shiny shoes. Elliott never even looked at Denny when he admonished him. He kept his eyes directed at Gage, and Gage saw the way the dullness of his eyes briefly gave way to something fierce and full of rage. Only for an instant.

"Sorry about that," Elliott said. "My little brother can get caught in a loop if it's not short-circuited, and it's best to do so with a bit of force. I know I probably sounded cruel, but his frustration can mount quickly if we don't act with a fair amount of sternness. And if his frustration is allowed to build … well, he can quickly reach a point where no amount of sternness can stop him. You can imagine, because of his size, what a problem this can be."

"I don't mean to," Denny mumbled.

Elliott, smiling thinly, held up his hand for his brother to stop. "This is more information than you wanted, Garrison, so we'll leave it at that. It is Garrison, correct?"

"What do you want?"

"Now, now. I know we didn't get off on the right foot, but can't we start over on good terms?"

"I guess that depends on how you answer my question," Gage said.

"Well, we just came to have a little conversation with you, that's all."

"About what?"

"About our father, of course."

Then Gage knew who they were. Ed Boone's sons. Of course. He should have known right off, but whether it was the dog, his conversation with Quinn, or just the general surprise of coming home to find strangers prowling around his property, he hadn't had the right mindset to even suspect along those lines. He looked from Elliott to Denny and back again. Could either have been the man he'd seen, or at least thought he'd seen, skulking in the trees Sunday night? Not Denny, certainly, he was too big to fit the part, but possibly Elliott.

The sun, high above them in a clear blue sky, produced shadows on the gravel underneath all of them like miniature manhole covers. Elliott had not directly threatened him, but there was still something menacing about his phony politeness.

"Your father," Gage said, deciding to play dumb.

"Ed Boone."

"Who?"

Elliott reacted with one of his off-kilter smiles, briefly meeting Gage's eyes before looking away.

"I wish you wouldn't do that," he said. "We know full well you were at his apartment this morning."

"You were misinformed."

"Oh, I wasn't informed at all. I observed your presence myself."

"What are you talking about?"

Elliott chuckled, seemingly delighting in Gage's confusion. "What, can't believe someone else can beat you at your own game, Gage? You're not the only one who knows how to do a bit of … sleuthing."

"You were watching his apartment this morning?"

"In a way."

"Well, either you were or you weren't."

Elliott shook his head. "I've read all about you, Gage. They say you don't even have a phone. Is that right?"

"What is your point?"

"You're quite the curmudgeon, but your inability to adapt to modern life does have its disadvantages. It can create a myopic view of potential solutions to problems. Let me show you something."

"I don't want to see your Amway card," Gage said.

"Funny," Elliott said, though he didn't laugh or even smile. "They also say you've got quite the sharp wit. I suppose that can be a useful tool in certain situations. But wait. This will be instructive."

He unbuttoned his blazer, holding one side fully open to reach into the inside pocket. The interior had the shiny smoothness of black silk. Considering the smallness of the object he eventually pulled out, he might have done this without fully opening his jacket, but it was quickly apparent *why* he had gone to such effort. Strapped to his chest was a leather shoulder holster similar to the one Gage wore, and it seemed especially large on such a slim chest.

Seeing the holster caused a jolt of adrenaline to course

through Gage's body, obviously the effect Elliott had intended. In an instant, the game had changed.

What Elliott actually pulled out to show him was a tiny white object, spherical, hardly bigger than a marble. When he held it up, he turned it so Gage could see the glass lens on one side.

"Do you know what this is?" Elliott asked.

"The first tooth you lost?"

Gage may have been startled, but he wasn't going to show it. He was keenly aware of his own gun: the obstacle his zipped-up leather jacket created, the strap over the holster that would further slow its retrieval, even the safety lever that would take a precious extra moment to disengage. He couldn't let Elliott know that any of this troubled him. "An Altoid mint from the reject pile?"

"It's a camera. A motion-activated camera, in fact. Look how small it is! What a marvel. Connects to Bluetooth to an app you can download to your smart phone, and whatever it records can be downloaded in seconds. Charges by USB. Technology can be a wonderful thing, Garrison. One just has to know how to use it."

Gage said nothing. Lady, unconcerned by the gun or any of this human business, had wandered over to the Douglas firs. She was sniffing a clump of clover that grew around the trunk of one of the trees. Denny, who seemed equally unconcerned about what was happening between Gage and his brother, watched the dog fondly.

"You see," Elliott continued, "I'm suspicious by nature. Comes from the line of work we're in. If you're not suspicious, you'll be … permanently unemployed soon enough. We haven't seen good old Daddy in many years. I just had this feeling—I do get these feelings—that maybe we weren't the only ones interested in his estate. While we were waiting for the lawyer, I thought it might be prudent to place one of these in the potted plant outside. Did you notice the plant? Being the great detective that you are, I'm sure you did, but you didn't notice this, did you?"

"What, you want an award or something?" Gage said.

"I want to know who you're working for."

"Who says I'm working for anybody?"

"People like us are always working for somebody, Garrison. I'm just less discriminating than you, since I am not motivated by anything less than monetary concerns. You, on the other hand, encumbered by inconvenient beliefs about right and wrong, good and bad, and all that nonsense, are *highly* selective about your chosen clients. You would not have entered my dear, departed father's apartment unless you had a very good reason for doing so. I want to know what that reason is."

"I heard the apartment would soon be for rent. I thought I'd get a jump on the competition."

"Who is it? Another relative?"

"I think it's time for you to go."

"I'll pay you double whatever they're paying you."

Now it was Gage's turn to smile. "If you think that's going to work, you really don't know me. It's those inconvenient beliefs about right and wrong, you see."

Gage saw another spark behind those dull eyes, but it was gone quickly. Elliott glanced away, his crooked smile more forced.

"You're not the only one the camera recorded going into the apartment," he said. "You had help. I'll get the truth another way."

"Is that a threat?"

"I'm just saying I have options. If you don't tell me who your client is, I'll find out by other means."

"That sure sounds like a threat to me."

Elliott shrugged. "Call it what you will."

"What I'm going to *call* is the police, if you don't get off my property in the next sixty seconds."

"Careful. There's no need to take such a harsh tone."

"Fifty seconds."

Elliott went on smiling impishly, but this time he was looking fully at Gage. No sideways glances. Good. That meant Gage had his full attention. Even Denny had pried his focus away from the dog to what was brewing. Gage unzipped his jacket, and, making sure to move slowly but deliberately, opened it so his own gun holster was clearly visible. Then, with a smile, he undid the strap on the holster. Elliott's smile faded a little, though he gamely tried to keep up the bravado.

"Thirty seconds," Gage said.

"Trust me," Elliott said, "you'd never even get your piece out of the holster."

"You sure you want to bet your life on that?"

"Garrison, if you knew who you were dealing with—"

"Twenty seconds."

"This is ridiculous! We just wanted to talk. Whoever hired you can't be worth dying over."

"I don't plan on dying. Ten seconds."

"Come now, this—"

"Nine."

"Garrison."

"Eight."

"All right! We'll leave. My God, man, there's no need to escalate to nuclear war when a little diplomacy will do. You think about what I said, Garrison. Denny, let's go."

At the mention of his name, Denny perked up, straightening his back and looking around as if newly aware of his surroundings, and Gage couldn't help but think of the way Lady was called to attention when she was addressed. Part of the same canine family, it seemed. Somehow Denny managed to fold his body into the passenger seat. Elliott started for the driver's side, then stopped, looked back at Gage with one of his trademark sideways smiles, and held up one finger. He walked toward the house—more of a slither, really, smooth, flowing steps that were both deliberate and unhurried.

"What are you doing?" Gage asked.

"I want to compensate you for the plant," Elliott said.

"What?"

Perennials in clay pots flanked both sides of Gage's stoop, bright, multicolored mixtures of flowers that Zoe had dutifully maintained the past few years. They were still in bloom. Elliott stopped next to one, took out his wallet, and retrieved a twenty-dollar bill. With a bit of melodramatic flair, he placed it under the pot on the left. Then he walked back to the Mustang and stopped by the trunk.

"We'll be in touch," he said.

"Do you want to explain—" Gage began.

What happened next, the speed of it, the precision, Gage wouldn't have believed unless he had seen it with his own eyes. It was the sort of rare talent he'd heard about over the years, from cops and other detectives, but he'd always attributed it to legend and myth, akin to the fish that kept growing in size each time a fisherman told the tale of its catching.

Somewhere between the word "to" and "explain," Elliott made his move with exceptional speed. It might have been called blinding speed if there had been anything blinding about it, but Gage saw every movement perfectly well, which was exactly why it was so hard to believe.

Hand moving into the jacket.

The Sig Sauer P229 pulled out and extended.

Shot firing.

Pot on the left exploding.

Sig returned to its holster.

The whole thing happened so fast that the debris from the pot—clods of dirt, ceramic shards, and a rainbow blizzard of petals—was still settling on the concrete and the gravel long after Elliott had returned the Sig to its original location. To say the display had frozen Gage on the spot wouldn't have been fair. It would have been more appropriate to say that the whole demonstration had happened too fast to allow him any reaction at all. The gunshot was still ringing in his ears before he even managed to take a breath.

Lady was quicker to react, cowering behind Gage's legs. A semi-truck had been rumbling past on Highway 101 at just the moment Elliott fired, partly drowning out the sound. Gage, his heart thudding away in his ears, wondered if Elliott had timed it just so. Elliott, tipping his head slightly, got in his Mustang. Gage watched as the brake lights glowed white, watched as they backed up to him. He didn't move, not so much out of defiance but because he was still dumbfounded, and the Mustang's tires came within only inches of his shoes. Elliott only swerved at the last second.

He drove past, smiling his infuriating and patronizing smile.

Chapter 12

"Assassins," Alex said.

A Harley motorcycle with a poor excuse for a muffler—was there any other kind of Harley?—roared past the grocery store on Highway 101 at just the moment Alex said the word. Even with the payphone receiver pressed tight to his ear, Gage wasn't sure he'd heard correctly. Or maybe he'd heard perfectly well but he couldn't quite believe that was what Alex was really saying. He asked him to repeat it.

"Assassins," Alex said again. "Hit men. Or, at least, that's what my sources in the FBI tell me. Nothing's been proven, but they've got files on both men. Where are you, anyway? Are you in Florence now?"

"No, Yachats," Gage said. "The lighthouse is about ten miles north of Florence. This seemed like the best place to stop."

"Sure. Of course, if you had a cell phone—"

"Skip it. You're seriously telling me that Ed Boone's sons grew up to become hit men?"

"That's exactly what I'm telling you."

"Man, the odds. Mercenary or working for some kind of

147

outfit?"

"Contract killers. Anyway, that's the rumor. Nobody's been able to make any charges stick. You still think that was a good idea, your little tough-guy act back at your place? You're not bad with that Beretta of yours, but from what my people tell me, this guy is about as good with a gun as someone can get."

"Based on what he did to my pot," Gage said, "I'm liable to believe it. What else can you tell me?"

"Hold on a second. I've got to ring up someone at the register."

There was the thunk of the phone being set on the glass counter. Gage, still digesting this news, surveyed the parking lot that ran along the market and the half a dozen stores adjacent to it, searching for anyone watching him. He'd been vigilant the entire hour-long drive south on the highway, constantly searching his rearview mirror, more than once pulling off at a wayside or a gas station just to make certain nobody was following him, and saw no one suspicious, but this news made him more alert than ever.

A steady stream of traffic passed by on the highway, the sun bright on the asphalt, but nobody seemed to be watching him. A kid licking a lollipop in a green Chevy pickup across the street, in front of a ma and pa video store, was definitely looking this way, but even in his present state of mind, Gage couldn't summon quite enough paranoia to believe a boy no more than ten could be a threat to him. Whirligigs, windsocks, and banners affixed to the overhang outside the kite shop next door rippled in a strong breeze—cool but not cold, smelling of the ocean.

Lady peered at him from the passenger seat of the van, standing on her hind legs with her black paws on the dashboard. He'd planned to leave her at the house, fix her up with food, water, and her blanket, but after his encounter with Ed's sons, he'd been reluctant to leave her alone. Now that he knew what Elliott and Denny Younger did for a living, he was even gladder he'd brought the dog along—for her own safety. It wasn't that he was getting attached. It had nothing to do with that.

On the phone, the cash register rang, the door chimed, and then Alex was back.

"Two greeting cards," he said. "You wouldn't believe how much I make selling those things. Hallmark must make a killing. I mean, it's just a little paper and some ink."

"Same could be said of books."

"Good point. Now back to your recent visitors. I don't have a lot on them, but I do have an interesting tidbit about why the younger brother is not quite with it."

"Yes?"

"Seems there was an unfortunate incident when they were in high school. This was when they were living in San Jose. There was a party at a friend's house, one with a pool in the backyard. The police report was that Elliott and Denny were horsing around in the pool by themselves while everybody else was inside, and Denny almost drowned. Paramedics revived him, but he was never the same after that."

"Lost a few brain cells, huh?"

"From what you told me, it sounds like more than a few. What makes it really interesting is the witness. A girl who had been sitting by herself in one of the bedrooms came to the police a week later to say she'd seen Elliott holding Denny underwater. Elliott wasn't that much smaller than him then. She said she'd yelled at him through the glass and he stopped, but she wanted the cops to know what had really happened."

"Interesting. Was there an investigation?"

"A brief one. Problem was Denny didn't remember the incident at all, so it was dropped. That's all that was in the file on them. But Garrison, I did a little digging myself, just a quick Google search because I had a gut feeling. The cops would have had no reason to see any connection here, but two years later that girl who saw him at the pool—she disappeared."

"What? How?"

"Nobody knows. She was a freshman at UC Davis, and one night when she told her sorority sisters she was going to the library, she never showed up at the library and never came home. There's a whole website on her. Very sad stuff."

Gage thought about it. "You think it was Elliott?"

"Considering what he became, maybe. Kid may have had a long memory and wanted to punish her."

"Nobody came back and questioned him?"

"Their paths hadn't crossed since high school. Nobody had reason to think of him. Even if they did, he and his brother took off right after graduation, and nobody really knows what became of them until they popped up on the FBI's radar."

Gage's hand, holding the phone, felt cramped, and he realized he'd been gripping the plastic too hard. For someone to wait two years to take revenge showed both deep malevolence and extraordinary patience, especially in someone so young. Had Elliott also come back last week to exact some sort of revenge on his father? Had Ed Boone been pushed off the lighthouse? If that was so, then why show up after the fact and draw suspicion? Maybe Ed Boone had more money than he was letting on, and Elliott and Denny were hard up for cash. As the surviving relatives, most of the estate would pass to them if a will didn't say otherwise.

It seemed a pretty clumsy move for contract killers who'd avoided both prison and all other threats this long, but maybe their financial situation was desperate enough to warrant such a move. Plus, Elliott did strike Gage as supremely confident in his own abilities, to the point that it might make him a bit reckless.

"Still think this is a suicide?" Alex asked, as if reading his thoughts.

"I don't know."

"It'd be a hell of a coincidence, these two being what they are."

"Yeah, but kids grow up to have all kinds of jobs. Some work at Starbucks, some shoot people for a living."

"Funny. Just be careful, okay?"

"Always."

"You going to the lighthouse now?"

"Yep."

"Buy a postcard for me."

HECETA HEAD LIGHTHOUSE was located on a high, rocky bluff only a short distance from Highway 101, in a cove at the mouth of Cape Creek. While the lighthouse itself was not far from the highway, the parking lot was actually down near the beach, part of a state scenic viewpoint, and getting to the lighthouse required walking a half-mile trail.

Fortunately, even though Gage had not been expecting this walk, the path was well-packed gravel the entire way. After letting Lady do her business, he left her in the van. With his cane to aid his bad knee, and his fedora to shield his eyes from the bright sun and the mildly strong gusts off the ocean, he even managed to enjoy it.

No matter how many years he'd lived on the Oregon coast, there was nothing like the smell of the ocean. The trail meandered through a grassy picnic area and into mossy Sitka spruce and wild rhododendrons that grew right up to the bluff, the trees becoming fewer and more sparsely limbed the farther up he went. The surf crashing against the rocks below grew louder. The ocean, full of subtle ripples and undulations, stretched out to the horizon, where a very fine afternoon haze blurred the azure blue of the ocean into the cobalt blue of the sky. A few seagulls rode the strong winds with only the occasional twitch of their wings. He'd looked up the lighthouse in a recent tour book he had on the shelf, and the description asserted it was the most-photographed lighthouse in the world.

He could see why. Though the most recognizable photo of the lighthouse was from a distance, some miles south, the view was fairly spectacular up close, too. The tall white turret capped with a red roof was like something out of a painter's dream.

He passed the Lightkeeper's Home, or what was actually the *assistant* lightkeeper's home, the head lightkeeper's home having been razed in 1940 according to the posted information and was now apparently a B&B operated by concessionaires of the U.S. Forest Service. Nice gig. The two-story white house with the steepled red-shingled roof, surrounded by a huge lawn and waist-high picket fence, couldn't have been any prettier, and Gage was inclined to talk to the managers at some point, but he knew the tours of the lighthouse itself were ending at three. By his watch, he had no more than half an hour.

The gift shop was a plain white outbuilding just past the B&B. Only a few cars had been parked in the lot, and he passed just one person on the way up, a man decked out in REI with a big Nikon camera slung around his neck. Gage reached the lighthouse just as five Japanese tourists were entering the one-story side building attached to the turret. The Japanese were all busy snapping pictures of anything in sight. The wind, much stronger on the bluff, forced Gage to keep his hat clamped to his head. Seagulls cried and squawked all around.

The lighthouse was smaller than he expected, about the size

of a small grain silo, maybe fifty feet tall and fifteen feet in diameter. From the narrow catwalk outside the lantern room, a glass enclosure surrounded by a waist-high iron railing, it was probably more like forty feet to the ground. Not that far. It bothered Gage. If a man wanted to commit suicide by jumping to his death, it didn't seem like an ideal location. Someone could easily, and probably often would, survive such a fall, especially considering most of the area around the lighthouse was grass. The harder, paved paths were far enough from the lighthouse that the jumper would really have to leap to have any chance of hitting them. The edge of the bluff would have been better. A rapidly sloping hillside was followed by a couple-hundred-foot drop to the rocks and then the ocean below.

No area designating where Ed Boone had died was marked—not surprising, since it had been over a week ago and no foul play was suspected. Gage stepped in behind the Japanese tourists, entering the tiny outbuilding and following them into the turret. It was cool and dank. He heard the tour guide before he saw him, a deep voice echoing off the red brick walls; the man was in the middle of explaining why the top was still not open for visitors: although most of the restorations of the tower had been completed a couple years ago, they were currently doing maintenance and inspections at the top, so there was no going up.

"This will give you all a reason to come back!" the tour guide said, with a hearty chortle.

Whether his audience understood him was debatable, but they did go on taking plenty of pictures. Gage, peering over the top of them, saw the tour guide standing at the base of a black iron spiral staircase, a black man wearing a green hat and tan vest, both clearly marked with Oregon State Parks logos. His beard, thick but trimmed, was just as white as his skin was as black. He had a deeply lined face and kind eyes. Seeing Gage, he waved for him to enter.

"Come on in, fella," he said. "Last tour of the day. Saved my best for last. Not that my best means much, but hey, I'm an old fart now."

He wore a laminated name tag pinned to his vest that read HAROLD, and it was clear that Harold's humor was lost on this particular crowd. No laughs, no smiles. There were a few appreciative nods, but then, they appeared to nod anytime Harold glanced at them. While Harold launched into what was obviously a well-rehearsed spiel about the history of the lighthouse and the construction and operation of the Fresnel lens, Gage studied the stairs winding up into the turret, thinking about the mindset of a man who would march up those stairs knowing he was going to jump from the top.

When it was over, and the Japanese tourists had departed, Gage approached Harold outside the front door. The man was fishing keys out of his vest. On this side of the lighthouse, they were shielded from the brunt of the ocean winds, but the gusts still swirled over the bushes that grew densely on the hillside behind them; the rustle of the leaves was almost as loud as the surf crashing against the rocks.

"Before you lock up," Gage said, "you got time for a few questions?"

Harold glanced at his watch, which, Gage was amused to see, was bright yellow and decorated with a Donald Duck's face. "Really supposed to finish at three," he said. "Is it something about the inside?"

"Kind of. It's about Ed Boone."

The next question Gage was going to ask was whether Harold knew Ed, but it was already obvious by the way the man winced that the answer was yes.

"Sad thing, that," Harold said.

"Did you know him well?"

"Just a little. But he wasn't a talkative sort, you know. Wish we'd tried a little harder. Why you ask? You related?"

Gage would have liked to tell Harold the truth, since he already liked him, but Nora's privacy was too important to risk it, especially with what he now knew about the Younger brothers. "No, I'm ... I'm a writing a book."

"A book?"

"That's right. It's about the history of Barnacle Bluffs, and Ed Boone has a couple pages in it."

"Really? Why?"

Gage told him about Ed's Diner, what an institution it was in town during its early days, and still was, in a sense. When he was finished, Harold shook his head.

"Amazing," he said. "He never said one word about any of that. I didn't even know he lived that far north."

"What *did* you know about him?"

"Oh, not much. Maggie—that's my wife, she's working the gift shop—she might know a bit more, because she actually worked with him when I came down with the flu a couple weeks ago. I know he liked to read a lot, and he knew his history, especially of Oregon. When he was doing our training, he was always recommending different books to read if we really wanted to dig deep into the history of the coast."

"He did your training?"

"Yeah, see, Ed was kind of head volunteer. Usually these places are staffed by RVers like Maggie and me, retired folks traveling around. This is our third lighthouse, actually. But I guess Ed filled in when they were between scheduled volunteers. And he told us to call him anytime we needed a day off. It's not rocket science, but you're supposed to have one person up here to do the tours and one person in the gift shop."

"Do you know much about how he died?"

Harold grimaced. "Well, I'm the one who found him."

"Oh. I'm sorry."

"Yeah. Glad it was me and not Maggie, though. Or a random tourist, I guess. Just pure luck, really. We don't have to be here until closer to ten thirty, since tours are only from eleven to three, but I sometimes walk up here with Fresco early in the morning. We got our RV a mile or so up the road at Washburn State Park, so usually I walk him there, but sometimes I drive up here and walk the path. You know, to check on the place. Kind of feel like since we're volunteering, we're responsible. It was barely dawn. Couldn't sleep that night. Not that I've slept through the night much since 'Nam."

"Fresco's your dog?"

"Yeah. Swedish bull hound. Sweet boy."

"You want another dog?"

"What?"

"Never mind. So you found Ed?"

"Well, technically Fresco did. I hate to say it, but I may not even have noticed. Light wasn't that good yet, and he was on the backside here, just around the turret on the grass. I walked up the path, saw the front door was fine, and started to swing back. If Fresco hadn't been pulling on his leash and whining, trying to get over to the spot where Ed was, I probably wouldn't have gone over there."

"So he was on the grass, then?"

"Yeah. Here, I'll show you the spot."

They walked over there. Except for one of the Japanese tourists who'd climbed the hill to take pictures, they had the place to themselves. The wind rippled across the grass. Gage could see how someone could miss the spot. It wasn't visible from the front door, and unless you walked all the way to the fence, it was hidden from view. The grass, lush and full of white clovers, felt soft and pliant, uneven enough that he leaned hard on his cane.

Harold swallowed. "See that spot there?"

Gage looked. There was an obvious divot in the grass, deep enough that some of the wet earth was visible. "Yeah."

"That's where he took a header. Paramedics who showed up when I called 911 said it probably broke his neck instantly. So there was that, at least. He didn't suffer. But man, to go like that? Think what that took, diving straight down, headfirst."

Gage studied the spot and then peered up at the railing. It seemed so close. Hitting headfirst was probably the *only* way someone could die from such a fall.

"So he had access to the walkway up there?"

"Sure. It's closed to the public, but all the volunteers can get keys in the gift shop. Those work for the causeway, too, though I don't know why. Only maintenance personnel are supposed to go up there. Probably just because it was easier to make the keys match, I guess."

"Any other security? Cameras, that sort of thing?"

"Nah."

"Keypads on any of the doors, you know, that record the time? Here or the gift shop? Any way of knowing when he went up there?"

"No, man, this is a low-budget affair. Lucky that we even have deadbolts."

"Any chance you could let me take a look up there?"

Harold shook his head. "Be my ass if anyone found out."

"I'll give you twenty bucks."

He shot Gage a look, as if disgusted with the very suggestion.

"Or not," Gage said.

"Why? Do you really need to see it for your book?"

Gage thought about his answer. The Japanese tourist who'd been taking a picture on the hill was now trudging down to join his friends, his back to them. There was nobody to hear or see them at the moment. A seagull, struggling against the wind, banked hard left and right high above them, barely moving toward the ocean, but Gage highly doubted his winged observer would let Elliott Younger or anyone else know what he was doing. What should he say? He didn't know if he could trust Harold, but he really did want to see that causeway. There might be a clue there, something the police would have missed because they weren't looking for foul play.

"I have a confession to make," Gage said. "I'm not writing a book."

"You're not?"

"At least not right now. Who knows, maybe someday. I'm actually a private investigator, and I'm looking into Ed Boone's life—and death—for a client."

Though Harold's eyes didn't lose all of their kindness, a veil of suspicion did fall over them.

"For real?" he said.

"For real," Gage said.

"Can I see your license?"

Gage was surprised. Though he was registered in Oregon, and actually had the little laminated piece of plastic to prove it, hardly anybody asked to see it. He took out his wallet and showed the license to Harold, who studied it for so long that Gage started to feel defensive. What, was the guy going to say it was fake? Finally, Harold handed it back to him.

"Garrison Gage, huh?"

"That's right."

"Who's your client?"

"I can't say."

"You can't or you won't?"

Gage put the license back in his wallet. "If it gets out who I'm working for … well, it would just make things a lot more difficult than they have to be. I need to keep that private as long as possible."

"And what's Ed's suicide got to do with things?"

"Maybe nothing. Maybe everything."

"And how is seeing exactly where he jumped going to help?"

"I don't know yet."

"You don't seem to know much."

"That's often the case, unfortunately. I just bumble around until I bumble into something interesting."

"Doesn't seem like a very methodical way to do things."

"Nope. Other people do methodical much better than me. I'm good at bumbling. Can you help me?"

Harold adjusted his cap, frowning. "I don't know, man. I'm a big mystery fan, read a ton of them since I retired. Robert B. Parker, Stuart Woods, Sue Grafton, love that stuff. But I don't want to get in trouble."

Gage thought carefully about what to say next. Was it really worth getting a look at the top? Probably not, but it would nag at him if he didn't. He could already see that Harold wasn't likely to help him out of curiosity alone, though the man's curiosity could also be used to Gage's advantage.

"Harold," he said, "if I tell you something, can I trust you not tell anyone?"

"I guess that depends on what it is."

"Fair enough. You strike me as a man of character, so I guess I'll take the risk. But after you hear it, please know that it would help me, and my client, an awful lot if you'd keep it to yourself."

Now he had Harold's full attention, which was exactly what

Gage had been hoping. There was something about being part of a secret that engendered a sort of trust that may be misplaced but was useful nonetheless. Even though there was no need because of the wind and because there was no one to hear them, Gage still lowered his voice to a conspiratorial whisper.

"I think it's possible that Ed Boone was murdered," he said.

Harold raised his eyebrows. "Murdered?"

"Shh. We've got to keep this to ourselves."

"But really?"

"I'm just saying it's a possibility that we're exploring."

"Why do you think that?"

"I can't get into specifics, but let's just say there's been a few odd things that have raised questions."

"And the police? Have you told them?"

"Not yet. I've got to have something solid first."

"And that's why you want to look up there? Because you think he was … pushed?"

"Again, it's just a possibility."

"Huh. Seems far-fetched."

"I admit, it does. But, Harold, in my line of work, far-fetched things sometimes turn out to be true. Not often but enough that I can't rule them out. I could really use your help."

Harold, chewing on his bottom lip, glanced down at his keys, then toward the keeper's house. Nobody was coming up the trail. Clouds that had been creeping in off the ocean moved partly in front of a sun that was already sinking toward the western horizon, graying the light. He sighed.

"You know," Harold said, "walking up fifty-eight steps is murder on my knees. Something about this Oregon weather really brings out the worst in my arthritis."

Gage pointed to his cane. "This isn't going to be a picnic for me either, buddy."

"Mmm. All right, let's go. We've got to make it quick, though, because Maggie wants to go to Old Town in Florence before the shops close. I can take you to the service room. Not outside on the gallery, though."

"The gallery?"

"Another word for the balcony outside the lantern. Some folks call it the catwalk."

"Are you sure? I'd really like to get outside and see the—"

"I'm sure you would. The service room or nothing."

"All right."

Gage was disappointed but it would have to do. Harold led Gage inside, shutting the door behind them. Without all the other people around, the inside felt larger—not spacious by any means, but certainly not cramped. Gage was also more aware of the smell of wet brick and plaster. Harold unlatched a chain over the bottom stair and the two of them started up, their footsteps on the metal stairs echoing off the walls. Gage was certainly capable of toughing it out at a faster clip, but he was thankful that Harold didn't push the pace.

Even though there was only one window halfway up and just a handful of small light fixtures along the way, the openness allowed plenty of light to penetrate. It only took a dozen steps for Gage's right knee to burn with excruciating pain, like a thousand hot needles jabbing from all sides each time his weight came down on the joint. By two dozen steps, he began to have serious doubts about his refusal to see an orthopedic surgeon.

He heard the hum of the machinery as they approached the top. The service room was a fairly tight space surrounding the electric engine that rotated the Fresnel lens above them, the shiny mirrors that he could see by peering up through indoor gangplank. The access to the very top, and presumably the outdoor gallery, was an extremely narrow staircase in the corner blocked by a chain.

"Well," Harold said, "make it quick. Not sure what you think you'll find that the police didn't."

"In my experience," Gage said, "the police usually miss a whole lot. And that's when they're *trying* to find things."

"Hey, my brother-in-law is a cop. A good one, too."

"There are always rare exceptions."

Searching the area, Gage didn't see any obvious clues. Of course, they wouldn't be obvious, would they? A heavy gray drop cloth covered some equipment in the corner, but looking under the cloth revealed nothing but paint cans, varnish, lots of brushes, files, and other tools, just what Gage would expect to find for restoration work. Dusty white walls. Four paned windows, one on each side. The machinery was interesting, but otherwise the area was so empty and plain that it was hard to ascribe any romantic wonder to the place, as would befit something that had graced so many postcards over the years.

Yet there was still something about the lighthouse that appealed to Gage, all those solitary hours of routine, providing vigil, making sure everything was working because lives depended on it. As Harold had said, almost all lighthouses worldwide were automated now, and Heceta Head was no exception, but if Gage had been born a hundred years earlier, he could easily see himself a keeper of a lighthouse.

He saw no obvious footprints. No signs of struggle—scuff marks, scratches, that sort of thing.

"Was the note left up here?" Gage asked.

"Note?"

"The suicide note."

"Oh, right. Yeah. I didn't see it, but I heard they found it by the stairs there, the ones to the top."

Gage went to the stairs, peering up at the locked door. "And you say the same key works on that door there?"

"It does. Not that any of us ever use it."

"This is the part where I ask very nicely one last time if you can take us up there."

Harold smiled. "And this is the part where I say again that I can't do it. But maybe the police could, you know, with a search warrant, that sort of thing."

"Now you're just taunting me," Gage said.

"Sorry. You done?"

"Give me just a second."

Gage leaned against the outer wall, thinking. The brick felt cold and rough even through his jacket. The wind whistled against the windows. He heard the gulls. It was hard to imagine a killer going to all the trouble of committing a murder in the lighthouse. Perhaps it was committed elsewhere, and then the killer dragged the body up to the top? That was even harder to believe. It was no easy feat to carry even a small man on level ground who wasn't aiding the effort. It wasn't just the weight. It was the ungainly nature of the human body. Add in all the steps? Not impossible but certainly quite a challenge.

No, if it was a murder, it most likely occurred on the gallery, or at least where Harold and Gage stood. But why would Ed agree to come here with his eventual murderer? Was it against his will? Did he know the person, and he had no reason to suspect what was going to happen? Suicide seemed far likelier, but Gage was finding that possibility increasingly difficult to believe, especially now that he'd been here. It wasn't just the short fall. It was also how difficult it would be to land headfirst, even if someone was trying. Forty feet would almost take a master diver, and then amazing willpower to suppress the normal instinct to flail or at least get hands in front of the face.

But if someone was held out over the rail by their legs, someone who was already dead? That body might drop like an arrow.

If, for example, Ed had been poisoned or strangled up here, that fact could easily be obscured unless a full autopsy was done—which nobody was doing, because everybody assumed it was suicide.

Gage was mulling all of this over when something small and red caught his eye. It was directly underneath the stairs to the top, partly obscured by the shadow of the step, an object no bigger than a thumbtack. He would have missed it completely if he hadn't been looking straight at it. When he bent down to study it, he found that it was a tiny red pebble. He picked it up, holding it between his thumb and forefinger. It was light and rough, speckled with tiny holes.

"What's that?" Harold asked.

"Lava rock," Gage said. "Pretty common east of the Cascades, but not so common around here. Except for decorative purposes, you know, in yards as a ground cover. There's nothing like this around the lighthouse, is there?"

"No. Not that I've seen, anyway. You sure it's not a piece of red brick? You know, like from the walls?"

"No," Gage said. "Red brick is usually made by cooking clay in a kiln. This is definitely lava rock. So who comes up here?"

"Well, maintenance personnel are supposed to be doing some inspections so we can open it up to the public, but I take it they haven't been up in a month or so. We're all hoping that changes soon, so people won't be disappointed when they come for a tour. Otherwise, only if there's a problem."

"And there hasn't been a problem lately?"

"Not that I know of. At least, not in the month since I've been coming here."

"Mind if I take it?"

Harold shrugged. Gage slipped the rock into his jacket

pocket. If it had been stuck to the bottom of Ed's shoes or the shoes of the person he might have been meeting up here, it might prove helpful.

At the bottom, Gage took one last pass around the perimeter but didn't find anything, and then the two of them walked to the gift shop. The door to the squat, plain building was locked, but Harold used his key to let them into a dim room with a low ceiling, packed with Oregon coast sweatshirts, Heceta Head snow globes, key chains, bookmarks, shot glasses, and every other kitschy thing one might expect in such a place. An incense candle that smelled of cedar burned on the front counter, only partly masking the faint odor of mold.

Maggie, a short firecracker of a woman with freckled, pale skin and long white hair braided down her back, teared up when Harold explained who Gage was and asked whether she remembered anything else about Ed, but it turned out she didn't have all that much more to say—only that he was exceptionally kind but didn't say much, and he always clammed up when she asked any personal questions. No, he never mentioned family.

Gage asked if they had a list of other volunteers, including contact information, and after some hesitation, they copied it from a laminated sheet behind the counter onto a yellow pad for him. Gage bought a postcard of a seal for Alex and a book on Heceta Head history for himself. After locking up, they walked outside. A group of five was approaching the gift shop, and Maggie stopped to explain to them that everything was closed. Harold walked on with Gage.

"One last thing," Harold said.

"Yes?"

"If I give you my email, will you promise to write me to tell me how this all turns out? Maggie and I are heading south to the California Redwoods day after tomorrow."

"I would," Gage said, "but there's just one problem."

"What's that?"

"I don't have email."

"Oh."

"I'll get the news to you some other way, though. Would carrier pigeon work?"

Fortunately, Harold laughed.

Chapter 13

Like many Oregon coastal towns, much of what lay along Highway 101 was not very interesting. After passing the Fred Meyer at the edge of town, which backed up to the Oregon Dunes National Recreation Area—huge, sloping hills of yellow sand—Gage drove his van past the usual suspects of gas stations, fast food joints, and other bland stores with the typical cookie-cutter architecture. The ocean, far from where the town was situated, wasn't even visible.

The Florence Police Department was located only a few minutes from the highway, as almost everything not on the highway was, a one-story tan and brick building that looked like an elementary school. Though he had little hope they'd help him, Gage couldn't leave town without at least trying.

He was right to be skeptical. A grizzled detective named Monroe wouldn't release any information other than to say it was designated a suicide. He didn't buy Gage's cover story about writing a book, and after a little give and take, it became clear he knew full well who Gage was. Gage had a certain notoriety in Oregon, after all, and unless he could be a little more forthcoming about who he was working for and why, Monroe couldn't say any more.

If Gage thought they actually knew something, he might have taken the risk, but he got the sense Monroe was just fishing. He did make sure to let Lady do her business on the grass in front of Monroe's window, however. Bonus points.

Next, with the sun a low orange orb in the sky and a stiff wind buzzing against the windows in the Fred Meyer lobby, he used a payphone to call the numbers on the volunteer list. For those who didn't answer—most of them—he left messages saying he was writing a book and Ed Boone was mentioned in it. He left Alex's phone number and told them if they knew Ed at all to reach out. For those that answered, two were in Eugene, and they didn't know him any better than Harold or Maggie. Three of the volunteers were local. Getting the same spiel from them—nice guy, not very talkative—Gage was about to say goodbye to the last of the three when she suddenly exclaimed, "Oh wait, there is something!"

Unlike most of the volunteers, Brittany Folsom was not a retired person with plenty of time to burn but a busy high school kid who fit in volunteering at the lighthouse between basketball practice and violin lessons. She'd only met Ed once, when he stopped by the gift shop to buy a bottle of water.

Outside the Fred Meyer lobby, someone was using a leaf blower to clear the sidewalk—it seemed silly in such windy conditions—and Gage had to cup his hand over his left ear to hear her better.

"What's that?" Gage asked.

"I almost forgot. When he bought the water, he smiled and said I reminded him of his daughter."

Gage felt a tingle up his spine. "A daughter?"

"Yeah. I'm pretty sure that's what he said."

"When was this?"

"Oh, maybe a year back. I haven't volunteered much lately, and really I just help out in the gift shop when they have a big load of stuff come in or when they're really short on the weekends. I only remember because he kind of got weird about it. I asked him how old she was, and he started to say something but then stopped and shook his head. Then he walked out without saying anything. I got the feeling it might be a sore subject or something."

Gage was now desperate to see how much Brittany looked like Nora, which made him ask his next question with perhaps too much excitement. "Can I come see you?"

There was a long pause. Silently, Gage castigated himself for coming off like a dirty old man trying to put the moves on a teenage girl. He heard the sound of screeching tires in the background, then gunshots. A video game?

"Um …"

"I can wait until your parents are home, it's no problem. I can even call back and talk to them before you give me your address. When will they be home?"

"Well, Mom will be home any minute, but I guess I don't know what else you want to talk about. It's really all I know. Why, does it mean something?"

Unsure if the parents would be all that willing to help him unless he divulged at least a little bit of the truth, he decided to get a running start by being more honest with Brittany. "It might. I'd like to see what you look like."

"What I look like?"

"Right."

"Well, you don't need to come over for that. Just find today's newspaper."

"Excuse me?"

169

She laughed. "I've had a good year on my basketball team. The paper ran a story on me, and there's a good shot of me standing at the free-throw line."

It was dark by the time Gage knocked on Nora West's motel room door. The moon, full except for a hint of shadow, spread its silvery light generously on the railing, the concrete walkway, and the tops of cars. It wasn't quite bright enough to read by, but if Elliott Younger or anyone else had been trying to hide in the parking lot below, Gage was fairly confident he would have seen them. The wind, so strong earlier, had died to almost nothing, and the surf was loud enough that it sounded like it was all around them.

He heard footsteps, then a pause. Looking through the peephole? Good girl. He heard the rattle of the chain and the sliding of the deadbolt. When she opened the door, he lifted the plastic bag of Chinese food.

"Oh, you're a lifesaver," she said. "I'm starving! Come in."

She locked the door behind him. It may have been a subconscious move, but he was glad to see that. They could no longer afford to mess around with her safety. The decked-out woman who led him into the kitchen had completely transformed herself from the harried creature in T-shirt and sweatpants he'd seen that morning. She'd been beautiful then anyway, to be sure, but the black turtleneck sweater, the designer jeans, and the brown leather boots all fit her perfectly, presenting her curvaceous figure in the best possible light.

When she looked at him, her eyeliner made her eyes pop even more than usual. She smiled.

"What?" she said.

"You haven't gone out, have you?"

She retrieved a couple of plates from the kitchen. "No, no. Really desperate to walk on the beach, but I did what you said and stayed put. Sometimes I just feel better when I gussy myself up a bit. What's that under your arm? You brought me a newspaper?"

Gage had forgotten about the newspaper. After placing the bag of Chinese food on the kitchen table, he held up the newspaper for her to see.

"It's the Florence paper," he explained.

"Okay. Why?"

"I'll explain in a little bit. Let's start on dinner first. I'm hungry too. But before we get to that either, I do have to ask you about something else. How do you feel about dogs?"

"Dogs?"

"Yes."

"Why do you ask?"

"Are you okay with them?"

"Of course! I love dogs. I had a dachshund for a few years, but it was just too hard when I was on tour. Jewel took him home to her kids, who love him, and I get to visit now and then. Wait a minute. I'm getting the sense this isn't a rhetorical question."

Gage shook his head, then explained who was waiting in the van. When he told her Lady had apparently belonged to Ed Boone, Nora insisted Gage bring her in at once. Gage, who'd felt bad about leaving the dog in the van for such a prolonged period, especially since she'd been cooped up in the van on and off most of the day, had been hoping Nora would say that.

Careful not to be seen, he fetched her from the van. The motel may not allow dogs, but Gage rationalized his rule breaking by telling himself that Lady was so small she barely even qualified as a dog. Nora lavished Lady with all kinds of attention, and the dog wagged her tiny tail and soaked it up.

Nora put out the plates and he opened up the boxes of chicken chow mein, steaming white rice, fried pork, egg foo young, and more, a wide assortment because he hadn't known what she liked. Turned out he had no cause to worry; she took heaping spoonfuls of all of it. Between bites, he filled her in on his conversation with Brittany Folsom. When he mentioned Ed's comment about Brittany's resemblance to a daughter, Nora froze, the noodles she'd been lifting to her mouth slipping off the chopsticks. On the floor next to her, Lady watched the noodles with rapt attention.

"He actually said the word daughter?"

Gage, never having mastered the art of eating with chopsticks himself, put down his fork and wiped his hands with his napkin. He turned the newspaper to the sports page and held it open for Nora.

"Notice anything about her?"

"That's Brittany?"

"Yep."

"Oh my."

"Looks a lot like you, doesn't she?"

"She ... does."

There was an excited tremor in Nora's voice. Gage glanced at the photo, then back at Nora, and in person the resemblance was even greater. Curly, dark hair, bosomy figure, eyes that popped. Even the slightly round face—the resemblance was strong enough that Brittany could have been Nora's little sister. Gage folded the newspaper so the picture was facing up and placed it on the table. Nora studied it for a long time, and when she looked back at Gage, her eyes had teared up.

"I knew he wasn't making it up," she said.

"Hold on, we haven't proven anything."

"But it's true. It has to be true."

"I'd still like to do a little more digging."

"Sure, sure, of course. I want more proof too. But why would that girl lie? Did she even know about me?"

"Of course not."

"See!"

"It's a good sign. It's just … there were other things that happened today that weren't so good."

"What do you mean?"

Gage caught her up on the rest of his day, starting with Ed Boone's apartment. He told her he was having Alex do a DNA test of her hair; he just needed a hair sample from her, too. She said she'd give him one before he left. She was disappointed when he said there didn't appear to be any of her music there, or anything else that indicated a fondness for her. He said maybe he liked her but not her music. She didn't find this funny. She didn't find Elliott and Denny Younger's surprise visit to Gage's place funny either, especially when he told her their rumored occupation.

"You're kidding," she said.

"Nope. Not according to Alex's intel."

"So I just find out I have a couple of half-brothers, and they turn out to be hit men?"

"If Ed really is your father, then it would seem that way."

"Did you warn that yard guy? What's his name?"

"Ron? Yeah, I stopped by on the way out of town, told him they might try to pressure him for information." Gage smiled. "He said he'd look forward to it."

"You think they're back because they want his money or something?"

"Probably."

"What if I paid them to go away?"

"I'd rather you not talk to them at all. They don't know about you, and I want to keep it that way."

"But if they just want money—"

"The problem, Nora, is that once you give them money, they'll just want more. That's how guys like them operate. Not only that, this may not be totally about money to them. Like you, they might have some unresolved issues regarding their father."

Nora smiled wryly. "Thanks."

"You know what I mean. It just makes them more unpredictable. I'd like to think they'd be overjoyed to find out they have a sister, but they might be jealous instead. We just don't know. I'm sorry to be the bearer of bad news. I wish I could tell you that your new brothers were Boy Scout troop leaders and members of the Lions Club. It changes how we think about your safety."

"What're you saying?"

"I'm saying I'm no longer comfortable with you by yourself here. I probably shouldn't have left you at all today. It was stupid, really, me leaving town, and you're alone in this motel room."

"They don't know I'm here."

"Right now, yeah. But for how much longer? No, I can't leave you here by yourself anymore. But you can't stay at my place either, not with them knowing where I live. I'm thinking we need to get you back to California."

"No," Nora said.

"I'd feel a lot safer if you had a bunch of big, burly security guys around you at all times."

"I'm not leaving. You can stop if you want, but then I'll ask people the questions myself. I've got to know this, Garrison."

"I'm not stopping. I'll tell you everything I find out."

"I know, I know, but I can't leave."

"Nora—"

"I don't want to argue about it. I've got to be here. This feels right. Besides, I'm doing some of the best composing I've ever done. Maybe it's all the stress, but I've already written two songs today. Two! And I think they're pretty damn good, too. Nobody knows I'm here, Garrison. Our plan is working. Let's just keep at it."

"Man, you're stubborn. We're talking about your life here."

"Yes, exactly. My life. This is important."

"Nora—"

"Our food is getting cold."

"Nora, damn it, I'm not leaving you alone."

"Well, I guess you better stay here, then."

"Fine. I'm sleeping with you tonight."

It took only a second for Gage to realize his unfortunate wording. They stared at each other over the boxes of Chinese food. Lady, taking this pause as some sort of invitation, whined pleadingly. Gage cleared his throat.

"I mean, I'm *staying* here tonight."

"I know."

"I'll sleep on the couch."

Nora looked down at her food. "Of course. I wasn't— I hope you didn't think I was … you know …"

"Of course not."

"I appreciate it. I do. You don't have to, though. I can take care of myself."

"I'm staying."

"Okay."

"And so is my Berretta. And so is Lady. I get the feeling she can be a vicious attack dog if need be. Don't be confused by her cuddly nature."

"Oh, I won't," Nora said. "I mean, just look at those teeth.

She could probably rip through metal."

Perhaps because they were both looking at Lady—partly so they could avoid looking at each other until the embarrassment passed—the dog started panting, revealing teeth that certainly couldn't cut through metal. Or probably even thick cardboard, really. They laughed. Nora asked what his plans were for tomorrow, other than looking for lava rock. He told her that the list of people to talk to about Ed Boone had only grown. He may have lived a mostly hermitlike existence, but there were still people that knew things about him.

As they cleaned up from dinner, he debated how much more he should tell Nora right now. He hadn't said one word yet about the possibility that Ed Boone's death had been a murder instead of a suicide. She had so much to deal with just absorbing that Ed was her father; he didn't want to bog her down with even more troubles until he had a very good reason to do so. She might be angry with him later for holding back, but he'd wait until he had more definitive proof.

She asked if he wanted a glass of the Chardonnay. He said sure. She poured two glasses and they sat out on the porch in the darkness. Neither of them wore jackets. The night was still, the surf and the sand bathed with moonlight; it was low tide and there was plenty of beach. He smelled smoke from a beach bonfire to the north, an orange flickering dot in the darkness, and thought he heard laughter from the same direction.

Sitting in the darkness as they were, he was fairly certain nobody could see them, but he still found himself scanning the beach for any sign of trouble. In time, his eyes adjusted and he could see both the beach and Nora much better.

"So you wrote two songs," Gage said.

"Yeah."

"You want to play them for me?"

"Nope."

"Oh."

She laughed. He liked the way the moonlight played on her cheeks, the way her eyes seemed to glow. "It's nothing personal. I just don't like to play songs for someone until they're really finished."

"And they're not finished?"

"Nope."

"How do you know when they're finished?"

"They're finished when I play them for someone."

"That logic seems fairly … circular."

She drank the rest of her glass. "What's logic got to do with it? I'm a musician. I don't have to be logical. But enough about me. Tell me something about you, Mr. Private Investigator."

"Oh, there's not much to tell," Gage said.

"Alex told me you have an adopted daughter."

"When did he tell you that?"

"Is it true?"

"Well, yes, technically."

"Technically?"

"It's true. It's just a long story. He told you this right after you met him?"

"No, he stopped by today with his wife. Eve, right? Sweet lady. Brought me some baklava she made. Yummy stuff. Now tell me about this daughter of yours. He said she just left for college."

"Jeez, did he give you my complete biography or the Reader's Digest condensed version?"

"Have I hit a sore spot? You don't have to talk about it. I'm certainly not one to judge."

She put her glass on the plastic end table between them, folded her hands in her lap, and gazed out at the ocean. The breeze stirred her curly hair over her eyes. Gage, not quite trusting himself to allow his senses to be dulled, seeing dangers not only out in the dark but also in the tantalizing possibilities that lay between them, took one little sip of his wine and put it on the table. It was cold and sweet, with only a hint of bitterness.

"Her name's Zoe," he said. "She left for PSU yesterday. Smart kid, tough as nails, been through a lot. I love her."

Those last three words were such a frank admission of his true feelings that he felt embarrassed. He certainly hadn't planned to divulge anything so personal. His face felt warm, his throat tight. He realized the pause was only drawing attention to his awkwardness, but he couldn't get himself to speak. He sensed Nora looking at him.

"Tell me about her," she said.

It was the sort of thing a psychiatrist said, and ordinarily Gage would have reacted with sarcasm, but he surprised himself again by answering honestly. He told Nora how Zoe came to be in his care. He explained how rough their early time together had been, the violent world he inhabited that had occasionally enveloped her, and the constant guilt he felt about not being able to shield her from it. He tried to put into words how complicated his feelings were seeing her leave for college.

"Honestly," he said, "I'm a little relieved. I miss her, but she's probably better off not being around me."

"Do you really think so?"

"Yeah, I do. Bad things always seem to happen to people who spend too much time with me."

"What do you think she would say?"

"I don't know. It'd probably be loud and profane, though." He laughed. "I *have* learned that I don't get to make those choices for others. I tried keeping people away from me for the first five years I was here. It didn't work so well."

"Mmm. After your wife died."

Gage looked at her sharply. She raised her hands in a gesture of helplessness.

"I didn't learn that one from Alex. I got that from the Internet."

"Right. Why should I even bother joining Facebook? Everything about me is plastered all over the place anyway."

"Sorry. I just wanted to know what kind of person I might be hiring."

"I guess I just hate that my personal life is out there for anyone to read."

"Tell me about it."

Gage heard the pain in her voice. When he looked at her, she tried a smile, but he saw how false it was. He'd never liked his own minor fame, but he knew it was nothing like what she experienced.

"I guess I shouldn't complain," he said.

" I didn't mean that. It's not a contest. I just meant I can relate, that's all. I mean, I found out my last boyfriend was cheating on me because one of the tabloids published a photo of him with this other woman at a club."

"I'm sorry."

"Yeah, well." She shrugged. "All I'm saying is that at least you have people who care about you. Don't take that for granted. It means a lot."

"Oh, I'm sure you've got people who care about you, too, Nora."

She snorted.

"What about your manager? Your band?"

"They just want things from me."

"I have a hard time believing that's true for all of them."

"Oh, it is. Trust me, if I wasn't the famous Nora West, the

big shot, they'd be gone in a heartbeat. That cheating boyfriend I just mentioned? Turns out pretty much everyone around me already knew he was unfaithful, but nobody told me. Nice, huh? And shit, right up until I found out, I was dreaming about when he was going to pop the question. What a fool I was. Jesus."

"I'm sorry."

"Don't say that any more. Don't say 'I'm sorry.' I hate that crap. I don't want pity. I'm fine, really."

"Okay. I wasn't offering pity, Nora. Just empathy."

"Right. Now I've pissed you off."

"You haven't—"

"It's okay. I know what you meant. I'm just not myself." She picked up her wine, took a sip, looked at it, then guzzled the rest. "This whole Daddy-o thing has just got me screwed up. I feel like, I don't know, like I'm outside looking at myself. And I don't like what I see. I just … I want you to understand why I have a hard time trusting anybody. They all end up screwing me over eventually. Jesus. Maybe it's the wine. I'm saying way too much. We've just met and I'm dumping all over you."

"It's okay," Gage said.

"No, no, it's not. It's not fair. You're nice. And look at me, whining about my problems. I'm rich! I'm famous! I've got my art! I shouldn't have anything to complain about. I'm bitching about a cheating boyfriend and your wife was … she was …" Her eyes teared up, and she shook her head forcefully. "It's dumb. I just have to grow up, that's all. You probably think I'm a pretty self-centered diva, huh?"

"I don't think that."

"Sure you do. Everybody does."

"Nora—"

"It's okay. It's what I am."

He touched her arm. He didn't do it in a sensual way. It was an instinctive act of comfort, of trying to quell the hysteria in her voice. Yet there was still something electric that happened when his hand touched her bare arm.

He would have pulled his hand away—his better judgment was already reminding him that he was crossing a line—but then she put her other hand over his. She stared at his hand, not looking at him, and slowly began to trace her thumb around his knuckles. Then he didn't know what to do. He couldn't pull his hand away. He didn't *want* to pull his hand away. What she was doing was both completely innocent and incredibly erotic, and he felt frozen.

This may have only lasted a few seconds, but it was long enough for Gage to become aware of the beating of his heart and the warmth in his face. Then, abruptly, she pulled her hand back, looking left and right, uncertain. She got to her feet.

"I'm going in," she said.

"Okay."

"I'm—I'm pretty tired. I know it's early, but I think I'll—I don't know. Probably just read for a while in bed."

"Sure."

She started inside, then paused midway through the screen door and looked back in his direction. The light from the living room left her mostly in silhouette, but he could see her well enough. She wouldn't look him in the eyes. "You'll be okay on the couch?"

"Yep."

"I'll get you some blankets and a pillow."

"That'd be nice. Thank you."

"Okay. Okay, good."

"Nora?"

"Yeah?"

She still wasn't looking at him, so he waited. She was like a hummingbird, ready to flit away, but he wanted her full attention. It worked. She looked at him, eyes big and watery, vulnerable. It was hard to believe that someone so in the public eye could be so easily bruised, and it made his heart go out to her. If there was anyone who needed a real friend, it was Nora West.

"I'll never screw you over," he said. "It's just something I don't do. When I say I'm there for someone, I'm there for them. Always."

For a long time, she did nothing but look at him. Was she trying to discern the truth? He realized that other people could say the same words to her, and probably had, and still betray her, but he hoped she could see his seriousness. He may have fallen short of the ideal more than once, but it was never from lack of trying. Maybe it sounded hokey to her, a corny truism of superheroes and medieval knights, but he didn't care.

In the end, he wasn't sure how she took it, because she merely bowed her head and went inside.

Chapter 14

For Gage, it was a long night with only brief periods of uneasy sleep. He could have blamed it on any number of things. It could have been the strangeness of the motel room, with all its unfamiliar sounds, the hum of the refrigerator, the gurgling pipes, or the pair of drunks who staggered back to their room at two in the morning. It could have been Lady, who punished his forgetting to let her out before going to bed by scratching on the front door at three a.m., prompting him to take her down to the parking lot where she could do her business in the bark dust. It could have been the couch, which wasn't particularly bad, especially with the pillows and blankets Nora gave him before wordlessly retiring to her room, but it certainly didn't offer him the comforting familiarity of his own bed.

Most of all, he could have blamed it on his anxious state of mind, worrying about the Younger brothers or other potential threats, his Beretta under the couch within easy reach, his heart occasionally jumping into a higher gear at the slightest strange sound from outside.

No, Gage knew his restlessness could be blamed almost entirely on Nora West.

He couldn't even lie to himself about it. He would prefer to believe that the reason he kept thinking about her all night long was because he was worried about her safety. That certainly would be a more virtuous explanation, one more fitting with what he had told her last night on the balcony—which was, of course, true; he *would* be there for her, no matter what. But this was different. This was more primal.

He wanted her.

He wanted her as much, if not more, than he'd wanted any woman in his life. As he lay awake on the couch, alternately studying the cracks in the ceiling and playing tug-of-war with the downy comforter, her face kept looming before him in a room dimly lit by the moonlight filtering around the edges of the curtains. Those luminous, soulful eyes. Those full, rich lips. How would it feel to kiss those lips? Not once was he tempted to knock on her door—he would never dare, *never*—but over and over again, he imagined her coming to him. He imagined rolling over and seeing here standing there.

Lust. That's all it was. He'd known her, what, two days? Not even that. He was primed for it. Tatyana hadn't been gone that long. The hurt was still raw. He was susceptible to a rebound. Zoe leaving made it worse. There was a yawning void in his life, and he was fixating on Nora as a quick fix. The beautiful musician. A fantasy.

But what was wrong with lust?

If two people could find comfort in one another, did it have to mean more than that? As long as both people had the same expectations—granted, an iffy proposition—then what was wrong with giving in to desire to abate the loneliness they both felt?

His attention kept returning to her door. There was so little separating them. A dozen feet, a couple inches of pressboard. Was she lying there thinking of him? He thought he heard sounds of restlessness from her bed, the rustle of sheets, the frequent movements of her body. He felt like a fraud. When she'd made her declaration to him that they wouldn't be sleeping together, he'd told her he hadn't been thinking about that at all, but he had. The lust was there even then.

At some point his exhaustion must have won the battle over desire, because he woke to the click of a door. His hand went instinctively to the Beretta just under the couch cushion before he realized the sound came from the bathroom. Rubbing his eyes, he sat up and saw the light under the bathroom door. A second later he heard the flush of the toilet, then the shower running.

He slipped on his pants, stretched, and moseyed to the kitchenette. His back felt like it was loaded with bricks. He would have killed for a toothbrush, too. Lady, who'd spent most of the night on loveseat, lifted her head briefly but didn't get up. He made some coffee, and, since he was already bustling around and the shower was still running, thought what the heck, and made up toast and scrambled eggs. At this point, Lady was more than a little interested, perching at the edge of the kitchen with her eyes wide and ears perked.

He was setting out two plates along with some orange juice when he heard the bathroom door open. Steam drifted along the ceiling.

"I smell something good," Nora said.

When she rounded the corner dressed in gray sweatpants and a black T-shirt, he felt mild disappointment that she wasn't standing there in nothing but a skimpy towel—then silently castigated himself. Her hair, still wet from the shower, lay shiny in long loose ringlets, water droplets leaving dark spots on her T-shirt. Her skin bore the shocking pink of being freshly scrubbed, a few freckles and red spots, but she had a nice complexion. If anything, her natural beauty, in its rawest form, drew even more attention to the power of her eyes. He did see just a bit of red in the whites, which may be from the shower but may also be because she, like him, hadn't slept that well. He knew he shouldn't be hoping that was the reason, but he was.

"Wow, breakfast," she said.

"Just toast and scrambled eggs. That okay?"

"Sure. But gosh, I hate to have you see me like this. You know, my hair like this, no makeup or anything. Ugh."

"Don't worry about it. You don't want the food to get cold."

"I must look hideous."

"No, you look beautiful, as always."

He said it without thinking, which was probably why she blinked a few times and some redness spread across her nose and cheeks. Really, the great Nora West, so adored by fans, could be embarrassed by such an innocuous little compliment? Saying anything else would only increase both of their embarrassment, so he pulled out her chair and asked if she was ready to eat. She was.

To his own mouth, the toast tasted ever slightly burned, and the eggs were just a tad on the runny side, but she complimented him profusely.

"You sleep okay?" she asked.

He thought he detected a hopeful note, and she conspicuously didn't look at him, focusing intently on her scrambled eggs.

"I've slept better," he said.

"I'm sorry."

"No, don't apologize. Just a lot on my mind."

"Yeah, me too. I just wish you didn't have to sleep on the couch. I mean, you know, just, I wish there was another bed. That's all I'm saying." The red in her face deepened. She picked up her orange juice and drank half of it. "This *really* is a good breakfast."

"Thanks," he said.

"You going out soon?"

"Yeah. Think I'll get cleaned up at my place, then do a little detecting on your behalf."

"And I imagine you want me to stay cooped up here?"

"I know it's no fun, but yeah, I think it's safer for now. But you don't have to stay in town, Nora. You can always—"

"No, no, I'm staying. I want to see this through."

"The DNA test should tell us one way or the other. You don't need to be here for that."

"Okay, sure, but I guess it's not just the biological proof I'm looking for."

"Well, what then?"

She struggled to put it into words, fumbling around for a bit, before finally shrugging. "Maybe it's just I know so little about him, you know? I just want to know anything you find out while there's still stuff to find out. And honestly, I kind of need to be here right now. I just need the space from … well, everything. This is good for me. This is helping. It's giving me some perspective on my life. On what's real and what's not. On what matters." She shook her head. "I know I'm not making a lot of sense."

"No, I get it," Gage said.

"You do?"

"Well, maybe not *exactly*. I don't have a Twitter account with a million friends."

She smiled. "Almost five million, actually. And they're called followers."

"Well, if I actually had a Twitter account at all, I doubt I'd have even one follower."

"*I'd* follow you."

"Well, that's nice of you. And if I set up one for Lady, maybe she'd follow me, too."

They both looked at her. She wagged her stubby tail. Nora took pity on her and tossed her a bit of scrambled egg, which she gobbled up before it even touched the ground.

"Anyway," he said, "I just meant I came to Oregon originally because I needed some perspective on my own life."

"You know, I never hated Barnacle Bluffs. I remember a lot of kids ragged on it all the time. They couldn't wait to leave. But I have a lot of fond memories of being here. I used to run with some fun kids in my neighborhood. My mom and I, well, we never had a great relationship, but it was at least somewhat functional back then, before she really took to the drinking hard. Maybe that's why I'm so desperate to find out everything I can about my father. It's like maybe that was the life I could have had, you know?"

He suspected she was romanticizing what her past could have been like, but he was smart enough not to say so. If finding out everything he could about Ed Boone was offering some kind of healing for her, then it was a good thing. They took their time finishing their breakfasts, sipping coffee and talking about more trivial matters. She asked whether certain stores, restaurants, and other public fixtures from her youth were still around. He boasted how smart Zoe was, and how he was eager to see exactly what direction she was going to take with her studies. They gave their plates to Lady, who did a thorough job, not leaving even one crumb behind.

"You'll be back tonight?" Nora asked.

"I will indeed."

"Fantastic. And, um, if I write it down and give you some money, will you pick up some stuff from the grocery store for me?"

"Sure, but you don't need to give me money. What do you want?"

She smiled. "That depends."

"Depends on what?"

"On what you want for dinner."

AT NORA'S INSISTENCE, and Gage's relief, Lady was left to spend the day with Nora at the Starfish Motel. Driving away, though, he realized his feelings about the dog were actually mixed. It *was* a relief not to have to worry about making sure she got food and water, or ensuring she got to relieve herself on a regular basis, but it was strange how quickly he'd gotten used to having her around. She was well behaved—no whining, random barking, or bouncing around unnecessarily—and exactly the kind of conversationalist he liked best. On the rare occasions when he wanted to talk, she was always willing to listen, but she never once interrupted his thinking by initiating a conversation of her own.

His feelings about Nora West were even more conflicted. Despite her insistence that nothing was going to happen between them, *something* was obviously happening. He needed to be careful.

Fog created halos around the headlights of the oncoming cars, but it was a much lighter fog than Monday's. The sun rising over the coastal range already pierced the thick air with lances of golden light. After a pit stop at the house to shave and shower, he stopped at Books and Oddities, catching Alex up on what he'd learned in Florence and giving him Nora's hair sample in a plastic bag. Alex said he'd overnight the samples to a tech he knew at one of the labs, who'd told Alex they were backed up and couldn't guarantee results in less than two weeks. This didn't please Gage, but Alex said they were lucky to get it that fast.

The next two places Gage wanted to visit were the library and Ed Boone's doctor in Newport. Since the library was open until seven p.m. on Tuesday nights and Dr. Joseph Keene was thirty minutes to the north, Gage decided to visit the good doctor first. By the time he dropped down onto Newport's bay front, the fog had completely burned off and the sun shone brightly enough that Gage had to fish his sunglasses out of the jockey box. Keene's clinic, Coastal Care, was on the east side of the bay near Embarcadero Marina, and when he got out of the van the air smelled strongly of fish. He heard sea lions barking nearby.

Gage guessed that the big, rectangular building had once been a warehouse, but if so, they'd done a heck of a job remodeling it. A brown brick facade, pastel-blue awnings over windows along the second floor, an entryway in the corner that was all glass—it could hardly have been built better if done from scratch. No lava rock decorated the landscaped areas, just plain fir bark. He told the receptionist he was writing a book about Barnacle Bluffs and wanted to speak to Dr. Keene about Ed Boone, who'd been a patient of Keene's. The skeptical receptionist said the doctor had a full slate of appointments, but she'd relay the message.

After a half-hour watching the fish in one of the three saltwater tanks in the waiting area, and about the time Gage began to think the doctor's curiosity wasn't going to win the day, he was taken to an empty conference room with a long walnut table and a view of Yaquina Bay Bridge. He waited there another fifteen minutes, counting the boat masts from the marina below, before a bald man in a white coat ducked his head into the room as if he expected to duck right back out again.

"Mr. Gage?" he said.

"The one and only."

"I'm Dr. Keene. I was Edward Boone's physician. What's this about?"

"Do you have just a minute?"

Keene glanced at his gold watch. He was short but broad-shouldered, his eyebrows a mix of blond and white. The baldness made him seem closer to sixty, but his smooth, unblemished skin lead Gage to believe he was closer to fifty.

"Two minutes max," he said, stepping into the room and closing the door. "I have patients waiting. There's a flu going around and we've been slammed. I was told this was something about a book?"

"Partly, yes. Doctor, can you tell me first if you diagnosed Mr. Boone's Alzheimer's disease?"

Keene frowned. "Mr. Gage, you understand that doctor-patient confidentiality prevents me from divulging anything about Mr. Boone's visits."

"I was afraid you'd say that."

"And what does Mr. Boone's ... medical condition have anything to do with your book?"

Gage sighed. He could see that his cover story wasn't going to get him very far today. "Well, not much."

"Excuse me?"

"Doctor, I assume you agreed to see me because you heard about Ed's suicide?"

"I did. Terrible tragedy."

"If I told you that his death unearthed a long-lost ... relative, one he'd had no contact with, but someone who has a lot of interest in his medical condition, would that help you bend the rules at all? Anything you could tell us could help this relative prepare for any unfortunate possibilities, if you know what I'm saying."

Keene regarded Gage silently for a long time, saying nothing, though looking obviously troubled. He stepped to the window, crossing his arms and staring out at the bay. He didn't turn around when he spoke.

"I don't fish much anymore."

"Sorry?"

"Fish. I have a Boston Whaler down in the bay. Haven't used it in two years. Used to go out on Sundays with my kids, when they were still here." He paused. "Is it a daughter?"

Gage felt his heart jump. "So he did say something?"

"You understand, I can't let you see his file. Not without a court order."

"I get it. But he did speak of her?"

Keene turned and looked at Gage, speaking to him across the length of the table. "When he told me he didn't want anyone to know about his … condition, I strongly encouraged him to change his mind, for his children's sake, if nothing else. There can be *some* genetic predisposition toward it, depending on several factors. He said the only person he might want to tell was his daughter, but she didn't even know who he was."

"Did he say anything else?"

He hesitated.

"Doctor?"

"Only that he didn't want to come barging into her life when it was too late to make amends. He didn't want her to know who he was, but maybe he'd find some other way to get her the news—an anonymous letter, perhaps."

"He said that? That he wanted it to be anonymous?"

Keene nodded.

"When was this?"

"Oh, perhaps six months ago."

"What else?"

"Nothing. He seemed to clam up after that, and I'm not one

to pry. I think in the moment, being a bit emotional, he said more than he wanted. I've seen it before."

"How did he take it, you know, when you gave him the diagnosis?"

"Well, again, we're venturing into territory I'm not all that comfortable with. I can tell you that I wasn't the one who gave him his definitive diagnosis. That would have been Dr. Hambly at OHSU. But as his primary care physician, and the one who spent more time with him, I can say this much: I was quite surprised when I read in the newspaper about his … choice."

"You're saying you were surprised he committed suicide?"

"Yes. He seemed quite resolute that he wanted to stay around as long as life gave him the opportunity. And the last time I saw him, a month ago, he was in fairly good spirits. He told me a funny story about a couple from New York who were visiting Heceta Head Lighthouse and asked him how long people in Oregon had had running water. His condition hadn't degraded that much. Perhaps in another year … But then, people do change their minds. All right, Mr. Gage, I think that's as much as I can say. Honestly, I don't know anything else. Let me walk you out."

Gage pressed him a bit more, but Keene wasn't having any of it. In the waiting room, they shook hands and the doctor wished him best of luck. He started to go, then pointed at Gage's knee.

"You know, my associate, Dr. Webster, could take a look at that for you. He's one of the best orthopedic surgeons in Oregon."

"I'll keep that in mind."

"What they can do these days with polyethylene inserts, there's a good chance you'd never have to walk with a cane again."

"But I'm so good at it now."

"Excuse me?"

"Never mind."

Back in Barnacle Bluffs, Gage grabbed a quick bite of lunch at the house, then headed to the police station to see if he could pressure Chief Quinn to get an autopsy of Ed Boone before it was too late. No luck. Quinn wasn't persuaded by Gage's flimsy evidence that Boone's death may not have been a suicide, or at least not enough to inject himself into a death that hadn't occurred in his jurisdiction.

So Gage needed better evidence.

It was going on three o'clock by the time he parked outside the drab concrete building where the library was housed, city hall and other government offices on the bottom floor, the library on the second. Heavy clouds had rolled in off the ocean while Gage was in Newport, blotting out the sun and cooling the air. It smelled like it was going to rain.

To spare his knee, he took the elevator. He'd already walked plenty. He hadn't been to the library much over the years, preferring to feed his reading addiction by frequenting Alex's shop, but he always enjoyed the ambiance: the air-conditioned stillness, the row upon row of orange metal stacks packed with books, and the plush purple reading chairs and couches. There was a reading session going on in the kid section, a woman wearing a white and red hat identical to the one from *The Cat in the Hat* reading to a dozen children and their parents.

Gage asked the young woman at the circulation desk if Al Bernard, the head librarian, was in. She called him on the phone and a minute later Al, an elderly black man with white hair so thin it looked like a dusting of snow, showed up at the reference desk. The gold, wire-rimmed glasses that hung around his neck may be twenty years out of style, but they were a good match for his brown tweed suit. He'd been running the library for close to forty years, an institution in his own right, and Gage guessed he'd owned the suit just as long.

"The great detective," he said warmly, extending his hand.

They shook. His hand was small and delicate, but the skin rough, his fingers like rolls of rice paper.

"I'm always amazed you remember me, Al."

"How could I not? You're famous around these parts, aren't you? How many times have you been in the newspaper?"

"I try not to think about it. How are those prize-winning poodles?"

"Ah, I just have one now. Frannie. I don't do shows any-more, and really, one is all I can handle. The other two passed away." His eyes, big, rich brown orbs that emanated a kind of genteel goodness, turned sad momentarily before he blinked a few times. "Getting old does have its downsides, you know. But enough of that. I heard you're writing a book about the history of Barnacle Bluffs."

"You heard about that, huh?"

"Word gets around. I didn't know you were a writer. How long have you been writing?"

"I haven't started."

"Oh."

"You mean you have to actually write something to call yourself a writer?"

"Um …"

"Just kidding. Let's just say that right now I'm in the re-search phase. That's actually why I'm here."

"Oh! Well, there are a number of books on Oregon history that I could point—"

"Actually, I have a very specific request." Gage looked

around. There was no one near the reference desk, but he still lowered his voice. "Did you hear about the suicide at Heceta Head a week ago?"

Al frowned. "Yes, I read it in the *Bugle*. Dreadful business. Why, what does that have to do with your research?"

"His name was Ed Boone. Did you know him?"

It was obvious, as soon as Gage said his name, that Al knew exactly who Ed Boone was. He reacted first with surprise, then his whole face sagged. He sank into the chair behind the reference desk.

"Oh no," he said. "Not Ed. That's terrible. I never would have guessed that Ed ... But why?"

"Did you know him well?"

"No, not well. A little better in recent years, but nothing that would make me think ... Oh my. I just can't believe he'd ... Are you sure there wasn't a mistake?"

"No, it was him. What did you mean, a little better in recent years?"

Al sat staring into space for a moment, then shook his head. He stayed like that for a while, until he finally sighed and leaned back in his chair. "Sorry. I'm absorbing this unfortunate news. What did you say again?"

"You said you knew him a little better in recent years."

"Right, right. Well, he's been a regular patron of the library for many years, really as long as I've been here, I think, but since he sold his diner he's been in at least once a week. Usually he just checks out his books and he's on his way, but a few times he's needed help. Not long ago, he wanted my recommendations on books on training dogs, since he knew my history. He said he had a Boston Terrier. We chatted about that quite a bit, probably the most we'd ever talked. Honestly, I always thought he was a bit cold, since he hardly ever even said hello, but that conversation changed my mind. I realized he's someone who mostly just wants to keep to himself. Kind of like you, Garrison."

"Yeah, it seems we had a few things in common. Did he say why he got a dog?"

"No, not exactly, but I assume it was for the same reason most people want dogs. For companionship."

"He didn't say he was planning on giving it to someone else?"

"No. No, in fact, I got the sense he was planning on working with her quite a bit. He really warmed up talking about it. I even remember something about the name, something about luck."

"Lady Luck?"

"Right! That was it. He said he was naming her Lady Luck because she was turning his luck around. He said it really helped him, having someone who needed him so he didn't just sit around thinking about his own problems. Hmm. I forgot that until just now. I guess if I'd known he was feeling blue, I might have seen that as a warning sign."

"Don't beat yourself up, Al. This came as a shock to everybody. Did he say anything else about his life? Anything at all?"

"No. As I said, he really did keep to himself."

"Okay. One more thing. Do you still have typewriters here people can use?"

"What? Oh, yes, we just have one in the back, by the copier. Why?"

"Do you know if Ed ever used it?"

"Um … Now that you mention it, I do remember him asking about it, maybe a year … no, I'd say six months ago, whether it was self-service or not. I don't know if he used it, or how much, because it's in the back and none of us might know unless there's a problem. You know, ink ribbon needing replacing, that sort of thing. Why, is it important? We could ask the clerks who work at the front desk, but they might not—"

"Could I see it?"

"Well, of course."

Al led him through the stacks, past a reading area surrounded by periodicals, to a small room next to the bathrooms and the emergency staircase. Through the window in the door, Gage saw a copier, a paper cutter, some staplers, and other supplies, as well as a metal desk with an electric typewriter on it. Could it be the same one?

The only thing adorning the off-white walls was an analog clock, big black numbers on a white background. Even with the door open, the thick walls muted all the noise of the outside world, leaving only the steady droning of the air conditioning from the vent on the ceiling. While Al talked about how often the poor copier broke on them, Gage retrieved a discarded sheet from the recycling bin and loaded it into the typewriter.

He typed a few sentences about the quick brown fox, surprised he still remembered it from his one typing class back in high school. When he typed the lowercase t's, and saw that the tops were chopped off, his heart began to race.

"It's the same," Gage said.

"Excuse me?"

"Ed used this typewriter. I'm sure of it."

"Oh. How do you know?"

"Well … probably best I don't get into that yet. So there's no log for this typewriter? No way of knowing who used it or when?"

"I'm afraid not."

"Security cameras? Here or up front?"

"Oh, heavens no. This is a library, a bastion of intellectual freedom. We would never invade on people's privacy in such a manner. There was talk of putting some in after 9/11, but I firmly rebuffed—"

"Would you do me a favor and ask your staff if any of them remember Ed being in here and when that might have been?"

Al said he'd be glad to do so, even though he doubted they would remember any better than him. Gage pulled out the paper, folded it, and slipped it into the inside pocket of his leather jacket. He had to accept the possibility that Ed really had committed suicide. The doctor's comment, the dog that was recently acquired ... maybe none of it meant anything.

Yet it was one thing for Ed to write his will six months ago, but why write the note to Nora and then sit on it? It *could* have been written earlier, but it felt as if it had been written more recently.

I am writing you now becaus I dont havemuch time ...

Story time had ended and the lobby was full of parents and children streaming out the door. Gage and Al asked the clerk on duty if she remembered Ed using the typewriter—she remembered who he was, after a brief description—but she said she couldn't say for sure. Gage thanked her, left Alex's phone number for Al, and turned to go.

"Oh," Al said, "I just remembered. That particular typewriter has only been there a month. I don't know if that's important or not."

Gage stopped. He felt one of those random shooting pains in his knee and had to lean hard on his cane.

"Excuse me?"

"Yes. The other one's not working right. This is a spare. I swapped them a month ago. We used to have two in the room, but we put the other one in the back when we got the copier fifteen, twenty years ago. It's exactly like this one, though."

"Do you still have it?"

"Yes. I'm planning on getting it repaired, but I was putting it off until—"

"Can I see it?"

"Um, well, I suppose. It's in the back, I think."

"I'd really appreciate it."

His pulse quickening, Gage followed Al into the stacks, this time to a door marked STAFF ONLY. Al unlocked the door and led Gage past his own office, which was cluttered with so many books that his desk was invisible, through an open area loaded with worktables, a couple of humming computers, and one gray-haired old lady affixing a Mylar jacket cover to a book. Al asked her where the other typewriter was, and she said it was in the broom closet. The closet was in a nook around the corner, and there, past a mop bucket and on a metal shelf next to cleaning supplies, was the typewriter.

"What's wrong with it?" Gage asked.

"I don't know exactly. The letters keep repeating. You hit A or B, and you get a dozen of them. So it's—"

"Can I try it?"

"Well, I guess."

"It'd be very helpful."

"All right. I guess we can carry—"

"No, there's an outlet right here. It'll just take a second."

Gage plugged the typewriter into the outlet next to the door, the cord just reaching. The machine whirred to life. He took out the folded sheet of paper from his inside pocket, smoothed it out, and placed it in the slot. He put his hands on the keys, then paused, thinking about what this might mean. The will had been dated six months ago, and it, too, had chopped-off t's. If this was the typewriter that had been used, it should have the same issue. If it didn't have that problem, then the will had been written more recently and backdated. Why would Ed backdate his own will? That didn't make any sense.

Gage only needed to type one letter, but the machine's particular malfunction gave him a whole slew of them.

ttttttttttttttttttttttttttttttt

Perfect little t's, all the way across.

Chapter 15

Gage brooded in his van. He was good at brooding, a champion brooder, if there was such a thing, and usually his brooding could help him see through just about any situation, no matter how messy, but this bit with the typewriter really had his mind spinning. Why would Ed backdate his own will? Without a notary and the proper witnesses, it was already a pretty shaky legal document, and anything that put the will in a suspicious light would only make matters worse. The logical conclusion was that someone else had written the will and wanted to make it *seem* like it had been around a while.

But who? And why?

Outside, the gray sky had deepened into a shade of charcoal. Most of the cars lurching along the highway had turned on their headlights, glowing a soft, gauzy yellow. The wind tossed a Jaybee's bag across the parking lot, and he felt the coolness sneaking its way through the many cracks in his van. He felt cold. His knee ached. Did he need all this nonsense? He could be at home in his armchair, perusing a *National Geographic* and nursing a glass of bourbon.

Alone. Just like Ed Boone had been.

Gage shook his head, trying to ward off the lethargy threatening to overtake him, a constant danger even in his early days as a private investigator. He never let it win, but it was always there, and he knew full well that the indomitable persistence he was known for was in many ways the end result of his constant need to prove to himself that his frequent stupors of passiveness couldn't beat him. Focus, Gage. If someone else wrote the will, what was the motivation? The money, if there was any, had been left to the library, and no matter how much Gage tried to see Albert Bernard, librarian extraordinaire, as a possible murder suspect, his mind just wouldn't go there.

Stranger things had happened, though. Maybe he'd have to dig into Al's life a little more.

But his gut told him there was still something he was missing. He was at the point where he needed to tell Nora about all of this, that she needed to know that her father, or possible father, may have been murdered.

Soon. Tonight, in fact. But there was still some day left, and people who'd known Ed and might have information that could make sense of the situation.

Keeping his hand on his fedora to prevent it from blowing off in a sudden gust, Gage ventured back into the lobby of the building. It was one of the few places in town that still had a public phone. He'd hoped for a phone book, or what was left of a phone book these days, but no luck on that score. He dropped in a quarter and called Books and Oddities. It rang ten times before Alex picked up.

After quickly catching up Alex on what he'd discovered, Gage asked if he could look up Ronnie Meyer, the waitress who'd worked for Ed, and locate an address.

"Let me get this straight," Alex said. "You're one flight of stairs from library computers that can give you free access to the Internet but you called me instead?"

"I don't know how to use all that fancy Google stuff."

"Bullshit. I've seen you do it hundreds of times. You're not nearly the curmudgeon you make yourself out to be."

"My knee's acting up."

"What's wrong with the elevator?"

"It's broken."

"Liar. Hold on two minutes. Somebody needs help in the children's section, then I'll do that fancy Google stuff for you, since you're too lazy to do it yourself."

It was more than two minutes. It was more like ten, and Gage was fairly certain, judging by the impatience in Alex's voice, that the wait had been deliberate. Alex had found an obituary in the *Bugle*. Ronnie had died two years ago. Gage asked him to look up the son, Howard or Howie Meyer, telling him he might be a local accountant or lawyer. This time Alex made him wait so long that Gage had to put in another quarter.

"Insurance, actually," Alex said when he returned. "Assuming it's the same guy. Howard F. Meyer, Northstar Insurance. I suppose you want the address?"

"If it wouldn't be too much trouble, my good man."

"And what if it was too much trouble?"

"Well, I'd want it anyway."

"Uh huh. I expect donuts on my counter tomorrow."

Gage jotted down the address. The street wasn't far away, on the north end of town near the casino. The clock hanging on the wall in the lobby showed that it was twenty to five o'clock. Maybe he could catch Howard F. Meyer before he left for the day.

Traffic on Highway 101 had picked up a little, what amounted to rush hour in Barnacle Bluffs, and it took him a few extra minutes to reach the two-story office complex with the brown shake siding. The Golden Eagle Casino, a massive rectangular building with a big amphitheater dome on the end, was across the street. Beyond the casino and the huge swath of parking lot that surrounded it, the ocean extended dark and turbulent to the west under an equally dark and turbulent sky. A storm was definitely approaching. He wasn't lying when he'd told Alex his knee was hurting; it was always worse before a storm.

He found Northstar Insurance in the back of the building, past a central courtyard and up an outdoor flight of wooden steps. Next to it was the Sand and Stars Yoga Center, and through the partially closed blinds in the front window he saw a dozen women stretched out on mats. A young couple with a baby, both dressed in black with tattoos up and down their arms, emerged from the insurance office just as Gage reached the door.

He held it open for them. Another man, dressed in a wrinkled white shirt and thin red tie, followed them to the doorway.

"Come see me again when you'd like to start a life insurance policy on little Benjy," he said. "It's a good deal at his age."

They murmured their thanks. The man, tall and pale, with a thick black mustache and a thick, unruly head of equally black hair above a wide forehead, had the kind of face that reminded Gage of Edgar Allan Poe, though heavier and with something of a double chin. But he had the same moody, dour face, everything sagging, the dark eyebrows, the mustache, the cheeks. Probably forty, maybe a few years older. He may have been smiling when he watched the young couple go, and smiling when he turned to regard Gage, but some faces were built for smiles, and his wasn't. He was well practiced, though, so the smile didn't seem entirely unnatural.

"You look familiar," the man said. His eyes, as piercing and dark as his hair, appeared wary.

"I do?"

"Yes, give me a second. I'm usually good with faces. Were you a guest speaker at the Lions Club?"

"Not likely. My name's Garrison Gage. I was wondering if I could have a few minutes of your time. That's if you're Howard Meyer?"

"Ah! The detective. I've seen your picture in the paper. Yes, sure, but call me Howie. Everyone does."

He motioned for Gage to accompany him. Stepping inside, Gage caught a whiff of Howie's cologne, some peculiar combination of citrus and leather. The office was a tiny affair, a reception area with an unoccupied maple desk, a couple of black plastic chairs, and an end table displaying a dozen fanned-out magazines. Beyond, an open door led to an office. The silver nameplate by the door read HOWARD F. MEYER. Northstar Insurance posters adorned the walls, each picturing different happy families doing the things that happy families supposedly did—having a barbecue, washing their dog in the front lawn, loading a cargo rack above a minivan. Nowhere did Gage see a grumpy guy with a gimpy leg drinking bourbon in his recliner. Not a big target market, apparently.

There was a cardboard box on the chair behind the reception desk, loaded with a potted cactus, some picture frames, and other odds and ends. Howie saw Gage looking at it.

"I had to let Kim go last week, sadly," he said. "Things have been tighter this year than last. She was pretty upset. I thought she'd be back to get her things, but she hasn't."

"I'm sorry to hear that," Gage said.

Howie shrugged. He was pear-shaped, with an ample gut, and he didn't have much in the way of shoulders, so his shrug came off like a turtle retracting his head into a shell. "Happens," he said. "I've survived leaner times, though the divorce really wiped me out. But what am I saying? Too much, like usual. Maybe if I kept my mouth shut I'd sell more policies, huh? Who wants an insurance agent who seems like he's on the verge of bankruptcy? Always my problem, saying too much. I like to talk. What can I help you with? That is, if there's still any hope I can get your business."

If the man had the face of Edgar Allan Poe, he certainly didn't act like him. It was an odd mix, that naturally frowning countenance with his gregarious demeanor. "Well, I'm not here for insurance, sorry to say," Gage said. "I wasn't to begin with, though, so you didn't lose anything."

"Car? Home? Life? Nothing you might need?"

"I'm actually here to talk to you about Ed Boone. Do you remember him?"

The man's brow furrowed. He waved for Gage to follow him into the tiny office. When Gage sat in the plastic office chairs across from a mahogany desk far too big for the room, the back of his chair was against the wall and his knees brushed the end of the desk. Howie squeezed around the side of the desk into the high-backed leather chair, also barely fitting into the space. Papers, brochures, and folders covered the desk. The two computer monitors behind him were open to different Northstar Insurance pages, each filled with charts and rows of tiny numbers. Awards and certificates filled the walls.

"Ed Boone," Howie murmured to himself. "Ed, Ed … Oh yeah! Uncle Ed!"

"Uncle Ed?"

"That's what my mom had me call him. He owned Ed's Diner. Or what was Ed's Diner, back in the day, when Mom worked there. Funny how even now I never really thought of him as Ed *Boone*. If you'd said Uncle Ed, I would have known who you were talking about right away. Why are you asking about him?"

Gage used the usual cover story, about writing *Barnacle Bluffs Blues: The Secret Stories of a Small Coastal Town*, and how Ed's diner was going to figure prominently. He said a few people at the diner remembered Ronnie and Ed being good friends. When Gage finished by telling Howie about Ed's suicide at Heceta Head, Howie stared at Gage with bewilderment.

"That was him?" he said. "Oh man, I'm sorry to hear that. I mean, I haven't had any contact with him in ages. Well, I saw him at Mom's funeral a couple years ago, but that was all kind of a blur. I don't think we even spoke. Suicide. Man."

"Can you tell me anything about him? You know, from when you were a kid?"

Howie rubbed his forehead. "Well, that was a long time ago. Let's see. Well, she always liked working for Uncle Ed, that was for sure. I think she was pretty sweet on him. Would have wanted more than friendship, know what I mean? She'd kill me if she knew I was talking this way, but I guess it doesn't matter now, both of them gone. But she definitely had a crush on him."

"So they didn't, you know …"

"No, no. I think he saw her more as a little sister. He was real nice to Mom. He'd dropped her off when her car was broken, which it usually was, and he'd stay for dinner. Come over to fix our toilet when the landlord wouldn't do anything. Move furniture. Anything we needed. Even helped me with math." Howie laughed. "A lot more than my own father ever did. He'd show up when he was on leave and spend most of his time drinking and yelling at Mom. Until he shacked up with that Filipino woman in Fresno. Then we didn't see him at all."

"Sorry to hear that," Gage said.

Howie shrugged his nonexistent shoulders. "I gotta tell you, back then I *wished* Ed was my real father. And I liked hanging out at the diner. It's interesting, thinking about it now." He nodded, smiling to himself, then his eyes turned sad. "But suicide? I wish I'd reached out to him, I guess. Kind of wrapped up in my own problems, you know? Why'd he kill himself?"

"That's partly what I'm trying to figure out. Do you know anything else about him? You say things between he and your mom were platonic—"

"Completely platonic. No way I would have missed that one. I was looking for it, too. *Hoping.*" He chuckled.

"Okay, but do you know if he might have had an affair with anyone else? Maybe confided in your mom about it, since they were close?"

"Huh. I don't know. I mean, I guess anything's possible. I know he didn't have the happiest marriage. And his boys, well, they were pretty bratty."

"What made you think his marriage wasn't good?"

"Overhead him talking about it with Mom. They didn't like to do it when I was around, but if I lay on the floor with my ear close to the door, I could hear them pretty well. I think that's one of the reasons they were close. They confided in each other. Wish I'd had someone like that when my own marriage was going south." He shook his head. "There I go again, saying way too much. You're not going to put all that in your book, are you?"

"No. I'll keep it mostly anonymous, anyway. Change the names, that sort of thing."

"That's good. Mom may be gone, but I'm sure not! Still hoping to turn my business around, you know. But boy, if you want stories about Barnacle Bluffs, I could really fill your ear for hours."

"Maybe another time. Right now, I'm really focused on Ed."

"Sure, sure. Hmm. Well, I know he was in Gamblers

Anonymous. That's something he talked about, hating the casino opening. He said he almost went back to his old ways. He was heading for the blackjack table a few days after the place opened, and it was only at the last second that he steered himself to the bar instead. I won't forget that story, because he was crying when he told Mom. The only time I remember him crying. He said the whole thing happened five years earlier and he hadn't told a soul—and it could still make him cry! He said a waitress in the bar saved his life, because he wanted to go back to the tables and she wouldn't let him, drove him to her place so he could sober up and get himself together before going home to the wife and kids. He said she not only saved him from going back to gambling, she probably saved his marriage too, because he said his wife would leave him if he ever set foot in a casino again."

"Did he say her name? The waitress, I mean?"

"What? No. Well, if he did, I don't remember it. I couldn't always hear everything he was saying anyway, especially if they were whispering. Why, is that important?"

This was the closest Gage had gotten to a confirmation that what was in the letter, about the affair with Deedee, was true. "Could be. I'm just trying to get an accurate sense of the man. Did he ever say anything about the waitress again?"

"I don't know. That was right after he started coming over, and I was pretty young, five or six. Hard to remember much. Wait, are you saying you think he and the waitress …?"

"Maybe, who knows."

"Well, geez."

"I wouldn't spread it around, though. There's no proof."

"No, no, I wouldn't do that. Hell, his boys, if they grew up to be bigger versions of what they were back then, would probably come back and beat me up. They were real turds."

This was so close to the truth that Gage had to suppress a

smile. If Howie knew exactly what Ed's sons grew up to be, he definitely wouldn't be spreading rumors about their father.

They talked a little longer, Gage probing for other details about Ed's life. Though Howie was the opposite of taciturn, there wasn't much more he could remember that was useful.

But what Gage had learned was plenty.

AFTER PICKING UP the things she wanted for dinner, Gage showed up at the Starfish Motel at half past six. Except for a mammoth RV, a couple of minivans, a Harley, and, of course, Nora's black Lincoln Navigator, the parking lot was empty. It made Gage aware of how conspicuous his mustard-yellow Volkswagen van would be, a van the Elliott brothers had seen, and he debated about parking at his place and walking to the motel. But fatigue and hunger won out over his caution, and he compromised by situating his van behind the RV.

The thick blanket of storm clouds, which was no longer approaching but fully upon them, brought upon an early dusk, the air hazy and cold. The sun was nowhere to be seen. The ocean raging against the beach on the other side of the building sounded close. He'd just reached the top of the landing when thunder rumbled over the city, and he felt the power of it deep in his chest. When Nora greeted him at the door, she ushered him quickly into the room.

"They say a pretty big one is going to wallop us," she said, "with an even bigger one in a couple days."

As if the storm had been waiting for her cue, the sky opened up and a torrent of rain poured down even before she'd closed the door. Nora took the bag and headed for the kitchen. In his absence, she'd dolled herself up, having changed into hip-hugging jeans and a pastel-blue V-neck shirt. He thought he caught a whiff of vanilla, from perfume or lotion.

Lady, who waited for him in the hall, wagged her stubby tail, and he stopped momentarily to pet her. He used the restroom, and when he came back Nora was putting away the groceries and humming to herself with her beautiful voice, her back to him, and he wished he could have gone on listening without disturbing her. She must have sensed his presence, though, because she looked over shoulder and smiled. That was almost as good, that smile.

"You weren't lying when you said you liked lasagna, were you?" she asked, fetching a rectangular glass baking dish from the cabinet.

"Oh no. I don't get to eat a good lasagna nearly often enough. You sure you're okay cooking it, though? I'm fine with just about anything."

"I don't want to make just anything. I want to make something special. And other than singing, cooking is the only other thing I'm good at. Lasagna is not exactly speedy, though, so why don't you catch me up on your day?"

He heard the hope in her voice, the expectation tinged with worry, and that was when he decided he wouldn't tell her about his murder theory quite yet. He would focus on the good news for now, or at least what he thought she would consider good news. While she hustled around in the kitchen, first cooking the hamburger, then preparing the pasta and the cheese, he told her all about his conversations with Dr. Keene and Howie Meyer, at least the parts that confirmed Ed Boone believed he had a daughter. He left out what he'd discovered at the library about the typewriter.

He thought Nora may have teared up at one point, but her face was masked by the steam from the cooking hamburger, so he couldn't be sure. Bored with all this human talk, Lady returned to the couch.

"I'm still doing some really good work on some new songs," Nora said. "Maybe I'll even play something for you later." She smiled over her shoulder at him, and he was sure his heart stopped a little.

"I thought you didn't perform works in progress?"

"Maybe it's not in progress anymore."

"Oh."

After she put the lasagna in the oven, he poured two glasses of an Oregon Pinot Noir and they settled on the couch to wait. The rain clacking on the roof and the balcony was so loud that they naturally sat nearer one another, their thighs so close he felt the warmth of her next to him. It felt right, totally natural. All the early awkwardness was gone. She'd only been in his life, what, two days? Yet it felt like she'd been a presence in his life for much longer. It wasn't long before the room was filled with the wonderful aromas of tomato sauce, roasted meat, and melted cheese. Lady curled up on Nora's lap as if she'd always been there. He wondered how hard it would be to convince her to take the dog when this was all done.

When *would* it be done? When she got her DNA test results, would that be enough for her? Would she get back in her Lincoln Navigator and disappear from his life forever, leaving him even more alone than before? It was a sad thought but a logical conclusion. She refilled his glass without him asking. Was she trying to get him drunk? Silly thought. She'd already made her intentions perfectly clear. They were going to be friends, maybe good friends, and that was just fine.

Dinner was served, and it was wonderful, of course. She hadn't lied. The pasta was firm without being brittle. The sauce had just a touch of garlic, but not enough to overwhelm the cheese. Before long, the wine was gone. Who drank most of it?

He didn't remember, and his head was swimming too much to care. They talked a little more about Ed Boone, mostly speculating about why, exactly, he felt he couldn't reach out to Nora, but there wasn't much more to say for the time being.

He again wondered why he wasn't telling her he now had doubts that Ed's death was a suicide.

"What is it?" she said.

"What's that?"

She swirled what was left of her wine around in her glass. When she spoke, her voice was slurred. "You were frowning there. Quite the sad face."

"Was I? Oh, sorry."

"What were you thinking?"

"I was thinking ... about how unfortunate it is that he never got a chance to know you."

Her eyes misted. She drank the rest of her wine in a single gulp, then put it on the table with a loud clatter.

"Well," she said, shrugging.

"He would have liked you."

"Maybe it's better."

"What do you mean?"

"I've built up all these ideas about what it might have been like. You know, to have a real father. I think my bubble would have been burst pretty quickly. Maybe it's better that I get, you know, the fantasy instead of the real thing. I mean, he is the guy that never bothered to get in touch with me. Maybe he wasn't so nice, you know?"

"Or he just had his own demons."

"Sure."

He thought she might cry, but then Lady, who apparently could endure the enticing smells in stoic silence no longer, whined a long, pitiful whine, a real doozy, and they both laughed. Nora, taking pity on her, put her plate on the floor. For such a small dog, Lady was able to inhale what was left with amazing speed, looking back at them with red sauce on her flat snout when Nora had barely sat back up. This got them laughing again, and then the dark clouds over their table—at least inside the motel room—had passed. Outside, the storm continued to rage.

Gage insisted on cleaning up. While he filled the sink with warm, soapy water, Nora sat on the couch and petted Lady in an absent-minded way, complaining how hard it was for her these days to get a quiet evening like this. He asked her why she kept doing it, and she said the music itself, writing it, playing it, and having people respond to it, was the one thing she truly loved. For that, she was willing to put up with a lot of crap.

"But sometimes I do have this little dream," she said, "of changing my name, my hair, and starting over as somebody else. Just travel around playing in little nightclubs and bars. I know it can't happen, but it's fun to think about. I even have a name picked out."

"Oh yeah?"

"Promise you won't laugh?"

"I will promise no such thing."

"Suzie Starlight," she said.

He laughed.

"It's silly, I know. But hey, you've got to admit, it's memorable."

"It is that."

"Oh, and you can think of a better one, I suppose?"

"How about Megan Moonbeam?"

"Now you're just making fun of me."

"Lucy Lazershow?"

"Careful, or I'll start calling you Grumpy Gary."

"I've shot people for less."

"Really?"

"No."

The tone was light, and they were both laughing, so it was all in good fun. When he finished the dishes, she got her guitar out of the bedroom, nearly dropping it on her way back. Settling on the recliner next to him, she looked at him uncertainly, a pink flush on her nose and neck.

"God, I'm nervous," she said.

"Really? But you've played in stadiums."

"It's always harder to play for one person than thousands. Especially if ..."

"What?"

"Never mind. Gotta warm up a little first. Tell me something that makes you nervous."

"Huh? Why?"

"It'll help me. Come on, tough guy, there's got to be something."

She strummed some chords. He marveled at how nimble her fingers were, how they danced over the strings with lightness and ease. Any anxiety, at least outwardly, disappeared as she became fully engrossed with her guitar. He could have watched her like that for hours, not even playing a song, just filling the air with random notes.

"Okay," he said. "I've got something. It's kind of embarrassing."

"Oh, good. Embarrassing is good."

"I'm nervous about ... motorcycles."

"Motorcycles?"

"Yeah. I had one in Montana when I was young. Took a bad spill."

"How bad?"

"Pretty bad."

"So bad that the thought of being on one makes you nervous?"

"Oh yeah."

She smiled. The rain subsided from a forceful pounding to a gentle drizzle, at least temporarily, so there was little obscuring her music. Even if the outside world had been engulfed in a hurricane, though, he didn't know if it would have mattered; he was so mesmerized by her that he was barely aware of anything else. She stopped warming and bowed her head. He thought something might have been wrong until she sat back up, her eyes with a distant gaze, and started to play.

The ships, the ships
They come and go,
And always I remain.
The ships, the ships
They come and go,
And me, I stay the same.

I can't teach you to sail
Or give you a course to chart,
But I'll guide you if you let me,
A lighthouse for the lonely heart.

The ships, the ships
They come and go,
And always I remain.
The ships, the ships
They come and go,
But me, I stay the same.

I can't stop the coming storm
Or make all the sorrow depart.
But I'll be here if you look for me,
A lighthouse for the lonely heart.

There were a few other verses, each as poignant. When she was finished, he wasn't sure if he should clap or just sit in appreciative silence. He settled on the latter, not really out of a conscious choice but because he was so moved. It wasn't just the tune, alternating mostly between G and C chords, or the lyrics, which her beautiful voice turned into something akin to gospel music, but that she had chosen him, of all people, to be the first person on this planet to hear it. She'd created something remarkable, something that had not existed in the world until she'd taken bits and pieces of her own life and pain and fashioned it into something that would move other people.

Gage had always been in awe of artists of all stripes, especially ones who'd achieved some level of excellence in their chosen trade. Musicians, painters, poets, even consummate players of the kazoo—it didn't matter what the art was, so long as the spark of creativity and mastery was there.

In the end, when she looked up at him with a vulnerability he found equally amazing, all he could say was, "Wow."

"You liked it?" she said.

"That would be an understatement. How did you do that?"

"What do you mean?"

"Just, you know, how did you come up with that? Did it just come to you all at once, perfect and whole?"

She laughed and put her guitar down next to her. "No. Usually I get a spark, one line, maybe part of a melody. It grows from there. There's some trial and error, some tweaking. Every now and then they come to me all at once, but that's rare. When it's right, I pretty much know it. People tend to know it, too."

"Could you always do it?"

"No. I had maybe some rough talent with my voice, but that's it. Nothing special. I sang in the shower. But then I picked up the guitar and it was like I was home, you know? I knew right away this was what I was supposed to do."

"Because you were so good?"

"No, I was terrible. But I *wanted* to work at it. That was the key, I wanted it, and I was really happy anytime I made even the smallest progress. Hours and hours and hours. Took lessons, read books, watched videos—I just knew I wanted to be really, really good, and I was willing to work at it. Because it didn't feel like work, you know? It started here, actually. In Barnacle Bluffs."

"Really?"

Lady, who'd been waiting patiently on the floor for Nora to get rid of her silly guitar, leaped onto the couch, and Nora started petting her. "Yeah. Maybe that was part of it. Things started getting so rough with Mom that I wanted something to focus on, something that was mine."

"How did you get your big break?"

"There was no big break, just lots of little ones. Lots of set-backs, too. But it didn't matter. I was going to keep playing any-way, for me. If I didn't think I could get better, I'd probably quit. I think that's what I'm hooked on more than anything else—al-ways striving to get better. Maybe one of these days I'll actually get good at it. I'm really just a beginner, you know."

It was the second time in less than five minutes that she'd done something that dumbfounded Gage. First she'd blown him away with a song that was obviously, in her words, *really good,* and now she seemed to sincerely believe that she was a begin-ner. Nora West, singer, songwriter, adored by millions of fans, a beginner. It boggled his mind.

"Well, I think you're pretty amazing," he said.

She looked at Lady, and Gage was fairly certain he detected a blush. This was no false modesty, either. She was the real deal. Though he shouldn't have been surprised at how genuine she was, based on the quality of her music alone, he still was. He didn't pay much attention to the tabloid world, whether that gossipy garbage was printed on the cheap newsprint that adorned the checkout racks at Jaybee's or posted on the Internet by attention-seeking celebrities and their Insta-something accounts, but somehow the warped and distorted view of Nora West had still seeped into his consciousness. This moment, right here, finally cleared the last vestiges of it away for him. He was glad to be rid of it.

"I'm just trying to keep it real, you know?" she said. "It's hard. It's like the rest of the world around me is totally insane. But the music, yeah."

"It's always there for you?" Gage said.

"Exactly. But sometimes I start to forget. Maybe that's why I like being here. In Barnacle Bluffs. In this motel room. It's like I can just be me."

"Maybe you should make it a regular thing."

"Come here?"

"Sure. Like a retreat. Just disconnect from everything and be alone with your music."

"It's a good idea."

"Well, I have a few now and then."

She smiled. Their eyes locked. It was one of those moments when the great movie reel of life seemed to stop. For a moment, there were hundreds of little details that came into sharper focus: the rain hitting the patio glass, the soft glow from the lamp behind her creating undulating waves in the dog's black fur, the tiny pinpricks of light in her pupils that seemed brighter than anything else in the room. Then she swallowed. He heard his heart beating louder in his ears.

Nora put down the dog and got to her feet, standing over Gage, looking down at him. The lamp painted the fringes of her hair with gold. She put her hands on his knees and leaned toward him, the whole lovely weight of her, all those wonderful curves, and kissed him.

He smelled the wine on her breath, tasted the tomato sauce on her lips, and felt her nose brush against his own, cold but not unpleasant. She pulled back, those dark eyes wide and unblinking, her hands still on his legs. When she spoke, he felt her breath on his face.

"Was that okay?"

"Um. Yeah, I'd say. But I thought—"

"Yeah, I know. I just said that because I started thinking about doing what I just did the moment I saw you, and I was trying to protect myself. Can it just be … you know, whatever it is? No past, no future, no labels?"

"I'm good with no labels."

"Good. Because I don't think I can wait one more second."

"Me either."

"I'm going to kiss you again."

"Okay."

"And then I'm going to do other things."

He was trying to think of a witty rejoinder, but it was no time for being witty, and even if he'd thought of something, she gave him no time to say it. She kissed him again, this time with much more urgency, climbing onto the couch and straddling him, moving her hands from his legs to both sides of his face.

No labels. He refused to analyze it and just surrendered to the moment. The first time was there on the couch, her on top, clothes coming off in a frenzy, lips only parting when unavoidable. Usually the first time was at least somewhat awkward, if not completely artificial, full of self-consciousness and uncertainty that made every action timid, but that was not happening here. They were like two starving people who'd stumbled upon a buffet. Even the brief respite to take the normal precautions, often done with haste for fear that delay would kill the moment, did nothing to quell their desire for one another.

The second time was on the floor in front of the bedroom. The third time they actually made it to the bedroom, barely, ripping into each other on the side of the bed, bodies dripping in sweat, skin on fire. Gage couldn't remember when there'd been a third time, for him, in the span of an hour. In his twenties, maybe? He attributed his newfound sexual fortitude to the power of her music. He hadn't even felt one twinge in his bad knee.

Finally, they ended up entwined in both the sheets and each other, listening to the rain. They slept for a while, easy and contented, then talked in low voices about nothing in particular, the laughter coming easy, the silences neither awkward nor profound. They simply enjoyed each other's company, which, Gage had long since learned, was the best a person could ever hope for—to be heard without judgment, to be accepted without agenda. Whatever came next, they had that, at least.

At some point, Nora started nibbling on his ear and fondling him below. He tried to beg off.

"You can sleep later," she murmured.

"The spirit is willing, but the flesh ... not so much."

"Well, your flesh is *starting* to feel willing, anyway."

"Hmm."

"What's that?" she teased. "Having a hard time speaking?"

"Mmm hmm."

"Don't make me go out and get some Viagra. The lady wants

what she wants and won't be denied."

"No. No … I wouldn't … dare."

"Oh, I know what I can do. Better than a pill, at least based on what I saw on your face earlier."

She slipped out of bed, giggling, and padded naked into the other room. She returned with her guitar. He'd been caught between the equally powerful gravitational forces of sleep and desire, the draw of sleep winning the battle until he saw her standing there with that guitar, a glorious nude goddess. Any thought of sleep was banished. She knew it, too, because she smiled that radiant smile. She sat on the bed next to him, the guitar in her lap and cradled against that lovely belly, hair spilling over bare, freckled shoulders, her breasts so full and wonderful.

No need for Viagra. He was ready to go, and he would have taken her then if she hadn't started playing. Gage had several moments from his past that he truly cherished, but he knew this would rank right up there. A naked solo performance from Nora West, who wasn't Nora West anymore, at least not the Nora West other people knew, the celebrity, but a wonderful and vibrant woman just as real to him as any other woman he had known—imperfect, full of doubt, beautiful.

When she was finished, he begged for another song and she obliged. He moved closer, kissing her shoulders, her back, caressing her with his hands, and she gamely kept playing though it was obviously a struggle. It became a game. How much pleasure could he give her before she had to surrender? The lyrics went first—it was difficult to sing between moans and gasps—and eventually the guitar was put aside too.

Finally, having spent all of their strength and then some, they finally collapsed in each other's arms and slept.

It was a deep sleep, Gage only briefly aware of her warm body pressed up against him and the gentle sound of the rain against the windows before he fell into that soothing and timeless place where there were no dreams and no worries, only peace. He slept for an hour. He slept for a year. It could have been either, but it was probably something in between, because when he woke—to the sound of a man snickering—it was still dark in the room.

His heart began to pound. He knew immediately somebody was in the room. It wasn't a dream. While Nora continued to slumber, he lifted his head and squinted into the darkness. There was only the barest amount of light, a pale white glow ringing the bedroom curtains, but it was enough for him to see the distinctive shape of a man standing at the foot of the bed.

"Time to talk," Elliott said.

Chapter 16

Calm. Gage tried to keep himself calm. No sudden moves. It was possible Elliott couldn't really see Gage either, which might give him a chance to get to his gun. But where was it? The wine had left his mind foggy. The Beretta and its holster were folded up in his jacket. The jacket was out in the—

"Looking for your piece?" Elliott said. "It's in my hand, pointed at your face. Don't do anything stupid, Gage."

This stirred Nora back toward consciousness; she fidgeted and murmured. Denny, who'd been standing behind Elliott, flicked on the light, and she bolted awake. The sheets had been wrapped around their torsos and legs, leaving them naked from the waist up. Nora, blinking through a tangle of hair, sat there with her breasts exposed until Denny snickered. That prompted her to shout and grasp the sheets, yanking them up to her neck.

"Well, well, well," Elliott said. "If it isn't the talented and beautiful Nora West."

He hadn't lied. The Beretta was in his right hand, pointed directly at Gage's face. Behind him, Denny, bearing the goofy grin and bugged-out eyes of a teenage boy who'd discovered porn on the Internet for the first time, also had a gun, a Sig 299 fitted with a suppressor—the same gun Elliott had shot Gage's potted plant with, by the looks of it, except for the silencer. His massive presence filled the open doorway. Rain droplets spotted their dark suits, and Denny's buzzcut glistened.

"Get the hell out!" Gage said.

"Tsk, tsk," Elliott said, wagging his finger at them. "You're not in the driver's seat here, buddy. Didn't think I could find you, huh? We cruised a couple dozen hotels, but we knew we'd find your van eventually. And the clerk was easy to bribe."

"What—what do you want?" Nora asked, her voice tremulous and breaking.

"Oh, a couple things. First, I want to see those pretty tits again."

"What?"

"You heard me. Put the sheets down. In fact, just toss them off the bed and show me everything you got. Bet you got a nice twat, too, huh?"

"I'm not—I'm not—"

"Elliott," Gage said, "just what the hell—"

While Gage was thinking, Elliott turned and nodded to his brother, who aimed his Sig at the edge of the mattress and fired. Even with the suppressor muffling the noise, the shot was a loud thump, like someone banging on the wall. Both Gage and Nora flinched, and Nora started crying.

"Aw, you're going to ruin it with the waterworks," Elliott said. "Come on, suck it up."

"Elliott—"

"You want me to shoot your leg next time?" Elliott said.

Gage tried to think of a way out of this. Rush him? He might stand a chance if it was just one of them, but not two.

Elliott grabbed the edge of the sheet and yanked it off both of them, leaving them totally exposed. Nora, really bawling now, tried to cover herself, and Elliott admonished her to let herself be seen or face consequences. Reluctantly, she complied. All Gage could do was seethe.

"Very, very nice," Elliott said. "Look at that body, Denny. Isn't that nice?"

He glanced over his shoulder at his leering brother, who nodded enthusiastically. Elliott went back to marveling at Nora for a while, then yelled at Nora to stop crying. She took a few shuddering breaths and held it together. Then Elliott slid the Beretta into one pocket and reached into another, pulling out an iPhone. Before Gage really knew what was happening, Elliott snapped a couple pictures.

"There, sent them to my email, too," Elliott said, "just in case something happens to my phone. Good to have backups, you know. Go ahead, sweetie. You can cover yourself up again."

Nora didn't need to be told twice, grabbing the sheets and retreating her whole body under them. "But—but why—" she sputtered.

Elliott laughed. "Oh, the look on your faces! What, did you think we were going to rape you or something? We're not monsters. Well, I guess I can't totally vouch for my brother there. I mean, just look at him. He has a hard-on the size of California. If I left him alone with you, who knows what he'd do." He faked a shudder. "Icky. I mean, you do have nice tits, but I have my limits. You are my half-sister, after all."

Gage and Nora stared, prompting a smile from Elliott. He took the Beretta back out, clearly savoring the moment.

"Yes, I know all about your secret," he said. "Got the court order giving me access to dear old Dad's apartment today, and I found the fake will. I figure Gage here planted it. Nora being the executor threw me for a loop. We did some digging, talked to some people, including the same doctor Gage talked to in Florence. So he had a secret daughter. Ah! Now it made sense. Somehow you got it in your head that being his daughter, you could hone in on his money."

"That's crazy!" Nora said. "We didn't plant the will! He wrote it!"

"You're an idiot, Elliott," Gage said. "She doesn't need his money. She's rich."

Elliott started to say something, then sighed and reached down with the Beretta and picked up Gage's jeans. He flung them at Gage, who caught them.

"Jesus, put them on already," Elliott said. "I don't mind looking at her, even if she is my sister, but you gotta put your junk away, man. It's distracting."

Gage yanked on the jeans. "I don't know where you're getting your crazy ideas, but two seconds after you leave, we're calling the police."

"Oh, I don't think so," Elliott said. "I don't think your lovely new girlfriend wants those pictures I just took plastered all over the Internet, does she? That's why I took them, see. It's called leverage."

"I don't care," Nora said. "Do whatever. You're going away for a long time, asshole."

"Sure, go ahead. I dare you. But I think you'll change your mind. You've cultivated this sweet American girl image, and this won't help. You see, the pictures are only part of the leverage. I may not be able to prove that you faked that will, not yet, but I do know something that Gage apparently doesn't know. And he's the private eye! Not much of one, it seems. This one's right under his nose."

"What are you talking about?" Gage said.

"I'm talking about how the great Nora West is flat broke."

"What?"

"Not only that, but she's in debt up to her eyeballs. And to the wrong people, too. People I happen to … well, let's just say I have connections. Seems her whole music empire is a bit of a house of cards."

"Nonsense!" Gage said.

"Is it? Look at Nora. The truth's written all over her face."

Gage looked at her. Her cheeks were flushed, her eyes bloodshot from crying, but it wasn't just shock he was seeing. When she looked back at him, he saw something else—shame.

"Nora?" he said.

"I'm—I'm not after his money! It's … I don't— I mean, I've had a few cash-flow problems. But it's not why I'm here. He doesn't have anything anyway!"

"Oh, don't play dumb," Elliott said. "You must have found out about the three quarters of a million he has sitting in that Fidelity account. Maybe old Daddy-o forgot about it. Or he didn't let himself think about it because then he'd go back to gambling. But when he sold the house, he put the money in an index fund and just let it ride. Twenty years of compound interest can do a whole lot."

"That's—that's not that much money! Not compared to what I have. Why would I … It's crazy! My boat is worth more than that."

"Sure, but not after you pay off your loans. You're way upside down, honey. I also know you're trapped in a pretty shitty record deal. So not only are you extremely bad at money management, you really don't have much coming in after everyone else takes their piece. Seven hundred and fifty thousand may not be that much, but it is when everything is going to collapse without it. The people you need to pay now don't give a rat's ass how many Twitter followers you have."

She started crying. "It's not true. I made some mistakes, yes, mostly by trusting the wrong people, but I'm not here because of that."

"Stick to singing, Nora. You'll never make it as an actress."

"I'm telling the truth!" She looked at Gage. "He's lying! I was getting on top of the financial stuff. This is about— It's about a lot more than money."

"It's *always* about money," Elliott said. "Me, I could really use three quarters of a million. I won't pretend otherwise. That will, whether Dad wrote it or not, is not going to hold up in Oregon. I checked. It'll all go to probate. So the library won't get a penny. But you might be able to prove you're his daughter and get a cut. Without a valid will, the judge will probably split the money among all his children. Or maybe he'll turn out to be a Nora West fan and things won't go my way at all. I've learned to expect the worst." He tapped his breast pocket. "That's where these pictures come into play, plus all the shit I know about your sorry financial state. But if you back out now, well, I'll just sit on it."

"So you're trying to blackmail her?" Gage said.

"I prefer to think of it as … expert persuasion. Look, I don't want her to have one fucking penny. Maybe that's petty of me, but he was my father. Not much of one, really, but he was nothing but a sperm donor to *her*."

"Get out," Gage said.

"Careful, careful. I'll leave you two to your little love nest, but first I want to make this absolutely clear. Nora needs to get back in her car and go home. If I find she's still in town tomorrow, I send these pictures to every gossip website I can find. If she still doesn't go home after that …"

"What?" Gage said.

"Let's just say I have other means of persuasion. Denny, let's go."

Denny, who had never stopped leering, wiped a line of drool from the corner of his mouth with the back of his sleeve. Nora tucked the sheets closer to her breasts. They started for the door, then Elliott turned back. He removed the clip from the Beretta, emptied the cartridge and the chamber, put the clip back, and set the gun on the edge of the bed.

"Wouldn't want you to think I was a thief," he said, grinning.

GAGE WAITED ONLY until he heard the click of the front door before jumping off the bed, grabbing the Beretta, and sprinting barefoot to his holster. There was so much adrenaline coursing through his body that he didn't even feel a twinge in his knee. He found the spare clip, loaded the gun, and darted back to the front door. He eased it open a crack and peered outside. When he saw no one on the landing, he opened it and leaned out. A light drizzle streaked through the lamplight over the parking lot, but he saw no one.

Then he heard the roar of an engine. Taillights flared down the road. It was too dark to make out clearly, but he thought the basic shape matched the Mustang. The car eased onto the road, no hurry, and headed north.

Gage, cool air on his bare chest, stood in the doorway debating what to do next. Call the police? Gage and Nora hadn't been physically harmed. There was no sign of forced entry. What proof did Gage have that anything had actually happened, other than a bullet in their mattress that could have been anyone's? He could pursue Elliott and Denny himself, but even if Gage thought that was a good idea, and he didn't, the Younger brothers would be long gone by the time Gage got to his van.

Instead, Gage closed the door and locked it again—they must have picked it, or stolen a key from the front desk—and returned to Nora. She hadn't moved, staring blankly into space and clutching the sheets to her chin. He sat on the bed next to her. Lady, who must have been hiding in the living room, hopped onto the bed.

"You okay?" he said.

She didn't move.

"Nora?"

Finally, she blinked hard. She looked at him, started to speak, then burst into tears. He held her until she got the worst of it out of her system. Then a whole bunch of stuff came gushing out, how she never meant to lie to Gage, how it was true that she was in financial trouble but she hadn't said anything because she was embarrassed and kept thinking her problems would be solved somehow—an HBO special, a book deal, something would come along if she just toughed it out. That wasn't why she was here. She really did want to know if Ed was her father.

"And the people you owe?" Gage said. "Was he right about that?"

Nora nodded. The skin around her eyes was so pink and puffy it looked like she'd been in a bar fight. "I didn't ... I didn't know who they were at the time. They said they were venture capitalists who wanted to get into the entertainment industry. There's always— I mean, lots of the Silicon Valley people throw money around just so they can be around Hollywood types. I didn't know. Then, when I couldn't pay, they sent other people ..."

"Did they hurt you?"

"No, but they made me sign other documents. I was too scared to say no. And it turned out later this gave them a lot more collateral—they'd own all my music if I didn't pay! This was all last month."

Gage said nothing. Nora must have seen the doubt on his face, because she grabbed both his hands. The sheet fell away, leaving her naked before him, but there was no feeling of arousal. There was just something burned out and hollow in the middle of his chest.

"Please believe me!" she said. "Please, I don't have anyone else. I don't even know who to trust! That's part of why I didn't tell anyone I came up here. I don't know who they got to, and I just wanted to get away from them. I was so ... so embarrassed ... Please, Garrison. I need you to believe me. I was never here for my father's money."

"I believe you," Gage said.

"Really?"

"Yes."

And he did. It may be stupid, and he wasn't so blind not to have some doubts, but he didn't sense any deception on Nora's part. Even if he did, it didn't matter. He wasn't abandoning her.

"We've got some decisions to make," Gage said.

"I don't want to leave."

"I'm not sure you have a choice."

"Another hotel—"

"You heard him, Nora. You don't leave, he's putting those pictures on the Internet."

She shook her head. "I don't care. Really, I don't. This is more important than that. I'm not ashamed to be with you. I don't care if the world sees us together. Does it bother you?"

"No."

She smiled. "You've got nothing to be ashamed of as far as your body is concerned, that's for sure."

"You're recovering pretty quickly for someone who just had

a gun pointed at her."

"Am I? I'll be honest. I'm still terrified. But I've been scared my whole life, Garrison. Even before I was famous, I was scared all the time. Scared Mom would drink too much and not wake up. Scared I'd get so depressed and lonely one night I wouldn't be able to see a way past it. Scared I wouldn't amount to anything, scared the men I loved would leave me, scared some crazy fan would rush the stage during a concert and … At some point, I just decided that I was going to be scared and that was okay, because I was going to get on with things anyway."

"This isn't some crazed fan," Gage said. "This is a trained killer who thinks you're homing in on what's his."

"Well," she said wryly, "nobody can say my family's normal, at least."

"Nora—"

"Ed Boone is my father. I know it my bones. I still want proof, and I want to know everything about him, but I know he's my father. Elliott Younger knows it too, and maybe that's what really bothers him. If my father wanted his money to go to the library, then I want to make sure that happens. I'm *not* keeping it for myself, I'll tell you that right now. I don't care how broke I am. I'll figure that out. I always do. I'll sell everything. Downsize until I can get on top of things. Maybe I'll even move up here with you. You know, trade rent for … favors." She grinned.

Gage was bothered by how quickly she was bouncing back. Even he, who was almost never without a wisecrack at the ready, was having a hard time thinking clearly. The need to find the Younger brothers and inflict a little payback—it was nearly overpowering. Only his concern for Nora's safety kept him firmly in place, a concern that she didn't seem to share.

The truth. She wanted the truth about her father. But if she wanted the truth, how could Gage withhold any part of it? The funny business with the typewriter. The unlikelihood that Ed would have jumped headfirst off the lighthouse. The dog not being mentioned in the letter or the will. After everything that had just happened, he hated to dump all this new information on her. Yet she needed to clearly see the danger. He also wanted to read her reaction. He may not want to believe she was involved, but he was still a detective, and no good detective would rule out any possibility without evidence to the contrary.

"What is it?" she asked.

"There's some things you need to know," he said.

He told her everything. She didn't cry or get angry, mostly just sat in grim silence. He studied her face carefully as he laid it all out for her, but if she knew any of it beforehand, he couldn't tell. Lady cozied up to her and Nora idly stroked her fur. With the earlier excitement fading, his body was cooling, and he felt the chill air on his bare chest. The rain outside had completely stopped.

"I should have told you before," he said, when he was all done.

"Why didn't you?"

"I don't know."

"I think you do. I think maybe you thought I might have been involved somehow."

"No."

"It's okay, Garrison. Really. You just weren't closing any doors. It's what makes you good at what you do."

"You're not mad?"

She laughed and cupped his face with both hands, kissing him hard on the lips. "Does that prove I'm not mad?"

"Okay. But you see why you need to leave? Elliott Younger may have murdered his father."

"If anything," she said, "it makes me more determined to stay."

"What?"

"If he killed my father, I want to prove it and make him pay."

"Nora, you *can't* stay here. It's too dangerous."

They argued, each of them getting increasingly heated. She saw leaving as giving up. He saw her staying as foolish and unnecessary. It took some time, but he eventually got her to see his point of view.

"*I* can keep working on this," he said. "Quietly, without Elliott really knowing. But it won't work if you're hanging around. The DNA tests will come in on their own. By then, maybe I'll have some solid proof that can put Elliott and his brother behind bars."

"And the will?" she said. "I'm supposed to just pretend it didn't exist?"

"No. We can honor his wishes. But without it being notarized, without witnesses—it would have been tough to prove it was real anyway, especially in Oregon. We always knew that. This thing was always going to go to probate. Which means—"

"But—"

"Which *means,* Nora, our best bet for getting the money to go where Ed wanted to go is back to what I said a minute ago. Put the Younger brothers behind bars. But come on, that's not the real reason you're up here. You're up here because you want to prove Ed Boone is your father, and you want to know more about his life."

"But you're saying he may not have even written the will *or* the letter. Maybe he's not even my father."

"I don't know. Nothing makes sense right now. That's why the DNA test will prove so useful. He either is or he isn't, right?"

She nodded slowly, with fading resistance. "I guess. Even if he's not, I don't want someone to get away with killing him."

"Me either. No matter what the DNA test says, I'm not letting this one go. I'm stubborn that way. But I can't do that if you're at risk. You have to give me some space to operate."

"Space," she said, nodding.

"Space."

"But you'll keep me totally in the loop? You won't hold anything else back?"

"Nope."

"Promise?"

He hesitated.

"If you don't promise," she said, "then I'm not going. No matter what you find out, you've got to tell me. Even if it's something I don't want to hear, you've got tell me, Garrison."

"All right, I promise."

"Good. But the probate thing—"

"It's a slow, slow process."

"But if I don't even make a claim—"

"Right now, you can't do anything without DNA proof. So we've got some time, anyway."

"How much time?"

"I don't know. But if I can get enough evidence that there was a wrongful death together, I might be able to get the police involved. That'll slow the process even more. We might be able to do that in a way where Elliott doesn't know we were behind it. He might still release his pictures—"

"I don't care about that. Really, I don't."

"Okay, but it will get ugly anyway. The state of your finances, the kind of people you're in hock to, that will all come out, too."

"I don't—"

"I know you say you don't care, and fine, I accept that. If you can live with the worst he can throw at you, then he doesn't have any power over you. We just want to make sure this looks like it all came out on its own. Now, tell me something. Is it safe for you to go home? Do you have bodyguards you can trust?"

"Yeah. It's fine. I mean, the people I owe, they're not really going to hurt me. How are they going to get their money if I'm not around to earn it for them? Besides, mostly I think these people, they just like having a music star around as a sort of pet. It's a game to them."

"It's not a game, Nora. That kind of thinking will get you into all sorts of trouble."

"Okay, okay, poor choice of words."

"I mean it. You've got find a way to pay them back and extricate yourself from them."

"I know, I know."

"So we're in agreement, then? You'll go back to California?"

She chewed on her bottom lip. "Can't I just head south, find another hotel room in another city?"

"No."

"Why? You've convinced me I need to get out of town, and I get that. Fine. I won't stay in Barnacle Bluffs. But what if I just hole up in another hotel? I wouldn't even have to tell you which one—"

"Nora, we need you to go home. Don't you see? I want you to go back to your life. Go out in public. Eat at your favorite restaurant. Be seen by the paparazzi. Elliott will think you've done as he asked and given up. That's important."

She stared into his eyes, searching for something. Up close, he saw tiny flecks of green in her brown irises, like blades of summer grass on rich brown loam. It was silent in the room. He couldn't even hear the ocean. No traffic from Highway 101. It was just the two of them, alone in their own little world.

"What about us?" she asked.

"I thought we were going to just let this be whatever it is."

"I know. I guess I just wanted it to *be* a little longer." She smiled.

"Me too. But this doesn't have to be goodbye."

"No. But it *feels* like goodbye."

"So let's not say goodbye. If we don't say it, then it's not goodbye, right?"

"Okay."

Her eyes had a watery tint. Exposed from the waist up, the sheets wrapped around her waist, she made him think of a model in an artist's studio. All those luscious curves combined with the poignancy of the moment—he almost felt bad that she *wasn't* a model. She would have brought even the worst painter's canvas to life.

It wasn't until she gasped that he realized he'd traced his finger from her chin, down her neck, and across the slope of her breast. He never would have imagined, even thirty seconds earlier, feeling any kind of arousal after what had just happened, but there it was. He shouldn't have been surprised. He'd felt it before, immediately after the heat of a crisis faded: that need to be physically close to someone, that powerful urge to touch and be touched.

"I have an idea," he said. "How about I *prove* to you this isn't goodbye?"

He let his hand drift lower. He waited for her to stop him, to tell him that this wasn't the time, that she couldn't do that right now.

She didn't.

Chapter 17

There was no point in trying to sleep the rest of the night at the Starfish Motel. After they showered, they packed and hit the road, her in the Navigator, Gage following close behind in the van. The storm had completely passed. The moon, shining brightly, gave them easy driving on a highway they had almost to themselves.

They reached Florence at dawn, a pallid gray light first in the east, then sweeping across the dunes they glimpsed to the west of the stores along the highway. The sand looked like ash to Gage's tired eyes.

They'd chosen Florence partly because it was big enough that it would be tough for someone to find them just by driving past all the hotels looking for their vehicles, but his eyes felt so heavy that he didn't think he could make it any farther. He knew the adrenaline would wear off eventually, but he hadn't expected to be so completely enervated, an energy crash that made it feel as if his veins were filled with lead.

They parked a few blocks away from the boardwalk in the Old Town district, behind a delicatessen that hadn't yet opened, then walked to the River Town Inn near the bridge. For the time being, they left Lady in the van. The sea lions were silent. A few tugs were already motoring their way out to sea. The air smelled of fish and baking bread—they saw a man and a woman inside a bakery hard at work.

At the hotel, the night clerk seemed surprised that anyone would want to book a room at such an early hour, but she happily did so. They even managed to get a room on the first floor near the back entrance, which made it easy for Gage to sneak Lady inside.

By the time he returned, Nora had already fallen asleep in her clothes on top of the bed. He wasn't far behind. He barely managed to put the chain on the door and retrieve a blanket from the closet, covering them both before he fell into a deep slumber. Lady joined them, squeezing herself between their spooning bodies.

They slept until late morning, made love, showered, made love again, each time more desperate and frenzied as if each of them suspected it might be the last time. Finally, after cleaning up for real, they ate breakfast downstairs—the eggs were cool, the pancakes doughy, but there was plenty of it, and they were hungry—then returned to the room. By this time, the sun was high enough that it cast rectangular bars on the bed from the slatted blinds in the window. He heard the distant horn of a ship. He thought about Heceta Head Lighthouse, not far away. He almost mentioned it, but he didn't want Nora to go there. For many reasons.

"So I'll head home now," she said, both of them sitting on the edge of the ruffled bed. She sounded like someone trying to make an argument she didn't believe.

"Call me along the way."

"How can I call you when you don't have a phone?"

"I mean, call Alex. Just let him know you're okay."

"Hmm. You know, there does come a point when not having a cell phone is a real liability."

"Uh huh. Somehow I struggle on, despite my liabilities." He pointed to his knee.

"That's something you can change, too, and you know it."

He smiled. Now he knew she was really part of his life, not just some fleeting dalliance. No matter what either of them told themselves, what they had here, even if it was never rekindled in quite the same way, would always be more than just two people finding momentary comfort in each other. He saw that as a good thing.

"But if I change everything that people want me to change," he said, "what would be left of me?"

"Cute," she said.

"You want to take Lady?"

They looked at her. She was curled up on the pillows like a big black pearl in a gift box lined with white silk. When she realized they were staring at her, she perked her ears and regarded them with her expressive eyes.

"You serious?" she said.

"I think it goes without saying that she likes you more than me."

"Does not."

"Okay, let's do a test. Lady, come here. Come here, girl."

The dog, instantly transforming from sleepy to eager, jumped to its feet and came to them. Yet, just as Gage expected, she crawled onto Nora's lap. Nora laughed and stroked Lady's fur.

"You made your point," she said.

"You don't have to, of course."

"No, no, I'll take her. I didn't want to admit it, because I didn't want you to give me her out of pity, but I've really bonded with her. But let's say we have joint custody, with me as the primary and you with guaranteed visitation rights. That way you have a reason to visit me, and vice versa."

"I don't need another reason."

"Mmm. Careful, buddy. You're starting to get me in the mood again, and I have a long drive ahead of me."

"Then we better get going before temptation overcomes us."

They checked out of the hotel and walked to their cars. He told her he'd let her know as soon as the DNA test results came in, and that he'd call her daily with any developments. After a final kiss, he watched her drive away, heading up under the Siuslaw River Bridge to the highway.

He got a last glimpse of Lady, in the passenger seat, peering back at him.

BY THE TIME Gage returned to Barnacle Bluffs, it was nearly noon, so he picked up some turkey sandwiches from the local sub shop and headed to Books and Oddities. The gravel was still wet from the night's rain, puddles in some of the deeper ruts. Only a few cars were parked in front of the boardwalk, and by Gage's memory, all of them belonged to the store owners. Alex was about to dive into a Greek salad Eve had made him, but he happily swapped the little plastic bowl for the sub.

"Twice already," he said, when Gage asked whether Nora had called. "I think she was more checking in on *you* than checking in, if you know I'm saying. It doesn't take a great detective to know that things have, um, changed between you two."

"A gentleman never tells," Gage said.

"There are exactly two people in this store right now, and neither of them are gentlemen, I'm afraid to say. More like dirty old men."

"Speak for yourself. I'm neither dirty nor old."

"You're a bit old compared to the lovely Ms. West, at least."

"Hmm. I'm detecting a wee bit of judgment in your tone."

"No judgment. Just stating a fact."

"Or sounding a note of jealousy."

"Now you're just being mean. Not that what you're saying isn't true, you understand."

They laughed. While they ate, Gage caught Alex up on everything. When Alex learned about the Younger brothers breaking into the motel room, he wanted to call the police right then, but Gage made him see that nothing good would come of it, at least not yet. One of the store's regulars showed up, an older woman, and they paused their conversation while Alex tallied up the paperbacks she'd brought in to trade. When finished, Alex sank back onto his stool, shaking his head.

"I agree this isn't a straightforward suicide," he said, "but it's hard to see how Elliott Younger is behind it. Why would he create a will that makes Nora the executor if he wanted the money for himself?"

Alarmed at how loudly Alex was talking, Gage nodded toward the stacks, where the old woman was browsing the mystery section.

"Oh, don't mind her," Alex said. "Sweetest lady in the world, but she's almost completely deaf."

"Okay."

"It really does make more sense that Ed wrote the will."

"Yeah, but why backdate it?"

Alex shrugged. "Maybe he had an original will with that date, and he destroyed it and put the new will on it with the same date. Who knows? We're talking about a man who was literally losing his mind, Garrison. Maybe that date had some significance to him. Maybe he was losing track of the days and he thought that *was* the real date. You shouldn't rule out the obvious."

"I'm not. It's just ... the whole thing is baffling."

"It's one of your stranger cases, that's for sure." Alex hesitated, thumbing the edge of one of the paperbacks on the glass counter. "I know this is difficult, but you haven't ruled out the possibility that Nora, you know ..."

"Is behind it?"

"Well?"

"No. Of course not. I have a hard time seeing that one, too, and it's not just because we've been ... intimate. So, what, she snuck up to Barnacle Bluffs, forged the will with the typewriter in the library, wrote herself a letter with the same typewriter, tossed him off the lighthouse, then showed up at your place hoping to cash in on his *enormous* fortune of seven hundred and fifty thousand dollars? Even if she *is* in financial trouble, that's peanuts compared to what she can make."

"People have done more for less."

"Sure. You may be right, though. Maybe Ed was just confused. Maybe he didn't mention his dog in the will because ... he didn't mention his dog. Right now, it makes more sense than anything else."

"So what are you going to do?" Alex asked.

"Keep poking around, but quietly. If nothing else, maybe I'll find out more about his life. That's what Nora's really after, anyway. At least, I think so. Hopefully we'll have the DNA results soon. One way or another, that will shed some light on the situation."

"What if they show that she *isn't* his daughter?"

Gage shrugged. "Well, then we have one hell of a confusing situation, don't we?"

The comment hung in the air between them, the store quiet except for the soft whisk of a paperback sliding against pine shelving. Then the phone rang. Alex answered it, listened for a second, then handed the receiver to Gage.

"The woman of the hour," he said.

SHE WAS FINE. Worried about him but fine. She was calling from a gas station in Brookings, just north of the California border. She'd already contacted her people in San Francisco to tell them she was on her way. Lady was enjoying the trip, but, Nora insisted, she missed Gage.

She promised to call Alex's cell phone a few more times, especially when she actually got home. Gage said he'd call from the gas station payphone near his house at least once a day to keepi her informed. Quite deliberately, neither of them said goodbye. Then, on his way home, he felt a pique of frustration with himself, and instead of turning onto his street, he drove to the shopping center and bought a pay-as-you-go phone from the electronics store plus a card for a hundred minutes of talk time.

It was the first cell phone he'd ever bought for himself. Would he keep it? Probably not. But he wouldn't be able to live with himself if Nora wanted to get in touch with him in an emergency and couldn't.

And someone else. That had been nagging him as well.

He picked up some groceries and headed home, getting the phone working in short order. He didn't even let the confusing array of menus on the phone's tiny screen detour him. He didn't call anyone at first, just sat at the kitchen table staring at it. The house felt like a big, empty mansion around him, cavernous and still.

Somehow the phone was in his hand and he was dialing. On the third ring, she answered, surprising him.

"Hello?"

Zoe. God, how he loved hearing her voice.

"So I distinctly remember," he said, "you telling me you didn't answer your phone if you didn't know the number."

There was a pause, not particularly long, but long enough that he was struck with a terrifying thought: she'd forgotten him. Or, worse, she was disowning him.

And then: *"Dad!"*

It was a breathless squeal totally unlike her, an exclamation of uncontained excitement. Dad. There it was again. He felt an ember of warmth in the center of his chest.

"I know you've only been gone three days," he said, "but it feels like three months."

She laughed. "You got a cell phone."

"I also saw the Virgin Mary in my toast the other day."

"Did you take a picture of it with your new phone?"

"It's not that kind of cell phone. At least, I don't think it is."

"What kind is it?"

"I don't know. What are the kind that have a hand crank on the side?"

She laughed, which was also a rarity for her, and he loved hearing her laugh because there was never anything phony or false about it when she did. He asked her how she was doing. She said she was settling in just fine, liked her roommates, bought her books, did a tour of the PSU campus, and was getting excited about her classes. She said the guy who worked at the coffee shop a block from apartment was pretty hot—hot, she actually used the word *hot*; who was this person?—and because of him she was already spending way too much money on nonfat lattes. Gage asked if she'd told this coffee boy that her dad had a concealed weapons permit.

"No," she said, "but I'll be honest, I've used your line of

work to, um, discourage unwanted advances in the past."

Unwanted advances. That sounded more like Zoe. All was not lost. "Is that so? Does it work?"

"It works beautifully."

"Good to hear. So how's Carrot?"

"He's … adjusting. He gets along with my roommates all right, but mostly he sits in the window looking sad."

"Maybe he misses me."

"I think he does. Maybe I should bring him down for a visit."

"Or I should come up to see him. Listen, about that, it's one of reasons I'm calling. I don't think you should come back to Barnacle Bluffs right now."

"Oh?" There was worry in her voice.

"It's about the case I'm working on. I don't want you to worry too much, but there are some … malcontents wandering about."

"Malcontents. Sounds like an Agatha Christie novel. Are you in danger?"

"Nothing I can't handle."

"I know. It's just … different when I'm not there."

Gage understood the feeling. She may be safer in Portland, at least in theory, but in reality he worried about her more when she was a couple of hours away. What would he do if there was an emergency? He'd be helpless. But for the time being, he was more relieved than worried that she was far from the epicenter of his crazy life.

"I'll come see you when this is all over," Gage said.

"And Carrot, too."

"And Carrot. Yes."

"And you'll call me to check in?"

"Sure."

"Or at least text me."

"What's a text?"

"Funny. Well, I've got your number now. So if you don't check in with me, I'm going to call you."

They talked for a few more minutes about nothing of importance. It was one of the few times in his life that he didn't want a phone call to end. He liked hearing her voice. Maybe there was something to this whole cell phone business. Maybe he'd buy another hundred minutes. Or go whole hog and get a monthly plan. It was worth considering, anyway. He wouldn't do anything rash.

He also kept her on the phone because he knew how stark the contrast would be once he hung up. She may be over a hundred miles away, but at that moment, she was right there at the kitchen table with him, just as she had been so many times the past few years. Eating potato chips. Cursing at her algebra. Paging idly through *National Geographic*. Snorting at his stupid jokes. Calling him out on his bullshit. He knew that as soon as he hung up that his house, *their* house, which had seemed so empty before he called her, would seem desperately empty once he was alone. He hoped, as he finally wrapped up the conversation and hung up, that he would be wrong about all this. He hoped, as he set the phone down on the table, the word *Dad* still ringing in his ears, that the deep, abiding loneliness he thought he'd vanquished so long ago would not sweep back into his life with such fearsome and overwhelming force.

But it did.

Chapter 18

The next few days did not provide Gage with new evidence that Ed Boone was murdered, but they did flesh out some surprising details of his life.

Not every contact added anything. He talked on his brand-new cell phone to Ed's doctor at OHSU, but unlike the general practitioner in Newport, this man wouldn't divulge anything at all, and said all further inquiries should go through their patient affairs office. Gage had better luck with Ed's mailman. Carl Talmack had been retired a few years, but Gage tracked him down through his former coworkers to a little cottage in the hills overlooking Pacific City, where he was in the process of sanding down an old Dory boat.

He was happy to talk. The *Bugle* had run Ed Boone's name as the identity of the suicide at Heceta Head, and Carl said he was still trying to wrap his head around it. While they drank lemonade on the porch, Carl told Gage everything he knew about Ed Boone from his years delivering mail to Ed's Diner, and it turned out to be quite a bit. The reason? They'd been in

Gamblers Anonymous together.

"He wasn't very talkative then either," Carl said, resting the lemonade on his rather rotund belly. Sweat and sawdust dotted his white T-shirt. He wore red suspenders and a red baseball cap. "But he was a real decent fellow. I stopped going to meetings years ago, so I don't know if he kept going or not."

The wind whispered through the spruce trees surrounding his property and stirred the tall blades of grass in the field below. Gage caught the barest glimpse of the ocean between the trees, but they were so far from the water that he couldn't hear it. What he heard instead was the buzz of traffic from Highway 101, much closer to the east.

"Were you his sponsor?" Gage asked.

"No, no. There was some Indian gal. She had a weird name ..."

"Storm-Tree?"

"Right! Deedee Storm-Tree. That was it. So you know about her, huh?"

"Just a little. So she was his sponsor?"

"Yeah. She even worked at the casino, which all of us thought was totally nuts. But she said it was tough to get a better job for somebody like her, and casino policy prohibited employees from gambling. She'd lose her job if she was caught. We were all plenty skeptical, but I have to say, it seemed to work. But she had bigger problems."

"Oh yeah?"

Clearly relishing the role of storyteller, Carl sipped his lemonade and wiped his lips with the back of his sleeve. It left a trail of sawdust around his mouth and on his chin. Gage thought about taking another crack at his own lemonade, but it had been so sugary that he feared another drink might instantly make him a diabetic.

"Yeah," Carl said, "she was what you'd call a functional alcoholic. Drank all the time. She carried around a water bottle, but all of us knew it was probably vodka. I have to say, though, she held it together pretty well. But Ed did tell me there were lots of times when she'd call him and need him to drive her home from the casino because she was drunk off her ass. Some sponsor, huh?"

"Interesting," Gage said. "I thought I heard Ed was kind of a drinker back then."

"Ed? That would have been a shock to me. His own father was quite a drunk, and Ed said he'd never touch the stuff. Maybe I'm wrong, but ... well, I did a fair amount of drinking myself back then. I think I would have seen him at least once at the liquor store or in one of the bars. Or one of my drinking buddies would have known him. We were a small club back then. What would make you say that, him drinking?"

Gage thought about the letter Ed had written to Nora, how he'd talked about all the drinking he'd done during those years. Was it another sign that somebody else had written it? Maybe they'd known he was a recovering addict and assumed it was alcohol. "Just some other information that came my way."

"Huh. Say, you never did tell me why you're investigating him. What's there to investigate if it's a suicide?"

Gage thought he might get more help if he offered up at least a partial version of the truth. "I'm going to tell you something, Carl, and I hope you can keep it to yourself. There's a possible family connection to Ed who's having me look into his life. Let me ask you something. Do you have any reason to think that Ed and Deedee might have ... had an affair?"

Carl raised his eyebrows. "Ed and Deedee? Well, I guess I wouldn't be totally shocked. One-night stand, maybe. Ed was a pleaser, you know. Part of what made him so good running that diner. So I can see him giving in to her one night in a moment of weakness. Then regretting the hell out of it." He scratched his chin. "Now I think about it, kind of makes sense."

"How's that?"

"Well, remember, this is all conjecture. I didn't really know Ed that well."

"I understand."

"It's just they both stopped coming to the meetings at exactly the same time. I tried to ask Ed about it once, you know, when I was dropping off the mail, just to make sure he was okay, but it's not an easy thing to talk about in public. Especially when I wasn't his sponsor."

Thinking about this, Gage raised the lemonade, remembered at the last second how sugary it was, and faked a tiny sip so as not to offend Carl. Even letting the tsunami of sweetness touch his lips sent a jolt through his body. "How did he seem when you tried to talk to him?"

"Hard to say. We were interrupted, but I could see in his eyes he didn't want to talk about it. I worried at the time he'd gone back to gambling, but now I wonder if it was because he and Deedee had a falling out."

"I see."

"Understand, I don't have no real reason to think this. I'm thinking out loud."

"I do most of my best thinking out loud. When I think at all, that is."

Carl nodded. "I've followed a few of your cases. Must be an exciting life. A lot more exciting than delivering people's mail, that is."

"Oh, I don't know," Gage said. "It's mostly just vast stretches of monotony and boredom punctuated by brief flashes of slightly less monotony and boredom. At least when you deliver the mail, you have a sense of getting something done. I almost never know if I'm getting something done until it's done."

"Mmm. So not many Dick Tracy-like gunfights with two-bit thugs, huh?"

Gage thought about his encounter with Elliott and Denny Younger in Nora's room a few days earlier. "Not many. Let me ask you something else. You were in and out of that diner a fair amount. Do you remember a waitress named Ronnie? Veronica Meyer was her full name."

"Ronnie? Oh yeah, sure! Sweetest little thing. Rain or shine, she always had a smile waiting for me when I walked in. I wonder what became of her."

"She passed away a couple years ago."

"Oh, that's too bad. When she left, that's when things really changed at the diner, even more so than when Ed sold it. It was still a good place, but it wasn't quite so special anymore, know what I'm saying?"

"How did Ed and Ronnie get along?"

"Fine, I guess. I mean, she got along with everybody." He arched an eyebrow at Gage. "What are you saying? Are you implying that they, you know ..."

Gage shrugged.

"*Well,*" Carl said. "You're really making Ed out to be some kind of Casanova, aren't you?"

"Just trying to get a fair picture of him for my client, that's all. They really want to know the truth of what kind of person he was."

"I see. Well, if he and Deedee were carrying on, they were sure good at hiding it. But I just don't see Deedee doing that. She seemed like the sort of person that if she tried to lie, she'd burst into tears. Naw. But who knows—the older I get, the less I seem to know people at all."

"I know what you mean," Gage said.

They talked for a while longer, though Carl didn't have much more to add. He gave Gage a few names of other employees that he remembered from the diner during the time, though he couldn't say where they all were now. Gage thanked him and stood to go.

"You know," Carl said, "now I think on it, Deedee did have a child around about that time."

Gage looked at him. Carl was studying him carefully.

"I delivered mail to her little bungalow for a while," Carl said. "Actually, both she and Ronnie. They were just a couple blocks apart. Funny, never really thought of them having Ed in common back then. I didn't get this route until after Ed sold the diner, and he'd kind of fallen off the map. They were just two ladies living in the same neighborhood. It was only a year. I was covering for a gal who was on maternity leave. Yeah, Deedee had a girl. Pretty thing, too. I remember seeing her running around with these cute little pigtails, always in the middle of a pack of kids. She was often the youngest one, but they sure all followed her around. Boys, girls, didn't matter. Something about her was special. I can't remember her name. Natalie, maybe? Something like that."

"Interesting."

"Mmm hmm. Boy, Deedee had a lot of men coming and going. But if I do the math back to when she and Ed were going to meetings … Who'd you say your client was again?"

"I didn't."

"Right. Probably not going to say now, either."

"Nope."

"I see. But if I were to … think out loud what happened to that girl …"

"I might also think out loud that it's my *guess* that she turned out just fine."

* * *

THE NEIGHBORHOOD WHERE Nora had lived with Deedee—
Gage got the address from Carl, who was nothing if not good
with addresses—was a few blocks from the casino. He drove by
it on the way home, hoping there might be a person or two still
living there who remembered Nora, Deedee, or even Ronnie. It
was like a lot of the neighborhoods on the west side of Highway
101. The houses on the bluff itself were a mixture of extravagant
mini-mansions built more recently and older but usually well-
kept cottages that dated back to before the price of anything
with an ocean view skyrocketed. Even the cottages, Gage knew
from real estate brochures that came in the mail, were worth at
least half a million now. Most weren't even primary residences,
but second homes and vacation rentals.

The farther east one got, and the farther from any glimpse
of water, the smaller and more dilapidated the homes became.
Deedee's street was only three blocks away, but it might as well
have been on a different planet. Gage doubted any of them were
vacation rentals—all tiny, one-story cottages, some with single-
car garages that could barely fit modern cars, others with garages
that had been converted to expand the houses. None had views
of anything but the bigger houses to the west. No sidewalks, no
trees, most of the bushes bent and twisted by years enduring the
harsh winds.

The few cars parked on the street or in the driveways were
at least twenty years old. The lawns were so small you could
hardly lie down in them. Gage always found the juxtaposition
interesting: it was one of the few places in the country, or maybe
anywhere, where people who had so much lived so closely to
people who had so little.

A few had been dolled up with fresh paint and fake shutters, lawns prim, flower boxes under the windows, but most were in sad shape, with rusted chain link fences and gray and flaking paint. Deedee's house was one of these, a boxy thing that had the look of a manufactured home even if it wasn't, the salmon-colored siding fading and chipped, cracks in the foundation, a children's yellow plastic playhouse in the front yard that looked like it hadn't been used in a decade.

Gage parked on the street, behind a trailer made from the back of a Ford truck, and knocked on the door. Nobody answered. He looked at the house, trying to imagine the woman who would become an international music sensation spending much of her youth here. There was nobody on the street. These were working people, most of them, so they wouldn't be. The wind was still, the sky so flawlessly blue it was hard to believe another storm was on the way. Even if he couldn't see it, he could both hear and smell the ocean; it would have been a constant presence in Nora's life.

He knocked on some doors. Mostly, nobody was home. In one, a girl that couldn't have been more than thirteen answered the door holding a baby in diapers. She said they'd only lived there two years. Gage told himself this was the baby's sister and tried to put it out of his mind. In another, a man shouted something inexplicable through the closed door about his water bill.

No red lava rock anywhere in sight. He walked two blocks. The last house on the street, one of the cheerier ones, brand-new banana-yellow aluminum siding with baby-blue awnings over the windows, was supposedly where Ronnie the waitress had lived. He wondered if they had known about their common connection in Ed Boone. Seemed hard to believe they didn't, but then, two families could live a hundred yards from each other for decades and never know of each other's existence. Still, he'd have to ask Nora if she had any recollection of Ronnie or her son. Maybe he should talk to Howie Meyer again, the intrepid insurance salesman.

It just seemed to Gage that there was something about the proximity that mattered here, something he wasn't seeing.

While he was standing on the sidewalk in front of the house, an old woman opened the front door, peering at him through a gray mesh screen. She wore a pink floral dress the same color as the dye in her hair. She hunched over, a big woman with a big bust, leaning on what Gage at first thought was a cane. He immediately felt a kinship, lifting his own cane in greeting.

Then the old lady lifted her cane and he saw it wasn't a cane at all. It was a shotgun.

"You from the govn'rt?" she yelled at him.

"Excuse me?"

"I'm not answering no questions!"

It seemed strange for such a cute house to be occupied by a madwoman, but then, Gage supposed even crazy people liked fresh paint now and then. "I'm not with the government, ma'am. You're not going to point that thing at me, are you?"

"Depends on how long it takes you to skedaddle! Get, now!"

Gage was about to do just that, since he had no desire, after all the many threats he'd faced in his life, to die in the driveway of a fanatical septuagenarian who'd mistaken him for a census worker, but then a man about his age appeared next to the old woman. He snatched the shotgun from her.

"Stop that nonsense, Mom," he admonished her. He wore an unbuttoned blue plaid shirt over a black T-shirt that featured Barack Obama's face. His black goatee was so thick that his mouth disappeared into it. "You're just going to get yourself in trouble."

"But he's trespassin' on my prop'ty!" she shouted.

"He's just standing on the sidewalk. Will you stop?" He

looked at Gage. "I'm sorry, sir. She was never like this until the last couple years. Did you want something, or were you just walking by?"

"Actually," Gage said, "a friend of mine grew up in this neighborhood and was friends with the people who lived in this house. I was just curious if you might have known them. I told him I'd ask."

"You mean the Meyers?"

"So you did know them?"

"What people?" the old woman said. "What people is he talking about, David?"

"The people who lived here before us, Mom."

"Oh!" She squinted at Gage. "You can't have the place back now. My little boy bought it fair and square."

Ignoring his mother, David focused on Gage. "Mom was friends with Ronnie. They were in a book club together. When she passed away, Mom told me about the house, and I got a chance to buy it before it got on the market."

"Oh." Gage concentrated on the old woman. "Ma'am, do you remember Ronnie at all?"

"Ronnie?"

"Yes. She had a son named Howie. Howard Meyer."

"Howard!" the woman exclaimed.

"You remember him?"

"Howard Cosell! Now isn't he the best!" She paused, then eyed him with suspicion again. "You're not with the govn'rt now, are you?"

Gage looked at David, who shrugged helplessly. David ushered his mother back inside and returned a moment later, sans shotgun. He apologized for the way his mother had threatened Gage and hoped the police wouldn't have to be called. Gage assured him he wouldn't, and asked a few more questions, but

David said he'd grown up mostly with his father in Portland and really hadn't really known Ronnie at all.

Disappointed that he hadn't gleaned more information, Gage thanked him for his time and turned to go.

"Oh," he said, turning back, "one last thing. What did you think of Howie? You must have met him. Or did you buy the house through the broker?"

"No, never met him. I think he sells insurance in town, right?"

"That's right."

"Yeah, it was all done through Green Willow Real Estate. But I think I gave you the wrong impression. Ronnie didn't own the place. She just rented it."

"Oh." Gage figured that made sense. Ronnie probably hadn't had enough money to buy a home. "Who owned it then?"

David scratched his beard. "Hmm. Let me see. I could probably dig through my boxes in the attic and find the paperwork for you, but I can't really remember offhand. But I do remember when I asked who it was later, somebody told me he once owned a popular diner in town."

BACK IN HIS VAN, Gage called Alex, asking him to look up the property's history on the online county records site. Alex grumbled about it, but did, and it was true: Edward T. Boone had owned the place until David Garland. On the way back to his house, Gage stopped at Howie Meyer's insurance office. Howie was there, talking animatedly on the phone, and he waved Gage to one of the empty seats. He was explaining to someone how their homeowner's insurance would cover flooding from a pipe breaking, but not a tsunami, and the person didn't seem to be getting it.

When he finally hung up, he leaned back in his chair and shook his head.

"Most of my clients are pretty reasonable," he said. "Unfortunately, it's not the reasonable ones who take most of my time. What can I help you with this time? Change your mind about getting a policy?"

Gage relayed his visit to Howie's old house. When he got to the part about Ed Boone being the owner of the property, Howie stared at him, slack-jawed.

"You're kidding!" he said.

"You didn't know?"

"God no. Wow, that puts Uncle Ed in a whole new light."

"Do you know if she was actually paying rent?"

"Well, if she wasn't, she sure was going to a lot of trouble of faking it. She always dropped off her check at Evergreen Property Management. I was with her a bunch of times when she did. Are you *sure* he owned the place? I could look it up online …"

"Already did," Gage said.

"Wow. Uncle Ed, our landlord. That's crazy. I guess that also explains why he was always there looking after the place, if he owned it. But why the property management company? Oh, wait." He looked thoughtful.

"Yes?"

"Maybe it *does* make sense. I don't think Uncle Ed's wife was all that keen on him being such good friends with Mom. He might have been hiding it from *her*, not Mom."

It was a good theory. Gage also wondered how much Ed was charging Ronnie in rent. Was he giving her a cut rate? Someone else might have found it hard to believe Ed wasn't having an affair with Ronnie, but not Gage. Again, he was seeing himself in Ed Boone. Gage had owned a house and rented it to his housekeeper—Zoe's grandmother, Mattie—and hadn't charged what he could have gotten on the open market. Why? Because it had been necessary, that was why.

"Do you remember the kids in the neighborhood?" Gage asked.

Howie's gaze was distant, and a couple of beats passed before he realized Gaze had asked a question. "Sorry?" he said. "I was just thinking about how nice Uncle Ed was. I should have stayed in contact with him."

"I was just asking if you remember any of the kids in the neighborhood around your mom's house."

"Why?"

"I heard there was a group that hung out together. I was just wondering if you were part of them."

Howie nodded. "Well, yeah, there a bunch of kids around my age. They ranged all over the place—the beach, the casino parking lot, riding skateboards, bikes, playing Frisbee. Just hanging out. I'll be honest, though, I was pretty shy back then. I didn't really hang out with them much."

"Would you remember any of their names?"

Howie's brow furrowed. "You're not really writing a book about Barnacle Bluffs in general, are you?"

"What makes you say that?"

"Well, it's one thing to focus so much on Uncle Ed. He did own a popular diner, and I bet there's all kinds of stories connected to it. But the kids in my neighborhood? What's this really about? It's his suicide, isn't it?" His eyes widened. "You don't think he was *murdered*, do you?"

Gage hesitated, trying to decide how much to reveal about his investigation, and that pause was all the confirmation Howie needed.

"Really!" he exclaimed. "Wow, a murder investigation."

"I wouldn't jump to conclusions," Gage said.

"Oh? Come on, you can tell me something, right?"

"I'll admit that writing the book is … not my primary purpose. Can you remember any of the kids who lived around you? Any of their names?"

"Why, is one of them a suspect?"

"Howie—"

"Man, this is interesting. Come on, you can tell me what this is about. Maybe I can help if I knew a bit more."

Telling an insurance agent about Nora West, especially an insurance agent who'd freely admitted he couldn't stop himself from talking about things he shouldn't, did not seem like a good idea to Gage. Still, Howie was right. If he knew a bit more of the truth, he might be able to help better.

"I'm looking into the possibility that Ed Boone had a child with someone other than his wife."

"Really!"

"Any thoughts?"

"And the client is the child?"

"Maybe."

"Man, you just won't tell me anything, will you? And this child, he doesn't want this information out, huh?"

"I never said it was a he."

"Excuse me, she."

"I didn't say it was a she either."

Howie laughed and raised his hands in defeat. "Okay, okay. But that's really interesting. Uncle Ed, an affair … Well, it's hard to believe. I mean, if he wouldn't with Mom … But I guess they were more like friends, no matter how much I wanted it to be different. I never heard him say anything about another woman, but I guess he wouldn't. Probably not even with Mom. So these kids in the neighborhood, was this mysterious child one of them or something?"

"I don't know."

"Or do you think one of them grew up to murder him?"

"Again, I wouldn't jump to any conclusions."

"Uh huh. Names, huh? Well, it's been a long time, and like I said, I didn't really hang out with that group all that much. There was a kid named Jimmy Long. Bob ... Bob something. He had bright red hair. There was a girl, too, one they all seemed to like. Norma or something. A lot of them were just faces to me. But I'll rack my brains and see if I can think of any more. You want to give me your phone number?"

"I don't have a—" Gage began, then caught himself. Of course he could do that.

He just had to make Howie wait while he looked up on the phone exactly what that number was.

Chapter 19

The DNA paternity results came in on Friday. Gage, sitting in his bathrobe at his kitchen table, was hardly off the phone with Alex and he was already calling Nora. It went to voicemail, but he'd only started speaking when his phone chirped and the screen showed him it was Nora calling. He tried to click over but hung up on her instead. Then he dialed her again and she did the same, and he managed to repeat the same foolish mistake.

"Hello? Hello?" he said.

"Yes, I'm here this time," she said. She sounded groggy.

"Sorry about that. Still new at this thing. I've got news."

"Oh?"

"Edward Boone is your biological father."

There was a long pause. In the stillness of his house, with no wind against the windows and no traffic from the highway, his thumping heart was loud in his ears. A band of sunlight fell across the table, illuminating each little divot and groove in the maple, each spot of dried milk or coffee. After a moment, he thought he heard sniffling.

"Nora?"

"Yeah," she said.

"Are you okay?"

"Yeah."

"You sound like you're … crying."

"It's okay. I'm okay."

"It's good news, right? It's what you wanted."

"It's good news. I don't—I don't know what I wanted. But it's good, yeah. It's good to know. It's just … so many people lied to me. Mom lied. He lied. Why? I don't get it. I would have liked to know him better."

"I know."

"You find out anything new about that whole house thing?"

Gage had been keeping Nora up on his investigation with nightly reports. Sometimes these were very late, since Nora had been doing her best to get out and be seen in public, at movie screenings, nightclubs, and various industry parties, but she had not gone one day without connecting with him. He sensed that he was acting as some sort of lifeline for her, keeping her from drowning in the chaos of her life, and he didn't mind. He just didn't know how much longer he could keep it up. What would happen when there was nothing more he could do for her?

"Not much more than you already know," Gage said. "That property management company is long since gone, so there was no one to talk to there. I think it's just what it appears. He was just trying to help out his friend. You really didn't remember her son, huh? Howie?"

"Well, I *think* I might remember him being in a couple classes with me, but I'm not sure. I'm sorry. I was pretty self-absorbed back then and people just kind of floated in and out of my life. Sad, huh? I should have paid more attention. I guess not much has changed. People are still just a blur to me."

"That's not true."

"Sure it is. Except for you, anyway. You are *definitely* not a blur. I'm counting down the days until I can see you again. I miss you so much. I know that's crazy, since we spent so little time together, but I do. Gosh, I sound pathetic."

"No, you don't. And I miss you too. But we want to put your safety first. I have some other news, and you're not going to like it. Elliott Younger was named the personal representative by the probate judge."

"Personal representative?"

"It's the legal term for executor in Oregon."

"Oh man."

"It's what we expected. And don't worry; these things take time, lots of time. From what I read, we have at least four months, because that's what the law gives any possible creditors to come forward and make their claims. They get their money before the heirs."

"I just don't want those weasels getting Ed's ... my *father's* money if they killed him. It's so wrong."

"I just need proof, Nora."

"I know, I know." She paused. "Maybe if I came up there ..."

"No."

"But maybe I can help. I might, I don't know, remember something useful if I'm up there. Those assholes went to the same school, you know? They were a grade ahead of me, and I didn't know them, but they were definitely there. I found them in my old middle school yearbook."

"You still have your middle school yearbook?"

"Yeah. Strange, huh? It's not like I even liked school all that much. But it's something solid, I guess. So much of my childhood is shaky, but the yearbook is solid. My picture's in here a bunch, too. Which is strange, considering how little I went to

271

school. I actually look happy in them. Maybe that's what I like about it. The pictures make me look like a normal, happy kid."

"It's nice, but I'm not sure how a middle school yearbook over twenty years old is going to prove anything."

"They do look kind of, I don't know, demented in their pictures."

"Hmm."

"Okay, I know it's not much, but I'm just saying, if I'm up there, maybe I'll see something that will help."

"I want you up here as much as anyone, Nora, but not until it's safe."

"But—"

"No."

"All right, all right. But I'm getting antsy. I've got to *do* something."

"Just hold on a little longer."

"Okay, fine. Keep me in the loop."

"Always. Something will change, and soon. I promise. It always does."

"I hope you're right."

"I am. It's the one thing I know for certain. If I keep poking around, the status quo always breaks."

GAGE WAS RIGHT. Something did break, and soon—the next afternoon, in fact, though it didn't seem to have anything to do with him poking around, at least not directly. He spent most of Saturday morning digging up and talking to some of the people who'd been part the neighborhood gang of kids who'd run with Nora, starting with one of the names Nora remembered from perusing her old middle school year book and going from there. It turned out to be the same name Howie had said to him:

Jimmy Long.

Jimmy, now in his early forties, owned Jimmy's Auto, a thriving three-bay repair shop behind Arrow Shopping Center. While taking a break from working on the alternator of a '67 Chevy Malibu, Jimmy wiped his greasy hands on a blue cloth and listened as Gage explained he was trying to track down an old friend for a client who wanted to be anonymous, and the person he was looking for, the client said, had run around in a group of neighborhood kids that Jimmy had been part of. Did he remember any of their names?

With the whirring of power tools and the roar of motors all around them, Jimmy pondered the question for a while, then rattled off a couple of names that Gage dutifully jotted down in little notebook. Then Jimmy mentioned Nora Storm-Tree and smiled.

"She was really something," he said. He was a big guy with a heavy mop of loose blond hair, which billowed in the breeze coming over the tops of the outlet stores. "All the boys had a crush on her. Even the boys who were a couple years older, like me. Man, I haven't thought about her in years. She kind of disappeared after middle school. I wonder what happened to her. Would that be the one your, uh, client is looking for?"

"No, but that's interesting. You know where I might find any of these other names?"

Jimmy said he didn't, that most of those kids got the hell out of Dodge after high school, though he did think one of them, Steve Schiller, lived in Portland. When he got home, Gage managed to use the Internet and the iPad Zoe had bought him to track down three Steve Schillers in the Portland area, one of whom actually answered the number Gage dialed and turned out to be the same Steve from Barnacle Bluffs. He had no new information, other than he, too, remembered the radiant Nora and wondered what became of her.

While Nora's effect on people was interesting, Gage did begin to wonder exactly what he was hoping to accomplish with this line of investigation. The proximity of Deedee and Ronnie's residences, and Ed's connection to both, seemed to imply something that might tie into Ed's death and possible murder. Why? Because coincidences were actually quite rare in his line of work, at least when it came to something of significance. He just didn't know what it was yet.

Early Saturday afternoon, he tried calling the Kayok Tribal Office, hoping someone might tell him something about the Deedee Storm-Tree, but he got an automated message saying they were closed weekends and to try again Monday. He'd just set down the phone on the kitchen table, rubbing his temples and staring at his muted reflection in the wood surface, when his phone rang again. It was an unlisted number.

"Yes?" he said.

"So this is how it's going to be, huh, Gage?"

It was Elliott. His voice was high and clipped.

"What are you talking about?"

"You know full well what I'm talking about. When I saw that Nora was back in California, I thought you guys got the message. But this afternoon she goes out and gives a statement in front of her fancy digs in San Fran."

"What?"

"Don't play dumb. This is something you two obviously cooked up—leaking the news about her long-lost father to the press. Then she gets to respond to it, so it doesn't look like it came from her. You're trying to throw a wrench into the probate process."

"I don't know *what* you're talking about, Elliott. And how'd you get this number?"

"Sure, sure, right. I warned you about that picture I took. Two can play this game. Maybe Nora doesn't care—"

"She doesn't." More than anything, Gage wanted to get off the phone to find out if what Elliott was saying was true. "Neither do I."

"Yeah, well, we'll see. I may hold it in my back pocket for now. There are other kinds of leverage."

"Is that a threat?"

"It is what it is."

"Elliott—"

He hung up. Uncertain, but feeling a growing sense of dread, Gage got out the iPad and went straight to CNN. Sure enough, there was a news item there, not a top headline but still on the front page: Nora West Responds to Rumors about Father in Oregon.

Gage clicked the link and plowed through the story. It seemed that Elliott was right. Around noon, about the time Gage was talking with Jimmy Long, one of the gossip sites had run a story about Nora's possible link to a suicide in Barnacle Bluffs. The strangeness of the story had been like catnip to the press. Rather than deny it, she'd come out with a statement confirming her past life in Barnacle Bluffs, her real name, Storm-Tree, and a request for privacy as she dealt with the death of a father she had never known. Gage wasn't mentioned.

He called her immediately. It went to voicemail. He left a stern message, then paced in his living room. The Douglas firs outside his window were wreathed in fog. He felt the moisture in his bad knee, wincing with each step, and the irritation only fed his anger. He called her again, left another message. He called Alex at the store, and the two of them brainstormed who might have leaked the news and concluded it could have been any number of people: Elliott himself, as some kind of ruse, someone Gage had talked to who had connected the dots, someone who worked for Nora, or maybe even Nora herself. Maybe she'd gotten impatient that things weren't developing quickly enough. But what would this accomplish?

A few hours passed, in which he left a couple more messages, and still she hadn't called. He was getting worried. Where was she? At dusk, when his windows were growing dark, Chief Quinn showed up in his F-150 and demanded answers. What kind of game was this? Seeing no reason to hold back, and temporarily overcoming his normal distrust of the police, Gage told him everything—the letter to Nora, who Ed's sons were and their involvement, and the little bits of information that made Gage believe Ed's death may not have been a suicide. Quinn, skeptical, didn't see that there was enough evidence to do anything, not yet, and they ended up shouting at one another until Quinn finally left in a huff.

So the police would be no help, at least not now. A little before midnight, Gage's phone rang. Nora.

"Where the hell have you been?" Gage shouted at her.

There was a long pause and crackling static on the line. Outside, in a night so murky and dark he couldn't distinguish the trees, he could still hear them: a whisper through the branches that rose and fell like someone taking a breath.

"I'm sorry I haven't called before now," she said. "I've been … out of cell phone range."

"What do you mean? Where are you?"

"You're going to be mad."

"Nora …"

"I'm in my boat."

"You're what?"

"We're bringing it up to Florence."

"Nora!"

276

"I knew you'd be mad."

"Why on *Earth*—"

"Look, I'm not even supposed to talk to you right now. I just … I couldn't resist. The bars on my cell phone are pretty weak. I'll probably lose the connection any second."

"What? What are you—"

"He said he has proof who killed my father. I'm going to meet him."

"Who? Elliott?"

"I … I can't say more. He was very clear that if I … Look, I'll be there soon. Should be tomorrow night. Ten or so, according to my captain. We're trying to get in ahead of the storm. Just trust me. I've got to do this. For me. For Ed." The static was growing louder; she was breaking up. "Trust … okay? I'll loop you in … soon as …"

"Nora!"

"… got Lady … me …"

"Nora, do you know who leaked the news about you and Ed to the press?"

The line went dead.

Chapter 21

Unlike the old days, when Gage actually had a landline in his house—or at least Janet had, and he'd tolerated it—there was no dial tone after a broken connection with his cell. Just dead silence. Somehow the silence was even worse. He called her right back, but it went straight to voicemail. He waited a few minutes and tried again. Same result. Clutching the phone, he almost hurled it against the wall, then caught himself at the last second. This was how she could get in touch with him. He couldn't afford to be without it.

The wind had died, and the night was so still he could hardly believe a big storm was coming late Sunday. But it was, at least according to the news, and she was bringing her boat up right in the middle of it. What would motivate her to do something so insane?

He said he has proof who killed my father. I'm going to meet him.

Who was she talking about? Elliott? If it was Elliott, wouldn't she have said so? Someone was moving levers behind the scenes, trying to make something happen. But what? Nora was coming up in her boat. Elliott was riled up. What was all of this supposed to accomplish?

Gage paced for a while, stewing, then collapsed in his recliner and stewed some more. The clock ticked into the wee hours of the morning. He couldn't sleep. He couldn't even think of sleeping. He tried calling a few more times, never getting an answer, and ended up staring at his phone on the end table next to the chair, just hoping. What could he do at this point? She had all the answers. His best bet was to meet her tomorrow at the docks in Florence and demand that she tell him what was going on.

"*Garrison.*"

He heard his name. He may have been dozing for a moment, but he thought he heard his name—not quite a whisper, but soft and high. A woman's voice? Was it the person he thought … No, it couldn't be. This was in his mind, a product of his anxiety and all the adrenaline coursing through his body that had nowhere to go.

"*Garrison.*"

There it was again, and this time he sat bolt upright in the recliner, because this was no phantom of his mind. Or was it? No, no, this was real, and it was coming from the direction of the kitchen. Most of the house was dark, how he usually had it when he was home alone, but the tiny oven range light cast its feeble glow on the walnut cabinets, on the vinyl countertops, on the small aluminum window cracked open just a hair … Yes, that was it. That was where the voice had originated. He left that window cracked open almost all the time, to get a little fresh air in the house, and if this sound was coming from anywhere, it would be coming from—

"*Garrison.*"

Now he knew for sure, and he felt the hairs on the back of his neck rise. His heart picked up its pace, a steady twitch behind his eyelids. He strained, trying to see a shape in the dark window, but the window was high off the ground and situated over the junipers, so there would not be a person there unless they were at least seven feet tall and could balance on thick but unsteady branches. But the voice, the voice, it could be her, couldn't it? Yes, it could.

But no. This was an illusion. Not real. He wanted it to be real, but—

"*Garrison.*"

And then he was up and moving, bad knee be damned. He flipped off the oven light and slid open the window the rest of the way, peering into the night. He had not turned on his porch light, he seldom did, and only a faint amount of moonlight penetrated the dense cloud cover, casting a silvery sheen on the familiar shapes of his property—the junipers below, the gravel path, the arbor vitae. Then, as he scanned east, into the grove of firs, filled with an endless array of shadows that all seemed to take human form … *something moved.*

It was back in the trees, obscured by more than one trunk, but he'd definitely seen it. Then he saw it again, and he knew for sure that it was definitely a person—hunched and moving, sprinting behind another tree. *A person with long hair.* That was what really set his mind on fire. Long black hair. She had not always worn it long, sometimes preferring the convenience of keeping it short, but he'd always preferred it long. He'd loved the feel of it against his face in the wind. He'd loved smelling it after she showered. He'd loved how it sometimes slid over her face like a veil when they were making love.

Outside. He was outside. He might as well have been teleported for how fast it happened. Somehow he must have had the presence of mind to slip on his shoes, because there they were on his feet, bare feet in tennis shoes. And what was that in his hand? His Beretta. While everything else felt like part of a dream, the gun felt so real, the metal handle cold and solid. His heart told him there was no need for a weapon, it was Janet, and if it was Janet there was nothing to fear, but some tickle in his rational brain told him that it could all be a trick. He'd keep the safety engaged, but he'd still be ready: fifteen rounds in the magazine and one in the chamber.

Real or not, it was hard to fool a 9mm.

Cool air nipped at his bare arms. He was in the trees, searching the shadows. A bed of leaves and twigs, made soft from the frequent rains, crunched under his shoes. Inside the house it had been still, but out here there was the slightest breeze, just enough to mask the sound of footsteps. He smelled fir and wet earth and just a hint of the ocean. Spindly branches, unseen in the poor light, raked at his face. In his haste, he'd left the porch light off, but that was fine, that was good; better that his eyes adjusted to the darkness.

Where was she? He couldn't see her. Was she going to leave him alone again? He didn't want to be alone anymore. He ventured deeper, toward the apartments, remembering he'd seen the person moving toward them a week ago. Had it been Janet? Yes. She'd come back to him. The house receded behind him, a dark shape among other dark shapes, but the apartments were still far ahead, unseen. He was in the thick of the forest and completely alone.

Something caught his eye, a yellowish glint. There was a clearing ahead, big enough to allow faint moonlight to filter through the branches and illuminate the rotting stump of what once must have been a proud oak tree. The yellow was there, hanging from the jagged bark that surrounded the top of the stump. A chain. A gold chain. He saw, clomping through the damp grass and clovers that grew thickly around the base of the stump, that it was clearly a necklace.

The tiny hoops were both fragile and brilliant, and he knew whose it was even before he saw the rest of the jewelry heaped in a pile on top of the stump. He knew it and felt the icy-cold hand of dread reach into his gut. He'd bought it for her on their fifth anniversary. The ruby earrings—for Christmas one year. The silver bracelet with three emeralds—on a whim, as they walked passed the window displays at Bloomingdale's.

And what was that diamond ring?

The one with the larger diamond surrounded by a dozen smaller ones?

The one with the band that was actually two bands threading back and forth through one another, like the intertwining fingers of two lovers?

She'd worn her wedding ring every day, from the day he'd married her to the day she'd died fighting a lunatic in their claw-tooth tub. Since then, he'd kept all of her jewelry in a drawer next to his bed. How could it be here? Someone had come into his house and taken it. Janet? *No, no, don't be foolish.*

Something moved in the shadows, to the east. He saw the hair, rippling like a mane when a horse was in full gallop. Seeing this, he felt a clenching in the middle of his chest, a tightness that made it hard to breathe. He sprinted, right knee throbbing, in that direction. She darted to the right, disappearing into the shadows. He heard the crunch of footsteps on the spongy forest floor. He tried to follow the sound, but lost it. He thought he caught another glimpse of her, this time off to the left, and he ran in that direction only to find nothing there.

Out of breath, he stood in the middle of that sweep of darkness, hands on his knees, straining to hear her footsteps again, but his ragged breathing and the quickening breeze made it impossible.

"Janet?" he called.

There was no answer. He heard a truck rumbling over the hill on the highway, a dog barking somewhere to the north, the wind speaking through the trees. He pressed through the forest all the way to the apartments, standing on the dew-laden grass under a yellow cone of light, but she wasn't there.

He headed back into the forest, tromping around in the darkness for quite a while, an hour, maybe more, tripping over the occasional log, slipping in a divot and scraping his hands on a jagged rock, searching, hoping to find some glimpse of her but finding nothing. He returned to the jewelry, his heart racing, and stuffed it all in his pockets. This, he couldn't explain away as some figment of an anxious mind. The precious gems and stones felt cold and slightly damp.

Strangely, now that the original shock had begun to wear off, he felt a little relieved. He wasn't crazy. Someone really had come into his house. A pale predawn light was just beginning to filter through the trees from behind him, the darkness lessening its grip on the leaves and twigs that littered his path, so he must have been out quite a while. The house waited for him, no porch light, mostly dark except for a faint glow from within, the front door ajar. Had he left it that way? In his haste, he must have.

Still, he felt uneasy. His rational brain was beginning to take hold again. Whoever was out there wasn't Janet, no way was it Janet, but the jewelry proved that this person was real.

And whoever it was could still be lurking.

Maybe even inside his house.

He'd made it easy for them, after all, leaving that front door open. He kept his Beretta at the ready, safety disengaged, a two-handed grip to give him maximum balance. Before even stepping up to his porch, he scanned his gravel drive, saw no one, peered under and around his van, got the same result, and waited a good two minutes anyway just to make sure. He could now detect the low rumble of the ocean below and to the west, but there was no other sound. Even the highway was quiet.

One step up. Then another. He eased open the door with his foot, waiting through the creak, waiting to see if anything would happen.

Nothing did. From the weak oven light, the only light that had been on, he saw the contours of his recliner, the edge of the kitchen table, and the vinyl flooring in the entryway that gave way to the carpet. He crept into the house, fully cognizant of all the blind spots, all the places someone could hide, and giving these places the bulk of attention. There were no surprises. The house beckoned, silent and dark.

He was alone.

Still, he remained cautious. What kind of foolery this was with the jewelry he didn't know, but someone was definitely trying to mess with him. Conscious that someone could surprise him from behind, he crept in a little more, saw no one, and shut the door with his foot. The wind slammed it shut, but he was expecting it and did not flinch. He waited a few beats, heard nothing but the normal creaks and whirrs of the house, and only then let himself relax—just a little. He'd still have to search the rest of his house.

Then his phone rang.

On the end table next to the recliner where he'd left it, the little black piece of plastic rattled and vibrated, the tiny screen glowing blue. The possibility that the caller could be Nora swept any other thoughts from his mind, and he sprang for it. He fumbled it open.

"Hello?"

His guard had been down for perhaps a tenth of a second. He'd never lowered his Beretta. He'd kept his attention on the room all around him, still expecting that someone was there. But the need to talk to Nora was so great that it did briefly overpower his better judgment, and that was it, that was all it took. The lapse wouldn't have been long enough for someone to get the jump on him physically, since he'd had a pretty good read on the room, but it was an opening and someone had been waiting for it.

The word *hello* was still ringing in the air when two pillows—his pillows, he had just enough time to see, with their white cotton pillowcases—hit him in the face. They'd been hurled from the hallway. They barely carried enough weight to knock him off balance, but they did distract him, drawing his attention in that direction. And that turned out to be just enough time for someone to spring from behind the recliner and sucker-punch him, a direct hit in the gap between his right eye socket and the bridge of his nose.

It was a hell of a wallop, and pain exploded across the side of his face. That would have been enough to bring down most men, even very strong men, but one of Gage's few useful attributes, at least as far as he was concerned, was his high tolerance for pain. His Beretta was up and firing even as his vision blurred and his mouth filled with blood, getting off one shot, two, shattering the lamp, spraying plaster from the wall, before someone else, the assailant who'd tossed the pillows, most likely, grabbed his gun hand.

There was a struggle. He saw Elliott's face flash in front of him, teeth gritted, before the other person—Denny, was it Denny?—slipped a black plastic garbage bag over his head.

The world was dark, shiny. Meaty hands clamped around his neck, holding the bag tight. Gage sucked the plastic into his mouth, choking. He clawed at the plastic and someone punched him in the gut. He doubled over, bouncing off the edge of the recliner before landing on the floor.

The fingers were tight but not choking him. He kicked out, landing his foot in his attacker's groin. The big man groaned and released his hold for just a second, enough time for Gage to get his hands on the bag and begin to pull.

Something hard knocked him on the head.

He instantly splayed out on the floor. The darkness inside the bag receded into a deeper darkness, consciousness fleeing as the pain flared up, white hot and intense at the back of his skull, before it, too, was swept into a void of nothingness. He tried desperately to cling to awareness, to not let go, but even Gage's high tolerance had its limits. He tasted blood, heard ringing in his ears, and felt tremors cascading across his skull, but it was all so distant and muted, like he was wrapped in layer upon layer of foam.

He was vaguely aware of his wrists and ankles being tied with a coarse rope, then bound together as if someone was going to hang him over a spit. The string on the plastic bag was pulled, knotted. Someone slit a hole in the bag and he breathed in fresh air.

Still, he swam in the distant ripples of consciousness, awake but barely. Someone hefted him onto their shoulders, holding him firmly with one hand on his leg, the other on his arm. He was aware that they were *his* legs and arms, but they wouldn't obey his commands. He heard a door slam, felt the night air on his bare arms, then other sounds: a beep, a click, the crunch of shoes on gravel.

He was dumped unceremoniously onto an uneven surface, carpeted but cold. Someone patted down his shirt and pants. Looking for another gun? Through the tiny hole in the plastic bag, he glimpsed the dark outline of a man, and behind him, the upper branches of his trees in the night. The man either missed the jewelry in Gage's pocket or didn't care. Some small amount of control was returning to his body just as a door slammed.

In a trunk. He was in a trunk.

Curled in the corner, his feet touched one side, his bound hands the sloped interior. He heard voices, laughter. Doors creaked, and the car wobbled as it absorbed the weight of a driver and a passenger. A faint whiff of gasoline tickled his nose. He tried to will himself back to alertness. *Come on, Gage. Move, move.*

An engine rumbled to life and he felt the vibrations through the metal chassis underneath the carpet.

Gage moved his legs, just a little at first, then pushed his tennis shoes against the side of the trunk. The rope cut hard into his ankles and his wrists. The car rolled forward, tires on gravel. Momentum carried him backward, then forward, a tilt as they headed down his driveway. Where were they taking him?

Somewhere to kill him.

Shoot him in the head and dump his body somewhere it wouldn't be found.

Not much time. What could he do? The engine roared, gravel spitting out behind them and pebbles knocking against the underside of the car. The tires hummed on bare asphalt. Highway.

A truck roared past, shaking the car. *Think, Gage, think.* There had to be a way out of this. He ran his tongue over his teeth, tasting blood. At least he *had* his teeth. That was something. What kind of car were they in? It was probably that white Ford Mustang, not more than a year or two old. The law required every modern car to have a safety release to allow someone to pop the trunk from the inside.

His wrists may have been bound, but he still had use of his fingers.

If he could pop the trunk, he might be able to jump out.

Not when the vehicle was moving sixty miles an hour, maybe, but at some point it would stop, and that would be his chance. Maybe all he'd be able to do would be call attention to himself from a passing driver, but that might be enough.

First things first. Could he get the bag off his head? Unlike the ropes, it wasn't on all that tightly, being held there by nothing but the tie string. With his wrists and ankles bound, he couldn't get his fingers up to the plastic even if he strained, pulling his knees up as far as they would go, craning his neck as low as he could manage.

But if he rubbed his cheek against his shoulder, he could move the bag. He kept at it, loosening it little by little, rubbing the smooth plastic against his shirt. The draw string released its hold. He worked more furiously, his cheek burning, his spine torque at an awkward angle and screaming at him to give it some relief. And his right knee—the pain was so excruciating he had to block it from his mind.

Finally, the bag slipped free.

He gasped for breath, blinking away the sweat in his eyes but not seeing much because he was still trapped in darkness. What was that sound? He heard music, a thumping bass, a crooning baritone. They'd jacked up the radio, those bastards. They were actually listening to music, enjoying themselves.

Or maybe it was to mask any sounds he might make, thrashing around in the trunk?

Smart, but he could use it to his advantage, too. It would make it hard for *them* to hear *him*.

He looked for the safety release. He knew the levers usually glowed in the dark, but he couldn't see it. Maybe it was small. Maybe the angle was bad. First things first: he had to do something about getting his arms free.

He still had Janet's jewelry in his pocket. Could that be of any use? No, he couldn't get to it, and even if he could, it was all too small and fragile. His wrists and ankles may be tied together, but it had been done in haste. There was still some slack. If he brought his knees up as far as he could and leaned forward … Yes, he could just get his fingers on the knots. The rope felt smooth but tough, the kind of thick twine someone might buy at any hardware store.

Gage felt each beat of his heart at the back of his head, like the tap of a mallet. They drove on for quite a while, Gage prying at the ropes, pulling and yanking, trying to get even the smallest amount of give. Which way had they turned? He'd been too out of it to know. But then, just for a second, he heard waves crashing on rocks to their right. South. They were heading south.

How far had they gone? Ten miles, maybe. Definitely out of the city.

Then the car slowed, coming to a stop. He heard the rhythmic clicking of the turn signal. A truck rushed by on the left. Now was his chance, but he was still bound. He pried at the rope, his fingers chapped and numb, and finally got the rope to move—just a tiny bit, but it was progress.

Come on, come on.

The car turned, picking up speed but slower than before. Gage moved the rope, only a fraction of an inch, but at least he was getting somewhere. The car tilted upward. Now he had the rope really loose and everything was coming undone. The uneven road, full of potholes, jostled him all over the place.

One hand was out, then the other.

He started working on the ropes around his ankles, everything coming faster now that he had full use of his hands. The car careened to the left, then the right, as they wound upward into some kind of hill.

Away from town. Not good.

The air felt cooler. He smelled fir and wet earth. He had a sense of where they were. The coastal range of mountains, for most of the Oregon coast, was ten or twenty miles east, but there were a few places that it jutted all the way to the beach. The Silverback River, and the estuary at its mouth, was one of those places. Follow the river a mile inland and there you were in the forested hills, ones that led to other, bigger hills, and eventually the mountains. Not *big* mountains by Oregon standards, but certainly big enough. Few people around, too.

A perfect place to murder someone and dump the body.

With renewed urgency, Gage kept at the rope until finally he got his ankles free. He rolled to face the back of the car. Where was the lever? He saw nothing glowing. He felt for the latch mechanism. The car slowed, turned to the right, and picked up speed again, even steeper now. He heard the caw of a crow. Asphalt full of potholes gave way to badly rutted dirt and gravel. His fingers, bleeding in places, searched all the nooks and crannies in the metal contraption. Where was the damn thing?

The car slowed again, turning left, right, rolling him this way and that, not making it easy to find the latch.

Then he had it.

There must have been a plastic lever, but it had been removed. Probably Elliott knew what it was and took it out. But the lever must have been fastened to a cord, because Gage could feel just a bit of what was left inside a hole. The car was moving, but not that fast, maybe twenty miles an hour as it curved left and right. Gage didn't know the exact road they were on, but he could imagine: dense forest all around, deep ravines on both sides. If he could get enough of his fingers on what was left of the cord, he could pull it, pop the trunk, and try for the forest. Maybe he could lose them there.

Or he could wait and surprise them. Pop the trunk before

they did and leap out at them.

No. They'd be more ready then. Better to do it now.

It took some time, but he managed to work just enough of the cord out of the hole that he could clamp on to it.

He yanked on it.

Nothing happened.

Had he not pulled hard enough? He pulled it three times, forcefully. Still nothing. Broken? The car slowed, stopped. He pulled the cord over and over with his right hand, using his left to push up on the trunk, thinking maybe it was stuck. The music stopped. He heard the doors open.

Then, with a cold, sinking feeling of dread, it occurred to him: the mechanism wasn't broken.

It had been disabled.

Chapter 22

Of course. Of course Elliott would do that, take precautions. This was a professional, after all. What could Gage do now?

Surprise them.

Gage rolled the other way, facing the front of the car. He tucked the rope in front of them, out of view. There was no time to fix the ropes in place to better fool them, so he just had to keep his wrists and ankles together and hope that was enough. The doors slammed, shaking the car. He heard feet clomping on dirt and gravel. Laughter. This was all a game to them, wasn't it?

There was a beep and the trunk popped open, letting in a rush of cool air and the gray, dappled light of dawn. Gage remained still. He could imagine them standing back a few paces, guns leveled on him, waiting for him to try something.

"All right, Gage," Elliott said. "Get up and out of there."

He groaned, as if struggling to come awake, but otherwise didn't move.

"Gage?"

This time he didn't do anything.

"Maybe he's dead," Denny said.

"He just made a sound, you idiot," Elliott said. Then, to Gage: "Come on, buddy. Roll on over and we'll get you out of there."

Nothing. No movement. Elliott sighed.

"All right, lift him out," he said. "Be careful, though. I've got you covered."

"Where should I carry him?" Denny asked.

"Where do you think? In the house, of course."

"Right, right."

"Wait, give me your gun. I don't want him trying to grab for it."

"Right."

"Okay, go."

"Go where?"

Elliott sighed again. "Pick him up and carry him in the house."

"Oh, right."

There was a pause.

"*Now,*" Elliott said more sternly.

Gage heard footsteps, the rustle of clothes, then a shadow fell over him. He had a second, maybe more, to race through the possible courses of action. So Denny had no weapon and Elliott had his gun trained on him. Not much chance here. Maybe better to play dumb a little longer. But wouldn't Denny see that the rope was missing? He had to chance it.

Wait, the rope.

It could serve as a weapon. He could choke Denny with it. No, Elliott would just shoot him. The rope could also be a *whip.* Smack Denny with his elbow, then whip out at Elliott with the rope and go for the gun hand. Best chance.

Gage felt Denny's big, meaty hands slide under his back and legs. Not yet. It was too early. Keeping his body slack and his eyes closed, Gage let out another groan. He pressed his wrists tight between his ankles, clenching the rope in one hand. It was balled up, ready to unfurl.

With a grunt, Denny lifted him out of the trunk. He started to turn, rotating. This was it. Now or never.

Opening his eyes, Gage swung out hard with his left elbow, aiming for the underside of Denny's chin.

Direct hit.

It felt like hitting wet clay. There was a loud smack. Denny cried out and staggered backward. Gage didn't have more than a split second to take in his surroundings—a moss-covered cabin surrounded by sagging Douglas firs and thick ferns—before both he and Denny were toppling. The world whirled around him and Gage struggled to stay focused. Just maybe, he had a tiny opening.

They crashed to the ground. Gage's face bounced off a mixture of gravel and dirt. He rolled away from Denny, unfurling the rope, swinging around to bring it to bear on—

Elliott.

He was looking right at him. Or rather, Gage, on his knees, was looking up at the long barrel of the Sig 299 and its attached suppressor. The end of the barrel loomed large and dark just a few inches from Gage's nose.

"Cute," Elliott said. "What, you think you're Indiana Jones? Go ahead, see what happens."

His voice was playful, but his eyes were as lifeless as polished granite. As Denny moaned and wobbled back to his feet, Gage and Elliott stared into each other's eyes. He and his brother wore the same dark suits and white shirts as before, looking just as out of place in front of the dilapidated cabin as their shiny white

Mustang. Out of place in Barnacle Bluffs, too. They belonged in glitzy cocktail lounges and smoky backroom casinos.

The morning sun broke through the dense upper branches of the firs to the east. He heard the trickle of a creek. There was nothing but trees. No houses. No one to hear him if he shouted for help, certainly.

"You'll kill me anyway," Gage said.

"Think so? I could have shot you at your place if that's what I wanted."

"What *do* you want?"

Denny staggered over, massaging his chin. "He hurt me!"

"Shut up," Elliott said. "You deserved it."

"But—but I did what you—"

"Quiet!"

Denny grumbled and rubbed his chin. Elliott's dead-eye gaze never wavered from Gage's face.

"The great detective," he said, grinning. "What the hell were you doing out there in the woods, anyway? Taking a leak?"

"What do you want?"

"Yeah, I heard you the first time. I want to have a conversation, that's all. You can still get out of this, Gage. Seriously, I didn't bring you up here to off you. Not my style. I brought you up here so we wouldn't be disturbed. Nice place, isn't it? Got a little porch there. Could have a glass of lemonade and enjoy the great outdoors."

"We should do that. I like lemonade. Why don't you two boys run into town and buy some?"

"I like lemonade," Denny said.

Elliott rolled his eye. "It's very simple, pal. All I want to know is what information Nora has on me."

"What?"

"See, playing dumb is not going to work here. It's not going to work at all. I ask a question, then you tell me the truth. If you don't, this isn't going to be pleasant."

"Oh, I'm sorry not to keep it pleasant."

"Are you? Sorry? Well, we'll see. Denny, take him inside. Gage, if you want your new girlfriend to live through the night, I suggest you cooperate."

The threat may not carry much weight up here in the Oregon woods, with Nora somewhere out in the Pacific Ocean, hopefully protected by a bevy of bodyguards, but the weirdness of Elliott's question made Gage doubt all of his assumptions. Maybe Elliott had her already. Maybe he had connections in the Bay Area, someone who could have helped him. Before Nora had been cut off, she'd said she was meeting someone—a man, she'd said *he,* so it was a man—who had information about who'd killed her father. Now here was Elliott claiming Nora had information on him. That certainly implied that Elliott wasn't the one she'd planned to meet, but the one she was meeting *about.* But then, who was she meeting?

Nothing made sense.

Denny seized Gage by the scruff of his shirt and yanked him to his feet. His right knee burned, but it was the least of his concerns. With Elliott keeping his Sig trained on Gage, they proceeded across an uneven driveway, half gravel, half dirt, to a weathered porch. The wood planks were mostly gray, but they did not appear to be in bad shape. When they stepped on them, the boards barely creaked. He saw fresh boards here and there, and evidence that new nails, glinting in the liquid dawn, had been put down in place of old ones. Someone had cared for this place, maintained it.

A rental? Or a hideout owned by a friend? Before they entered the cabin, Gage tried to get some sense of where they were, but other the dense canopy of firs, oaks, and the occasional birch, he saw nothing that could indicate their location. A blue jay fluttered overhead. The stream, down the hill, trickled over rocks. Somewhere not too far away, a little to the west, the whine of a small engine briefly broke the stillness.

So there *was* someone not too far away. But where?

Denny opened the door and shoved Gage inside. It was a single room lit by the daylight coming from two framed windows. There was a queen-size metal-frame bed in one corner, a kitchen in the back, the sink piled with dishes, a hide-a-bed couch that was unfolded into a bed, sheets messy, next to a wood stove and massive television that would have been too big even for a house ten times the size. The couch and the loveseat were both dark leather. The floor was hardwood, a cherry color, and freshly stained. Gage smelled garlic and baked bread.

Was this where Gage would meet his end? In a place that looked like a mix between an old logger's cabin and an IKEA showroom?

After flicking on a couple lamps—they provided very little extra light, but they did create a softer, gauzier glow—Elliott grabbed one of the oak chairs from the matching oak table and slid it into the middle of the room. Denny deposited Gage roughly in the chair.

"Want to play some Scrabble?" Gage asked.

Denny laughed, and started to say something about not having a Scrabble board, but Elliott cut him off by thrusting the rope he'd brought with him from outside into Denny's gut.

"Tie him up again," he said, "and this time, do it right. Ankles to separate legs of the chair. Wrists also separated behind him, tied to the frame. Think you can handle that, little brother?"

He said the words *little brother* with such disdain that a smarter recipient may have reacted in anger. Denny, on the other hand, only bobbed his head like an eager dog and set to work. Under Elliott's watchful supervision, Denny did as he'd been asked, looping each ankle and wrist so many times, and so tightly, that even as Gage bulged his muscles to create some slack, there wasn't much slack anywhere when it was all done. Elliott inspected the final knot, tied far out of reach of Gage's hands, and murmured his approval.

It was then that the windows darkened, just a bit, and Gage heard the first tapping of rain on the roof.

Elliott glanced at the window, where a few droplets of water had appeared. "I'm guessing that's the storm they've been talking about. Hope your girlfriend gets to land before it gets really bad."

Gage said nothing.

"A lot of questions in your eyes," Elliott said. He tapped the Sig against his pant leg. "I have questions, too. It seems we both don't know everything."

"You better talk," Denny said.

"Shut up," Elliott said.

Denny hung his head. Elliott returned his attention to Gage.

"But see," he said, "I'm in a position to ask questions, and you aren't. So I'm going to ask you a question. You will answer said question. If I don't like your answer, Denny will demonstrate my disapproval."

Denny looked at Elliott, dumbfounded, and Elliott sighed and made a fist.

"With this," he said.

"With your hand?" Denny asked.

"No, idiot, with *your* hand. You're going to punch him."

"Oh. Right now?"

"No. When I tell you to."

"Oh."

Elliott closed his eyes, breathing slowly through his nose, and when he opened his eyes, Gage expected to see rage, but it was like looking through peepholes into an empty room. "My poor brother," Elliott said. "Ever since his unfortunate accident, he has not had his full faculties. It has fallen upon me to make up for his deficiencies. The cross I must bear, I'm afraid."

"You bear it well," Gage said. "But then, I heard you had something to do with that unfortunate accident in the first place."

Denny, eyebrows raised, glanced at Elliott, who merely shook his head.

"What does he mean?" Denny asked.

"Nothing. It's babble. Please show him my displeasure."

"Huh?"

"Punch him, you fool!"

"What? Oh."

Like an automaton, Denny stepped forward and smashed his first against the side of Gage's face. It happened so fast that all Gage had time to do was to try not to tense up or resist, just let his whole body snap back with the blow. As it was, it still felt like a rock slamming into his temple.

His eyes welled up, blurring the two figures before him. His face puffed up like a balloon. He felt a trickle of blood down his nose. It was all he could do to hang on to consciousness. Another blow like that and he'd be gone for a week.

"Jesus," Elliott said. "Not so hard next time or you'll kill him."

"Sorry," Denny said.

"Gage?" Elliott said. "You still with me, pal?"

Gage liked Elliott thinking Denny had to let up. So he lolled his head around and pretended he was trying to focus. He was still fully there, enough to hear that the rain outside had picked up, loud taps on the roof and the windows.

"Stay with me now," Elliott said. "No more bullshit. I ask, you answer. What information does Nora have on me?"

Gage still had no idea what Elliott was getting at. Information? It made no sense. He cracked open his eyes and blinked away the film blurring his vision. His nose was so blocked that he had to breathe through his mouth.

"What are you talking about?"

"I'm warning you!"

"Why—why do you think she has information on you?"

Elliott shook his head. His usual cool, controlled demeanor was fraying, and it made Gage think of the kid who'd almost succeeded in drowning his brother. He had to be careful. A calm Elliott was dangerous enough, but at least somewhat predictable. But Gage could see what a monster Elliott could become when all of his carefully practiced defense mechanisms withered away.

"This is seriously how you're going to play it?" Elliott said. "One minute you're threatening me, the next you're acting like nothing happened?"

"What?"

"What you wrote!"

"I don't—"

"It was in your fucking text message!"

Elliott groped into his pocket and thrust a cell phone in Gage's face. It was hard to focus, the cell phone blurry enough that it could have been anything from a giant cockroach to a stapler, but it appeared to be Gage's pay-as-you-go phone.

"I didn't write a text message," Gage said.

"Really? That's what you're going with?"

"But I didn't."

"You're calling me a liar?"

"I'm just—"

"Gage, Gage, I have the proof in my hand." Elliott punched a few buttons. "Right here. Three hours ago. *We've now got proof you killed your father, asshole. Better run like the coward you are.* You telling me you didn't write that?"

Gage blinked a few times, his vision finally clearing. His mind was also starting to kick into gear. A text message? What kind of nonsense was this? If Elliott's goal was to confuse him, he was succeeding, but Gage didn't see …

But then he did. Even in his addled state, he saw the truth all at once.

Someone had come into his house and sent a text message from his phone.

His heart thundered in his ears. Something cold and nauseating slid into the pit of his stomach. The realization hit him on a visceral level, and yet he suppressed any outward surprise, not wanting to give away whatever advantage this knowledge provided him. Who had done it? His first thought, irrational as it may be, was that it had been Janet. But no, that was nonsense. It was someone else. They'd lured him out of the house just so they could send the text message. But why? Just to enrage Elliott?

"Gage," Elliott said, "are you *seriously* telling me you don't remember sending this?"

"Maybe he was drinking," Denny offered. "Maybe he was drinking when he wrote it and he forgot."

"Shut up, Denny."

"Okay, sorry."

Elliott paced away, turning at the door and staring at Gage. "No more crap. We didn't kill our father, man. I don't know what makes you think that, but whatever fake info you have, I want it. My feeling is Nora offed him somehow. She's hard up for cash and saw an easy score. Faked the will. It seems bonkers, but she's an artist probably high on coke all the time, so who knows. So you got something you can toss to the police to get us out of the picture. I see on your phone you talked to her tonight, so don't bullshit me. What is it?"

Gage had no idea what to say. It was still possible Elliott was playing some kind of three-dimensional chess, but if so, what was the endgame? Gage didn't see it, and honestly, he didn't think Elliott was capable of such a convoluted strategy. For as much as he lorded over his brain-damaged brother, he didn't strike Gage as all that smart himself, not really.

But Gage couldn't give him nothing. In his current, edgy state, Elliott may just shoot him. He had to play for time.

"Denny," Elliott said with a sigh, "show Gage here what—"

"Nora wouldn't tell me," Gage said.

"What?"

"She said if she did, I'd be in danger and it may not work. That's why she's heading out in her boat. She's—she's afraid you'll come after her. She said she's going to stay at sea for a while until the info surfaces. She's already made arrangements."

Elliott stared at him. He tapped the Sig against his thigh, nodding to himself, his eyes returning to their flat, dead state, until finally he smiled.

"Lying," he said.

"I'm not," Gage said. "I don't have the info. She does."

"Not about that," Elliott said. "I haven't decided if you're lying about that. But if you know something, I can see that you're not going to tell me. I've always had that gift, the ability to read whether someone will crack. You're tough, Gage. I'll give you that. I could have Denny here beat you senseless and you still wouldn't tell me, even if you knew something. But maybe you don't. Sure. And part of me just wants to let dear brother beat you to a pulp just so I can watch him do it. Then I'd put a bullet in your head, bury you in the woods, and be done with you."

"Not a bad final resting place," Gage said. "I think I'd like being close to nature."

Elliott nodded. "Joking even now. I get it. Some other guy, I'd say joking is a way of trying to fool yourself that you're not scared shitless. But you? Nah. You just joke because you like spitting in people's eyes. Fine. But see, I already know Nora is coming up to Florence. You know how I know? Because she's surrounded by people who will do anything for money, people who see her as the piece of meat she is, and they stay in contact with the people she's in hock to, people I know. I promised them a certain amount of work if they could keep me informed."

Gage said nothing. Elliott looked down at Gage's cell phone. He clicked a button, held the phone up and positioned it steadily, and snapped a picture of Gage. He studied the screen, smiling, then hit a few more buttons.

"See," he said, "the real reason I brought you up here wasn't really to interrogate you. I wanted to get the measure of you, sure, but I have a whole other plan. The people Nora belongs to, they'd be real unhappy if I even roughed her up. But they don't care a shit about you. So I brought you up here for leverage. There, I just sent a lovely picture of you to Nora, along with a message that we need to talk."

He put the phone back in his pocket. Gage's face felt like a misshapen melon. He couldn't breathe through his nose, and his mouth was still filled with the taste of blood. It was difficult to think at all, but he knew he couldn't let Elliott leave without trying to change his mind.

It had been a mistake to deflect toward Nora; he saw that now. He'd only made the situation worse.

"I didn't write the text," Gage said.

"What?" Elliott said.

"Someone's playing us."

"What are you talking about?"

"I was lying. I didn't know how else to get you to back off. But that text, I didn't write it."

"Bullshit."

"I'm telling you, someone snuck into my house while I was … while I was out in the woods. They sent that to you. They were hoping to get you riled up. Get you to, I don't know, go after me and Nora."

Elliott shook his head. "Uh huh. Why?"

"I don't know."

"Right. You should have stuck with your first story. It was pretty lousy, but it was better than this."

"I'm *telling* you—"

"Shut up!"

"Elliott—"

"*Shut up!*"

The Sig was suddenly jammed into Gage's nose. Whatever deep reservoirs of self-control that Elliott possessed were gone. Gage, his head shoved backward, stared down the barrel at the contorted face of a madman.

"God help me," Elliott said. "God help me, I so want to pull the trigger. I don't—I don't want to look at your smug face one more second. But I still need you. I need you a little while longer. But I want you to know something, Gage. I may just kill your girlfriend after I've gotten what I want out of her, no matter what the California people want. I'll kill her and everybody else on that damn boat. You hear me? I want you to think on that."

Gage's nose was shoved back so far he could barely speak, but he had to try.

"Elliott," he began, "please—"

With a roar of fury, Elliott pistol-whipped him hard across the face. For just a second, Gage felt himself spinning, tumbling to the floor along with the chair, his mind whirling even faster than his body.

Then the world went dark.

Chapter 23

Gage woke to someone humming.

He drifted, for a time, in that purgatory between the conscious and unconscious world, a dark and painless void, knowing that all he had to do was open his eyes to be fully awake, yet finding it difficult. His eyelids felt like they were taped shut. It was an unpleasant feeling, but it was nothing like the other feelings that lurked a little further beyond that mild irritation, a tsunami of pain that repelled his consciousness from fully inhabiting his body. *Don't go there*, it seemed to be saying. *Stay in the dark.*

If not for the thought of Nora, which was like a knife blade of urgency piercing the thick wool that covered his mind, he certainly would have let himself stay in the dark. An hour, a day, a month, whatever it took until at least some of the pain subsided. Yet he couldn't. Nora's life was at stake.

"What—what time is it?" Gage mumbled.

The humming stopped. With great effort, he managed to pry his eyelids open. He saw a person hunched over the kitchen sink, turning to face him. His eyes began to focus. Denny. It was Denny, rubbing a blue plastic plate with a dishtowel. His dark jacket was hung over the back of one of the kitchen chairs, and the sleeves of his dress shirt were rolled up to the elbows. His massive shoulders and bulging biceps stretched the thin white fabric. He was a hulking presence in the kitchen, filling the space; the oven, next to him, seemed like a child's toy.

"Oh, hello," Denny said. "You're finally awake."

Gage smelled baked beans. Heard wind and rain, a full-throated storm. Behind Denny, water streaked a dark kitchen window. How long had Gage been out? A surge of panic swept aside the fogginess clouding his mind. The pain also joined him in full force, a pulsing cut on his forehead, dried blood around his nose, a steady pounding at the base of his skull. None of this mattered. Elliott was on his way to Nora.

"What time is it?" Gage asked.

"I just had a burrito," Denny said. "It's the microwave kind, Elliott showed me how to make it, but it wasn't too bad. Not like Taco Bell but still good."

Gage closed his eyes and tried to get his bearings. It was dark. It had been dawn on Sunday before. No matter what time it was, another whole day had passed. Or maybe even two days? No, it couldn't have been that long. Sunday night, then. With his eyes still closed, he cleared his throat.

"Where's your brother?" he asked.

"Gone," Denny said.

"Florence?"

Denny didn't answer. Gage opened his eyes and saw that Denny had turned back to the kitchen, opening a cabinet and sliding the plate inside.

"Is he in Florence?"

Denny closed the cabinet and hung the dishtowel from the

bar on the oven. "I'm not supposed to say."

"He's gone to meet Nora, right?"

"I'm not supposed to tell."

"But it's true, right?"

Denny gripped the counter with both hands and dropped his head.

"You've got to stop asking questions," he said. "Elliott said if you keep asking questions I was to hit you a bunch in the face. But you been punched a lot already and you may not wake up if I punch you again. So I don't really want to punch you but I will if you make me."

"I see," Gage said. "Sorry, then. I'd rather not be punched either. It does get old, to be honest."

Denny turned around, his troubled expression so exaggerated that Gage would have thought Denny was mocking him if he didn't know that emoting like a mime was the usual for Denny.

"I really have to take a leak," Gage said. "Any chance you can untie me just for a second so I can use the bathroom?"

"I can't untie you," Denny said.

"I really have to go, man."

"I can't untie you."

"If I don't get to take a leak, I'm going to wet my pants."

Denny blushed and stared at the floor. Gage rocked back and forth for good measure.

"Really, man, if I don't get to the can in the next thirty seconds—"

"You just have to go where you are," Denny said, still looking down.

"What?"

"Elliott said you might ask to go to the bathroom. He said that would be a way you would try to trick me. He said to tell you to just go where you are." Denny had a pitying look in his eyes. "I'm sorry."

"Even if I promise I won't try to trick you?"

"Yeah. I mean, no, I can't. Elliott would be mad."

Gage lowered his voice to a conspiratorial whisper, speaking just loud enough to be heard over the storm. "I won't tell him, you know. When he comes back, I won't tell him. It will just be our little secret."

"I can't."

"All right, I don't know how long I can hold this."

"Sorry."

Gage nodded, making sure to look frustrated and glum. It wasn't hard. He *was* frustrated and glum.

"I'm dying of thirst," he said. "Any chance I can get a glass of water?"

"No."

"Really? Not even water?"

"Sorry."

"So you're just supposed to stand there and stare at me? You can't do anything?"

Irritation flashed across Denny's face. "I'm supposed to watch you. I'm supposed to make sure you don't get away. That's important."

"Oh, I'm sure."

"It is!"

Gage fell silent. Denny's irritation was sliding into anger, and the last thing Gage wanted was an angry Denny. Or did he? Gage remembered how Denny had asked what Gage had meant when he mentioned the incident that led to Denny's condition, and how Elliott had quickly silenced him. It was a sensitive area, obviously, but Denny's curiosity might be the hook Gage could use to manipulate him.

There was danger in flirting with a piece of Denny's past that might trigger all kinds of unpleasant emotions, but what other choice did Gage have?

"I'm sorry," Gage said. "I didn't mean to upset you. I know you're just doing your job."

"I am!"

"I know. And I won't bug you anymore, I promise. No need for us to make this more difficult than this has to be, right?"

Denny's lips were pursed so tightly that he could have crushed a walnut with them. Not looking at Gage, he took his jacket from the chair and slipped it on, buttoning with great care. Gage used the time to choose his words. They had to be just right.

"I always wished I had a brother," Gage said.

Denny looked at him. Just like that, the embarrassment of the previous moment was gone, curiosity rising in its place.

"You don't have a brother?" he asked.

"No, I'm an only child."

"Oh."

"And man, looking at you two, it really makes me jealous. I mean, you're so *close*. You're really there for each other."

Denny beamed. "We're not just brothers, we're best friends. Elliott says so."

"See, that's what I wished I had. And he's so lucky to have you. Especially …"

Just as Gage had hoped, Denny's raised his eyebrows. If Denny was a dog, they would have had to rename him Pavlov.

"What?"

"Sorry?" Gage said.

"You said, you said, 'specially. What were you going to say?"

"I did? Oh, nothing. I shouldn't talk about it. It would upset you, and I'm sure Elliott is very sorry."

Denny stared. Gage could almost see those broken gears in

his head lurching and sputtering as he tried to process this information. The rain, which had been a steady drumbeat against the roof this entire time, picked up its pace.

"We really shouldn't be talking," Gage said. "I know your brother doesn't want it. And you're a very good brother, doing what he wants … despite … you know …" He shrugged.

"Despite what?" Denny asked.

"Huh?"

"You were going to say something."

"I was? Oh, right. Well, like I said, better to let sleeping dogs lie. I wouldn't want you to think less of him. You're so loyal. And I know Elliott probably said that anything I say or do, I'm just trying to trick you, right?"

Slowly, Denny nodded.

"Right," Gage said. "So we better just let it go. You always do what he tells you, and that's good. It keeps things smooth between the two of you. I mean, I bet sometimes Elliott just does what he wants, and you're a grown man, too, and you know that you can also do what you want, but making sure things stay smooth between the two of you is more important, right? Sure it is."

Gage nodded and turned his focus to the floor. All he could do now was wait and see if the lure would work. He took steady and easy breaths through his mouth—breathing through his nose was still impossible—and tried to look like he didn't care what happened next.

Denny cleared his throat. "Maybe …" he began, then, like a toddler who'd reached for a forbidden candy and realized it at the last second, hesitated. When Gage looked up at him, Denny was chewing on his lip. "Maybe, if you tell me, it's okay. Elliott—he doesn't have to know."

Gage tried not to show his glee. The door had opened.

Denny had given him a way inside.

"Oh, I don't know, Denny," Gage said, studying the cracks in the hardwood floor. "Probably not a good idea."

"No, really. It's okay. I won't tell."

Gage pretended to think about it. "No. I don't want to get either of us in trouble, and I don't think you'd believe me anyway. Let's just drop it."

"Tell me."

"No, Denny."

"Tell me *now.*"

Gage looked up and saw the anger sliding over Denny's face. This was the most dangerous part, the part where he'd flagged down the bull and they were about to begin their risky dance. Yet it was critical that Gage didn't give in no matter what happened. He had leverage. If he didn't use that leverage to get what he wanted, none of it mattered.

"No," he said firmly.

Denny balled his fists. "You tell me now or I'm going to hurt you."

"No."

"I'm warning you—"

"You *could* hurt me," Gage said. "It's true. But you remember what Elliott said? No amount of beating will get the truth out of me. You'd be so mad, you'd probably kill me, and then what? You'd never know the secret about the pool. Oh, man, I shouldn't have said that. I'm done talking."

Denny, showing his teeth, advanced a step, but then Gage's words seemed to register. He stopped, blinking hard, his feeble mind trying to make sense of it all. Thank God there was still enough self-restraint in Denny to make this possible.

"What pool?" Denny asked.

Gage said nothing.

"Please," Denny whined. "Just tell me. I want to know the secret."

"No."

"Please."

"You'll just get mad. And then you'll tell Elliott, and we'll both be in trouble."

"I won't get mad. I promise. And I won't tell. I won't."

Gage sighed and looked at the floor again. He wasn't much of a thespian, but he knew he didn't have to be much of one in this case. Just scrunch the eyebrows, purse the lips, and give it time. Gage would have waited even longer, but there was Nora out there, and he just couldn't.

"Well …" he began hesitantly.

"Yes?" Denny said.

"Look, I know you can't do much for me. I get it. But how about a trade? Something little? I *really* need to take a leak, man. I swear, I'm going to piss all over myself if I don't get to that bathroom in the next five minutes. No man wants to sit in his own piss. It's about having a little dignity. You get that, right, Denny?"

Some confusion washed over Denny's face. The hook was coming loose. *Easy now, Gage. Reel him in, nice and slow.*

"I tell you what," Gage said. "You take me to the bathroom. You can leave the door open. You can stand right behind me. You're a big guy. You know there's nothing I can do. And I'm in bad shape, anyway. Just look at me. Jesus. I just want you to untie my hands long enough that I can take a leak on my own. Is that too much to ask? I mean, Elliott wouldn't do it, but you're not Elliott, are you, Denny? You make your own decisions."

Denny stared. It was good sign. He hadn't said no.

"Tell me the secret first," he said.

"If I tell you the secret first, you won't let me use the bathroom."

"I will, I will!"

"You say that," Gage said, "and I know you mean it. But this secret, it's going to upset you. You've got to trust me on this. I know you can handle it, Denny, or I wouldn't tell you, but let's do it my way. You can tie me right back up, and I'll tell you as soon as I'm done."

Denny looked at the floor. Outside, the storm continued to rage. This was the moment of truth. What was stronger, Denny's desire to please his brother or his desire to find out a secret about his past? Gage was sure some part of Denny knew this secret history existed, which was why it gnawed at him.

"You promise not to try something stupid?" Denny asked.

"I just want to take a leak, man."

"You won't tell Elliott?"

"Of course not. We'd both be in trouble."

Denny chewed on his bottom lip. "You gotta tell me a little piece of it."

"What do you mean?"

"Maybe you're just making this up. You gotta tell me a little piece of the secret, enough so I know it's real."

Gage nodded. Denny may be slow, but he wasn't a complete idiot.

"When you had your accident in the pool," Gage said, "there was a girl there. Do you remember? Elliott may have told you something about her, something that made you think that you two needed to … make sure she didn't talk. But what if I told you that what Elliott said about her wasn't the whole truth?"

Judging by Denny's wide eyes and gaping mouth, this was exactly the piece of the secret that Denny needed to hear.

"What's the whole truth?" he blurted.

"Aw, not yet," Gage said. "You gotta hold up your end of the deal."

Denny seemed to debate internally for another moment, then nodded solemnly. He approached Gage from behind, grabbed the chair, and tilted it backward. Then he slid Gage across the hardwood toward the little door next to the bed, stopping there. He opened the door and there was the bathroom: the toilet, the sink, and the tub all squeezed into a space not much bigger than a coffin.

Maybe it *would* be Gage's coffin, if this didn't go well.

Denny slid him right up to the toilet. The rain pounded against the glass, the yellow daisy curtains not quite covering the window completely and giving Gage a glimpse of the utter darkness outside. Caps from beer bottles lined the shelf above the sink, but there was nothing Gage could use as a weapon.

It was just as well. Gage already had a weapon in mind, one Denny was already unfastening for him. The ropes binding his wrists loosened, freeing his arms from the chair. Because his ankles were bound with the same rope, that meant Gage would be able to completely free himself if he had the chance.

Denny grabbed him under the armpits and lifted him into a standing position. It was an easy, effortless move, as if lifting a pillow, and Gage actually had second thoughts. He was going up against King Kong here. But what other choice did he have?

"Go ahead," Denny said.

Gage swayed on his feet.

"What's wrong?" Denny said.

"Just a bit dizzy," Gage said. "Don't feel all that well."

"Oh. Can you go or not?"

"Yeah, yeah. Just … give me a second." Making sure he seemed unsteady, he bent slowly to the lid and lifted it. "You know, it really is … really is a shame what happened at the pool when you had your accident. I'm sure if your brother … Well, if he could do it over, he wouldn't do it the same way."

Except for the rain, there was silence. Gage couldn't see Denny's face, but he could imagine the surprise. He pretended to work on his zipper, swaying more.

"What do you mean?" Denny asked.

"Oh, I'll tell you … I'll tell you in a second. But you know, that girl saw it all. She saw him put your head under the water. But she can't see in your brother's mind. She doesn't know him like you do."

"What?"

"She says he looked like he was happy to do that to you, but she can't … she couldn't see in his mind. She doesn't know what he was thinking. I'm sure he hated himself even as he was doing it."

"I don't …" Denny began, the anguish in his voice growing. "I don't understand. Are you … What are you …"

Gage, who'd been swaying this whole time, realized this was it. Do or die—literally.

He let himself crash into the tub, only bringing his arm up at the last second, as far as it would go with the rope, to soften the impact. His ankles were still bound to the legs of the chair, so the chair flipped with him. He put on quite a show. Maybe he had a future in theater after all.

Denny grabbed him and hauled him back into his chair, scooting him out of the bathroom. Gage lolled his head side to side, groaning, eyes closed. His hands were in his lap, the rope pooled between them. Denny hustled around in front of him, gently shaking his shoulders.

"Hey, man," he said. "Hey, you okay? You can't die now. You got to tell me everything. I want to know."

Gage moaned, lifted his head a little, then let it slump back to his chest. "W-w-water," he said.

"You want water? Okay, man. Okay, just a second, I'll get

you a glass."

When Gage heard Denny turn toward the kitchen, that was when Gage cracked open his eyes. Denny's expansive shoulders were like a receding stone wall. Gage's performance, with all the moaning, wasn't entirely an act. He *was* in pain. Getting himself to jump out of the chair took a lot more willpower than just pitching himself forward.

But that was what he did: put every last ounce of strength he had to spring out of the chair.

Denny, oblivious, was still walking away. The rope was up, extended taut between Gage's two extended fists.

He slammed into Denny.

Yet he couldn't quite get the rope over Denny's oversized cranium. It was going to fall just short.

Fortunately, Gage the human cannonball did hit Denny with enough force to knock him off balance, and the two of them crashed to the floor. That allowed Gage to keep his focus on the prize: getting the rope over Denny's head.

Which he did.

Looped it over, then yanked back hard.

There was a second when Denny didn't react, but then the bull jolted to life. First, a violent bucking. Gage held on even as Denny sprang to his knees. To let go meant certain death. He didn't want to kill Denny. He even felt a little sorry for him. But if only one of them could come out of the cabin alive, Gage intended on being the one.

Denny gasped and choked, prying at the rope. He lurched to his feet. He was so tall that he actually pulled Gage—who was not a short man himself—right off the ground. The tips of Gage's tennis shoes brushed against the floor. He tightened the noose even as he hung on for dear life. There was not much strength left in his body, but dear God, he would use every last bit of it to keep that rope as tight as humanly possible.

The storm howled against the thin walls, the wind whipping around the house and their own violent maelstrom inside. They might as well be a ship at sea, there was so much water washing against the windows. Denny flung himself left and right, but Gage held fast. The ropes encircling his wrists actually helped: even as his fingers slipped, the rope, clamped to him like a shackle, kept him from flying free.

Denny charged toward the front door, turning at the last second and smashing Gage into it.

It jarred Gage's whole body. His fingers slipped free for an instant, but the rope did not lose its hold, and he refastened his grip.

Three, four, five times—Denny smashed into the door.

With each jarring blow, Gage's determination was starting to crumble. His vision narrowed to the smooth black material of Denny's jacket. The muscles in his arms trembled. His back felt as if it had been run over by a tank.

Denny staggered away from the door. Finally, he let go of the rope and clawed at Gage, managing to clutch Gage's hair with his right hand. He yanked hard, sending tremors of pain searing across Gage's scalp, but Gage did not let go.

Tighter.

Hold the rope even tighter.

Denny's spasmodic movements began to slow. Was this it? Was Gage finally winning? Then, with a strange, gurgled cry that must have used up whatever oxygen Denny had left, he hurled himself backward toward the door with even more force.

Gage felt as if he'd fallen from a ten-story building onto his back. All the air in his lungs wheezed out of him. The door, in an explosion of wood and plaster, finally surrendered to the onslaught. One moment they were slamming against it, the next they were toppling onto the deck.

Hitting the door was bad enough, but having Denny land on top of Gage was even worse. With his lungs spasming for air, it was finally more than his chapped and bleeding fingers could handle.

He let go of the rope.

Gage's vision darkened. The rain and the wind, uninhibited by the cabin walls, rose to a guttural roar before suddenly falling silent. He slipped into a soundless, formless void. A second or two may have passed before he came back to himself, feeling first the massive weight on top of him, that sweaty bulk of flesh, then the rough wood boards beneath him.

He grabbed the rope, fearing that the momentary lapse was all Denny had needed to get a bit of air in him. Yet the wall on top of him didn't move.

Was he dead? Gage could barely take in short, shallow breaths. He tried to push the body off him, but his muscles were rubbery. Somehow summoning an even deeper reservoir of energy, Gage managed to push Denny off to the left. He gasped for air. He got his upper body free. Still, Denny didn't move. Gage got one leg free then the other.

The storm, muted during his struggle, grew in volume; he heard the distinctive swish of the wind through the tops of the firs, the dull thumping of the rain on the cabin's shake roof, the rattle of his throat with each breath.

As he gathered energy, he gave himself a few seconds to take inventory. His right knee felt like it had been severed at the kneecap. His face was a lumpy mess of bruises and cuts. A ringing in his left ear wouldn't stop. The rope, cutting into his wrists and ankles, felt like barbed wire. There were so many sharp jabs, dull throbs, and deep aches from all over that, in a way, the totality of his pain muted any particular wound.

Nora.

Her name sprang into his mind. Whatever sorry state his body was in, it would have to do. He got himself on hands and knees, wheezing for breath, then willed himself to sit up. Denny lay motionless next to him, eyes closed. If his chest was moving, Gage couldn't tell. Gage felt for a pulse. It was there, faint.

Lucky fellow, Denny. He'd live to see another day. But if he woke anytime soon, he wouldn't be happy, that was for sure. As quickly as his numb fingers would allow, Gage untied the rope from his wrists and his ankles. Then he set to work on Denny, binding his wrists behind him, then his ankles, making sure to knot the rope tight enough. During all of this, a wave of dizziness passed over Gage, black cloudbursts flashing in front of his eyes, and he steadied himself with a hand on the deck. What now?

Call for help.

As much as Gage detested the police, it was not the time to let his personal feelings get in the way. He had to help Nora, but Florence was over an hour away. Did Denny have a car? The porch light did not shine far into the rainy murk, but it was obvious there was no white Mustang or any other vehicle parked in the gravel around the cabin.

He searched Denny's jacket and pants for a cell phone and didn't find one. Elliott didn't trust his brother with a phone? Gage searched the cabin, just to be sure. No phone there either. Fine, then. He was going to have to hike down to Highway 101. Along the way, maybe he'd find help at another house. In the closet next to the kitchen, he found some shirts, a pair of overalls, and a black rain jacket. He put on the jacket; it was obviously Denny's, several sizes too big for Gage, but it would keep him dry. Flashlight? He searched and found none.

A clock shaped like a salmon, hanging next to the door,

caught his eye on the way outside. It was twenty to nine. Didn't Nora say she'd be arriving in Florence around ten? That didn't give him a lot of time. She might have arrived early. Maybe Elliott was already with her. But she might be late. If he hustled, Gage might still be able to intervene.

I may just kill your girlfriend after I've gotten what I want out of her.

That was what Elliott had said.

The clock ticking, Gage hustled into the storm.

Chapter 23

It only took a few steps—painful, agonizing steps—beyond the porch for Gage to be glad he'd worn the jacket. The rain pelted him with all the force of a nail gun. The hood helped. The vinyl-like material may do little to keep him warm, but it did keep him dry. At least his upper body. It was nearly impossible to navigate around the puddles that littered his path like landmines, especially when he'd ventured beyond the reach of the porch light into the deeper darkness. One tennis shoe was quickly submerged, then the other, soaking right through to his toes.

The only saving grace there was that he'd been in such a frenzied state earlier—yesterday?—that he'd never put on socks. At least he wasn't weighted down by a lot of soggy cotton.

Mud clung to the treads of his shoes. When he rounded the bend into the trees, the darkness was so complete that more than once he ventured off the road into one of the ditches. He stumbled, fell, and bounded back up again, now with mud on his jeans and his hands. His right knee threatened to buckle, and it was only through intense concentration that he stayed upright.

The wind blew back his hood repeatedly. He finally gave up on it and let the rain soak his hair and face. He bumbled along through the darkness, feeling his way from one tree to another.

He came to a silver mailbox. A driveway through the firs, and past a massive woodpile, led to a cabin similar to the one he'd just been in; the soft glow of solar-powered lanterns lined the walk to the front door, though the cabin itself was dark. No cars. He was glad to get under the tiny overhang. The top half of the front door was paned glass, but it was too dark inside to see anything but the vague outlines of a couch and wood stove. He tapped on the glass, but got no answer. He tried the knob and found it locked.

Maybe there was a phone inside. He found a rock and smashed a lower pane, managing to cut his knuckle in the process. On another day, the clatter of the glass might have carried, but today the sounds were swallowed by the storm. He reached through the opening, unlocked the door, and stepped inside.

"Hello?"

No answer. He saw a lamp on the end table. He clicked it on. A sprawling Native American rug, fish decor all over the walls, and a few cobwebs hanging over the kitchen sink—no one had been there in a while. No phone in the living area. There were two bedrooms. No phone in either. He was starting to remember why he hated the era of the cell phone.

The cut on his knuckle was bleeding profusely. He washed it in the bathroom and patched it up with Band-Aids in the cabinet. He drank straight from the faucet for a long time, easing his parched throat. When he stood, he looked at himself in the mirror and saw the haggard face of a man who'd been through hell and back, an ugly quilt of bruises and dried blood. He saw more purple than pink. One of his eyes was completely hidden behind a swollen mass as big as a golf ball.

A wave of fatigue washed over him, powerful enough that his legs buckled and he collapsed onto the toilet seat.

For just a second, Gage lingered. It would be so easy to let go.

But then he was up. Moving out of the house, faster than before. The next house was also dark, and there was no easy way to break inside, so he walked on. The third house, ten minutes later, was much more promising. More than a single porch light, this place was all lit up, which meant people. He felt hopeful. The lower part of the driveway was paved, and the house was a big single-story ranch with lights on in the kitchen and the living room. There were no vehicles in the drive, but there was a trailer with two red and white motorbikes parked next to it, the kind used primarily for sport.

The bay window was open. He saw the kind of cheap, generic furnishings that made him think it was a vacation home and not a principal residence. There was also a lockbox next to the door. No people. He knocked and nobody answered. He tried the knob, though, and was surprised to find it unlocked. Trusting folk.

"Anybody here?"

No answer. He smelled pizza and saw the empty boxes on the kitchen counter. As he searched the house, he called out a few more times, afraid he might surprise someone who was napping. There were suitcases, rumpled beds, but no people. No phone, either. His frustration rose, which only made all the aches and pains even worse. How many houses would it take?

Then he spotted a key on the kitchen counter, a single key attached to a Honda chain. He stared at it, thinking about the motorcycles outside.

"You've got to be kidding," he said.

* * *

Outside, straddling the motorcycle, Gage tightened the straps of the helmet he'd found by the front door. As he'd told Nora a week ago—had it really only been a week?—he hadn't sat on a motorcycle in decades. He'd certainly never ridden a bike so small and ungainly, more fit for dirt tracks than slick asphalt. He hadn't lied to Nora; it was a particularly bad spill on a hairpin turn on the switchbacks outside of northeast Yellowstone that not only gave him a broken collarbone but also sapped him of any desire to ride again. He'd come *this close* to a hundred-foot drop to jagged rocks. So he'd sold his ruined Harley for parts and swore he'd never touch another motorcycle. And he hadn't.

Until now.

What he *hadn't* expected was the fear—not just nervousness, but outright fear. Once the exhilaration of the engine starting wore off, he felt a growing trepidation. What he wouldn't give to be that eighteen-year-old kid again, afraid of nothing and no one, the vastness of his life stretched out in front of him with endless possibilities. *That* person didn't know that sometimes, when you put yourself in harm's way, harm's way was only glad to be there to greet you—usually wearing brass knuckles, to boot.

Yet this was now, this was who he was, and there was nothing to be done but shift into first with his right foot and *go.*

Which was what he did.

It had been so long that he nearly killed the engine, easing up on the brake too fast, a common rookie mistake, but the motorcycle roared back to life and away he went. The headlamp cut through the gloom, streaks of rain in the yellow beam of light. It being an off-road bike, the suspension was excellent. There were a few wobbles as he found his balance, but it was amazing how fast all the old knowledge came back to him: when to shift gears, based primarily on the pitch of the engine; the subtle dance between the two brakes, right hand and right foot working in tandem; counterturning, the non-intuitive act of pre-turning a little in the opposite direction, forcing a tilt the way you wanted to go and creating a sharper turn.

Even so, he was so nervous that he actually drove *too* slow, easing around the dark bends at barely over ten miles an hour. Almost all motorcycles performed terribly at slow speeds, needing a certain a moment of momentum to maintain balance and create steadiness for the rider. So he picked it up as best he could, staying in third but giving it more throttle.

Down the road he went, rain splattering against the visor, dirt and gravel spraying his jeans. He passed a few driveways, and considered stopping, but how long would that take? He'd have to explain this whole crazy thing to the police, and that would waste precious time. They definitely wouldn't want him going to Florence. And once he got off the damn bike, would he be able to get himself back on?

Before long, he reached the highway, his headlamp shining on the guardrail. The ocean, beyond a rocky bluff, was invisible. No traffic in sight. He slowed but didn't put his foot down, turning south. He shifted into fourth, then fifth, and was surprised when there was a sixth gear. That was new. Most of the motorcycles he'd known had only gone up to five.

A Safeway truck roared past. Should he stop and flag someone down? He knew exactly where he was, a few miles south of Barnacle Bluffs. But again, that would take time. The speedometer showed the bike climbing up to fifty, then sixty, the engine reaching a feverish whine that indicated it couldn't go much faster. It wasn't designed for high speeds.

The tank was full, though. He could ride without stopping.

* * *

LATER, WHEN GAGE TRIED to remember the drive to Florence, it would come back to him as a series of images and sensations. The steady roar of the engine. The way the rain seemed to fly straight him. His fingers so numb they no longer felt like they were attached.

He knew, even then, that the drive must have taken over an hour, but in the present it seemed he buzzed onto the highway and seconds later saw the sign welcoming him to Florence. It was still windy and raining, but the storm seemed only tepidly annoyed instead of madly enraged. He hoped it would last—not just for the safety of Nora's boat, but for his own sake. It would make it easier to find her if he could see more than ten feet in front of him.

He roared past the more rural outskirts of the city, full of spindly spruce trees and dark dunes, then the main commercial drag, Fred Meyer, Rite-Aid, Dairy Queen, plenty of cars out even in the bad weather. Some kids in a jacked-up truck yelled at him as he passed, saying, "You go, man!" He must have looked like a crazy person out on this dirk bike on a night like this. He was completely soaked, the windbreaker he'd nabbed from the cabin doing little to keep him dry when the water was coming from every direction. His face felt speckled with mud, and he smelled it in his nose, too. He was lightheaded with hunger, not thinking straight. When was the last time he'd eaten?

A bank clock showed that it was a quarter past ten.

He might be too late.

Nora had a big boat, so she'd certainly dock at a marina. But where? Florence was at the mouth of the Siuslaw River, and the main marina was around Old Town, if he remembered correctly, but in his frenzied state he couldn't remember which side of the bridge they were on, and missed any signs telling him so. He was halfway across the double-arched Siuslaw Bridge when he realized the main marina was on the side he'd just come from, the north. He'd have to double back. He scanned the water below, both to the west of the bridge and to the east. And that was when he saw it.

The yacht.

He realized, seeing the turgid river, that few people would be crazy enough to be out on a night like this unless they had no choice, and that made the sleek and modern yacht heading *west,* up the river leading to open ocean, all the odder. Most of the windows on all three levels were aglow. There was a flybridge on top, a secondary bridge that was exposed to the elements, and Gage saw two figures under the awning. Blinking away the water in his eyes, he tried to make them out.

It looked like a man and a woman. The woman had the wheel. The man stood next to her.

The woman had lots of dark hair, billowing in the wind. She gesticulated wildly.

The man was pointing something.

A gun.

After that, Gage was over the bridge, his heart hammering so loud in his ears that he heard it even over the motorcycle. The man had her at gunpoint. But why? And why head out to sea, unless he really intended to kill her? Gage made a U-turn right in the middle of the highway and gave the bike plenty of throttle, zooming back over the bridge. He took the exit to the Port of Siuslaw Marina hard, skidding so much he nearly lost the bike, but then he gave it more throttle and roared down Second Street until he reached the marina. A grizzled old man driving an RV, who was pulling out of the parking lot, gawked at him.

Faster. He had to go faster. He raced across a mostly empty

parking lot and screeched to a stop at the boat ramp. He jumped off the bike and ran—staggered, more like, his legs cramping—toward the rows of landing slips. The rain was already picking up, crackling on the water. He had to find a boat. Coast guard? No time.

The wind cleared most of the fishy smell, but not all of it. There were boats everywhere—fishing tugs, double-masted sailboats, even a pontoon boat—but most of them were dark and tied up, and the chances of the keys sitting in them were slim. Then he came across a teenage boy in a bright red jacket who was tying a tiny aluminum boat to the dock next to a Catalina sailboat. He looked up as Gage raced up to him. His hair, plastered to his forehead, was nearly as red as his jacket.

"Can I help you, mister?" he asked. His surprise turned to shock when he took in Gage's appearance, which must have been like something out of a horror movie. He swallowed. "Um, my dad is just over—"

"I need your boat, kid," Gage said.

"What?"

"There's a woman on that yacht that just left who's in trouble. I've got to stop it."

The kid, who couldn't have been more than fifteen, blinked hard at Gage, then sputtered nonsensically for a moment before the words actually turned into something coherent. "My dad—he—he—he just went to go get some dinner for us. We're—we're sailing up to Vancouver."

"I don't have any money on me, but I'll pay you a thousand dollars for it."

"I don't—"

"Look, there's no time. My name's Garrison Gage. I want you to call the police and tell them I stole your boat, okay? I'll pay your dad a thousand dollars either way, but I have to go *now.*

Do you have a gun?"

"A gun?"

"Please, I'm not going to hurt you. I just need the boat. You and your dad call the police. Tell them what I said. If you mention my name, they'll come. Garrison Gage. I'm a private investigator, kid. It's okay."

The kid stammered, a hopeless case. Gage didn't have time to make him understand. He hopped into the little boat. It was hardly more than a rusty bathtub, but there was no time to find something better. He didn't plan to take it onto the open ocean anyway, hoping to catch the yacht when it was still on the river. The kid, seeing that Gage really was going to do this, scrambled onto the dock. He jumped onto the Catalina and disappeared through the hatch into the cabin.

Going for his cell phone, probably. It was just as well. Gage yanked the cord on the motor and nothing happened. He tried again and it sputtered to life. As it idled, he untied the rope, and that was when the kid emerged from the hatch. He was pointing what looked like a toy gun at Gage, bright red, with and over-sized barrel, and then Gage realized it was a flare gun.

Uh oh.

The kid had decided to play hero.

Gage, defenseless, raised his arms. "Don't do anything rash, kid. If this is the way it has to be, then I'll …"

But the kid turned the flare gun around and handed it down to Gage.

"It's all we have," he said, then smiled a little. "I hope you stop the bad guys, mister."

GAGE DID TOO. He'd already stopped one, but the bad guy on Nora's boat was much more dangerous. Gage was broken, beaten, and bruised. He was armed only with a stupid flare gun zipped in the pocket of his windbreaker, and his wits—whatever those were worth in his present state. Other than that, as he motored away from the dock into the Siuslaw River, numb fingers on the cold rudder, he had his determination. That was worth something, wasn't it? Maybe some luck, too. He usually had luck on his side, when things were most bleak. Sometimes all you needed was a little luck to have a chance.

"You hear that?" he said, tilting his face into the rain and speaking directly into the impenetrable darkness. He'd never been a believer, not in the way other people usually defined it, but right now he'd take whatever help he could get. Or maybe he was just out of his mind. "You hear that, up there? Just help me out a little. This one time, that's all I ask."

As if in answer, the rain turned into a furious torrent, and a fierce wind roared out of the west.

Chapter 24

"*Janet?*"

The word had barely fallen from his lips when a fiery explosion—an outline of a yacht briefly visible within the most intense oranges and yellows he'd ever seen—lit up the western sky.

For a fraction of a second, no longer than it took to flinch, Gage thought he also saw the profile of his long-dead wife mixed with the silhouette of the ship. The spread of her hair in the wind. The slope of her nose and her chin. But then she was gone, maybe never there at all, and the boom of the explosion finally caught up with the light and hit him like a battering ram.

The force of it, the sharp, ringing pain, was so great that Gage cupped his hands over his ears. It also brought him back to himself. The wild ride over mountainous ocean swells, Heceta Head Lighthouse shining its beacon through the worsening storm, the mental dalliance with ghosts from his past—all these had been fragments from some discombobulated dream. But the explosion, this was *real*.

The boat, with his hands off the rudder, drifted to the right, and a particularly large wave nearly capsized him. The explosion disappeared behind the wall of water. At the last second he managed to get his hands on the rudder and veer hard to the left, throttling into the wave. With icy water spraying him from every direction, he didn't know he'd caught air until he felt it in his stomach, a precipitous drop. Water sloshed in from all sides. Too much water. It was pooling at the bottom of the boat.

It wasn't until he again saw the black, burning hulk of the ship—when the waves parted in front of him like a curtain—that he finally had a chance to react, emotionally, to what he was seeing.

Nora.

Nora was in there.

Plus whoever else was on board. He didn't give a rat's ass about Elliott, but what about her crew? And little Lady Luck. The dog would have died, too. He felt an anguished rage, both at Elliott, for inflicting such needless harm on the world, and at himself, for being incapable of intervening in time.

Yet maybe there was hope. It was such an all-consuming fire that the rational part of his brain doubted anyone could have survived, but maybe some had jumped ship before the explosion. It was possible.

He guided the boat toward the explosion, up a wave, down another, the fiery reds and yellows ahead of him bouncing in and out of view. Salt water stung his eyes. There was so much water in the air he might as well have been underwater; it was difficult to take a breath without choking. Her boat had seemed so close, but it took an eternity to get there. The boat couldn't take much more of this. Yet he couldn't turn back. She might be out there.

Fifty yards from the fire, he passed the first debris, a white chunk of the hull. It bumped against his boat when he came off a wave. A foot to the left and he would have hit it dead on, probably sinking him. After that, debris littered the ocean everywhere:

a half-melted plastic chair, a shredded orange life preserver, lots of twisted plastic and metal that could have been anything.

Twenty yards away, the heat from the fire pulsed and pushed at him. Even in the swirling wind, the air was choked with smoke. He smelled gasoline, burned wood, seared plastic, and something that could only have been the terrible, acrid odor of charred flesh. He saw someone reach out of the water and turned toward it, his hope rising until he saw that it wasn't someone at all ... only a dismembered arm.

It got worse after that. As he rode the swells up and down, running in a wide circle around the wreck, he saw horrors he would never be able to un-see. Part of a scalp. A bloodstained leather armchair. Black heels partly melted into a shiny silver refrigerator. Though the heat of the ship was still too great to get close, smaller fires burned all around him.

"Nora!" he cried.

Only the storm answered him, a primal scream of wind and rain. In his despair, as he searched for survivors, he turned his attention away from the ocean—only for a moment, but it was enough.

A wave much larger than any he'd encountered so far sucker-punched him from behind.

One second he was scanning the ocean. The next he was flying through the air.

End over end, he somersaulted through the darkness, plunging headfirst into the ocean. Icy-cold salt water gripped him from all sides. There was a moment of disorientation. It was too dark to know which way was up by sight alone. He started to swim, thrashing wildly, then his sense of gravity took hold and he realized he was swimming down and not up.

He reversed course. Only when his lungs were about to burst did he reach the surface, gasping for breath before a coughing fit seized him. Breathing the air was not much better than breathing the ocean; it was so thick with smoke that it burned in his throat. He spat out salt water and tried to keep his head above water.

He was just getting his bearings when he turned and saw another giant wave swooping down on him.

"Oh no," he said.

Then he was underwater again, spinning. His back crashed into something hard. He hoped it was his boat, but when he surfaced and spun around to look for it, he saw that it wasn't the boat but a long, rectangular object with a metal cylinder sticking straight up from the middle—some kind of table.

He swam for it, bumping against smaller debris. He tried not to think about what the debris was. He got hold of the edge of the table and tried to climb on, but it kept sliding forward and dumping him back in the ocean.

Cursing, he held on to the metal bar as his best he could, and spun around, searching through the churning water and the burning air for some sign of his boat. But the ocean was too rough and the light too poor to spot anything. Another wave crashed down on him, but this time he managed to ride it out by holding fast to the table.

He was so cold that he felt disconnected from his body. Did he have toes? Fingers? He was conscious of gripping the metal bar, but his fingers did not feel like his own. His ears felt like rubbery stubs. His clothes—the windbreaker, the jeans, his tennis shoes—might as well have been lined with lead for how they felt, weighing him down, trying to drag him under the sea.

Was this how it was going to end? He was going to drown in the dark, alone?

Mixed in with the moaning wind and the roaring sea, he heard the occasional crackle and fizz of the burning bits of boat that still remained. Other objects floated past: wine bottles, ripped paper, a bundle of toilet paper in a plastic bag. Something bumped him from behind; he turned and saw that it was a person— facedown, a shard of glass as big as Gage's fist embedded in the middle of a bloody red scalp.

Suppressing his horror, Gage rolled the body over.

It was Elliott.

His eyes stared ahead, unblinking. His boyish mouth was open in a silent scream. Gage shoved the body away from him. The sea brought it back. He shoved again, harder, shouting at the man who'd taken Nora from him. The body drifted away with the next wave, but the effort robbed Gage of the rest of his strength. His fingers started to lose their hold. He felt as if something was grabbing his ankle, pulling him under. Maybe it was Janet. Maybe she was telling him it was his time.

Don't give up hope.

No.

No, she wanted him to live.

He saw now that her words had been about him, not Nora. His wife didn't want him to give up on himself. He was no Ed Boone. He may prefer a hermitlike existence if given the choice, but he did have friends. A daughter. There was a lot to live for, and even if there wasn't, Gage would go on anyway. That was what you did. In the end, that's all hope was—finding a way to go on anyway.

So if he was going to die out here in the dark, it wouldn't be willingly. He would fight to the end.

It was in that moment he heard something above all the cacophony around him—a strange, rhythmic whirring. It grew louder. Gage rode the waves up and down, searching for the source of the sound. What was it? Briefly, as one of the waves dipped, he thought he spotted a beacon of yellow light off in the distance. He felt a leap of joy. Of course. A helicopter.

The coast guard.

Brave souls, coming out on a night like this. The kid at the marina must have called them. Or they'd gotten reports of the explosion. When the wave dipped, he saw that the helicopter was quite a ways off, and that the bulk of the wreckage was some distance from him. The length of a football field, maybe more. The currents had pulled him away. The fires had already mostly burned out, but what was still burning was centered in that area. That was where they would obviously concentrate their search.

He only got brief glimpses, but could see the helicopter struggling to remain aloft, strong gusts pushing it left and right. A spotlight swept across the water. The helicopter was moving outward in an ever-increasing spiral. He cried for help. It was no use. He could barely hear his own voice with all the wind and waves. The spotlight was approaching, the *whup-whup* of the helicopter blades growing louder. It was going to be close. Would it miss him?

It did.

It swept just off to his right, mere feet away.

He shouted at the source of the light as it receded, but it was no use. Would they try again? No. When the ocean pushed him higher, he saw that the helicopter was already turning back, away from the wreckage. With the conditions the way they were, it was too dangerous to stay out long.

Yet this was Gage's only chance. He sensed a heavy presence in his jacket pocket. Yes! The flare gun. But would it work? It had been sealed up in his windbreaker, but there was no way the jacket was completely waterproof. Still, flare guns were *meant* to work in extreme conditions, and most guns would even fire underwater as long as the cartridge was completely sealed and the gunpowder inside was dry.

He unzipped the pocket, submerging for a second while he struggled. He hated taking the flare gun out underwater, but it didn't matter at this point. Either it would work wet or it wouldn't.

The *whup-whup* was almost gone. He couldn't see the helicopter, but knew they would soon be beyond eyesight. He shook the flare gun hard, shaking loose whatever water he could. His arms were so weak.

He pulled the trigger.

Nothing.

It didn't work. Then he realized that the trigger hadn't really moved. It had been hard to tell, since his fingers felt like ice. A safety. That had to be it! Even as another wave crashed over him, he felt around for a lever and found it on the left side. Yes! He clicked it forward with his thumb.

He aimed high and squeezed the trigger again.

This time there was a loud bang and a burst of smoke. The gun jerked back. A smoky streak of red sliced through the storm, bursting high above. The flare lasted a few seconds before the storm smothered it with all its fury. Gage searched the sky and saw the helicopter's blinking beacon. Would it turn?

For a few agonizing seconds the helicopter didn't seem like it would, then it banked hard to the left and swung back around.

Chapter 25

Five days later, Gage watched the sunset.

Ensconced in one of the leather chairs in the turret atop Alex's bed and breakfast, a glass of bourbon resting on his lap, he watched the sun sink underneath what was, finally, a tranquil ocean. It was a welcome change. There was a little choppiness, the waves like stuffing tearing through an emerald-green couch, and a few clouds that masked much of the vivid reds and yellows that painted the horizon, but the scene was nothing like the ceaseless turbulence that had been their companion for so long that people had started to wonder if the storm would ever end.

But it did, as storms always did. At least he had his bourbon to help see himself through it, though he usually nursed a single glass for so long it could hardly be called drinking. He felt the coolness even through the thick jeans, the ice already half melted. He didn't *want* to drink much. He didn't want to throw himself such an easy lifeline, not when there was so much stewing in guilt to do, not when he deserved to feel the full weight of his failure without anything to lessen the load.

"Dad?"

That was a voice he had not expected. He turned, expecting to see Zoe, *his* Zoe, the teenage Goth girl with the attitude, and was surprised when a young woman stepped into the room. Who was this tall, lean person in denim, white blouse under the designer jean jacket, black leather boots giving her height she didn't need, Ray-Ban sunglasses holding back her auburn hair? It was almost like he was seeing her for the first time in years, not weeks.

"Can I join you?" she asked.

"Of course. So good to see you."

"I told you I was coming."

"Yes. But you said Friday night. I wasn't expecting you until tomorrow."

"Um, it *is* Friday."

"Oh. Right."

He gestured to the chair next to him. She sat, the two of them transfixed by the sunset. Or at least he was. He was conscious of her repeatedly glancing at him.

"You okay?" she asked.

The concern in her voice was so genuine that he couldn't give his usual flippant answer. Everybody else who'd asked that question lately—the coast guard rescuers when they'd pulled him out of the water, the paramedics who'd met him when they landed, Alex when he'd picked him up in Florence—he could lie his ass off and just tell them what they wanted to hear. But not Zoe. He could still duck and weave, though. A good fighter, when the punches were coming too fast, could always duck and weave.

"I feel like shit," he said, "but I'll live."

"You certainly *look* like shit. Better than when I came down that first night and saw you in the hospital, but still like shit."

He'd forgotten she'd visited him in the hospital. Of course, he remembered almost nothing of the two days he'd spent there.

"Thanks," he said. "You're so kind."

"They could put you in an art gallery. 'Man Beaten to a Pulp.' People would pay a fortune."

"Keep going, you're doing well."

"Uh huh. But I can see how you're doing physically. Are *you* okay?"

"Like I said, I'll live."

She said nothing, smart enough to wait him out. Most people weren't. Most people had to fill the silence. She would make a hell of a psychiatrist, if that was the route she decided to go. The thought annoyed him. He didn't want her to be a psychiatrist. She should be an astronaut who went to Mars, a scientist who cured cancer, or president, and even those things seemed too small.

The sun was nearly gone, filling the room with a warm amber light. The western half of the hexagon was a series of floor-to-ceiling windows that provided a 180-degree view of the ocean. The back half was filled with bookshelves, giving the room the comforting smell of aging paper and stained walnut. The room was Alex's pride and joy, the reason it was called the Turret House Bed and Breakfast, and Gage was one of the few people—maybe the only one—who didn't need to ask if he wanted to spend time in it.

"I don't like failing," he said.

"I know."

"I failed Nora."

"I'm sorry."

Still, he didn't look at Zoe. If he looked at her now, he might lose it, and *that* wasn't going to happen. He took a drink and swallowed it all in one gulp. The burn in his nose, the warmth spreading across his face—it helped for a moment. But only a moment.

"Do you want to talk about it?" Zoe asked.

"Not really." And then he surprised himself by saying: "But this doesn't feel right. We're missing something. The police, the press—they've got it all wrong."

She was silent for a moment, maybe waiting for him, and when he didn't answer, she got up and went to the liquor cabinet. He heard her open the fridge. He watched her from the corner of his eye and saw her pour 7 Up into a glass and add nothing but ice. Same old Zoe. She might have a glass of wine during the holidays, but alcohol just wasn't her thing. He thought about her parents, meth addicts whose only saving grace was that they'd died before they could screw up her life any worse, and felt another surge of anger. There was so much failure in the world. Failure all around.

"I only read one article," Zoe said, returning to the chair, the 7 Up still fizzing. "And Alex told me a few things. But I really don't know much about what happened."

That was it. She didn't tease him with something pat like "Tell me about it," or "I'm interested in your point of view," but it was still a tease. Yet even though he saw right through it, subtle as it was, it worked. He found himself talking without even making a conscious decision to talk.

He started at the beginning, from the night he met Nora, focusing on the things that unsettled him. He told her about the letter Nora had received from Ed Boone—or so they all thought at the time. Was it really from him? He explained the strangeness with the library typewriter. And what about the dog? If he loved Lady Luck so much, which he seemed to, according to Ron, why did he not even mention her in his will or his letter? If he'd made arrangements with Ron to take care of the dog whenever he was gone for long periods, why didn't he do so the night he committed suicide?

Then there was the text message, the night when everything went down. Who sent the text to Elliott? It certainly wasn't Gage. He said nothing about his repeated forays into the forest chasing ghosts. She was worried enough about him.

But the text. There was no denying the text. It was real.

"Didn't that other guy confess?" Zoe asked. "The one you got away from? I thought he said he sent the text just to psych you out."

Gage snorted. "Denny would confess to blowing up the World Trade Center if he thought it was what the police wanted to hear. He's got the brains of an inchworm."

"So who do you think sent it?"

"I don't know! That's the point. Somebody else was playing us like puppets, jerking our strings from a distance."

"But why?"

"Yeah. Why? That's what I don't know. But nobody wants to believe me. Even Chief Quinn told me the text *seemed* like something I would write, poking somebody in the eye like that."

Zoe took a moment to respond, and when she did, she spooled out her words very carefully.

"When you were in the hospital," she said, "you were … pretty out of it. You were mumbling some stuff about Janet."

"So now you don't believe me either?"

"No, I believe you. It's just, Chief Quinn was in the hospital for part of it. It might … explain why he's a little skeptical."

"I did not write that text."

"I know."

"But the police, they have their bullshit story, the same one the press has. Denny Younger, criminal mastermind. Elliott Younger, the expert marksman who bizarrely fired a shot in anger on Nora's boat and accidentally hit the gas tank. Nonsense!

And making it worse, it's a madhouse around here. I can hardly go anywhere without some damn paparazzi taking my picture. I just wish …"

There was something there, something about cameras and photos, something nudging against the edge of his mind.

"What?" Zoe said.

He shrugged, dismissing the feeling as just more random anxiety. "Nothing. Did you bring Carrot?"

"No."

"Aw."

"I thought about it, but … well, the craziness you mentioned. When I came down when you were in the hospital, there were all kinds of strange people coming to the house. I kind of figured that's why you're holed up here."

"It's part of it," Gage said. "But I did fire a few rounds into the air the other day back at the house. Told the press if they set foot on my property, I'd shoot first and ask questions later. That at least kept them at the end of the driveway."

He glanced at Zoe and saw that she was smirking.

"Yeah," she said, "I read about that one on CNN. Nice bluff."

"Bluff? You really think the world would care if I shot a few paparazzi?"

"The people who work for CNN are not paparazzi."

"They are if they set foot on *my* driveway."

"Uh huh. So what are you going to do, just stay up here the rest of your life?"

"Why not? Good chair, good bourbon, good view. What more could I ask for?"

"Seriously."

He sighed. "I don't know. I'm just hoping the craziness dies down eventually. But it's not just the press. It's Nora's fans.

They're starting to show up in droves, like this is some kind of Graceland. Florence has it worse, but it's bad enough here. I worry about that more than anything else. There are few things more dangerous than an obsessed fan." He stopped again, because that strange feeling came back. Photos. Obsession. What was it? He shook his head, looking at Zoe. "Maybe I'll move. You got a spare bedroom?"

"No, but we have a broom closet under the stairs."

"Ah! Like Harry Potter. I could be the detective who lived."

"Mmm."

"You're not warming up to this idea? I'd pay my way doing housework."

"I'll have to run it by my roommate."

"You do that. In the meantime, how long can you stay?"

She stayed the weekend.

It was a good couple of days, as good as they could be given the circumstances. She only stayed on the condition that he would promise her that, once she left, he wouldn't just return to spending his time in the turret at Alex's place, and he reluctantly did so. Even worse, he knew that when he told Zoe he would do something, he would actually do it.

The weather remained pleasant, though mostly they stayed indoors. The one time they ventured out for a walk on the beach, on a crisp Saturday morning, a gaggle of reporters and cell-phone-toting Nora West fans followed them. Even swinging his cane like a wild man, threatening to beat anybody who didn't leave them alone, did little to detour them. So Gage and Zoe played hearts and pinochle and hoped this other kind of storm would pass soon enough. Zoe, less recognizable, went to the grocery store and bought him a month's worth of food and supplies.

Gage figured that would be long enough. If not, he really would move. Or kill someone.

It was good having Zoe around. Not just good. Wonderful. The problem, of course, was that when she drove away in her Corolla Sunday night, seeing those taillights disappear around the bend felt even worse than when she'd gone off to college a few weeks earlier. The emptiness, the deep pang of loneliness that opened up inside him, was so much stronger than before.

Someone must have gotten ahold of his cell phone number, because the press started calling. Then the fans. So he took the cell phone outside—it was only a few days old, a replacement for the one Elliott had taken—and shot it with the Beretta. The first bullet turned it into a blizzard of plastic and circuits, but he shot it twice more just to make sure. He drank himself to sleep that night, then felt terrible in the morning and vowed not to give in to depression again. If not for himself, then for Zoe. *Don't give up hope.* No, he wouldn't.

For the rest of that week, he filled out crossword puzzles, his old mainstay when he'd first moved to Barnacle Bluffs, and focused what little energy remained on projects around the house. A dripping faucet in the bathroom. A loose piece of baseboard in his bedroom. It was amazing how easy it was to fill your time if that was your goal. There was always a way to fill the time.

Then, the next weekend, he got a stroke of luck—though it was a bit macabre to call it luck. There was another shooting, a really bad one this time, at a mosque in Missouri. Fourteen dead before the shooter put a bullet through his own brain. Gage found out about it only when he walked down to the gas station late at night—surprised not to find any news trucks camped out waiting for him—and used the payphone to check in with Zoe. Terrible as the tragedy was, he admitted to her he felt some relief that at least the press would be moving on.

The fans were another matter, though even they dwindled over the coming days. He ran into an emaciated young man with dirty blond dreadlocks who hounded him at the checkout stand at Jaybee's, asking him where Nora really was, whether there was a conspiracy at the highest levels of the government, and what, exactly, she had to do with Area 51, but mostly these types just ogled him from a distance. A few determined journalists—not brave enough to come up to his drive, but still determined—accosted him when he went out for his walks, but he never answered any of them.

On a whim, one Sunday afternoon he drove to Heceta Head Lighthouse and was surprised to find it crowded with people wearing purple T-shirts adorned with Nora's face. He turned and went home before anyone noticed him. Would it ever end? He didn't want these constant reminders of his failure.

Still, when he stopped to buy some milk at the little market near his house, he also picked up the copy of *People* magazine that had a special section on the life of Nora West. He couldn't help himself.

He also couldn't help himself from buying the *Bugle* and the *Oregonian*, scanning for any news that the police had found clues to make them revise their theory. Had they sent divers to the wreck? No such luck. Even though the ocean was calm enough to finally conduct an underwater investigation, it turned out that the *La Vie Sans Regrets* had sunk in waters far too deep, at least for the kind of equipment local law enforcement had on hand. And since the police had their man, no one was all that interested in taking on the logistics of a much more complicated (read: expensive) operation.

That left Gage, late one Tuesday night in early October, over three weeks since Nora's boat exploded in front of him, paging through that *People* magazine for the first time. He'd bought it but then left it on his kitchen counter without touching it, afraid that if did he'd open some Pandora's box of grief. But with sleep once again proving elusive, he found himself settling into his armchair at two in the morning with the magazine in his lap hoping some words of appreciation about Nora's career might mitigate his despair, at least for a few minutes.

It didn't work. The articles were written well enough, but the portrait they painted of Nora was not the Nora he knew. It was the Nora the world wanted her to be—with flaws, certainly, but only the kind of imperfections the world could tolerate. She grew up poor, so of course she was easily seduced by wealth. She had an ego, so that meant she took part in petty feuds with other musicians. She grew up without a father, so of course that meant she was always looking for a father figure in the men she dated.

Some of that may have been true, but it wasn't complicated enough, and Nora was a complicated woman, as almost all people were when you peeled back the surface layers and the quick judgments and the tallying up of this or that the world used to sum up a person's life. She may have had an ego, but she was also incredibly self-conscious about her music, preventing anyone from hearing it until she thought it was ready. On one level, she may have liked money and the pretty things money could buy, but he had no doubt, after the brief time he'd spent with her, that if she had to choose between money and music, she'd take the music in a heartbeat.

She had a way of looking at you that made you feel you were the only person in the room, but you still got the sense she was holding back part of herself.

She had a smile that was always genuine, even though she must have smiled for cameras a million times.

She made love, every time, like the world was going to end.

She was Nora. She couldn't be summed up in ten thousand

words or ten million.

Still, the photos were nice—most of them either too glossy to be real, or too off guard to be fair, but a few at least hinted at the real Nora. Maybe it was just the bleariness of his eyes as fatigue finally started to take hold, but he thought he saw the essence of the real her in a few of them. Maybe some of the photographers caught glimpses of it too.

Photographers.

There it was again. Something about photos, or the people who took them. All at once the mushiness of his tired brain was gone, energized by this vague but tantalizing feeling that kept needling its way into his mind. What *was* it about photos? He got up and paced back and forth across the living room. There had to be a reason this kept coming back up. He paced for so long that he began to feel warm. He cracked open the window in the kitchen. The air was cool, but it was so still that he needed to stand next to the screen and breathe it in to enjoy it.

The ocean, usually a distant murmur, was so loud it could have been at the bottom of his drive. He stood there until his eyes adjusted, but even then he could not see into the forest beyond his house—it was one shapeless, dark mass.

Would she be out there?

No, he didn't want to let his mind go there. These past few weeks, he'd resisted the temptation to search for her. He knew she wasn't real. He'd *always* known, even when he'd let himself believe otherwise; he'd simply allowed himself the fantasy because the fantasy felt good.

Yet someone *had* texted from his phone while he'd been in the woods that night. And he *had* seen someone. He'd been afraid to go out again because he didn't know if his need for the fantasy would outweigh his need for the objective truth, but something told him he should go out now. It was a good night for it. Maybe they were watching him at this moment. Maybe, if he hurried, he could catch them.

So he did. He did it before he could convince himself otherwise, slipping on his hiking boots and his black leather jacket in a rush, grabbing a flashlight on his way out the door—a Maglite he'd bought at the Fred Meyer in Newport, one big enough to use as a weapon. His heart was pounding before he'd even closed his door behind him.

He didn't take his cane. There was so much adrenaline coursing through his body that he didn't even feel a twinge in his knee.

There was only a sliver of a moon, but it was high in a cloudless sky and shed more than enough silvery light on the fir trunks and spongy ground for him to see. He decided not to use the flashlight for now.

If someone was out there, he didn't want them to see him.

The forest usually smelled pleasant, of fir and fertile earth, but the utter stillness of the air allowed other, fouler odors to take hold, the smell of rotting wood and moldy leaves. While the air had felt pleasantly cool from within his house as he'd breathed it in through a screen, it quickly felt colder, his jacket and T-shirt no longer enough to keep him warm. Didn't matter. He wasn't going back, and it wouldn't take long for his walking to warm him up. Five minutes, maybe.

It was less than three before he heard the first sounds.

There was a rustle in the darkness off to his left, something crashing through a bush. That was followed by the patter of feet on leaves and fir needles. It sounded small, like a child, but perhaps that was because the person was trying to move stealthily.

Gage ran toward the sound. The patter of feet became a scamper. Maybe an animal? Whatever it was, he was going to see it for himself.

The person, the creature, whatever it was, scurried one way, then another. Gage chased it the best he could. Then he didn't hear it all. He turned on his Maglite and scanned the forest. No luck. He kept walking, emerging on the western parking lot of Hidden Hills Village, Ed's complex, his breath fogging in the yellow cone of light under the street lamp. He saw no one. The cars were still. A few of the apartments lit up but most of the windows were dark. He walked just far enough to see Ed's apartment, the windows dark, then turned back the way he'd come.

Dejected, he walked more slowly on his return trip. He stopped frequently, listening for sounds, and heard nothing. Maybe it had just been a big squirrel.

Oh well. He'd needed a walk. Maybe now he'd be able to get some sleep. This was what he told himself, though he was so dispirited—and embarrassed, too, for latching on to something so incredibly irrational—that he doubted sleep would be any easier than before. Now, when the excitement wore off, he'd have a throbbing knee to go along with his depression.

No.

No depression.

It was time to get on with things, one way or the other.

This was his vow as he emerged onto his driveway. Dusted by moonlight, the packed gravel resembled thousands of tiny clam shells. He trudged to his porch, his flashlight off, and only looked up when he heard a plaintive whine ahead of him.

He knew, even before he saw the source, what this whine was. He'd heard it before, a noise that had seemed annoying at first but was now the sweetest sound he could imagine. Even as his eyes adjusted, taking in the small black-and-white shape sitting outside his door, she trotted out to greet him.

Lady.

Or Lady Luck, as the dog was officially named.

Gage froze, not wanting to believe his eyes. He'd already been fooled once. What kind of trick could this be? Was she even real at all? Yet Lady dispelled this notion instantly by pressing her tiny front paws against his leg.

She was real, all right.

He bent down to her. She licked his face. On another day, it would have annoyed him, but not today. Alive! How could it be? And then, of course, everything else her arrival meant came rushing at him: Lady had been with Nora on the boat. She'd said so herself on the phone. So if Lady didn't go down with the boat …

Nora.

Nora might be alive, too.

But how? His heart pounding, Gage picked up the dog and carried her into the house. She felt the same, no major weight loss. Her coat was clean and soft. He put her on his armchair and examined her thoroughly. Her eyes were clear and bright. Though she bore no collar, this was not a dog who'd been on her own the past few weeks.

No, someone had taken care of her. Maybe Lady had never been on the boat. He'd seen Nora and Elliott, after all, not Lady. Maybe she'd jumped overboard before the explosion and swam ashore. A dog so small? Not likely. But somehow she was here. Florence was a long ways away from Barnacle Bluffs. Maybe the dog had escaped, but *someone* had brought her up to the city first. She probably tried Ed's apartment, then came looking for Gage. Maybe all his hypotheticals would amount to nothing and Lady's new owner was just a random person who found the dog. If Gage took a picture of Lady, and put it on posters all over town, the person might even come forward.

And, just like that, Gage realized what his mind was trying to tell him about photography.

Chapter 26

At a quarter to eight the next morning, Gage waited in his van outside Deering Middle School.

He was fortunate it was a Monday and the school was open. A few minutes earlier the bell had rung, and the diesel-spewing buses and the parents in the overstuffed minivans, having deposited their cargo, were mostly gone, but he waited a few minutes to let the classrooms settle. Not too long, though. He'd already been parked outside for two hours, tapping his steering wheel and watching as the sun rose over the school and the surrounding houses. He'd taken Lady on three walks around the track field. He tried to take her on a fourth, but she'd curled up in the passenger seat and ignored him.

The pin oaks flanking the arched metal entryway of the school—a recent addition to an old brick structure, someone's attempt at modernizing a building that had no business being modernized—were already showing signs of fall, a few fringes of yellow and orange amidst all the bright green leaves. The weather may not change all that much on the Oregon coast, the temperature usually falling within a band of cool to slightly cooler, but the trees still changed color.

He liked that. It made him think of New York. Not that he wanted many reminders of his old city, but he didn't mind a few.

"All right," he said to Lady, "time to put on the charm. Don't go anywhere, okay?"

Lady perked up her ears. Gage almost said something else, then realized that he was talking to a dog and that he'd vowed not to be a person who talked to dogs.

He may not have slept more than a few hours the previous night, but he'd made sure that he didn't look it: a cleanly shaven face, newly washed jeans, even a tie underneath his leather jacket. He left his Beretta under the seat, of course. He also made sure to take his cane, trying to look as non-threatening as possible. In a world where school shootings had sadly become commonplace, no stranger was going to be allowed to waltz into a school without being interrogated.

Yet when he hit the buzzer and told them who he was— seeing no point in lying, since his face had been all over the news—he didn't get the third degree. Instead he got the school principal, a short man who was just about as wide as he was tall, ushering him through a crowded front office full of ogling women to his room at the end of the hall. The enormous collection of keys attached to his belt jangled with each step. He closed his office door, removed a stack of books from one of the two chairs, and gestured for Gage to sit. He did.

"Sad, sad business," the principal said, settling his bulk into his own chair behind his desk. "I'm Marv Brown, by the way. Read all about you. I'm really sorry about Nora West. Honestly, we didn't even know she'd attended here until … well, you know the story better than us. What can I do you for?"

There were ocean-themed photos on all the walls—not professional ones, but still quite nice. One of the largest, and best, was a picture of Heceta Head Lighthouse at dusk.

"Ironic," Gage said.

"Excuse me?"

"Nothing. I just like your picture there."

"Oh, thank you. My wife took it, actually. Oh, right … Heceta Head. That's the place where her father … Um, yes, it's a nice photo. My wife does like to take her pictures."

"She's very talented. Actually, that's the reason I'm here. It has to do with photography."

"Oh?"

Gage had to be careful. It was only the hint of a theory that had led him here, after all, something that might be nothing, and the last thing he wanted to do was get the rumor mill started.

"I'm wrapping up some notes about the case," Gage said. "I'm kind of here on a whim, really. I just thought it might be nice to see any photos you might have of her. She did mention at one point that she was in her middle school yearbook a bunch."

"Oh!"

"Do you have any of them?"

"Oh, yes! We have a full run in the library, plus another set in storage. I like to page through them myself, sometimes, especially the older ones."

"Would it be possible to go to the library and see them?"

"Certainly, but there's no need."

"Excuse me?"

Marv searched for one of the keys on his ring—the whole thing was attached to some kind of retractable string—until he found the one he was looking for and unlocked one of his desk's side drawers. He pulled out two slim yearbooks, both glossy blue leather with worn corners and heavily scratched laminated covers that pictured the whole school gathered in the field, shaping themselves like a giant D. He deposited them on a stack of file folders at the edge of his desk.

"Seventh and eighth grade," he said. "That's before the re-structuring and we started doing sixth at Deering. She's in both of them. A lot more in the bottom one there, eighth grade. She was right about that. Don't know why. It wasn't like she was involved in much, from the looks of it. Just lucky, I guess. Happens sometimes, and kids who *aren't* in the yearbooks a lot like to complain. Why is Mary Sue in all these photos and not me? Well, because Mary Sue happened to be walking by when the photo was taken, that's why." He chuckled. "Go ahead, take a look. I just locked them up because I was afraid they might get stolen."

Reaching for the yearbooks, Gage felt his hands trembling and hoped it didn't show. He wanted to seem nonchalant. He was just taking a look for curiosity's sake, after all. But in his mind, he heard Nora's comment to him very clearly. She'd been trying to convince him that she might be of some help, and she'd mentioned seeing the Boone boys in her middle school yearbook.

So much of my childhood is shaky, but the yearbook is solid. My picture's in here a bunch, too. Which is strange, considering how little I went to school. I actually look happy in them. Maybe that's what I like about it. The pictures make me look like a normal, happy kid.

That was what had been nagging him the past few weeks, though it wasn't until the previous night that he'd finally realized it. Photos. She'd said she'd been in her a yearbook a bunch, more than she should have been. Gage had nodded at the time and, just like Principal Brown now, figured it was nothing but luck.

But what if it wasn't?

What if someone had *wanted* her in those photos?

The thing about photography: there was always someone

behind the camera, meaning that photography was in some sense a record of the moments the photographer noticed. Some photographers may be drawn to lighthouses, others to particular people, even if they were not consciously aware of it. Someone on the yearbook staff may have been particularly taken with young Nora Storm-Tree.

Perhaps even obsessed.

As he flipped to the index in the eighth-grade yearbook, Gage knew there was a distinct possibility that if his theory proved true, *that person* might turn out to be either Denny or Elliott Younger—or Denny or Elliott Boone, as they were known at the time. For the police and the press, that would only confirm a theory they were determined to believe. Gage hoped that wasn't the case. No matter what he found in the yearbook, he still couldn't believe that Denny and Elliott were behind all this. It didn't add up.

Nora was right. The index listed her in a bunch of places. Page three, seven, eleven, fifteen … A dozen in all. Gage skipped the official portrait. There was Nora singing in the choir—though in the background, because the subject of the picture was the retiring choir director. There was Nora in the art room—though off to the side, the photo about two girls in front of her, sisters, apparently, who were painting a picture of their mother to give to her on Mother's Day. There was Nora walking in the hall; the bespectacled boy in the foreground holding a blue ribbon for first place in the Oregon State Science Fair was clearly the intended target. On and on they went, none of the photos seeming to focus on Nora directly, though she was always pictured in a very flattering light. Unlike a lot of middle school kids, she didn't have that awkward, haven't-grown-into-my-body way about her; she was beautiful even then.

Gage had been hoping that the photographer would be

credited under the photos, but was disappointed. Then he realized that the whole yearbook staff was probably listed at the front of the book. How many photographers could there possibly be? Sure enough, there was a page that listed the staff: an editor in chief, four writers, two graphic designers ... and three photographers.

The first two names were girls he didn't know. The third, however, jumped off the page at him, so much so that the book slipped from his hand and he barely prevented it from falling to the floor.

It wasn't Denny.

It wasn't Elliott either.

It was someone Gage should have been paying more attention to all along, and he finally had some hope that Nora was alive—and where, exactly, she was.

Chapter 27

![L] ess than an hour later, Gage waited in a van for the second time that day.

This time it wasn't *his* van, the Volkswagen being a little too loud and distinctive for this particular stakeout, but Alex's green Toyota Sienna. It was possible that the owner of the house Gage was watching—a big two-story at the end of a quiet residential street near Big Dipper Lake—would recognize Alex's van too, but Gage was willing to take that risk. He certainly wasn't going to involve the police. Nora's life could be in danger, and he wasn't going to let them bungle the rescue.

After the lightning bolt in the principal's office, Gage had gone straight to Books and Oddities, discovered Alex not there yet, then raced across town to the Turret House, where he found Alex enjoying his morning coffee and the *New York Times*.

He didn't just go for the van. To be safe, Gage also wanted someone else to know his theory. Alex was appropriately skeptical. But he said he'd watch Lady, insisted that Gage take his van, and also forced Gage to take Alex's cell phone—with instructions to call him in one hour no matter what happened. Otherwise, Alex would call the police.

The only question was where this person lived, but it didn't turn out to be too difficult. It *wouldn't* be, of course, given the man's occupation. It wasn't the sort of job that lent itself to a desire for anonymity. Five minutes on Alex's laptop, without any help from the FBI, and they'd found the address all over the Internet. In this day and age, unless someone tried very hard to keep that information private, the same was true for almost everybody, especially a person who'd lived in the same house for a decade and wanted to be seen as a pillar of the community.

Howie Meyer.

That was the name that jumped out at Gage from the three photographers listed in the Deering Middle School yearbook. Howie Meyer, the big, pear-shaped insurance salesman who could have passed for Edgar Allan Poe, at least from the neck up. Howie Meyer, the son of Ronnie, Ed's waitress and close friend, who'd apparently lived down the road from Nora when they were teenagers and most likely watched her, fondly, from afar. Howie Meyer, who'd gone through a recent divorce and also lost his secretary, showing signs of a man whose life may be coming apart at the seams.

Howie Meyer, who somehow found out that Ed Boone, a father figure he probably wished he had, was actually Nora's father ... and snapped.

But why? Obsession was a strange animal, causing people to behave in all kinds of unpredictable ways. And Gage didn't even know that Howie *was* obsessed. Conjecture, theory, possibilities—that was all he had, which was why Gage still sat in the van and watched the house through his rearview mirror even though everything inside him was screaming to get into that house. Every second that passed might mean he was too late.

Yet making his move now also might get Nora killed.

That was because Gage not only didn't know where Nora

was in the house, if she was there at all, but also if Howie was inside. Before coming there, Gage had visited the insurance office and found it dark. There were no cars parked in the driveway or on the street in front of the house, but that didn't mean anything; there was a detached two-car garage.

So Gage had spent the last fifteen minutes studying the house and the neighborhood. It was quite a house—not a mansion, by any means, but still large and very impressive in a somewhat Victorian style, a trend that had cropped up for a brief time in pockets around Barnacle Bluffs during the thirties, with wraparound porches, dormered windows on the second floor, and high-arched roofs. Some of these homes, Gage had seen around town, had fallen into disrepair, but this one had been well cared for: blue paint and yellow trim fresh and new, boxwood bushes lining the sidewalk to the front door well trimmed, ivy growing on the white picket fence kept neatly in line.

It was probably the nicest house on the street, with the biggest sweep of property around it. The undeveloped valley on the other side likely gave the owner a view of the lake, or at least a glimpse of it, though Gage could not tell for certain with the fences, oak trees, and arbor vitae hedges blocking his way. Judging by the small, mostly ranch-style homes that lined the street around it, Gage guessed that Howie Meyer's house had predated the others by a few decades at least. Maybe business had tightened enough that Howie had been forced to let his secretary go, but, like any good insurance salesman, he certainly wasn't making this fact obvious.

If Howie was crazy, he was hiding his crazy from the world well.

The curtains on the bottom floor were closed. The ones on the top were open, though covered with some kind of sheer curtain. Gage saw no activity. Except for a yard service mowing the lawn at the first house on the street, the rest of the houses were equally sedate. There were some cars in the driveways but no people. A German shepherd in the backyard to Gage's left, probably annoyed at the lawnmower, occasionally showed his annoyance by poking his head through the gap in the chain link fence and barking, but otherwise it was just another peaceful residential street.

Gage tapped the Beretta on his knee. If Nora was alive, Howie could be doing awful things to her right now. Could Gage really just sit here? If he was afraid of going at the house directly, maybe he should drive around to the bottom of that undeveloped valley and look for a way to hike to the house from that side, giving him the element of surprise. He was pretty sure that the valley bordered Big Dipper Road, though he'd need to drive down there to be sure.

In the end, he was glad he hadn't moved, because it was only a few minutes later that he saw Howie Meyer, the man himself, emerge from a side door and enter the garage. He was dressed in a navy-blue suit and carried a briefcase, walking briskly but not really in a hurry. A minute later, the garage opened and a silver Lexus backed out.

Gage ducked low in his seat. That Howie was apparently headed to the office was, on one hand, exactly what Gage wanted; he was hoping to get a crack at the inside of the house without having to confront Howie just yet. On the other hand, Howie's dress and manner had seemed so ... normal that Gage couldn't help but feel a pang of disappointment. Was this *really* a man who had Nora West locked in his house? Was this chatty insurance salesman really the sort of person who had somehow orchestrated a complicated charade that involved duping not only Gage but two professional hit men, as well as blowing up Nora's yacht while somehow ferreting her away in another boat without being seen?

Impossible.

That was what Chief Quinn would say, and Gage knew he would think the same thing if their positions were reversed. He partly thought it even now. And yet …

Hunched in the seat, making sure to keep his head away from the window, he heard the Lexus drive past.

The dog, angered by this apparent transgression into his space, barked even louder. Gage waited until he was sure the Lexus was gone, then peeked up over the dashboard to make certain. No Lexus. Still, even though he was itching to get out of the van, he waited. He knew from hard-won experience that the time people were likeliest to return was in the first twenty minutes—when they remembered they'd forgotten something and weren't yet far enough away to convince themselves it wasn't worth going back.

Gage made it ten before he said to hell with it.

He slipped the Beretta into the shoulder holster under his leather jacket. No cane. He'd just have to tough it out. When he got out of the van, the German shepherd went crazy, and went on going crazy until Gage was out sight. Gage reached the end of the cul-de-sac and crossed into Howie's driveway. He didn't hesitate. The key was to always act like you belonged.

A few gray clouds had crept in from the west, but otherwise the sky was clear. The breeze, cool and only faintly smelling of the ocean, was just strong enough to make the bamboo wind chime hanging from the end of Howie's porch knock softly.

His hand inside his jacket and gripping the Beretta, Gage circled to the back of the house, passing through the ivy-laden arbor and the unlocked gate. His right knee, still recovering from his ordeal a few weeks earlier, ached. The house's location at the end of the street, and the tall hedge of arbor vitae that separated the property from the neighbor's, meant Gage was quickly out of view.

He'd only taken a single step through the gate when he saw the red lava rock.

His heart kicked up a couple of gears. The lava rock formed a walking path that led to the back of the house, plush grass on either side.

If it was just a coincidence, it was a hell of a one.

Still, even though the discovery fueled his hopes, it meant nothing by itself. Either Nora was here or she wasn't. There was a kitchen window immediately to his left but high enough that he couldn't see more than the top of the refrigerator: very plain, no magnets, no notes. Gage pushed himself to keep moving. If someone had seen him and called the police, he might have two minutes, maybe less.

The first incongruity was apparent to Gage when he passed through the cozy area just behind the gate, where there was a tidy area for the garbage, recycling, and yard bins all harbored inside a red plastic enclosure, to the back of the house. The path sloped to a third floor, a daylight basement hidden from the front. There the grass could hardly even be called grass; it was so high and unkempt that it was more of a jungle. The cracked concrete patio was almost invisible underneath all the weeds.

If there was a view, it was obscured by a wall of blackberry bushes at least ten feet high, much higher than what was left of the wooden fence that was trying, and mostly failing, to hold back the bushes. The few remaining gray and crumbling boards, positioned under all those crazy, tangled vines, resembled rotten teeth in the mouth of a witch with frizzy hair. The bushes were so overgrown that he almost missed the gate at the end, which seemed to lead to a path through the bushes.

Probably to the street below. Good. Now he had a backup

means of escape, if Howie should come home.

A pile of debris at least as tall as Gage leaned against the side of the house—mostly branches and leaves, but he also saw a milk jug, wrinkled magazines, and other random garbage, the odor of rot and mildew strong. There was a rusted old barbecue, a blue plastic cooler full of empty beer bottles, and a cast iron bench stacked with what appeared to be flower boxes. Mold and moss pervaded everything. There was also a sliding glass door, what lay beyond hidden by sun-bleached drapes.

So there was a side of Howie Meyer that he presented to the world and another part he kept hidden away. It bolstered Gage's spirits even more. *This* was the sort of man who might have kidnapped Nora West.

He tried the screen door. Locked. He tried the two windows behind the refuse pile, the blinds shut tight. Also locked.

The hard way, then. He searched the yard, found nothing that satisfied him, then spotted a big rock under the blackberry bushes. It wasn't a rock after all. It was a chunk of concrete half coated with red clay, large enough that Gage could hardly hold it in his hand.

Perfect.

He would have liked to wait until there was another sound to cover him, even the barking dog, but the neighborhood stayed stubbornly silent. No matter. After a good wind-up, he really let the window feel the full force of all his pent-up frustration.

The shattering glass was just as loud as he feared, but at least the window yielded. Glass rained down on the curtains and clattered to the concrete patio. Now the clock—since no doubt someone would have heard—was really ticking. After pulling out the Beretta, he kicked through the remaining shards and yanked the curtains aside.

It was so dark he couldn't see much but the edge of a plaid

couch and a couple of green plastic totes. He felt inside for a light switch and found it.

Weak light from an overhead fixture illuminated what might have been intended as a family room, with a couch and loveseat, a wooden rocker, and a couple of throw rugs over a polished concrete floor, but it was more of a giant closet now: the green totes labeled with black magic marker were everywhere (*spring clothes, taxes 2013, office supplies*), as well as Amazon boxes, piles of newspapers, a ten-speed bicycle missing the front wheel, a free-standing clothes racked packed with coats, shirts, and pants … Wood-paneled walls. A musty smell. He saw a wood stove, carpeted stairs to the left, and two dark-stained wood doors to the right.

"Hello?" he called.

He tilted his ear, listening. No one answered. He leaned in farther.

"Nora? Anyone?"

Still nothing. He stepped into the house, glass crunching under his feet. His heart was really going now. There were movie posters between the two doors, one of James Dean, the other of Marilyn Monroe. Gage tried the door on the left. It was a half bath: a toilet and a wall-mounted sink. The other room was some kind of office, though it was even more crowded than the family room—filing boxes, newspapers, magazines, and other assorted papers piled all around a metal desk. A dusty mobile of the planets hung by the window, spinning slowly.

Had someone just been in there? No, it was just from him opening the door.

Gage navigated around the boxes and gritted his way up the stairs. He called out a few times, hoping maybe Nora was locked somewhere and would hear him, but nobody answered.

The second floor—a country-style kitchen, a living room

with wing-back chairs and a leather couch, polished hardwood floors—was nicer, but it still didn't seem quite normal. It was sterile, like a show house. The fruit bowl on the counter, the copies of *Architectural Digest* on the coffee table, the plush tan pillows arranged on the couch just so: it was all too perfect. It even smelled too nice, like lavender. An air freshener of some sort, most likely. Perhaps good old Howie Meyer needed to be ready in case a prospective client stopped by unexpectedly.

The furnace kicked on, blowing hot air out of a vent just to Gage's left, and he jumped. Otherwise the house remained quiet. A humming refrigerator, a ticking clock, the slight crackle of an old window—these were the only sounds. He peered through the living room blinds. Alex's van was still there. The neighborhood was quiet. Maybe no one had called the police after all.

Upstairs there were three bedrooms. Nobody was in any of them. They were all tastefully decorated, in blue and pink pastels, but only the master bedroom showed signs that someone lived in it. There were three cabinets packed with clothes. There was a wall-mounted television, speakers in each corner, plugs next to the high wire-frame bed for various devices. A bag of Doritos, a half-filled bottle of Coke, some M&M wrappers.

One wall was dedicated to black-and-white photos in silver frames. Gage hoped he might see Nora in them, but they all pictured Howie and a woman who must have been Ronnie, his mother, at various ages. In one of them, she lay in a hospital bed hooked up to intravenous tubes, her hair grayish white, her limps shrunken and her face gaunt even as she smiled with happy, beaming eyes.

Gage felt his hope slipping away. He'd searched the whole house and found no sign of Nora. Maybe this was all for nothing.

Yet one of the photos showed his mother sitting in an aluminum fishing boat, ocean all around her, nobody else in the picture. She didn't look much younger than when she'd been in the hospital, but her hair was dark brown—dyed, most likely. The boat was so small that the photographer was probably the only person in it, and that photographer was most likely Howie.

So he was familiar with boats.

Lava rock. Boats. These things had to matter.

Gage looked through all the drawers and cabinets, pawing through the clothes, searching for any clue. There was nothing. There was also nothing unusual in the medicine cabinet, under the bed, or in the walk-in closet—not unless you counted far more suits than any man should ever need in his life. There wasn't even a hidden stash of porn.

He searched a little more on the main level, didn't find anything, and headed back downstairs. Dejected, he paused by the broken sliding glass door and called out to Nora again, really listening. But still there was no answer.

So that was it. Howie wasn't involved. Time to go.

Yet he couldn't quite make himself leave. He stood with one hand on the frame, the other still gripping the Beretta, and allowed the curtain to billow against his face. He told himself to think it through. If Gage had kidnapped someone, where would he put her? In a basement, most likely, hopefully with thick walls that would block any sounds. But he was in the basement.

Or was he?

This was a daylight basement. Could there be *another* basement underneath this one? Perhaps a hidden opening, something in the floor. Yet the floor was concrete, making such a passageway unlikely.

But there were rugs.

Giant, thick rugs.

In a frenzied state, Gage pulled back the most easily accessible rug. Nothing but concrete. Undaunted, he turned to the next one, pushing aside the couch and some boxes to get to it. He thought for sure he'd find a door. But no. Concrete again.

Wasn't there one more rug in the office? Sure enough, when he returned to the office, he saw the edge of it underneath the desk, a black and burgundy rug in alternating colors. He'd have to move the desk. Or did he? No, he could lift the back half of it. He didn't even have to move the chair; it was in the corner off the rug, three filing boxes stacked on it.

Gage lifted the rug.

And there, to both his relief and surprise, was a door.

It was a gray metal panel set in a recessed area of the concrete, with two finger holes on either side—like a manhole cover, but square, perhaps four feet across and two feet deep.

Gage stared at it in astonishment. Like the boy who'd found a hidden stash of candy, he perked up, listening, expecting at any moment to be found out, but the only sound was the low hum of the furnace. He stuck his finger in one of the holes. It went in deep, touching nothing. He leaned low, peering inside, but could see only darkness. Cool air blew through the hole—not fresh air, by any means, but it was not dank or moldy. Whatever was down there was ventilated.

After placing the Beretta in his shoulder holster, Gage slipped a finger through each hole of the panel and lifted. The plate was two inches thick and heavy. He saw a ladder of wall-mounted iron bars leading down into the darkness, and a dangling chain hardly thicker than a spider's web. He placed the cover under the desk, then pulled the cord.

Sure enough, a bulb that must have been just out of view flickered on and bathed the passageway with faint yellow light.

Perhaps ten feet down, in a square passageway with slick concrete on all sides, was a metal door.

"Hello?" Gage called.

His voice rebounded in the tight space, but there was no answer. The walls were thick. If Nora was behind that door, it explained why he couldn't hear her upstairs and she couldn't hear him.

Gage massaged his bad knee, preparing for the agony sure to come, then started climbing into the hole. He wasn't wrong. The pain was unbearable. The light bulb was on an exposed fixture wired through the support beams and the insulation. He was surprised to see the support beams. That meant sound should have more easily traveled from below, not exactly ideal for a hidden dungeon.

Everything still had the gleam of newness about it—the concrete, the metal bars. When he got to the bottom, and saw that the simple lever handle on the metal door had no lock, he began to suspect *why* there was no soundproofing on the ceiling. If this room wasn't locked, there must be another locked room inside; otherwise, Nora would have escaped.

If Nora was alive.

No, she *had* to be alive.

Holding his breath, Gage turned the handle.

The room inside was nothing like the plain concrete passageway. It was well lit, for one, with two rows of fluorescent lights. The ceiling was low, perhaps seven feet high, and the room was maybe twenty feet by ten, no windows, carpeted with the sort of low-nap tan pile common in office buildings. Gage's first impression, at a glance, was that the room was a command center. Bulletin boards filled all but one of the walls, each of them filled with newspaper clippings and other documents. He saw a detailed map of the Port of Siuslaw, a wetsuit hanging from a hook, and a deflated yellow raft. There was an outboard motor next to the raft, a small one, but certainly powerful enough to motor two people back to shore even in a bad storm. There were two large-screen computers, three filing cabinets, a stereo system, a small fridge, and a big-screen television currently tuned to CNN, the sound muted. A vent on the ceiling fluttered the paper cluttering one of the desks.

Gage's second impression was that the room was a shrine.

For the farthest wall was not covered with bulletin boards, but instead oak shelving packed with items related to Nora West.

He saw the framed photos of her from across the room and felt his gut tighten. Stepping closer, he saw rows of CDs, vinyl records, magazines, and books, everything about her. There was even an action figure, complete with a free-standing microphone. It was a wall of shelving ten feet wide by seven feet tall dedicated to Nora West. Gage even saw that the very first item, far to the left, was the same Deering Middle School yearbook he had flipped through only hours earlier.

There was no Nora, though.

She *should* have been here but wasn't. So there were two possibilities. Either Howie kept her elsewhere or he'd already killed her. Gage didn't think he would have killed her, though, not with this kind of obsession. But where would she be? Some little cabin in the woods? A man who would go to this kind of effort to construct a hidden bunker would probably not risk putting her in a cabin in the open. His hiding place for her would be more elaborate.

But where?

Gage knew he had to leave the house soon. His advantage now was that Howie Meyer did not know Gage was onto him. That meant Gage had options. He could stake him out, hope to follow him to his other hideout. Or bring in the police. There was enough evidence now.

He turned away from the shelving, heading for the exit, and

that was when he heard the clinking.

It was very faint, barely audible over the whistle of the air through the ceiling vent. But yes, there was a sound, a rhythmic clinking like two pieces of metal tapping against one another. Then it stopped. Then it started again, the rhythm changing, changing again … A repeating pattern.

A song!

All at once, Gage knew the rhythm. It was from the song Nora had recently written, the one about the lighthouse.

Turning back to the shelves, he listened intently. The clinking sounded as if it was coming from the other side of the shelves. A secret room? If the situation weren't so dire, Gage would have allowed himself a smile; it was like something out of a James Bond movie, a secret room within a secret bunker. He searched for hinges or handles. He ran his hands along the tops of the books and other items, feeling for some kind of lever, and came up empty. It was dust-free, though. This was a man who liked to keep his collection tidy.

Frustrated, Gage stood under the buzzing fluorescent lights and stared at the shelves. Maybe the latch or lever wasn't *behind* the books or CD cases but *was* the books or CD cases—or something else among the collection.

Her first album?

He located it, the one with her sitting on a stool in front of a plain white background, and pulled it out. Nothing happened. There was a mug from her first live concert, featuring aliens with microphones for heads floating over the city of Los Angeles. He picked it up. Nothing.

Then Gage saw the Deering Middle School yearbook, the first item all the way to the left on the top shelf. Could it be? He tried to pull it but it wouldn't budge.

Jackpot.

If it wouldn't come out, would it go in? He pushed, and sure enough, it slid backward—only a few inches, but there was an audible click. Yet nothing special happened. All right, maybe it just unlocked some kind of mechanism. He pushed on the shelving ...

... and all of it slid back three feet.

It slid right into what had appeared to be a solid wall but turned out to be only a third of a solid wall, one that dropped from the ceiling and stopped exactly at the top of the shelving, creating the illusion that it went all the way to the floor. Metal tracks were recessed into the floor, the shelves on wheels. Gage squeezed into the gap and found himself in a narrow hall with a single square of light in the center.

As his eyes adjusted, he saw that the square of light belonged to a window in another metal door.

This, finally, was what he'd come for, and he held his breath as he approached, hoping that the person on the other side of that door was not only Nora, but that she was unharmed.

It was her.

Yes, it was her, though her appearance seemed both familiar and foreign. Through a glass pane thick enough that it would have been home on a submarine, he saw her crouching on a pine futon with a black mattress, staring gloomily at the floor, one hand chained by handcuffs to a metal ring bolted to the wall. She was dressed in a denim jacket and a black leather skirt a bit on the small side, designed for a body not quite so curvaceous. The tank top under her jacket practically pushed her cleavage right out of her shirt, though she also seemed ten or fifteen pounds thinner than the last time Gage had seen her. Fishnet stockings, with a deliberate tear up the inside of her thigh, disappeared into her *very* short skirt. She wore eyeliner almost as dark as her tall leather boots. Her fingernails were painted a garish green.

When she looked up at the window, first with dread, then with relief, he realized why the outfit seemed familiar. It was a similar getup to what she'd worn in middle school. He'd seen it in the middle school yearbook.

The bastard had dressed her that way.

The whole room was a portal back in time, as if it had been scooped out of a teenage girl's past—Nora's, he assumed—and deposited in this dungeon of dark memories. Posters of Nirvana, Alanis Morissette, Radiohead, and dozens of others layered walls that had been painted a similar green as Nora's fingernails. Ceramic dragons, trolls, centaurs, and other mythical beasts adorned her cheap pressboard dresser. There was an acoustic guitar leaned against a hamper that was actually full of clothes. There was a water cooler and a plastic camping toilet next to the bed. Somehow Gage didn't think those two prison necessities were in Nora's teenage room.

Nora jumped from the bed and was jerked back by the hand-cuffs. He heard the barest *tink* of sound and knew that was how she'd produced the rhythm, by clinking the handcuffs against the metal loop. The dark eyeliner and purple lipstick couldn't hide the gauntness of her face, the deep groves under her eyes.

She shouted something but there was no sound. He shook his head and tried the lever door handle. Locked. Now that his eyes had adjusted, he saw a keypad next to the door, the numbers zero through nine barely illuminated. It made sense, in a twisted way. There was undoubtedly a keypad on the other side, and only Howie knew the combination. After he let himself into the room and closed the door behind him, only then did he unlock Nora's handcuffs. If she tried to hurt him, she'd just be locked in there with him.

Gage looked at Nora again. She was still shouting at him, crying now, her mascara spider-webbing down her cheeks.

"I can't hear you!" he shouted at her. "I'm going to find something to break the glass!"

Nora stopped long enough to watch him intently, then shook her head, frantic. She pointed at her mouth. He understood. She wanted him to read her lips. He nodded. Slowly, with greatly exaggerated mouth movements, she said the following words:

Howie ... was ... just ... there.

On the last word, she pointed at the window to punctuate her point. Gage squinted at her, fairly certain he'd made out the words correctly, but how could that be? Gage had seen Howie drive away in his Lexus. The only way that would be possible was if Howie had somehow circled back and ...

With a chill, Gage remembered the gate in the backyard, the one that led to a path through the blackberry bushes and the road below.

He started to go for his Beretta, but it was too late. Down the short hall past the door, the shape of a person emerged from an alcove that had been hidden from his view.

"Hello, Gage," Howie said.

There was a loud pop and Gage was consumed by fire.

Chapter 28

I t wasn't fire, though Gage didn't know that until a few seconds later. It certainly *felt* like fire, a sizzling buzz of agony that gripped his entire body. Every muscle went taut against his will, turning him into an electrified statue. It was only when he stumbled backward that he also felt the darts sticking into his chest.

A Taser.

He hit the concrete floor hard, knocking the wind out of his lungs, and he would have gasped for breath if he could have even managed that much control over his paralyzed body.

Howie materialized out of the darkness, the light from the window shining on the side of his pale face. With his black hair and black mustache, his skin seemed all the whiter, ghostly, even.

The nodes attached to Gage's body went on doing their work, electrifying him, producing a steady, clicking buzz. How long would it last? Even physically immobile, Gage's mind was strangely clear. He remembered the charge on Tasers lasting half a minute or so. Howie didn't waste time, rifling through Gage's coat until he had the Beretta and Alex's cell phone. Then he took two pairs of handcuffs out of his pocket, snapping one on Gage's ankles, the other to Gage's wrists behind his back. It was then that the Taser stopped and the spasmodic twitching racking Gage's body was finally ceasing. Too late.

Gage heard the faint beeps of Howie typing on the keypad, a loud click, then felt a whoosh of cool air spill into the hall.

"Don't hurt him!" Nora cried.

Howie grabbed Gage by the ankles and dragged him into Nora's room. The big, doughy man with the beer gut didn't seem so doughy after all. He left Gage next to the dresser, far from Nora's bed, then delivered a sharp right foot straight to Gage's kidney. The pain cleared away whatever remained of his paralysis, and Gage rolled onto his side and hugged his knees to his gut, all that he could do with his hands pinned behind him.

"It was the damn dog, wasn't it?" Howie muttered. When Gage didn't answer, he glared at Nora, gesturing with the Beretta. "I told you I should have killed that stupid animal. Take her outside once to go the bathroom and she ruins *everything*."

"Please," Nora said. "Please don't hurt him."

Gage saw the furious expression on Howie's face soften, though only a little, a boiling rage percolating just under the surface. Gone was the garrulous, aw-shucks insurance salesman with the glad-to-see-you smile, which was an act, Gage had known from the first, but a very good one.

"Yes," Nora said. "Yes, I'll ... How about another backrub? You want that? Or—or something else." She sat down on the futon and patted it. "Come here, Howie. *Please*. Garrison doesn't matter. This is—this is about us. I want to show you how I feel. Come here."

Gage heard music playing faintly from the stereo. *Nora's music.* Howie smiled at her, took a step toward the door, then stopped abruptly.

"Oh, how I'd like to," he said. "I would indeed. You know how much I like you, Nora. You've always known. But I can't. There's things to do."

"Sure you can," she said. "Sure, sure, there's no hurry. Do what you always do. If you lock the door, you know I won't escape. Garrison won't go anywhere either. Let's just sit with each other."

She rubbed her hand suggestively up her stocking. Howie leered. Gage, even as he hated watching her debase herself, didn't want to say anything for fear of breaking whatever spell she was trying to cast. There had to be something else he could do. The door was open. As long as it stayed that way, they had a chance. The keys to the handcuffs had to be on Howie's person, or at least somewhere in the house. Gage's ankles may be cuffed, but he could still kick with both legs at once.

But then what? He might be able to take Howie down momentarily, but Gage would still be helpless.

"No," Howie said, with a forceful shake of his head. "There will be time for that later. Right now we have to go."

"But Howie—"

"*No!*"

His bellow echoed off the walls. He pointed the Beretta at Gage.

"One more word and I shoot him," he said. "You hear me? One. More. *Word.*"

Nora, cowering behind her hands as if she didn't want to see what might happen, said nothing. Gage thought about Howie's ankles. If Gage swung his legs hard at them, maybe Howie would go down. Maybe the Beretta would drop right into Gage's hands. Maybe he could even get off a shot with his hands behind his back.

It was a lot of maybes, too many. Howie, satisfied that Nora wasn't going to defy him, bent down next to Gage.

"Smart guy," Howie said. "You figured it out, I have to hand it to you. When I followed Nora from California to your friend's bookstore, and saw you meeting her, I knew I'd have to deal with you somehow. My little mind games didn't work, did they? But they almost did. You saw her boat explode and thought … Hmm. I'm saying too much again, aren't I?"

He pressed the Beretta against Gage's temple. Gage closed his eyes. If this was it, then this was it.

"I'm not going to beg," Gage said.

"I don't care," Howie said.

The muzzle was pressed harder against Gage's skin, and he felt his pulse taping against the cold metal. Who would have thought he would die by his own gun? Seemed appropriate, somehow. Nora whimpered. Finally, the muzzle relaxed. Gage opened his eyes. Howie was sneering at him.

"I'd like to," he said. "Maybe it wouldn't matter that much. But I don't want your bloody, exploded skull in her mind the rest of her life. We've made so much progress, her and I. We have something special. So I'm not going to do that to her."

"That's very kind," Gage said. "How about letting me go, too? I promise not to tell anyone about your special relationship."

Howie sighed. He stood, slipped the Beretta into the side pocket of his suit jacket, then reached into the inside pocket and pulled out what looked like a walkie-talkie, the homegrown variety with lots of duct tape and a very long antenna.

"Do you know what this is?" Howie asked.

Gage was more interested in the Beretta dangling from Howie's pocket. It wouldn't take much for it to fall.

"Your TV remote?" Gage said.

"It's a transmitter," Howie said. "You see, I always have backup plans, Gage. Always. Did you think I knew Ed Boone's sons were hit men? No. I had to adapt, use a backup contingency. Play along until I got my way. And this device, this is my adapting, too."

"Does it get HBO?"

"I have a special little contraption hooked up next to my natural gas line. When I push this button, the line will be cut and gas will flood the house. Twenty minutes after that, the device will detonate. You know what kind of fireball it's going to create when it does?"

"You planning on having the neighbors over for a barbecue? Count me in. I like a good hamburger."

Howie's skin was so pale that even a bit of pink would be visible, but his flush was a full-on sea of red. "Always joking. Fine, joke away. But see, I get the last laugh. My plan all along was to blow up this house. Don't think I have a nice insurance policy? Of course I do! I'm an insurance salesman! And believe me, the way I've done it, nobody will suspect arson. But I was going to wait. Make sure Nora and I got to know each other better. Make sure I could trust her. Now I have to speed up my plan. They'll never find this little place of mine, Gage. You'll die down here and nobody will even know."

"I already told a few people I was coming here, Howie. Your plan is shot. You'll never get away with the money."

"Oh, I know. I figured I wouldn't get the money now. That's sad, but I still get to blow you up. That's almost as good."

Howie held up the device, his thumb on a silver button. He was grinning. Was he really stupid enough to push the button while he was down here? What if the device misfired? It might cut the line and blow up at the same time. Then he'd die too.

"Listen," Gage said, "you don't have to—"

Howie pushed the button.

There was a loud click. Gage froze, as did Nora.

"Didn't think I would, did you?" Howie said. "But I have confidence in myself. I know what I'm doing. Nancy never understood that about me. She never understood how I could be so sure of myself. But it's just how I am. I see things others don't see. I know things will go a certain way." He shook his head. "Ten years she's been gone, and I still can barely stand to say her name. That's how long I worked on this place down here, Gage. Ten years. A long ten years, but at least I had my work."

"Let's call her," Gage said, trying to sound more confident than he was. "I'm sure she'd like to apologize."

"Shut up!" Howie cried. "No, no, no, I'm not letting you get me angry. I'm saying too much. I know it. I like to talk. It's a weakness, like I told you. But we're going now. In a few minutes you'll start smelling rotten eggs, a smell they put in natural gas that's otherwise odorless just to let you know you should get the hell out of your house. But you won't be able to, Gage. Unless …"

"Unless what?"

"See, this is how it's going to work. If Nora comes willingly and doesn't try anything stupid, I'm going to give her a chance to call the fire department. If we go now, they may still have time to get down here before the explosion. But we have to go now. You think you can do that, Nora? You think you can play nice?"

Nora nodded. Gage had no doubt Howie was lying, that he had no intention of letting her call the fire department, but saw no advantage in pointing it out. Howie was just trying to get Nora to play along. Was she falling for it? Gage couldn't tell.

"Here's what I'm going to do," Howie said. "We can't do things the normal way, since we're leaving. I'm going to toss you the keys to your handcuffs. You unlock yourself, then walk nice and slow right by me out this door. As long as you don't try anything, I'll keep my promise. I'll let you call 911 to help poor Gage here. Try anything else and I'll tase you just like I tased him, then carry you out anyway and let him die. Got it?"

She nodded, glancing at Gage. The Beretta appeared to hang even more precariously from Howie's right pocket. He reached into his left pocket and tossed a ring of keys at her.

It should have been an easy catch, but Nora made a mess of it, not only lunging unnecessarily but actually batting them away from her. They landed with a jangle. Howie groaned. She tried to reach for them, but the chain wouldn't allow her to go far enough. She tried with her foot, stretching, but could only nudge the edge with her boot.

"You did that on purpose," Howie said.

"I didn't! It was an accident, I swear!"

"I don't believe you. You—you are being very *bad!*"

"I'm sorry."

Growling in frustration, Howie crept forward with great care, keeping his gaze fixed on her and the Taser zeroed in on her chest. He crouched down, and only at the last second did he glance away to locate the keys.

It was during that glance when Nora stuck him in the balls with a club.

That was Gage's first impression, that she'd swung a club straight into his groin, but it wasn't a club at all. It was her left *boot*. One second it was on her leg, the next it was being gripped by the top half so the thick heel side could be swung as a weapon. Even in the intensity of the moment, Gage had to appreciate both her nerve and her preparation, because she'd obviously loosened the long zipper and torn away enough material to make such a quick grab and swing possible. She'd been waiting for her opportunity.

Howie doubled over and grabbed his privates. Neither the Taser nor the Beretta fell loose, however; the only thing that he dropped was the key ring. It might have all been for naught, except Nora swung the boot again even harder, slapping the hand with the Taser.

It looped high in the air, landing with a thud in front of Gage.

He scooted toward it, an awkward shuffle with his bound ankles. It would be a million years before he got there, and then what would he do, with his hand behind him?

Nora dove for the keys. Howie, having at least slightly recovered, saw what she was doing and lunged after her. She got her hands on the keys but Howie smacked them away. The keys bounced high off the wall and slid to the floor. With a roar, he tossed her back on the bed and climbed on top of her. "You *will* obey me!" he shouted, slipping his hands around her neck.

Nora grabbed at his hands and bucked about, but physically she was no match for him. Howie went on screaming, telling her he loved her, why didn't she understand, why couldn't she just be nice, all the while choking the life out of her. Gage, still crawling, realized there was a faster way, and rolled end over end until he reached the Taser. He felt for it, fingers brushing against the handle, and finally got it into his grip. Nora was gagging. How the hell was Gage going to point this thing?

It had to be now.

Now.

Somehow he managed to struggle up to his knees, the stun gun in his right hand behind him. Looking over his shoulder, he lined up Howie's back as best he could. There was a good chance that the darts might hit Nora instead, and then Gage would really be screwed, but what choice did he have?

Gage pulled the trigger.

There was a bang. One dart missed the mark completely, hitting the futon mattress, but the other landed on Howie's back. The effect was instantaneous. While the thin cord delivered its clicking pulses of electricity, Howie jerked upright as if he'd been stabbed, then rolled to the left, off Nora and onto the bed. While Nora gasped for breath, his body spasmed and convulsed.

Now the clock was ticking.

They had thirty seconds, maybe less, until the Taser stopped and Howie recovered.

"Get the gun!" Gage shouted at Nora. "Hurry!"

She took big, shuddering breaths but didn't acknowledge Gage. He scooted around to face her, walking on his knees in her direction. He wasn't going to be much use to her, handcuffed as he was. But getting control of the Beretta was the bigger concern.

Twenty seconds.

"Now!" Gage cried.

Coughing and hacking, she groped for the keys with her free hand, misunderstanding Gage or just instinctively wanting to free herself. He shouted at her again to get the Beretta. She reversed course and reached for Howie, trying to find the gun, but his right jacket pocket was buried underneath him. She tried to roll him, but moving a two-hundred-pound slab of flesh would have been difficult for anyone, and especially for a woman who'd just about had the life choked out of her.

Ten seconds.

While Nora struggled to roll Howie, Gage picked up the keys. It was hard enough manipulating them into the keyhole even if he *could* see, since handcuffs weren't designed to allow a prisoner to unlock them. Without being able to see, it was almost impossible. The first key he got into the hole didn't work.

Five seconds.

Nora had finally gotten to the pocket in Howie's jacket that had the Beretta, but it was snagging on the material. With a howl of frustration, she yanked the Beretta free.

Time was up.

The Taser stopped delivering its charge, falling silent. With anyone, the effects of a Taser weren't exact, and Howard F. Meyer could have taken a lot longer to recover. But in this case, he must have realized what was happening, and he rolled over into Nora just as she was scrambling to point the Beretta at him. With one hand still chained, it wasn't easy.

The Beretta fired.

The boom reverberated in the soundproof environment and Gage felt it right down to his bones. His ears rang. The bullet left a red streak on Howie's cheek. There was the pungent odor of gunpowder. Howie wailed and lunged at Nora, so much bigger than her that the sheer weight of him pressed her down, made it hard for her to aim the gun. He got one hand on her right wrist, her gun hand, and now it was a battle of strength. Half his face was smeared with blood. Howie was pulling her arm toward him even as she torqued herself around, trying to keep the keep the gun from his reach.

There was no more time to mess with keys. Howie almost had the Beretta. He might not shoot Nora, but he'd definitely shoot Gage.

If Gage was going to intervene, he had to do it now.

One chance. It all came down to perfect execution, because he'd be completely helpless if this didn't work. With great effort, he rocked onto his heels, then up, ignoring the pain, staying balanced. No way he could fall now. Then he was on his feet—ankles chained, but on his feet. Howie had the gun. He was turning, bringing the gun around, his face coming into view even as Nora scratched and clawed at his arm.

Howie's face was what Gage was hoping to see.

The human head could either be the most vulnerable part of the body or the deadliest, depending on which part was exposed. The nose was soft cartilage. The upper skull was almost like steel. Gage, pretending for one adrenaline-filled moment that he had the best knees in the world, bent low and propelled his upper skull at Howie's nose.

In the brief span before Gage made contact, the Beretta fired again, ripping through his jacket, but then Gage smashed into Howie like a battering ram. He heard a sickening crunch, and pain vibrated across his skull. They were a mash of three bodies slamming into the corner of the futon.

Howie was yelling and screaming, flailing wildly, and all Gage could do was absorb the blows and try to keep his weight on him. He hoped Nora was going for the Beretta. Then Howie managed to push Gage off him, throwing him onto the floor. Gage bounced off the carpet and rolled over, expecting, through his bleary vision, to see Howie pointing the Beretta at him.

But Nora had it.

She was pointing it at Howie's face.

Everything became very still. Howie was crouched, partially twisted away from her, his face like a half-closed red curtain. Even though her hand trembled, and her arm seemed bent and unsteady, she had her finger on the trigger. Her face didn't even seem like her own. There was something primal about her expression, something bared and exposed that Howie saw right away.

"Please," he said. "I—I will be good to you. You'll see. Neither of us have to be lonely anymore. Just—"

She pulled the trigger.

The bullet went right in the middle of his forehead and blasted the wall behind him with red.

For a few beats, while the bang of gun echoed around them, it was as if Howie didn't realize he'd been shot. His mouth kept moving, his eyes blinking, but then it all stopped as if someone had flicked a switch. He fell backward and lay still.

Gage smelled rotten eggs in the air.

Of course. The natural gas.

The bomb.

How much time did they have? Nora was whimpering and crying. Ordinarily Gage would have been more sympathetic, but he couldn't afford such a luxury right now. The keys lay between them on the carpet. He barked at her to get them. She blinked at him.

"Now!" he shouted. "Or we'll die!"

It was enough to propel her into action. She put down the gun and reached for the keys, stretching the chain as far as they would go, and scooped them up. A few seconds later, she'd managed to free her cuffs. Gage was upright by then, and soon she'd freed his hands, too, then his ankles.

"Should—should we call—" she began.

"No time," Gage said. "Go!"

Helping each other, they staggered out of the room. Gage afforded himself one backward glance at Howie, saw that he was a lifeless form in a deepening pool of red on the futon, then they were both into the hall behind the secret room. Then up the stairs. Faster, faster. If Howie wasn't lying—and the foul odor was a good sign he wasn't—this whole place was going to blow.

Once in the daylight basement, they bolted for the sliding door. The sunlight and fresh air were a relief, but they still weren't safe. To the van? No, too far. They headed for the rotting gate and the passageway through the blackberry bushes. The vines scratched at their faces as they sprinted through the tunnel. Were they a safe distance away? They should be, or at least close, though Gage began to wonder if either the device didn't work or Howie was at least partly bluffing.

They were halfway down the hill when the house behind them exploded.

Chapter 29

The chief of police of Barnacle Bluffs was known, among the locals at least, to be an extraordinarily patient man. To remain in his position as long as he had—going on twenty years now—he would certainly have to be, dealing with not only the usual nuttiness of an Oregon beach town, with its regular, massive influx of tourists who seemed to treat a trip to the coast as an excuse to dispense with their best behavior, but also with Barnacle Bluff's more *unique* characteristics.

For no other town on the Oregon coast could match its recent history of weird crimes, strange happenings, and enough national attention to last a lifetime.

Yes, Percy Quinn was a patient man, Gage had to give him that. Yet as they both sat at Gage's kitchen table, and Quinn ticked off a long list of murders, betrayals, conspiracies, and other assorted unpleasant events that Gage had somehow gotten mixed up in over the years, Gage would have to say to say that the man's patience appeared to be waning. Each time the chief counted an event, he stabbed his finger into his palm with more force. His left eyelid twitched. His voice, usually slow and measured, just what you'd want in a man charged with keeping the peace, was rushed and ragged.

"So what I'm telling you," Quinn said, after finishing his litany of horribles, "is that I find it highly unlikely—I think most people would find it highly unlikely—that all of this crap didn't somehow start with *you.*"

Gage shrugged and took a sip of his coffee, wondering if the bags under Quinn's eyes were darker than usual.

The sun from the high windows filled the room with warm, rich light. Dust motes floated in the shaft of sunlight that fell next to the table. It was an unseasonably warm day for mid-October; even with the windows cracked open, and a slight breeze, the room felt stuffy. Gage wasn't complaining. It had been a nice stretch of good weather, and he had taken advantage of it by taking lots of walks on the beach—gingerly at first, then with increasing confidence. He barely felt any aches or pains now, except for the usual twinges in his right knee. After everything he'd gone through a month ago, it was nice for his body to feel almost normal again.

"So," Gage said, "you just stopped by to ask me to leave town again? How many times have you done *that* over the years?"

Quinn sighed, spinning his coffee mug a little but not picking it up. He hadn't taken a drink since Gage put it in front of him. "You know why I'm here."

"For fashion advice? Well, before we get to your clothes, I'd say you need to start laying off the eyeliner. Your eyes are looking too dark."

"Gage."

"I'm just trying to help."

"Gage, I know you know something. You're just not telling me."

"About what?"

"Gage."

"Seriously, I'm drawing a blank."

"Uh huh. Ed Boone, Nora West, Howie Meyer, exploding boats, burning houses—none of this rings a bell?"

"Oh, *that.* You're still worrying about all that stuff? The world's moved on, chief. Haven't you noticed?"

Quinn drummed his fingers on the table. "I'll move on when I finally get the real story."

"We went over this weeks ago. I told you everything I know."

"Uh huh. Let's go over it again."

"Okay. I don't know anything. There, we're done."

"You're lying."

"Ah," Gage said, "now that's not very nice of you. After I gave you a tasty cup of coffee, too."

"See, here's what I don't understand. One minute you're harassing me night and day to dig deeper into Nora West's death, telling me that even if Ed Boone's sons are involved that there's more to this whole thing than the press believes, and the next you're telling me that I should move on. And that's *after* Howie Meyer's house explodes in a terrible natural gas disaster—and the man himself has been missing ever since!"

"Maybe he was inside?"

"They didn't find a body."

"Hmm. Well, it's a very sad thing. I'm not sure what the death of a local insurance salesman has to do with me, though."

"Yeah," Quinn said, "I might have thought the same thing. But see, there's a couple of weird elements to it that make me think differently."

"Oh?"

"First, as you well know, your friend Alex's van was found parked a block away."

"Yeah, he told me about that. Didn't he report it as stolen?"

"He sure did. Said he thought someone might have grabbed

his keys when he was in the back of his store and taken it for a joyride. It's strange, though. A Toyota Sienna is not exactly the kind of vehicle that someone steals to take for a joyride, is it?"

Gage shrugged. "Some people are really into vans. Take me, for instance. You might even say I have a van fetish."

"And I also found it fascinating that Alex's call reporting the van as stolen came in about an hour *after* Howie Meyer's house went up in flames."

"An interesting coincidence."

"Right. Then there's this other odd bit of information. During their investigation, the fire marshal's team came upon something pretty strange—what seemed to be some kind of hidden basement."

"You don't say?"

"I do. And here's something else that's weird. They found a lot of … Nora West stuff. The foundation pretty much collapsed. It was like the house just melted, so there's not much intact in all that rubble, but still enough bits of magazines, CD cases, and other things to create an unusual picture. The guy was really into Nora West."

"Well, she was a popular singer."

"And you know what else I found?" Quinn said. "It made me curious, this Nora West stuff, so I did some digging. It turns out that Howie Meyer and Nora Storm-Tree both went to Deering Middle School."

"Huh."

"Not only *that,* but when I talked to the principal there, you know what he told me?"

"That it's never too late to get an education?"

"He said *you* were there asking to look through old yearbooks *the very same day* Howie's house burned down. Now how's *that* for a coincidence?"

"It is that."

Quinn sighed. "Gage, come on. Are you really going to tell me that you don't know anything more about this whole thing?"

"I *told* you. I was just desperate, looking for any possible clue that might help me explain what happened to Nora. The middle school was just one of the places I went. Probably because you're right about me. Maybe I just want things to be more complicated and weird than they sometimes are. But in the end, I realized that you were right. I needed to let the whole thing go. Just like you need to now. Denny and Elliott Younger killed Nora because they didn't want her to get any of their father's money. Elliott just botched it. Case closed."

Quinn regarded Gage for a long it time with his tired eyes. Finally, he lifted the coffee mug to his lips, took a drink, and winced.

"It's cold," he said.

"Well, you waited too long to drink it. That's what happens."

"Thank you. Brilliant advice."

"Just trying to help."

"Oh, sure you are."

Quinn put down the mug and stood, moving more slowly and deliberately than when he'd entered. He may not have gotten the answers he'd come for, but perhaps his usual frustration with Gage had provided a valuable distraction. Gage decided this was a good thing, and vowed silently to go on frustrating him.

Quinn started for the door, then turned back. "One last question."

"Yeah?"

"That photo sitting on your kitchen counter. It looks just like the one I saw in Principal Brown's office. Is that a coincidence, too?"

Gage looked at it. The photo, in a simple silver frame, was indeed the same one from Marv Brown's office, or at least an exact copy: Heceta Head at dusk. It wasn't what Gage would consider professional-level quality, but there was a beauty and simplicity to it that he found quite profound. It wasn't exactly associated with a happy memory, not when it came to poor Ed Boone, but that might have been part of its poignancy.

"I'd use the word serendipity instead," Gage said. "I was quite taken with it when I saw it, and Marv's wife was kind enough to sell me a copy."

"Seems awfully sentimental for you."

Gage shrugged. "Maybe I'm getting more sentimental as I get older."

"Uh huh. I'll believe that when I see it. Where are you going to hang it?"

"I don't know. I'm sure the right place will call to me."

GAGE WAS RIGHT that he didn't know where the picture would hang, but not because he hadn't decided. It was because it wouldn't be up to him.

Since it was nearly noon, he was going to have to hustle. Another few minutes with Quinn, who'd shown up unexpectedly, and he would have had to come up with an excuse to show him the door, and he hadn't wanted to arouse any more of Quinn's suspicions than he already had. Hence the proffered coffee and easygoing manner.

Gage wrapped the photo in newspaper, sealing it with tape; he did this partly to protect it, but also because he wanted it to be a surprise. Then he was out the door and tearing down the gravel drive in his van.

Even though he was running late, he turned north first. Paranoid that Quinn or one of his lackeys would be watching, Gage crossed through the shopping center, ducked in and out of the parking garage, then took some side streets on the east side of the highway before dropping down and heading south on Highway 101.

He probably needn't have worried. It may be October, but it was a sunny Saturday and just about any sunny Saturday brought out the tourists, regardless of the time of the year. The highway was choked with cars. Tough to keep a tail in this kind of traffic.

Gage tapped the steering wheel nervously. He knew this day was coming, but he'd just wanted a little more time.

The road he turned on, east into the woods, was only a quarter mile before the one that led to the cabin where he had been held captive. The road narrowed and wound up into the Douglas firs, leaving the ocean and the highway behind. The houses were mostly hidden from view. Lots of privacy—just what he'd wanted. The place he'd rented was down a side dirt road, grass growing between the tire grooves, a crumbling stone wall covered in ivy making the house invisible from the road.

Still, when he rounded the corner and saw her emerging from the little blue cottage, he felt a flash of panic.

Then he let the feeling pass. If she couldn't go outside today, of all days, when could she?

She smiled at him, waving just a few fingers because she was carrying two paper sacks of groceries. While he parked, she carried the sacks to the open hatchback of a red Subaru Outback with gray trim, which was amazingly loaded to the brim with belongings despite how few things she now owned. The fourteen-year-old car was a bit dinged up, with nearly two hundred thousand miles on it and a nice cloud of black smoke out the tailpipe every time it started, but it ran well enough. The plates had two more years before they needed to be renewed, which was the important part. In two years, she'd be able to figure out something else.

The truth was, even if someone would have ventured down the driveway at that moment and seen the woman putting the bags into the back of the car, they probably wouldn't have known it was the famous Nora West.

A woman who'd died.

This was Penny Martin, who now had a Social Security number, a driver's license, and even a Visa card, all courtesy of some of Alex's less savory connections from his FBI days.

Straight black hair, horn-rimmed glasses with thick black frames, bright ruby lipstick—he'd known how she was going to change her appearance, because she'd told him, but he was still amazed at how effective a few adjustments were in completely changing her look. Would *he* have known it was Nora if he'd walked by her on the street? Maybe, but only because he'd spent so much time with her lately—lots of time, much of it in intimate proximity.

Having left the cottage door open, Lady took the opportunity to scamper out and greet Gage by jumping up and landing her front paws on his leg, adding in a little shake of her tiny tail. He scratched her behind the ears, making sure not to drop the wrapped photo under his arm or let go of his cane.

Gage was going to miss that little tail. Just like he was going to miss the woman walking over to embrace him.

"Hello, Penny," he said.

"Huh? Oh, yeah, I guess I should get used to that real quick, shouldn't I?"

"You better."

"What do you think?" she asked, twirling her hair.

"You look good."

"Hmm. You wrinkled your nose when you said that."

"Did I?"

They embraced, though there was a hesitancy, an awkwardness that hadn't been there for weeks. She'd been distant the first couple nights after escaping Howie's underground prison, while they holed up in a third-rate hotel and figured out what to do, but as soon as he brought her to the cabin, all of that changed. It was as if the remoteness and the privacy of the place was just what she needed to unleash all of the emotions she'd bottled up while she suffered through those long weeks as Howie's prisoner, determined not to let her fear take control of her.

She'd told Gage that nothing physical had happened between her and Howie except her giving him backrubs, although Howie had watched her while she changed into the outfits he provided her. And more than once, she looked up while using the camping toilet to see him ogling her through the little window.

He may not have raped her, not technically, but somehow the sense of violation and abuse was just as strong.

And he was definitely working up to doing more. Gage was just glad he'd arrived before it happened.

She'd also found out how Howie had killed Ed, plying it out of him a little at a time. It was true that Howie had seen Ed at his mother's funeral a few years earlier. They'd formed a casual friendship, meeting for coffee a few times, but it wasn't anything close, and Howie didn't find out Nora was his daughter until Ed, knowing he was going to lose his mind to Alzheimer's, confessed it to him a year ago. Ed said he wanted at least one person to know, since he wasn't planning on writing Nora; he didn't want to intrude in her life. Howie believed it was divine fate. Here he'd been preparing for years for Nora to be with him—he'd already figured out that Nora West was the same Nora Storm-Tree he'd admired from afar—and suddenly the universe provided him with a means.

Howie lured Ed to the lighthouse with an anonymous letter, saying his daughter was in danger if he didn't comply, and that was where he knocked Ed out and dropped him from the top of the lighthouse. He left a suicide note. Then he wrote the letter to Nora, using the same library typewriter Ed had said he used to write his will. He also wrote up a new will, since Ed hadn't made Nora the executor, and Howie wanted to make sure Nora had a very good reason for sticking around Barnacle Bluffs.

The only thing he'd missed was Lady Luck. The last time he'd seen Ed, the old man had said nothing about a dog, and there'd been no evidence of one when he snuck into Ed's apartment to put in the new will, since Lady had been with Ron at the time.

"You're really sure about all this?" Gage asked Nora, when they separated.

"What, the hair? I'm just trying it out. I might change to a redhead after a while."

"No, I meant the whole starting over with a new identity. Are you *sure* this is what you want?"

"More than anything. And I'm going to pay you back, I *swear.*"

"It's not about that. I don't care about the money. You know that."

"I'm still going to pay you back. Just give me a few months."

"But what will you do?"

"Wait tables. Work as a bartender. Teach guitar." She smiled. "That's part of what I find so exciting about all this. I get a second chance, Garrison. The world thinks I'm dead. Nora West is gone. I'm Penny Martin. See, that rolled off the tongue much better, didn't it? Penny Martin's life is a blank slate. I was thinking I'd eventually start singing in nightclubs. Maybe I'll get a teaching license and teach music in schools. Who knows? I can't wait to find out! Maybe I'll even work as a stripper!"

"Um ..."

"Relax. It's only if I get really desperate."

"Okay, well, I'm going to be paying that credit card as long as you need me to, you know."

"I'm kidding. Man, you're easy." She laughed and kissed him hard on the mouth, no reservations this time. "And I can't thank you enough for what you're doing for me. I mean, I've *tried* the past month to thank you every single way I know how, but somehow I think all that ... thanking ... was benefiting me more than you. It was like some kind of healing, you know? Thank you for that too, I guess. Now, before I ruin this meticulously applied makeup by getting any more teary-eyed than I already am, what's that you're holding?"

Gage had almost forgotten about the photo wrapped in newspaper. He handed it to her.

"A gift," he said.

"Should I open it now?"

"Of course."

She unwrapped it. When she saw that it was a picture of Heceta Head, she teared up. He'd been worried how she'd take it, and when she started to cry, he thought maybe he'd made a mistake, but when she looked up, she was smiling.

"It's perfect," she said.

"Really?"

"Yes."

"I just thought, you know, it would be a good reminder that even good things can come from bad beginnings. New connections, a fresh start, that sort of thing. It's a metaphor, of sorts ..." He realized, by her blank expression, that he was losing her, so he shrugged. "Plus, you know, it's also a really nice picture of a lighthouse."

She laughed and kissed him again. This time, they really put everything into the kiss, because both of them knew it would probably be for the last time.

AFTER HE'D SEEN Nora and Lady off on their new life, Gage headed home.

Home … Nothing but an empty house would be waiting. The loneliness he'd felt swelling in his heart when he woke that morning, knowing that Nora would be leaving him later that day, was only heavier now. It felt like a physical thing, a lead ball residing in the center of his solar plexus. The sun may be shining on the highway, but Gage felt his own storm clouds brewing inside him.

Then, just like that, it was okay.

It wasn't that the loneliness was gone. No, it was still there, just as strong as ever. It was that he was fine with it. He wouldn't fight it. If he was lonely, he was lonely. It was just a feeling, like other feelings, and they all came and went just like the weather. As long as he didn't obsess about it, life would go on. It always did. There was a glass of bourbon waiting for him. A walk on the beach. A few hours with a good book.

Gage told himself he believed all this, and he probably did. But when he rounded the corner of his driveway and saw Zoe's Toyota Corolla parked outside the house, he was very, very glad.

He even found himself hoping she'd brought Carrot.

About the Author

SCOTT WILLIAM CARTER's first novel, *The Last Great Getaway of the Water Balloon Boys,* was hailed by *Publishers Weekly* as a "touching and impressive debut" and won an Oregon Book Award. Since then, he has published many books, including the popular Garrison Gage mystery series set on the Oregon coast, as well as the provocative Myron Vale Investigations, about the private investigator in Portland, Oregon who works for both the living and the dead. In past lives, he has been an academic technologist, a writing instructor, bookstore owner, the manager of a computer training company, and a ski instructor, though the most important job—and best—he's ever had is being the father of his two children. He lives in Oregon with his family.

Visit him online at www.ScottWilliamCarter.com.

Made in the USA
San Bernardino, CA
29 May 2017